Nowhere to Hide

As the son of a bookshop owner, Max Luther grew up immersed in literature, reading the likes of Roald Dahl and the Biggles books, before discovering crime fiction in adulthood. A lover of fast paced stories, whether on the screen or the page, he decided to try his hand at writing one of his own. *Nowhere to Hide*, a crime thriller starring private bodyguard Alex Drayce, is the first.

NOWHERE
TO
HIDE

MAX LUTHER

CANELO

First published in the United Kingdom in 2023 by

Canelo
Unit 9, 5th Floor
Cargo Works, 1–2 Hatfields
London SE1 9PG
United Kingdom

A CIP catalogue record for this book is available from the British Library.

Print ISBN 978 1 80436 580 9
Ebook ISBN 978 1 80436 583 0

Cover design by Andrew Smith

Look for more great books at www.canelo.co

Printed and bound in Great Britain by Clays Ltd, Elcograf S.p.A.

1

For my dear Mum, Manya.

Mick kept his eyes busy. The dark woodland and fields surrounding the grass verge offered little to see, but staying alert was vital. The engine off, his window open a crack, he listened for any sound that didn't belong, not easy with the strong wind assaulting the trees. Branches thrashed back and forth; leaves rustled, mimicking the white noise from a broken radio. Lightning illuminated the hills on the horizon, the distant rumble of thunder echoing seconds later. The big all-wheel-drive BMW rocked from side to side, bouncing on its giant springs as the wind jolted the bodywork.

Rain spattered his cheek through the small gap in the open window. He wiped it off just as the heavens truly opened, the giant raindrops slamming into the glass, propelled by the storm. The sleeve of his waxed jacket soaking wet, he turned on the engine and closed the window. Half a mile from the house, this was the last stop before going back in. He slipped his right hand under his jacket and rested it on the Glock in his shoulder holster: a comforting reminder that he had something to fight with should the worst happen. With his left, he raised a pair of night-vision goggles to his eyes, and turned his world bright green as they amplified the dim moonlight that had broken through the storm clouds, relieved to see nothing moving in the woods and fields, with no sign of any vehicles on the single-track road. His view, both ahead and behind for over a mile, was clear: no headlights and no human figures stalking him. He could continue to the house, confident no one had followed him. He let the goggles hang from the cord around his neck, took his hand off the pistol, and pulled out into the road.

Half a mile later, he turned onto the gravel driveway of the derelict country house, his home for the past week. He parked in one of the garages, grabbed the bag of shopping from the boot, closed the big wooden doors, and hurried to the front door.

Something about the imposing empty structure unsettled Mick. The crumbling plaster and pungent smell of mould, along with the dearth of furniture, pictures, and decorations, radiated soullessness and neglect, a crying shame, considering it had stood for over four hundred years. This past week he'd often lain awake thinking of the families who had lived in the house, worked the land, and thought it strange that nobody had seen fit to use it as a home for a long time.

It certainly still had potential: a huge eight-bedroom house, built with giant blocks of stone, high ceilings throughout and original features, for which many wealthy families were willing to pay obscene sums of money, hence why it was going on sale at auction soon, and would probably be bought by some multi-millionaire from London as a second home in the countryside. However, the millionaires would have to wait a while before they squabbled over this diamond in the rough. Most definitely until after the three of them had moved out.

Mick shut the front door behind him, copycatted a wet dog as he shook off the water droplets, and walked down the dark hallway to the kitchen. The occasional battery-powered lamps were the only source of light to mark his route, the wooden shutters closed on all the downstairs windows to guarantee they weren't displaying any signs of life to the outside world. As with every other room in the house, the kitchen was little more than an empty square. A lamp rested in each corner to illuminate the space where they'd set up their living quarters. Danny, perched on a folding chair he'd brought with him, gazed at a camping stove between his feet, boiling water for their next cup of tea. Wayne sat on a stool in the nearest right-hand corner, his shoulder against the bare wall, eyes lifeless and miserable. The sleeping area at the far end of the room comprised three air mattresses against the back wall, with individual grab bags next to each one, should a hasty departure be required. They'd set up in that room, in the centre of the house, because of the choice of several escape routes in the event of an emergency.

'All right?' Danny asked when he saw Mick walk in.

'Yeah, fine. I got everything you asked for.'

'What about my fags?' Wayne asked in his pronounced south London accent.

Mick turned to Wayne and frowned. Everything that came out of Wayne's mouth had a hateful tone.

'I said everything, didn't I?'

Mick dropped the bag on the floor next to Wayne and turned his back on him, curling his lip in disdain as the man rummaged through it, desperate to inhale poison. The blue Nike tracksuit was the only thing Mick had ever seen him wear, the filthy polyester material clinging to his skeletal frame. His fingernails had blackened from the build-up of grime during their time on the run, his hair and skin layered with grease, his face unshaven, and his body odour had achieved an antisocial level. Mick hoped he didn't smell as bad as Wayne. It wasn't easy to maintain standards, living as they had.

Mick walked over to the old open-fire cooking facilities – little more than a large brick arch with a firepit underneath the chimney – the only source of heat in the entire house; another reason why they'd chosen this room to set up camp. The embers were a subtle glow amongst a bed of ash. He threw on a couple of lumps of smokeless fuel, and watched as they caught fire.

'See anyone while you were out?' Danny asked.

'Just the staff member behind the till at the Co-op. Other than that, not a soul. It's not exactly Piccadilly Circus out there.'

'You make plenty of stops on the way back?'

'Of course I did,' Mick said, rubbing his hands in front of the growing flames. 'Six in total, so there's no way anyone could have followed without me knowing.'

Danny nodded, visibly relieved. 'Nice one. You want a brew?'

Mick pulled off his jacket. 'You bet I do.' He turned his head sharply to Wayne at the scratch of a disposable lighter. 'Don't you dare light that thing in here!'

'What's your problem?' Wayne mumbled through the cigarette dangling between his lips.

You are, you scrote, Mick wanted to say, but instead, he said, 'These cold, wet living conditions are bad enough. I don't want you adding the stench of your miserable addiction to the equation as well. Smoke it outside.'

'But it's raining.'

'I don't give a shit. You're not smoking in here.'

Wayne threw up his hands in exasperation. Mick threw Danny a hard look.

'What?' Danny's expression suggested he knew very well why Mick was glaring at him.

'It's your turn.'

'But I'm making the tea.'

Mick sighed and shrugged his jacket back over his shoulders. 'Fine, I'll take him.' He pointed a finger at Danny. 'But when I get back, I'd better be handed the best cup of tea I've ever drunk in my life.' He took hold of Wayne by the arm and lifted him out of his chair.

'I can stand up myself, you know.'

'Stop whining and do as you're told.' Mick lifted him upright with one arm, the skinny man's body no challenge for the nineteen-stone ex-rugby player. 'You're our responsibility until your permanent handler takes over, so whenever you step out of this room, I want to keep you nice and close. Our reputation relies on you staying alive.'

He marched Wayne down the hallway and out of the front door where they stood together at the back of the porch.

Smoking at the front of the house wasn't ideal as they were in view of the road, but the wind was driving the rain away from them, meaning they could stay dry. At the back, they'd have been drenched and Wayne wouldn't have been able to light his cigarette. Mick watched Wayne's face glow brightly above the lighter as he lit up. The deep lines and pockmarks on his hard-lived face were more prominent when cast in moving shadow from the flickering flame, imbuing his features with an even harder and more menacing appearance than normal.

'Turn and face the house while you light that thing,' Mick said.

'What for?'

'Because I don't want you lit up for the whole world to see. We're supposed to be keeping you hidden, remember?'

Wayne grumbled, but did as he was told. 'How much longer do we need to stay in this shithole?' he asked.

'Another couple of days and we'll hand you over to live your new life.'

'Can't come soon enough. I'm sick of it here.'

'This might surprise you, Wayne, but moving around with you this past month hasn't exactly been a picnic for Danny and me, either. The sooner we can get rid of you, the better.'

Wayne took a deep drag, the glowing red tip prominent in the dim light. 'Likewise,' he said on the exhale.

Mick ignored the current human headache for whom he had responsibility and peered out through the horizontal rainfall pelting the countryside. But he was unable to see much, other than the faint outline of the horizon beyond the countless acres of farmland, marking a line in the sky where the dark woodland met the silver haze, barely cast by the moon through the black clouds. The lightning was getting brighter, the thunder louder, as the worst part of the storm headed their way.

Mick stiffened.

'What's the matter?' Wayne asked.

'Be quiet a second,' Mick replied, unnerved by his shaky voice.

The 'matter', as Wayne put it, was headlights in the distance, travelling at a steady speed along the single-track road to the farm's driveway. A vehicle on a road wasn't normally something that would cause Mick to worry, but a car on this particular road, in their current circumstances, meant that his pulse throbbed in his neck.

With a swipe of his hand, he knocked the cigarette out of Wayne's mouth and stamped on the bright red tip.

'Oi!' Wayne pointed at the cigarette he'd only just lit, crushed on the wet porch paving stone. 'What d'you do that for?'

'Shut your mouth.' Mick's tone made it clear he wasn't in the mood to repeat himself.

He lifted his NVGs for a better view of the headlights and identified a 4x4, the silhouette of the driver too far away to make out any detail. He watched the vehicle continue down the approach to the entrance of the farm and held his breath, praying it was just one of the locals. Perhaps they were out lamping, or ferreting, or another form of poaching, although they'd picked a hell of a night to do it. The road went on for miles and miles and led to nine different farms, covering about a thousand acres in total. There was every chance the car would just pass by, that it had nothing to do with them. Mick's body temperature rose despite the weather, a nervous sweat breaking out across his back. He crossed his fingers and said a prayer, watching the vehicle closely.

Brake lights.

'Are they turning in here?' Wayne asked. 'Are you expecting one of your lot?'

'Get inside,' Mick ordered. 'Now.'

He pushed Wayne ahead of him into the hallway, shut the door behind them both and slid across the deadbolts he had fitted as extra security at the top and bottom, before he manhandled Wayne down the hallway, switching off each lamp as they dashed back to the kitchen.

'Did you put in a call?' he asked Danny, still crouched over the stove, patiently waiting for the water to boil.

'What? Of course not. I'd have told you if I had. Why? What's the matter?'

'There's a vehicle out on the road… looks as though it's going to turn into the driveway.'

The expression on Danny's face dropped.

'You told me I'd be safe here!' Wayne said to the pair of them, moving from one foot to the other with nervous energy.

'You are,' Mick said.

'Where did you leave the car?' Danny asked.

'I put it in the garage, so there's no indication that anyone's here.' He eyed Wayne. 'I'm sure these people are nothing to worry about, but we need to take precautions.' He turned back to face Danny. 'Fit your goggles and kill the lights.'

Danny ran to each corner of the room to switch off the lamps. On the fourth click, the room fell into total darkness, a split second before Mick wrapped his NVGs around his head. In the green tinge, he strode to the other side of the kitchen and picked up his grab bag.

Wayne's voice trembled in the darkness. 'Have they found us? Is that them out there? Oh, God, we're dead. We're all dead!'

'We don't know who it is,' Mick said. 'But we must be prepared for the worst, so pull yourself together and do as you're told.'

He reached inside his bag and removed the Heckler & Koch MP7, pulled out the retractable stock and racked the charging handle to chamber the top round, before placing it between his feet. He took out a set of body armour and threw it at Wayne, who yelped as it hit him in the face.

'What the bloody hell was that?' he asked in shock.

'Sorry, I forgot you can't see. It's body armour. Feel for the armholes and straps and get it in place. Hurry up, we don't have time to mess about.'

As Wayne fumbled with the Kevlar protection, Mick and Danny fitted their body armour and radio earpieces so they

7

could communicate with one another, before slinging their carbines across their torsos. Mick's bag secured to his back, he helped Wayne with his and then turned to face Danny. His green figure with circular lenses for eyes made for a terrifying image.

'I'll take Wayne out the back and sprint to the treeline,' Mick said. 'Go upstairs to a room at the front and get a view of whoever steps out of the vehicle. If their faces match any of those on the watch list, radio through to me and we'll make ground through the woods. If they're nobodies and it's just a wrong turn, we'll wait for them to leave and come back inside.'

Danny nodded then ran to the stairs. Mick gripped Wayne's arm.

'Don't make any noise outside. I'll keep hold of you and lead the way. We'll move directly away from the back door and keep the house between us and the driveway, so there's no chance of being seen. Got it?'

'Yeah, got it,' Wayne said with quivering lips.

Mick guided him to the back door and opened it as smoothly as he could, avoiding unnecessary noise, and took care to close it behind him before the force of the wind slammed it. He pushed Wayne in front of him, keeping his body between Wayne and the threat, and encouraged him to run straight for the woods as planned. The cold rain took his breath away, more forceful than before now that the storm had picked up.

A few metres into the foliage, he pulled Wayne to a stop and whispered for him to get on his knees and out of sight. Mick turned to face the house and dropped onto one knee, too, bringing the stock of the MP7 into his shoulder as he scanned the area.

The glare of the vehicle's headlights shone across the open space at the front of the house, reflecting brightly off the garage brickwork. The tyres grinding on loose pebbles were barely perceptible over the noise of the wind and rain battering the leaves and branches surrounding him. He hoped the driver would make a U-turn in front of the house, realise he'd taken a wrong turn and rejoin the road.

Instead, the headlights crept into view along the side of the house, followed by the rectangular body of something big and heavy, steadily coming to a stop in front of the garage doors. The lights went out, and the almost indiscernible rumble of the engine vanished.

These were not comforting signs.

Mick pushed the transmit button on his radio, keeping his voice down. 'Danny, you in position yet, mate?'

'Yeah, I can see the front aspect through a bedroom window.' His voice came over the radio in a series of breathless whispers. 'Are you seeing this, Mick?'

'My view isn't great. What're you looking at?'

'Two vehicles. The one you saw was a silver Range Rover SVR... must be the advance vehicle, scouting ahead, because it was promptly followed by a big black Mercedes van.'

'I can see the van by the garages. You see any registrations or faces yet?'

'No. The headlights were too bright for my goggles when they drove up, and they've parked and killed the engines in spots where I can't see them.'

'Maybe they're just travellers searching for somewhere to bed down for the night,' Mick said optimistically.

'Doubt it. No caravans or motorhomes.' Danny's voice died and Mick heard him frantically take a couple of breaths, his heart rate sure to be through the roof. 'I'm worried, Mick. This could be bad news.'

Mick took a deep breath. 'Just sit tight, mate. Let's watch what they do.'

He took his hand away from the transmit button and wrapped his fingers around the grip of his MP7. He kept a close eye on the van he could see. A man's silhouette in the driver's seat was just sitting there in the dark, waiting for something. Danny was right, Mick thought. This could be really bad news.

Danny's voice exploded in his earpiece. 'Jesus Christ! Evac-uate! Evacuate right now!'

His voice cut out at the same time as a bright flash of light erupted at the front of the house, overwhelming Mick's goggles with a burning green, followed by the *boom* of an explosion, forcing him to turn away from the glare.

'What the fuck was that?' Wayne asked.

'Be quiet,' Mick hissed.

Smoke rose above the roof, the source somewhere at the front where the explosion occurred. Disciplined enough not to transmit on the radio – one person could talk on the frequency at any one time – Mick waited for an update from Danny. Seconds had the feel of minutes, a clock full of treacle, his fingers dancing on his weapon as he fought the urge to press the transmit button to find out what had happened. Then, finally, Danny spoke up.

'They're an assault team,' he whispered, as though trying to remain hidden from a threat in the house. 'Seven or eight of them breached the front door with explosives and are searching the ground floor. Are you receiving this, Mick?'

Mick fought the urge to be sick. 'Received that,' he said. 'Can you get out?'

'I don't know. I think—'

Gunfire, loud and overwhelming at first, discharged through Mick's earpiece, then dull and subtle through the walls of the house after the transmission dropped out. The punishing report of heavy-calibre assault rifles subdued the rapid rat-a-tat-tat of Danny's MP7, the consistent flashes from the firing muzzles visible through the landing window on the first floor. Everything stopped, the remote countryside returning to the storm.

With a shaking hand, Mick reached for the transmit button.

'Are you still there?' No reply. He turned around, his eyes searching deeper into the dark woods. Unable to bear the thought of giving up on his friend, he turned back to the house.

'Danny, are you receiving me?' Still nothing. 'Say something, damn it!'

A figure appeared around the corner of the building from the front of the house. A flash of lightning right over Mick's head overwhelmed his goggles; forced to pull them off, he blinked repeatedly amidst the roar of the thunder, to dissipate the bright green that burnt into his retinas, until another bolt revealed the figure in brilliant clarity: a man, tall and broad, dressed in black, a balaclava over his face, and an assault rifle slung across his chest. The man turned to the treeline. A shiver ran down Mick's spine as the man stared straight at him. Behind balaclava man, three sinister figures emerged from the same corner, lit up intermittently by lightning. They gathered around the first man, all of them facing the woods, in the hands of each one the distinctive outline of an AK-47.

Abandoning the goggles, Mick watched them closely, braced to make a run for it through the trees. Four more armed men exited the house through the back door, swaggered across the yard as though taking a stroll in the park, then stood still and aimed their weapons at the treeline. Yellow flames swept through the landing window and rapidly spread through the upper floor of the house, forcing black smoke out of every gap. Almost frozen to the spot, terrified to move an inch, Mick prayed Wayne wouldn't open his big mouth. Wayne visibly shook in his tracksuit.

The first man let his assault rifle hang from his sling and reached up to his neck with his right hand. In a single movement, he pulled the balaclava off his head to reveal a thickset jawline above a muscular neck, and a close-cut head of dark hair. Mick squinted; the man had an ear missing, a rough patch of old scar tissue left in its place. He watched his hand raise something to his lips.

Danny's radio handset.

'You won't get far.'

Mick shuddered when he heard the deep, gravelly voice in his earpiece. He kept his gun up on aim as he eased to stand –

he and Wayne had to get out of there. Danny was dead; there was nothing Mick could do for him now. The only thing to concentrate on was surviving long enough to get Wayne to safety.

As he stood and turned around, the line of gunmen opened fire into the woods, a hailstorm of steel-plated lead shredding trees, branches, leaves, and shrubs. He grasped Wayne's clothing from behind, shouting for him to move. He hoisted him to his feet as Wayne screamed in terror and pushed him forwards, desperate to move deeper into the woods.

The first bullet hit Mick in his lower back, slipping underneath his body armour, a sharp, hot, punchy thud in his kidneys. The second and third hit his rucksack, stopped by the ceramic plate in his vest; the assaulter's point of aim climbed with the power of the weapon, sending the fourth above the collar of his armour. A red-hot metallic force passed through his spine at the base of his neck and out of his Adam's apple, where it went on to hit Wayne squarely in the back of his head.

The thunderous clap of the fifth was the last thing Mick ever heard.

2

'How many times do I have to tell you? Get away from that window!'

Sarah put her phone on the ledge, blew her fringe out of her eyes, and brushed the fingers of both hands through her long black hair, tucking it behind her ears. An old habit, something she did when stressed and her hair was down; just as she was now, with that painful excuse for a human being barking commands at her. She didn't bother to turn around to face the woman, merely pushed herself off the window ledge and winced as a bolt of pain erupted on her palm. Three vicious semi-circles tracked from her wrist to the base of her thumb, the product of a sadist and an electric hob, still raised and angry two weeks after the event. She returned her gaze to London's cold, dark streets for a moment longer, a chill wafting over her cheeks through the open window: her only means of tasting fresh air. The view from the second floor flat in Enfield she'd been forced to call home wasn't great, but it was better than sitting in her room, staring at the same blank walls all day long, wondering when, or perhaps *if*, she'd be able to walk the streets again without constantly checking over her shoulder.

'Are you deaf? I said—'

'I heard what you said.' Sarah snapped her head to the side as she glared at Francesca, standing square to her, hands on hips, the Glock 17 bulging underneath her black fleece. 'I'm not an idiot, so don't speak to me as though I am.' She turned back to the window, allowing herself one more glance at the group of kids playing in the park. People watching: it was all Sarah had for entertainment. 'You can't expect me to be happy about sitting around this flat for the past fortnight. My only sense of hope is watching others live normal lives through this window, imagining that one day that might be me again.'

Sarah thought Francesca far too cheerful and uplifting a name for someone so cold and clinical. She often thought if the woman's parents had known at birth what kind of person she'd grow up to be, they might have been more inclined to name her something similar to Robocop, or perhaps Terminator.

Francesca's blank expression and emotionless eyes regarded Sarah with contempt, the incarnation of a disapproving android who couldn't understand why the pathetic human wanted to gaze out into civilisation, desiring contact with someone who didn't bark orders all day long. To appease her, Sarah took a few steps back from the window, invisible from the pavement, but stayed facing the glass, as an act of defiance. She avoided eye contact with Francesca, who had just stepped between her and the window, the scornful expression on her face unmistakable.

'The only hope you have is right in front of you,' Francesca said. 'And what I expect is for you to be happy about us keeping you alive when you wouldn't have lasted five minutes in this city on your own.'

Taller than Francesca – at six foot one, Sarah was taller than most women – and able to peer over the top of her short black haircut and out across Bush Hills Park on the other side of the road, she continued to watch the group of kids playing by a set of goalposts, even though it was late in the evening and only about five degrees. The torches on their phones lit up the area around them, fireflies dancing in mid-air. They didn't have a ball; it was too dark and the ground too soggy. Instead, they took it in turns to climb onto the horizontal top post and swing from it, no doubt daring one another to perform the riskiest, and therefore most impressive, feat possible. Testing themselves in the process, they were learning to become competent in the face of danger, a skill Sarah knew the importance of all too well.

She'd been watching them for twenty minutes and resented Francesca for making her move away from the window ledge where she'd had the best view of the happy children. So far, the most impressive stunt she'd seen was from a little boy with bright blond hair, who had managed a full rotation of the bar, earning high fives and numerous back slaps from his friends. A surge of envy for their stage in life enveloped her.

'Did you hear what I said?' Francesca asked.

'I heard you,' Sarah replied, without meeting her eyes. A moment later, a convoy of vehicles pulled over across the street, bumper to bumper in a line, blocking her view of the kids.

A silver Range Rover SVR and a black Mercedes van.

She turned around, ignored Francesca, and walked down the hallway to the small kitchen, where she filled the kettle and dropped a teabag into a mug. Over the rumble of the boiling water, she heard the toilet flush and the tap run in the bathroom, and turned around to see Craig, Francesca's partner, or sidekick, or whatever cops called one another, rush past the kitchen doorway to the living room. Sarah smiled because his hands still fumbled with his belt that he hadn't yet fastened properly.

'Did I hear you pair arguing again?' she heard Craig ask.

Sarah turned back as the kettle clicked off, and filled her mug, listening to the robot and her sidekick – yes, she was going with sidekick – argue in the other room while she mashed the teabag.

'She was by that bloody window again.'

'Well, next time, maybe you could try an approach that isn't quite so hostile.'

'Have you forgotten who wants her dead? They've got eyes everywhere and we cannot afford for her to be recognised. She might not care about her safety, but it's our job to, so when she goes near the window, we've got to tell her, in no uncertain terms, to get away from it.'

Sarah lip-synced Francesca's words, having heard her lecture before, with an exaggerated scowl on her face as she spooned the soggy teabag out of her mug, dropped it in the bin, poured in a splash of milk, and restrained the urge to walk into the living room to tell that bitch what she thought of her. She knew very well how serious the threat was, but where was the harm in gazing out of the window? It's not as if they'd be driving around London on the off chance of spotting her. The people who wanted her dead were rather more sophisticated in their methods than that.

She reached into her back pocket and took out the small, laminated photograph of her mother that she carried everywhere. Her mum's head and shoulders nearly filled the entire square, apart from a patch of blue sky and a few waves crashing in the distance behind her. Taken when her mum was thirty years old, which Sarah was due to turn next month, she was on a beach in winter, in the process of wrapping a thick wool scarf around her neck and smiling from ear to ear. Sarah hadn't had the chance to really get to know her mum – she'd died when Sarah was eight years old – but that picture always made her feel better.

'All right, just relax,' she heard Craig say over the metallic jingling of his belt buckle being fastened, snapping her out of her happy thoughts. 'Deal with her however you want next time, if you feel that strongly about her enjoying a view of the park.'

'Don't be so ignorant, Craig,' Francesca said. 'Being relaxed will get us killed. And there won't be a next time. I'll stand guard by this window all night if I need to, and then we'll hand her over tomorrow and she can be someone else's problem, God help them.'

The door buzzer made Sarah jump, and immediately silenced the other two. She imagined them both staring at one another, each expecting the other to have an answer for who it could be. She slipped the photograph back in her pocket and listened.

'You expecting someone?' she heard Craig ask Francesca.

'Of course not, nobody knows we're here. It must be some door-to-door salesman.'

'At this time of night?'

'Well, maybe it's one of the nosy neighbours wanting something. If it's that old woman from next door scrounging milk again, tell her to clear off.'

Sarah walked up to the kitchen doorway with her mug of tea and looked down the hallway, wondering who might be on the other side of the front door. A chill introduced itself to the surface of her skin.

'No, I won't be telling her that,' she heard Craig say in an exasperated tone. 'And try not to have another row with our witness before I get back.'

Sarah stepped back from the doorway and blew on her tea with a lot more concentration than necessary: a poor attempt at masking the fact she'd been eavesdropping.

'You okay?' Craig asked her when he came into view.

The rolled-up sleeves of his checked flannel shirt showed off his thick, muscular forearms as he leant up against either side of the kitchen doorframe, his green eyes sharp against the background of his olive skin. She met those eyes with her own. Hard not to.

'As can be, I guess.'

He smiled and leant forwards so his face wasn't in view of the living room, then whispered, 'Don't let her get to you. It's just one more night and then you'll be going somewhere a lot more comfortable, with a lot more space, and things will get back to something resembling normality.'

She smiled before mouthing, 'Thanks'. Craig gave her a thumbs up and then vanished as he walked in the direction of the front door. She stayed in the kitchen, hugged her thick woollen sweater to herself and sipped her tea, craving some time on her own. That was the worst thing about that flat: not only could she not leave, but she was stuck in the tiny space with the same two people for company, one of whom was barely a person. Another knock on the door, louder than the first, prompted Craig to call out that he was on his way. Sarah heard him slide the deadbolts across and open the door, the chain rattling until pulled tight.

'Who are *you*?' she heard him ask. The worried tone to his voice concerned her.

The shock of a gunshot made the mug of tea slip out of her grip. As it fell to the floor, a gruesome dark red substance splattered the hall walls and around the kitchen doorframe, as though a pound of minced beef had been thrown into a ceiling fan. At the crack of her mug smashing on the tiled floor, she shielded her eyes from the horror by staring at the dozen or so pieces of white ceramic scattered in the pool of expanding tea.

Frozen to the spot, her wide, unblinking eyes gazed at her feet.

All hell broke loose.

More gunfire made her snap out of it as chaos erupted. She heard Francesca fire shots from the living room, her attempts to fight off the intruders overpowered by three or four much louder weapons fired from the front door. The noise of the shots and the smell of the burning gunpowder, mixed with the iron scent radiating from whatever was left of Craig, swamped her.

The sheer carnage made Sarah scream and bring her hands up to her ears, her lower back hitting the edge of the kitchen counter as she backed away from the horrific scene in the hallway. Tears ran down her face and mingled with the fear-sweat that had broken out across her skin. After everything she'd been through, and after every order she'd followed, somehow, her worst fear had come true.

They'd found her.

Terror coursed through her as she stood completely defence-less against the men forcing their way in. The inevitable happened: Francesca stopped shooting. Footsteps walked cautiously into the flat, followed by the presence of a man's shadow, darkening the crimson blood splatter on the wall. The man would reach the kitchen doorway and see her, and that would be the end of it. There would be no negotiations. They would shoot her on sight; after all, that's why they'd tracked her down. Not to abduct her, or steal something from her, or frighten her into doing something for them. They were there to kill her. This was a clinical execution by a group of the most well-equipped and ruthless criminals in the country.

And now she was on her own.

More movement caught her attention, the sinister tip of a gun appeared from the corridor. Her chest seized, too scared to breathe. She shut her eyes tightly, unable to witness her impending doom a moment longer. Helpless, totally vulnerable, and devoid of any options, how stupid was she to think she could run from them and go on to live a safe, happy life. That notion was utterly ridiculous now, in the presence of their ferocious capabilities. There would be no more running. She'd done her best, but this was the end of the road.

It'll all be over in a second. The thought almost brought a sense of peace, as she accepted the inevitable.

Footsteps at the kitchen doorway changed the energy within her and forced her eyes open. Shaking even harder, her primal instinct to survive overpowered her fear. Adrenaline fuelled her innate desire to run away from the danger, but now, stalked by killers, moments from certain death, the primitive section of her brain overpowered her more rational frontal lobe, and demanded a new plan. Giving up was not an option for this part of her brain. It knew all too well that her DNA hadn't survived tens of thousands of years, passed on over countless generations, by giving up when all seemed lost. Rational or not, action was imperative, and unable to run away, that ancient portion of her brain offered only one other option: fight.

A knife from the kitchen block materialised in her hand and pure survivor's instinct drove her to the doorway. Before the gunman could peer into the kitchen, Sarah pushed their black weapon out of the way and followed through with the knife, plunging it deep into the man's neck as she screamed at the top of her lungs.

Wide eyes glared back at her through the holes in a balaclava. She let go of the knife, leaving it embedded, shoved him hard in the chest and sent him crashing into the man behind him.

Despite the chaos, her frontal lobe threw another idea into the savagery. She pictured the open window in the living room. They were on the second floor, but so what? A broken ankle was better than a bullet.

The hallway blocked by the man bleeding on the floor, Sarah seized her opportunity and turned to the living room, running for her life. As she cleared the doorway, a gunshot rang out from behind, the bullet cutting through the air next to her ear before embedding in the far wall. Propelled by an energy she'd never experienced before, she barely even noticed Francesca's body slumped against the far wall of the living room, her chest punctured by a series of gruesome holes.

Without hesitation, Sarah ran to the window and threw herself at it, hitting the glass hard with two open hands. She reached up to grab the top of the window as it swung open and followed it out, her entire bodyweight relying on the flimsy hinges. Her legs dangling in mid-air, her hot breath billowing up into the cold night air, she heard her nails clawing at the plastic as she slipped. Voices of men with guns coming after her gave her no time to think: she let go.

A weightless sensation engulfed her for a split second before she hit jagged branches, then the unrelenting impact of the dirt. The landing forced the air out of her lungs and for a terrifying moment, she couldn't breathe. She rolled out of the bush, barely noticing the thorns and splinters, and crawled a few feet across the lawn until she was able to stand, grateful she hadn't broken any bones. Her lungs frantically gulped breath as she staggered to the road, slowly at first, then briskly, then as fast as she'd ever moved in her entire life. As she reached the pavement, she saw a man sitting behind the wheel of a black van parked across the street. The sinister whites of his eyes peered at her through his balaclava. She turned left at the same time as the man opened his door to come after her, and sprinted as fast as her legs would carry her.

Gunfire from behind made her stumble, and something kicked up the tarmac a few feet ahead of her. She turned her head to see a man shooting at her from the window she'd just jumped from, and to make matters worse, the man from the van was gaining on her, along with another three figures in dark clothing and balaclavas who had joined him. She saw the guy at the front of the group reach into his jacket for something. Fearing it was a gun, she darted off the pavement into the congestion of the housing estate. The park would make her an easy target.

Another shot rang out as she neared the corner of a line of garages, the bullet just missing her right arm and hitting the brickwork in front of her. She legged it behind the garages and followed the wall in the direction of a car park. It wouldn't be long before those men had her in sight again; spurred on, she followed the wooden fences alongside the car park, which marked the rear boundaries of a row of terraced houses on the next street. She crouched low as she moved, desperate for somewhere to hide as she brushed past the leaves and branches growing over the wooden panels. She slipped through a gap in the fence into someone's garden, doing her best to break through the bushes on the other side without making too much noise. She stood in the middle of a neglected lawn, the thick, wet grass up to her knees.

On the other side of the fence, she heard her assailants talking as they searched for her. She breathed a sigh of relief when it was clear they hadn't seen her enter the garden. The scraping of their boots on the concrete was so close, she held her breath for fear she might give away her position. The house at the other end of the garden was dark, but she couldn't see any security lights that might illuminate her if she approached. Desperate to think of something – it wouldn't take them long to find the gap and clamber through – she had to move or they'd find her frozen to the spot in the middle of that garden.

More noises from the other side of the fence, accompanied by the bright glare of a torch shone around the car park, impelled Sarah to take a tentative step closer to the house, followed by a more confident second, until she was almost running, taking high strides to clear the tall grass so it didn't rustle too loudly. She ran down the alleyway to the side of the house, intending to get out onto the next street and put some distance between herself and the men chasing her.

The end of the alleyway was blocked, first by three big bins, and then by a gate with a padlock fixing it to an iron latch bolted to the brickwork. Too terrified to turn around and retrace her steps, she lifted the lid on one of the bins and climbed inside, gently lowering her feet onto the bags of rubbish at the bottom. She hunkered down her tall frame and closed the lid above her head, her muscles clenched to control her trembling.

At the sounds of footsteps in the alleyway, she clamped her hands over her mouth to stifle a scream. At least two people talked to one another in gruff, hushed tones. She pictured the guns in their hands, and imagined how she would die if they found her inside that bin. Just her laboured breathing alone was deafening; she tried her hardest to take slow, steady, quiet breaths through her nose. The padlock rattled as they tried to pull open the gate. Sirens sounded in the distance.

Hope flooded Sarah's mind as she heard the two men run away, their heavy boots tapping out a fast rhythm on the concrete, no doubt fleeing the area now the police were on their way; undoubtedly after dozens of calls reporting gunfire in the area.

Sarah stayed exactly where she was, too frightened to move a muscle. Her hands remained clamped over her mouth as tears ran down her fingers and her shoulders gently shook. Only once she was sure they were gone did she allow herself to cry properly, expelling the stress of the past fortnight, and the unbearable terror of the last few minutes.

3

The following day. 4:30 a.m.

Julie Adler was already awake when she got the call. She'd barely slept, which wasn't exactly uncommon these days; insomnia had plagued her for years and it only ever got worse. She fought her hands out from under the covers and rubbed her sore, itchy eyes in the dark, before fumbling around on her bedside table for her phone. It sounded so loud it was almost a physical presence in the room, beating her over the head with its incessant high-pitched jingle. *Good job I'm single and not at risk of waking up anyone else*, she thought bitterly as her fingers found the phone and lifted it to her face. She squinted at the bright screen. John Foster: her boss. She answered with a croaky, 'Hello?'

'Why isn't your work phone switched on?'

His Belfast accent was even harsher than usual through the haze of her half-asleep state.

'I'm not on call, John. What's the matter?'

'I want you to get into work as soon as possible. In the meantime, find your work phone, switch it on, and keep an eye on your emails.'

The first question on Julie's lips spluttered to a halt when he hung up on her, morphing into a groan as she reluctantly switched on her bedside lamp, climbed out of bed, and staggered into the en suite; by the tone of Foster's voice, her shower would have to be a quick one.

Braving the harsh white glare of the LED ceiling lights, she brushed her teeth with one eye shut as she showered. Having taken care not to get her hair wet – she didn't have time to mess around with the dryer – she towelled herself down, then tied her blonde hair back in a ponytail as she walked to her wardrobe, accidentally bumping her Star of David wall hanging with her elbow; something her mum bought her years ago when she moved out of the family home. She set it straight and read the inscription: *May those who live here know only blessing and peace.*

Yeah, right…

She rummaged around in her underwear drawer for pants and a bra, yanked a clean white shirt from the wardrobe, and unhooked her black suit from the back of the bedroom door; there was never any point in putting it away. With the hours she worked, her suit needed to be close by at all times.

She jogged downstairs to the kitchen, her mind whizzing through all of her case files to try to figure out what had gone so wrong overnight that it would warrant the call.

Relax, she told herself. *It's probably nothing to do with anything you're working on; it's probably a brand new, time-critical investigation. Don't be paranoid. You've done nothing wrong.*

But the paranoia remained, despite the pep talk, and she walked quickly to the coffee table in the front room while the kettle boiled, grabbed her work phone and switched it on with panicky, fumbling hands, to the sight of a red batter symbol in the top right.

Damn it. Won't be long before the thing dies on me.

She searched for five long, frustrating minutes for her phone's USB cable, but couldn't find the damn thing anywhere. She carried her phone back to the kitchen, rested it on the work surface, and glanced at the screen from time to time as she poured thick, coarse coffee grounds into her cafetière and filled it with hot water. Once her phone had started up properly, she tapped her email app and watched intently as it loaded. Nothing yet. She finished brewing her coffee and filled her biggest travel mug, grabbed her phone and car keys, stuffed them into her handbag, and rushed to the front door. Outside she half ran, half walked to her car, slowed only by her eagerness for that first sip of hot coffee to help her face the brutal cold of an early morning in wintry London. Muttering as she fumbled to get her ridiculously big mug of coffee into the cup holder, she drove out into the dark streets of Tooting to her office in the National Crime Agency's headquarters in Vauxhall.

The journey was quick at that time in the morning, the drive faster on the clear roads than the law allowed. When she wasn't checking the screen of her phone to see if the email from Foster had come through yet, she kept her eyes out for any Black Rats: a term she and her colleagues had for the traffic cops, back when she'd been a young DC with the Metropolitan Police.

A *ding* forced her eyes back to the screen of her phone: the email had arrived. She tapped on it, but there was nothing in it apart from a PDF attachment. She tried to open the attachment but was met with the circle of doom as it struggled to upload, presumably because of how low the charge was. The screen went black. She punched the steering wheel with the palm of her hand.

'Typical. The one time I forget to put it on charge and this is what happens.'

Minutes later, she pulled through the front gates of NCA HQ, abandoned her car in the nearest space, grabbed her handbag, coffee cup and phone, and hurried to the main entrance, through reception to the lift, and pressed the button for the top floor.

Her watch read 5:33 a.m., meaning she'd probably be the first one in, as usual. Julie, who struggled to sleep, normally beat everyone else into work when she eventually got sick of just lying in bed and decided to get on with the day. Even something as miserable as insomnia had to have its upsides, she supposed. At times she wondered how she functioned the way she did.

As the lift shot up, she took another sip of her coffee and felt her mind focus on the real world rather than the hazy, dreamlike state in which she'd spent the night. She kept the mug tilted back as her tongue spoke to her brain, registering how good it tasted, and only moved it away when she felt her top lip burn.

There we go, she thought as she sighed with heavy coffee breath. *This stuff is how I function the way I do.*

By the time the lift doors opened, her mug was empty. Breakfast is next on the list, she thought, once this meeting is over.

She stepped out into the dark corridor, the automatic light sensors a line of dominoes triggering ahead of her one by one, proving she was right about being the first in. She dipped into an office and found a phone charger plugged into a socket, grabbed it, and then marched to the conference room where she'd been summoned at such an ungodly hour. She took a seat at the big table and plugged the charger into one of the desk sockets in front of her, watching the screen eagerly as the device slowly sucked up some juice.

Minutes later, it had enough power to switch on. A briefing document opened. As Julie read, the fear and paranoia she'd felt earlier hit her system tenfold.

A sick feeling stripped away her desire for breakfast.

Something terrible had happened last night; something very much to do with one of her cases. Two safe houses, each containing a witness, whose safety Julie was ultimately responsible for, had been attacked. Both were high-value key witnesses for the same case, protected by two separate teams.

Correction, Julie thought, as she read on, they *were* protected. Past tense. As in, you can no longer protect the dead.

'No, no, no, no, no.'

Julie's fingers turned white as she gripped her phone and read fast.

The four officers who made up the two protection teams were all dead, as was one of the witnesses, the whereabouts of the second currently unknown.

Oh my God. This is bad. Really bad.

Julie had no idea how this could have happened. The department she worked for within the NCA dealt specifically with witness protection: the staffing, the logistics, the communica-tions, as well as the skilful deployment of every single method known to law enforcement regarding how to keep a witness's whereabouts secret. The officers guarding them were experts: highly trained and heavily armed, they had never lost a witness. Never.

Until now.

Julie read to the end of the document where it repeated the stomach-churning fact that one of the witnesses was dead and the other missing.

Missing? Or kidnapped?

She laid her phone on the table and bowed her head, covering her face with her hands, wishing, hoping, this was all a nightmare and she would soon wake up.

No such luck.

'Morning.'

The voice, abrupt and stern in the quiet room, made her jump. Foster, wearing his standard navy suit and ugly face beneath a mop of yeti-white hair, stood at the other end of the table. As a former handler of informants for the Police Service of Northern Ireland, Foster had a wealth of experience organising the protection of witnesses whose lives were under serious threat, hence his recruitment by the NCA following retirement from the police. The stress of his long career in Belfast, a substantial chunk served during a time when the city was at war, had left its mark. Overweight and under-exercised, Foster's blood pressure readings were always in the triple digits.

She noticed the door was shut.

Can this man walk through walls or something? A little heads-up would be nice in the future, please, universe.

'You read the document yet, Julie?' he asked.

'I've just fini—'

'How could this happen?' he demanded. 'How on earth could the brothers have found them?'

On the 'b' of brothers, several drops of saliva cleared the six-foot length of solid wood that separated the two of them and landed on the back of Julie's hand. A pro, she subtly moved it out of his view and wiped it underneath the table, without changing the expression on her face.

'I'm as shocked as you are, John.'

He leant forwards and placed the knuckles of his clenched fists on the tabletop. 'I very much doubt that.'

The doors burst open and in walked the other three people Julie had expected to turn up: Fiona Mitchell, Chris White, and Dereck Reid. They all worked under Foster in the UK Protected Persons Service, each one of them case managers like Julie. Young Fiona was dressed smartly in black trousers, a white shirt, and a terracotta raincoat; Chris was in black chinos and a light grey sports jacket; and Dereck had chosen a navy suit, his crisp white collar an attractive contrast to his dark skin. None of them appeared pleased about being called in so early.

'What's the emergency?' Fiona asked as she took a seat.

'It'd better be good, I'll tell you that much,' Chris said.

Foster shot them both a face that made them shut their mouths and take a seat. Dereck opted to go a different route from his two colleagues and sat down without making a comment, knowing better than to say something that might make their ill-tempered boss even angrier. The door swinging open and crashing against the wall cut through the silence. Foster's assistant — a scrawny young man named Dominic — scurried into the room clutching a phone, his hand cupped over the microphone. By the expression on his face, he was holding an important call.

'Sorry to interrupt, sir,' Dominic spluttered. 'But you need to take this.'

Foster assessed his assistant's demeanour and then turned to face the team. 'Check your emails and read the briefing document I've sent you.'

While he left the room with Dominic to answer the call, Julie watched the other three read through the document on their phones, subconsciously digging her fingernails into her palms to dissipate her anxiety.

Fiona leant forwards, concentrating hard on the screen, brimming with the energy of the young and ambitious. A twenty-six-year-old graduate from UCL, with a BSc in Crime and Security Science and an MSc in Countering Organised Crime and Terrorism, Fiona reminded Julie of a younger, better-educated version of herself.

Fiona's introduction to the team had come about after her hard work on an operation led an arrest team to a group of people traffickers, an achievement that not only earned her the current specialist role she had in witness protection, but also a commendation from the Director General of the Agency. In her late forties with nothing but a thirty-year police career behind her – a hard-earned skill set that didn't elicit as much respect from management as you'd think – Julie had already stepped carefully through the minefield that Fiona was rushing headlong through.

Julie's eyes moved to Chris. A young graduate with a similar background to Fiona, he slouched in his seat and barely paid any attention to what he was reading. Slightly older than Fiona, he came across as younger. His skinny, boyish frame and floppy brown hair gave him the appearance of a schoolboy on work placement, rather than someone responsible for the safekeeping of people at serious risk of harm from organised criminals and terrorists. Like Fiona, he had no experience in policing, and had joined the NCA straight from university on the graduate scheme.

Julie tried hard to nurture more respect for him, because ultimately he wasn't a bad lad, just a bit lazy and timid for her tastes. Unfortunately, he didn't make it easy for her. Whenever she saw him or heard him speak, all she saw in front of her was a scared little boy, constantly avoiding risk and seeking others to do the hard work and make the difficult decisions for him.

Her eyes slid across to Dereck, an entirely different kettle of fish. He'd been the first to finish, which Julie suspected might be because he'd read the first part in the lift on the way to the top floor once the email had landed in his inbox. He'd had a long career in the police as a detective in the West Midlands before joining the NCA, and although it sometimes pained her to admit it, he was the most switched-on of the lot of them. Tall, strong, and a former Commonwealth boxing champion, Julie knew from experience Dereck was a good man to have around in messy situations. She watched him from across the table, sitting back with his arms crossed, a bracelet of the Jamaican flag that he'd worn for as long as Julie had known him dangling from his right wrist. His five-mile gaze suggested he was pondering what he'd just learnt from the briefing document, tossing the thoughts around in his mind as he tried to make sense of it all.

The caffeine was well and truly in Julie's bloodstream now, and by the time the others had finished reading, she already had a list of ideas for how they could try to bring some order to this chaos.

'Is this the work of the Marlowe brothers?' Chris asked, keeping his voice low so Foster didn't hear him from the corridor.

'I'd say so,' Julie replied. 'They're the ones with the motive for wanting these two witnesses dead, and they run one of the few organised crime groups in this country capable of making this happen.'

'But they're in prison awaiting trial,' Chris said.

Julie shrugged. 'Well, somehow, they've been able to communicate with their associates on the outside to plan this attack. Their dirty fingerprints are all over it.'

'Are they both your witnesses?' Dereck asked Julie.

She nodded. 'Yeah, I'm case manager for both of them, Wayne Hardwick *and* Sarah Bennett.' Guilt stabbed in her chest as Wayne's death weighed down her conscience.

'How the hell did the killers know where they were?' Chris's young, pale face was shocked. 'They were in witness protection, for God's sake!'

Julie's heart sank as she prepared to say aloud what she'd suspected as she'd read the briefing document. 'Someone is passing them information, either from the police,' she paused to take a deep breath, 'or the Agency.'

Silence descended on the room, the enormity of the night's events hitting home for each of them.

'Holy shit,' Fiona said, her face flushing red.

'Holy shit indeed,' Foster said in response as he walked back into the room. 'But the good news is that the missing witness is being tracked as we speak.'

'How?' Julie asked, a flare of positive energy igniting within her.

'That was tech support on the phone. Sarah used her bank card overnight, and our facial recognition software has picked her up on CCTV in Tottenham.'

Julie emptied her lungs with relief. 'Thank God she's alive.'

'Yes. She's still in London, and our analysts think they can narrow down where she'll be to an area quite manageable in terms of a search. I want some ideas for where we go from here.'

Julie stood up. 'I think I know where we can start.'

Foster tucked his hands into his trouser pockets.

'Go on,' he said.

Julie cleared her throat. 'Well, we need someone to liaise with the police forces whose jurisdictions these crimes fall within, namely Suffolk Constabulary and the Met. We need to be kept up to date with everything their investigations uncover.' She paused and licked her lips, wishing she'd taken the time to fill her water bottle before leaving home. Her mouth was as dry as scorched earth on a hot summer's day. 'It's important we learn the methods these criminals used to attack our witnesses, because those details will help us keep Sarah alive. But the most urgent of tasks we face is to locate Sarah, so while we're learning from the police investigations, we require wheels and boots on the ground to search the area where our analysts believe she is.'

'Agreed,' Foster said. 'And they'll want someone with them who knows both Sarah and the ins and outs of this case. Well volunteered, Julie.'

Yes! Julie almost punched the air, relieved she'd be in the thick of it as she fought to salvage what remained of her case. She smiled, and Fiona frowned. Julie knew it would eat the ambitious young girl alive if she were assigned to be a liaison with one of the police forces, rather than directly involved in finding Sarah and securing her safety.

'You'll go with someone else from our department, along with a small tactical team; make sure you find Sarah before the Marlowe brothers' people do.'

'So you think it's them as well?' Julie asked.

'Of course. The only question is, how?'

'Wouldn't be too hard for them to organise it from prison,' Dereck said.

'That's not what I meant,' Foster said. 'When I asked how, I meant how on earth did they find out where our witnesses were?' Four worried faces stared back at him. 'That's the question that needs answering, but before that, I want one of you to go with Julie to secure Sarah. Her safety is our overriding priority.'

Foster scanned the room. His eyes fell on Chris.

Oh God, Julie thought. *Not Chris. I don't want to have to babysit that boy all day long.*

His eyes moved on to Dereck.

Yes. DereckpleaseDereckpleaseDereckplease.

But his eyes scrolled past and came to rest on the only other person in the room.

'Fiona,' he said.

Bollocks.

Fiona's smile was perfectly framed between the curtains of her shoulder-length brown hair. Julie simply nodded her head. Making a bid for Dereck – the only person on her team with a similar level of experience as her – would get her nowhere.

'What else?' Foster asked her.

She looked at him quizzically.

33

'I got the impression you had more to say,' he said. 'You were on a roll.'

Julie cleared her throat once again. 'Well, while it's true our initial priority is to locate Sarah, it's also true that we need a plan for what to do with her once we've found her. The attackers are clearly extremely dangerous individuals, well-trained, well-equipped, and willing to do anything to eliminate the people who can ensure the brothers stay in prison for the rest of their lives.' Julie paused to allow herself a moment of sobering clarity at the thought of heading right into the firing line of these killers to bring Sarah in alive. 'That they executed the armed protection units the Met put in place, tells us a bulletproof plan is crucial to keep Sarah alive once we've tracked her down.'

'I'll contact the Met,' Foster said. 'We'll want their help to guard her again once we have her back.'

'No!' Julie exclaimed, the word far sharper than she intended. 'We can't involve the Met again.'

'Why not?'

'Because after what's happened, we can't rule out the possibility that the brothers have someone inside the Met's ranks, feeding them information. Also, I think we should seriously reconsider using one of our tactical teams to help with the search. We don't know how the locations of the two safe houses got into the brothers' hands, and until we do, I'd say the only people we can trust are inside this room.'

Foster wasn't happy, but he didn't reply, signifying to Julie that he couldn't think of a good reason to shut down her observations. His stiff posture and tight lips indicated he had the same concerns.

'Well, you and Fiona can't go hunting for Sarah on your own,' Dereck said. 'Not with this level of threat.'

Julie considered that statement for a second. She tested an idea in her mind, worried it'd be too crazy for Foster.

'But there is nobody else,' Chris said.

Not quite, Julie thought. She turned to Foster.

'Dereck's right. If Fiona and I come up against the people the Marlowe brothers have sent after Sarah, then we simply won't have the firepower capable of defending her, or ourselves for that matter. And even if we do find her, what then? If we think the Agency outside of us five has been compromised somehow, we can't just put her back into the programme with another protection team. The brothers' informant could be anywhere along the intelligence chain, and for all we know, have access to our database, our communications channels, and even our movements. All our phones have GPS that can be monitored by anyone with the appropriate clearance within the Agency… they might be able to feed everything back to the brothers' people in real time. If we bring Sarah in ourselves, it stands to reason that we might risk what happened last night happening all over again.'

Foster nodded.

Oh, sod it, she thought. *Might as well tell them my idea. It's not as if we're spoilt for choice in our current circumstances.*

'I think I might know how we can solve both those problems,' she said.

Everyone's eyes were on her.

'Do tell,' Foster said.

She cleared her throat. 'Well, I think I might know someone suitable for protecting Sarah once we've found her.'

'Who?' Foster asked.

'Someone I know from my time in the police. He's a bodyguard now.'

'You can't be serious,' Dereck butted in. 'You want to bring a civilian in to protect a key witness under our protection? Are you crazy?'

Julie folded her arms and glared at him. She'd thought he would be the one to have her back. 'Well, we can't use the police, or the Agency teams, because, as I've just pointed out, we don't know who this corrupt officer is, or how far their reach is. Therefore, it seems a civilian is the only option we have.'

Dereck leant forwards, resting his forearms on the table. 'Think of the vetting that's required to do that job. And you want to bring in someone we know nothing about? Do you know how dangerous that is?'

'It seems that vetting has already proven worthless, doesn't it? Since we don't know who to trust in our own organisation. I know this guy, and I know his reputation. We can trust him.'

Chris turned to Foster. 'We're not seriously going to entertain this idea, are we?'

'Dereck and Chris are right,' Fiona said, chiming in only when Julie was on the back foot, as always. 'And you say you *know* him. Well, I guess that's all right then, isn't it? For a minute, I thought you were considering handing a client, who is under an extreme threat, over to someone who has undergone zero security vetting. But if you say you know him, well then, that's just fine.'

Julie didn't appreciate her aggressive sarcasm and calculated how painful today would be with her, but she knew better than to fight fire with fire at a time such as this.

'I know it sounds crazy,' she said. 'But this guy is one of the best in the world at this sort of thing. He's worked across Manchester, Birmingham, and London as a Counter Terrorist Specialist Firearms Officer, as well as a close protection officer with the Royalty and Specialist Protection unit. I briefed his team numerous times when I was on SO15 counterterrorism and he was a CTSFO. On the back of our warrants, they carried out countless dynamic entries into buildings all over the city to arrest armed criminals and terrorist suspects. He's the best there is in his field of expertise. He's the man who saved the Prime Minister's life a few years ago when there was a kidnap attempt during a visit to Leeds.'

'What kidnap attempt?' Foster asked, his tone full of scepticism.

'Yeah,' Dereck said. 'I don't remember hearing about the Prime Minister nearly being kidnapped.'

'You wouldn't have done,' Julie said, 'because this guy stopped it from happening, killed the entire plot dead in its tracks and kept it out of the papers. I'm telling you, his reputation is second to none. He's extremely well trained and his morals are carved into bedrock. We can trust him more than anyone.'

Another silence fell upon the room.

'What's his name?' Foster asked, eventually.

'Alex Drayce,' Julie said. 'Feel free to run some checks, but all you'll get back is what I've just told you about his time in law enforcement. He's kept a low profile since leaving the police. He'll be the perfect man for the job of keeping Sarah hidden until we can secure a more permanent team for her. And anything the brothers send her way, believe me, he'll be able to deal with it.'

'And what makes you think he'll agree to help us?'

Julie smiled. 'He owes me.'

Foster thought it through in silence. The others didn't make a peep as they all waited.

'Fine,' he said.

'What?' Chris asked, almost standing from his seat in shock and disbelief. Sharp eyes from Foster made the boy settle down and hold his tongue.

'I must say I'm not entirely comfortable with the idea of handing Sarah over to the Met again, after what's happened,' Foster said. 'And it appears our organisation, outside of this room, may have been compromised. Therefore, we have little option but to go with a private contractor.'

Julie sat a little taller, glowing in her victory over the negativity from the others, none of whom were yet to offer anything useful.

'And use whatever you need to track this guy down,' Foster said. 'No technology is off limits in the circumstances. Find him, find her, and make sure he keeps her alive. Got it?'

'Yes, sir,' Julie said. 'I'll get right on it.'

'You all will,' Foster said. 'Chris, you're police liaison for Suffolk. Dereck, you've got the Met. And Fiona, as I've already mentioned, you're working for...' he fumbled with his words to correct his mistake, '...*with* Julie on this.'

Julie barely kept the smile off her face; Fiona didn't appear quite so happy.

Foster's eyes moved between the two of them. 'Make sure you both sign out a pistol from the armoury, for your own protection.'

'Yes, sir,' Julie said as she picked up her phone, the newly acquired charger, and the empty tumbler, and marched to the door. 'This way, Fiona. Chop-chop, we've got work to do.'

An irritated growl was all she heard in response.

4

As Julie and Fiona left the armoury with their pistols, the man they wanted to track down walked into a snooker club three miles away in Bermondsey. The entrance was through two slabs of old English oak, stained with various oils over the last hundred years, and led directly off the pavement in a part of the East End not yet gentrified. The only option was up, so Alex Drayce climbed the creaky wooden staircase in front of him to the first floor, each step groaning under his weight. A pair of swinging doors, fitted with frosted glass windows from the waist up, greeted him at the top. On the other side, he heard a gruff voice, loud enough to address a crowd of people, with perhaps half a dozen silhouettes in the room. He hoped the voice belonged to the man he'd come to see.

As he pushed open the doors, he saw the half a dozen estimate was inaccurate: there were double that, only four of whom were playing snooker. Five giant tables lined either side of the big room, creating a funnel leading to the other eight men. The blinds shut, the green lamps hanging above each table were the only sources of light in the room, casting a dim ambient glow through the smoky haze. Drayce walked down the funnel, right between the two rows of tables. The second on his left and the fourth on his right were the ones in use, the people involved no doubt having been at it all night. He guessed all four players were in the region of fifty to sixty years old, but they appeared much older after a night of smoking and drinking around a snooker table rather than in bed asleep, their eyes bloodshot and their backs rounded from stooping over the table, taking shot after shot. The games had probably started around dinner time the day before. Like Drayce, these boys clearly had scores to settle.

Drayce examined the other eight men; the group arranged as seven gathered around one: Peter Talbott. The rest were his henchmen, taking their morning briefing before heading out into the city to collect the numerous debts 'owed' to them for various protection rackets they ran.

Talbott was an ugly old man, with a bad back and breath that made you wonder if his insides might be rotting. Drayce had seen healthier people in mortuary drawers. Talbott's face reminded him of one of those warnings on cigarette packets. As for the seven men hanging on his every word, they all had the bodies of successful powerlifters and the faces of incompetent boxers: big men with flat noses, broken several times, and maybe only a few dozen teeth amongst them. Without exception, the knuckles on their hands were deformed in one way or another – the mark of men long accustomed to violence.

Drayce stood still behind the seven and waited until he'd caught Talbott's eye.

'What do you want?' Talbott asked in his croaky cockney accent.

The seven all turned around. Drayce assessed each of them in turn with a blank expression, making his presence felt, before returning his gaze to Talbott.

'Where's Lynch?' he asked.

'None of your business where he is. I'm still running the day-to-day operations for the time being, so anything you've got to say can be said to me.' Talbott licked his cracked lips and smiled, showing two rows of dark yellow teeth. 'And that's *Mr* Lynch to you.'

Mr Steven Lynch was Peter Talbott's boss, the leader of this group of criminals, who for the past couple of months had been at war with a Turkish element based in the north of the city. It had something to do with who controlled what and where, which was as far as Drayce understood the mentality of these things. Beatings and arson had culminated in a shoot-out that left several members of each gang wounded, and since then, the Turks had threatened Lynch that they would kill his eight-year-old son, Matthew. Lynch had sensibly kept his head down and left Talbott to take care of the daily business while he stayed within the relative safety of the walls of his home.

But of course, the same wasn't possible for Matthew; he had to go to school. The question of how to get Matthew safely from the Lynch household to the school gates and back every day had become a serious problem.

The first option his father undoubtedly considered would have been to have two or three, or maybe even five or six, of his ugly employees handle the school run. But this came with risks. The men Lynch employed were leg-breakers, chosen for their ability to be violent and not much else. They were not subtle, and they were not, by any stretch of the imagination, clever. Added to these issues was that, given the number of steroids and stimulants they took, they were almost as paranoid as a person could be. These men might see a threat where there wasn't one and beat a father half to death, who was simply dropping his child off at the school gates, but was unfortunate enough to 'look Turkish'. This, in Lynch's words, was 'an unacceptable risk'.

Nobody at the extremely expensive private school knew how he'd earned his fortune. They all thought he was a property developer, and he wanted to maintain that façade. Well thought of amongst the teachers and staff, Lynch wanted to protect his reputation, so the job of guarding his son couldn't have gone to the thugs. Instead, he needed a professional. Someone capable of correctly identifying a threat and dealing with it in the most efficient way possible. Someone with experience in planning for every contingency, while blending into the background, unnoticed, until they were required.

He'd needed a professional bodyguard.

He'd chosen Alex Drayce.

Drayce was sure Lynch had just as much trepidation about employing a former police officer as Drayce had about working for a serious criminal, but as a former CTSFO and RaSP officer, he had all the requisite skills, subtlety, and professionalism Lynch required. And, when it came to his son's safety, capability was what really mattered to him.

From Drayce's point of view, he'd initially laughed at the offer, but then thought about it and pictured Matthew, who had no idea who or what his father really was, or how his school fees were paid. He was just an eight-year-old boy, wanting to go to school to learn some things and see his friends, unaware he ran the risk of being kidnapped by Turkish gangsters. In Drayce's opinion, an innocent child should not suffer for the sins of his father.

He'd taken the job, driven Matthew to school and back, and watched over him from far enough away to be discreet, while staying close enough to remove him from his surroundings in the blink of an eye if a threat presented itself. As time went by, deals were made, hands shaken, and lines drawn and agreed upon; the Turkish threat vanished, and life returned to normal for the Lynch family.

Drayce's job had lasted six weeks.

He'd only been paid for four.

'I've come for the rest of my money,' he said to Talbott. 'If you're running things for Lynch, I suggest you resolve the issue.' Talbott's expression didn't change much, his face as gormless and hateful as ever. 'He only owes me three grand, and I'm sure you've got ten times that in cash on these premises.' He stared directly into Talbott's eyes. 'The quicker you give me what's mine, the sooner I'm out of your life.'

A smile slowly spread across Talbott's face as though invisible wires gently pulled on the corners of his mouth. Then he chuckled, a gurgle rising from his chest, the product of a chronic smoking habit. The laughter spread amongst the other seven, keen to show their boss they were onside, even though they probably had no idea what they were laughing at. A few seconds was all Talbott could tolerate before he took out a tissue and coughed up something black.

Finished, he stuffed the wet ball back into his pocket and took a step closer to Drayce, the smile returning. 'You've got a nerve,' Talbott said. 'But then, you filth always have been a bunch of arrogant bastards.' The smile vanished in a heartbeat, replaced with something else entirely. The exact opposite of a smile. 'Whatever Mr Lynch paid you is all you were worth. And I'm telling you now, you'll either leave here with whatever you arrived with, or significantly less, if you catch my drift. Those are your only two options, sunshine. As you are, or missing some bits.'

Talbott moved closer, the seven parting ways to allow him through. 'And what you do manage to limp out of here with depends entirely on how soon you turn around and walk away.'

The energy of the seven changed, their aggression escalating with their boss's. Drayce's right hand balled from a mixture of instinct and muscle memory. He scratched the dark stubble on his cheek as he studied the seven leg-breakers. The biggest was perhaps six feet tall and probably weighed a solid eighteen stone. He lifted his chin to meet Drayce's eyes, as if measuring himself against the guy he might have to lay hands on. His eyes darted across to Drayce's cauliflower ears, his face suggesting he was working out whether it was from rugby, or fighting. Unfortunately for him, it was the latter.

Drayce assessed the challenge: maybe two stone of lean muscle in Drayce's favour, and six inches in height; a trained Malinois eyeing up the cocky neighbourhood mutt for breakfast. But, of course, a violent encounter in this club would not be a one-on-one affair. Drayce would have all seven to tackle, probably all at once. Messy stuff.

Negotiate, he told himself.

'Listen, I haven't come here for trouble,' he said to Talbott. 'I've come to collect what I'm owed by your boss. I shook hands with the man, Peter. You remember, you were there. So please, do what's right, and pay me the rest of my fee.'

Talbott examined him carefully, squinting slightly as he processed his options, and for a moment, Drayce believed his attempt at negotiating had worked.

That feeling didn't last long.

'Piss off!' Talbott said, flinging saliva in Drayce's direction.

Drayce took a deep breath, allowing himself a moment to open his fist, stretching his fingers wide. 'I'm not leaving here without my money.'

Fleeting surprise crossed Talbott's eyes; Drayce knew he wasn't accustomed to people standing up for themselves.

'Are you really that stupid?' Talbott asked.

Drayce undid the button on his tailored suit jacket, parting the grey wool material to make room for the movement he feared might soon be necessary.

'Listen, I'm sure you've got a lot of money to pick up today, and if this kicks off, none of these men will be in any fit state to collect it for you. I also know you keep a decent amount of cash here, which means you can easily make the problem of *me* go away, without the risk of your workforce sustaining any injuries.'

Talbott's arrogant expression made it clear he was unlikely to opt for the easy road. Even if he'd perceived Drayce as the threat he was, backing down and coming across as weak was something he'd be extremely reluctant to let happen, especially with four witnesses over by the snooker tables, all of whom would be quick to spread the word of how soft the Lynch firm had become. It was obvious he felt safe to reject Drayce's demands while nestled amongst his seven leg-breakers.

Drayce gave the peaceful resolution one more try.

'The decision's yours,' he said. 'Either do the right thing by paying me what I'm owed, or set your dogs on me and risk failing to collect your boss's takings, which probably amount to fifty times as much. Think about it… which do you think he'll be angrier about?'

Talbott backed away, slowly, grinning the entire time. Drayce watched the void between them fill with the seven, a pack of wolves crowding around him. As Talbott's lips moved, Drayce knew the old man was about to make the wrong decision.

'Gentlemen,' Talbott said. 'Please do me a favour and introduce this prick's face to the pavement.'

The seven inched forwards to close the net around Drayce.

Time to embrace the savage within him, to park his more civilised self in the wings for a later performance. Perhaps another day, he thought. For now…

Drayce appraised the solid wooden cues, the rock-hard snooker balls, and pictured in his mind how he might use them over the next few minutes.

Then he sighed, clenched his fists, and got to work.

5

He waited until he was out on the street before he counted the money. There had been close to a hundred thousand pounds in cash inside the safe in Talbott's office, but Drayce wasn't a thief; he'd taken what he was owed, plus a little extra to cover the dry-cleaning costs to remove the small splatters of blood decorating his suit.

Counted, he folded the notes in half, wedged them into his jacket pocket, and clenched his hands a few times, testing them out. They were sore, but from experience, he knew the damage was limited; nothing broken, that was for sure. It might have been a different story if he'd been forced to put down all seven, but once the third jaw hit the floor, the rest backed off a little and turned to Talbott, who conceded the loss and resorted to Drayce's original offer of paying him his money to make him go away. Happy he'd been paid – and left the snooker club relatively unscathed – he stuffed his hands into his trouser pockets and set off down Southwark Park Road.

Next on the to-do list was a trip to the gym. He favoured an old black-iron venue in the city. Kong's Barbell Club was an old-school facility: nothing but barbells, cast iron plates, and kettlebells, with a dusting of chalk over every surface.

'Heavy lifting only' was the main rule in that place, which suited Drayce just fine. He'd once seen a guy thrown out – a literal description – for doing bicep curls in a squat rack. Kong's survived the modern fitness industry era because of a group of loyal powerlifters and strongmen who kept the place going. For that reason, it didn't attract the Instagram types. Those folks tended to prefer the clean, commercial gyms the city had to offer, with their walls of mirrors and tanning booths. Drayce's worry was that in the future, they would be the only gyms left, with places like Kong's deemed too rough for most people. He shuddered at the thought.

Today was squat day, so he was glad he'd fuelled up with a big cooked breakfast after he'd woken up that morning. He'd rented an apartment in Southwark since taking on a job in the city a few months back and extended the contract with the landlord when he took on the Lynch job. He thought about the programme he'd follow at the gym after he'd gone to his apartment and changed clothes, planning his training in his head as he walked away from the snooker club.

He hadn't made it far when his phone rang. He took it out of his pocket: a private number. Although tempted to ignore it, it could be work, and as a freelance bodyguard, he took the offers whenever they came; he never knew how far away his next pay cheque was.

He tapped the answer icon. 'Hello?'

The faint background noise of traffic on the other end of the line was dull, as though heard from the inside of a moving vehicle. Then, 'Is that Alex Drayce?' a woman's voice asked.

'Who wants to know?'

'Julie Adler does.'

'Jules? Is that really you? It's been a while.'

'It certainly is, and it certainly has.'

'What can I do for you?'

'It's better we discuss it in person. Are you still at the snooker club?'

Drayce stood still, spooked at what she'd just said. He turned on the spot.

'Where are you?'

'We're on our way to you.'

We? From a woman he presumed was still a detective with the Met, 'we' could mean bad news.

'Just stay where you are,' Drayce heard her say.

A jet-black BMW with no police markings hurtled down the road in his direction, the flashing emergency lights hidden behind the front grilles. He made eye contact with the driver – a youngish female – and then recognised Julie in the front passenger seat, pointing a finger in his direction. The vehicle swerved to the pavement, right next to where Drayce stood. As it stopped by the kerb, the lights switched off and the two front doors opened in unison.

Drayce put his phone away as the two ladies stepped out of the vehicle and approached him. It occurred to him for a split second that the men he'd just assaulted had called three nines on him, but then he discounted it as a realistic possibility. The reputation of Talbott and his goons was already tarnished; they wouldn't want to add snitching to the list. And of course, even if they *had* picked up the phone, the call would elicit a response from the uniforms at the local borough, not the Criminal Investigation Department. That is, unless the snooker club was under surveillance, he thought. Julie and her friend might have just listened to, or even worse, watched him beat three men unconscious.

Drayce wondered if this reunion might be bad news.

Julie's driver was perhaps in her mid to late twenties, slim and attractive, wearing black trousers, a white shirt, and a copper-coloured raincoat that looked expensive. Julie was wearing the same black suit and white shirt he remembered her always wearing from his days in the force. Everything about the pair of them signalled 'serious' as they approached him, as though whatever was behind the phone call and subsequent meeting was the most important thing in their lives right now.

'What can I help you with, Jules?' he asked.

She raised her eyebrows. 'Nice to see you too, Alex.'

He smiled. 'I assumed we were skipping the pleasantries after that arrival. Seems like you two don't have a second to spare.'

'You could say that.'

'Where are you working now? Last time I saw you, you'd hit the big time on the Met's homicide teams.'

'Not anymore. I work for the NCA now.' From habit, she reached inside her jacket pocket and pulled out a black leather wallet, flipping it open to show Drayce her ID. His eyes flicked down to it and then straight back to her face. 'I've gone to great effort to track you down.'

Good job you didn't get here ten minutes earlier, Drayce thought. *Or you might have seen something that would have inspired you to put handcuffs on me.*

'Speaking of which, how exactly *did* you track me down?' he asked.

'Our people pinged your phone.'

He frowned. 'Is that legal?'

Her eyes dropped down to his jacket and bounced straight back up to his eyes. 'Is that blood on your suit?'

Drayce raised his eyebrows. 'Touché.'

'Given the circumstances, it won't cause us any issues if you complain. It needed to be done.'

'And why is that?'

'We had to find you. I know you left the police to work as a bodyguard and I called around some old colleagues to get your number.'

'Sounds serious.'

'It is. I'd like you to come for a ride with us. There's something I want to discuss with you.'

Drayce examined her closely, intrigued. His eyes flicked to the lady next to her, who nodded her head, an attempt at friendliness.

'This is Fiona,' Julie said. 'She works for me.'

Fiona's head whipped round to glare at her colleague. Drayce thought it might have been Julie's use of the word 'for' that upset her.

'What's this all about?' he asked Julie.

She shook her head. 'Not on the street. Let's take a ride.'

'And if I don't want to?'

'Then I'll remind you of what I did for you back in 2012.'

Drayce's eyes narrowed. 'I see.'

Julie took a step closer. 'You owe me, and all I'm asking is for you to hear me out.' She turned her body and held her hand out to the rear door of the BMW. Her expression radiated an insistent quality; she wouldn't take no for an answer. 'Please, Alex. I need your help.'

6

They drove north, with Drayce sitting in the back next to Julie. He was behind the empty passenger seat, which was pushed all the way to the front of the rails. His right shoulder nudged Julie's left, even though she was right up against her door. She had her phone in her hands, swiping and tapping the screen.

From what he could see, she was flipping between a mapping app and a conversation thread on a messaging app regarding the location of someone called Sarah. His chin tucked in and his head pressed up against the roof, his scruffy brown hair rustled every time he turned his head to glance at what she was doing. He hoped this was a short journey. His size had advantages, but being comfortable in the rear of a sporty BMW was definitively not one of them.

Despite his discomfort, he kept a close eye on their surroundings, surprised when they crossed the Thames over Tower Bridge and carried on north, rather than heading west to Vauxhall. He turned to face Julie.

'Aren't we going to your headquarters?'

'No,' she replied, firmly, without looking at him. 'I don't want to walk you through that building. Too many people will see you and the fewer who know of your involvement in this, the better. Besides, we don't have any time to waste… I'll brief you here in the car while we're en route.'

'En route to where?'

She peered at him out of the corner of her eyes. 'You'll find that out only if you're willing to help me after you know what it is you'll be getting into.'

Drayce shrugged. 'Not much choice... a debt's a debt. So how about you crack on and tell me what this is all about?'

Julie finally took her eyes off her phone. 'I tracked you down because I need to make use of your professional capabilities.'

'And once more in plain English?'

'You're a bodyguard. I want you to protect someone for me.'

'Let's start with the basics. Who and why?'

'I'll give you as much background as I can, but there are key pieces of information I must leave out. Not by choice. I'm bound by the Official Secrets Act, and you're a civilian now. This is an extremely sensitive operation. I've got to be careful.'

Drayce nodded. 'Understood, but give me something to work with. The more you keep me in the dark, the less able I'll be to do my job properly.'

Julie grappled with this for a moment. Thinking about exactly how much she could say, Drayce presumed.

'Okay, here goes. I'm a case manager in the NCA's wing of the UK Protected Persons Service. Last night, two of our teams were attacked. Both were short-term protection details designed to keep the witnesses safely hidden until they could be transferred to their permanent handlers with their new identities, due to happen later today. The officers were killed, along with one of the two witnesses. The precise whereabouts of the other is unknown.'

'How on earth did that happen?'

'That's what we're trying to find out.'

'So where do I come in?'

'The second witness. She ran from the safe house when it was attacked, and we believe we know roughly where she is in the city.'

'How?'

'She used her credit card to pay for a taxi, and her debit card to withdraw cash in the early hours of this morning. CCTV footage from the cashpoint shows her alive and well. Once we've located her, I need you to protect her.'

Drayce squinted at Julie. *Need* was a strange choice of word, he thought, especially for someone who worked for an organisation as powerful and well-funded as the NCA. She shouldn't *need* anyone outside of the Agency – not for this.

'Why me?' he asked. 'Why not your own people?'

Julie hesitated. 'Our witness protection programme is the best in the world. The people who were after them should not have been able to find them. That they did, tells me there's a rat somewhere in the system. Until I find out who it is, I don't want to use anyone from the Agency, or the Met. I want an outsider: someone with no involvement in any of this, who I can trust to do the job.'

Drayce took a deep breath. 'I see.'

'I'm one of only five people who know about what I'm offering you. If you accept this job – and I sincerely hope you do, because I have nowhere else to turn – it'll stay within that select group.' She took a moment, eyeing him as she nervously turned her phone in her hands. 'So, what do you think? You interested?'

He smiled at her. 'Of course. Like I said, a debt's a debt.'

Julie smiled back, clearly relieved to have him on board.

'Tell me how you want it to work,' he said.

She was back on her phone, reading messages and tapping away as she replied to him. 'Fiona and I will lead you to her, and then you'll take care of her from that point on. You'll be protecting her on your own, with no support and minimal communication with me. I want her kept safe by someone who doesn't have any current ties to the police or the Agency, at a location where she can't be found by the people who want her dead, just long enough for us to get to the bottom of what's happening and get her safely back into the programme.'

'What did she witness?'

'I can't tell you that.'

'Who wants her dead?'

'I can't tell you that, either.'

Drayce sighed, the tail end of which came out as a grumble, which made Julie look up from her phone.

'I have substantial funds at my disposal,' she said. 'The debt was repaid when you said yes. I'll make doing the actual job worth your while.'

He thought about the cash in his pocket and the figure in his bank account. 'The money doesn't make any difference.'

Julie shrugged. 'All right.'

'But that doesn't mean I won't take it. I just wanted to let you know I'm helping you because it's you. No other reason.'

She smiled. 'That's good to know.'

'How crucial is this witness's evidence to the case?'

Julie's smile morphed into a more sober expression. 'Without her, they walk.'

'And just how much of a threat are *they*?'

Julie stared into his eyes. 'Let me put it this way… during my thirty years of tackling organised crime in this country, I have never met a group of criminals as ruthless and as well-connected as these men. If we don't find her soon, they will. This isn't just about a court case. It's about a woman's life.'

Drayce nodded. 'I want to reiterate a few points before we go any further.'

'I'm all ears.'

'I work on my own, so once she's in my care, I'll take her off the grid and handle things from there on. Tell your hierarchy they shouldn't expect to know where we are. And that includes you.'

Julie raised her eyebrows.

'If I'm doing this, then that's the way it has to be,' Drayce said. 'I don't want to run the risk of our location getting back to whoever's leaking information from within your organisation. For that reason, the only people who'll know where we are, will be me – and her. Deal?'

Julie's eyebrows collapsed into a frown. 'Fine. It's a deal.'

'Good. What can you tell me about your witness?'

Julie slipped a hand behind the lapels on her suit jacket and pulled out a folded piece of A4 paper. She handed it to Drayce, who unfolded it and examined it. It was a passport photograph, scanned and blown up to cover almost the whole sheet. The first thing that caught Drayce's attention was how beautiful she was, strikingly so. Long dark hair framed a face that reminded him of a young Kate Beckinsale, her bright amber eyes razor-sharp with intellect. Wouldn't be hard to pick her face out of a crowd.

'Her name's Sarah Bennett,' Julie said before pausing. Drayce waited expectantly. 'That's all you're getting from me. If she decides to tell you more, then that's up to her, but she's been instructed not to divulge anything to anyone, so she shouldn't.'

'How will she know she can trust me?'

'We'll make contact with her first and introduce you to her, then the two of you can vanish from that point on.'

'Sounds like a plan. I'll keep in regular contact with you and you alone, and I'll want to know precisely what you know of any emerging threats.'

'Understood.'

'Good.' Drayce turned to his window. 'So now we're all up to date on things, can you please tell me where we're going?'

'Not much point now.' Julie's eyes flicked up and down, from her phone to the windscreen. 'We're here.'

7

Sarah shifted her position slightly to ease her discomfort, the flesh on the underside of her body numb against the bare concrete. The cardboard boxes she'd covered herself with were wet from the morning frost, and moving her lower back rattled the steel shutters she leant against. She shook from the cold and her jaw tapped out a rhythm against her knees, which were tucked up to her chin, her body caving in on itself in the effort to retain body heat. She closed her eyes, her mind drifting back to the night before, when her life had taken a monumental turn for the worse.

After the approaching sirens made the gunmen run off, she'd counted to ten, climbed on top of the bin, and vaulted the locked gate, too scared to venture back out through the same gap in the garden fence, knowing it was the way her pursuers would have gone. Staying hidden in the bin might have been the most sensible option, but her desire to run was too overwhelming, wanting to put as much ground as possible between her and those men. Exhausted, she was forced to come to a stop further down the long street. She had listened out for the police, but the sirens she'd heard from the bin were now even more distant, leading her to believe they might have been heading elsewhere, to another emergency somewhere in north London, and weren't coming to rescue her.

After she'd run from the flat in a blind panic, she had been relieved to find her bank cards in her pocket, but her heart sank when she thought of everything she'd left behind, including her phone. Craig had told her to always keep her cards and phone on her, so if she ever had to make a run for it, she'd be able to pay for a bus, tube, or taxi, and would always have a means of dialling 999.

Craig.

The disgusting dark stains on the hallway walls rocketed to the front of Sarah's mind. She tried to blank them out but it was pointless. The image had been so terrible she wondered if she'd ever be able to forget it, or the smell of his blood, mixed with the burnt gunpowder that had hung in the air like a thick fog.

She flung her head back, rattling the shutters in her angry outburst. Tears streamed down her face, just as they had done the night before, her skinny jeans saturated up to her knees from the long, wet grass she'd run through, her limbs shaking from fear rather than the cold, despairing about what she should do next. She remembered panicking about not having her phone on her, stamping her feet in the street as she pictured herself holding it in her hand while looking out of the window at those kids in the park. Then her mind had regurgitated the image of it resting on the window ledge, moments before Francesca had barked at her.

She made me put it down, Sarah had thought. *If it wasn't for her hassling me, I'd have remembered to pick it up and put it back in my pocket. It's thanks to her I'm completely alone.*

A powerful surge of guilt washed over her for thinking that thought. Her panicked, terrified mind was desperate to find someone to blame for her circumstances, but despite how little the two of them had gelled, Francesca didn't deserve to be that person.

She died protecting you, Sarah told herself, the tears flowing freely down her face as she stood alone on that dark street.

Minutes later, having cried out the stress of narrowly avoiding death, she caught her breath and walked on. Eyes peeled for any black vans full of hitmen, she'd waved down a taxi. A moment's silence had elapsed when the driver asked her where she wanted to go. Further north and out of London was a good idea, but she wasn't familiar with anywhere outside of the M25. London she knew, so deeper into the heart of the city it would have to be. At least for now.

She'd asked him to drop her off on the High Road in Tottenham – an area where hopefully there was less risk of being spotted by the people who were after her. There she had withdrawn money from a cashpoint, and wandered around for a while, searching for somewhere safe to sleep. None of the hotels she'd passed were willing to take guests in the middle of the night without a booking, and given how exhausted she was, a quiet industrial estate was the best of a bad bunch of options.

A length of chain, fixed together by an old padlock, secured the gate at the entrance. Suitable for stopping a vehicle from getting in, but with just enough slack to allow Sarah to slip through sideways. She'd found some shutters on the side of the main building and curled up there for the night.

The main downside was how unbearably cold it had been. Some old cardboard boxes in a recycling bin helped her to stay relatively dry by preventing the frost from settling on her, but the cold had seeped down to her bones. Jeans, trainers, a thin white t-shirt, and a grey woollen cardigan were not ideal garments for rough sleeping in London in January; the glee of having survived the initial attack had been well and truly beaten down by the misery of shivering in the freezing night air.

She needed a plan. Sarah kicked the cardboard aside and stood up. To generate some warmth, she marched back and forth in front of the shutters, rubbing her hands together vigorously. She was still alive and free, for now. Ultimately, she had to decide whether she could trust the NCA enough to make contact. She could easily purchase a burner phone from somewhere, but the contact numbers for witness protection were in her phone, back in the flat, not in her head. Besides, last night's experience had shown the authorities weren't capable of keeping her safe, so what was to say they would do a better job given a second chance? Would she be better off disappearing on her own? After all, if she only had herself to trust, then only she could let herself down, and for some strange reason, that was a more palatable option.

A loud metallic clatter rang out across the yard as she booted the shutters with the ball of her right foot from pure frustration. She'd never felt more alone, suddenly overcome with a desire to run to the nearest police station and cry her heart out to the first officer she could find. The thought of falling into the arms of a big law enforcement organisation was comforting, to say the least, but so was the idea of staying hidden, keeping her movements to herself. One thing was for sure: to survive and prevent the people hunting her from finding her, she'd have to take things one step at a time. The big picture was far too chaotic to make sense of. Focusing on little bite-sized chunks of time and surviving from one meal to the next would be a good way of keeping an attainable goal on the horizon.

She stopped pacing and stood still, her numb hands on her rumbling stomach. The thought of food brought home to her just how hungry she was. The stress of the last twelve hours had taken its toll, and her body cried out for energy. She walked purposefully away from the shutters and retraced her route to the gate, to the city streets that by now should be busy enough for her to walk around unnoticed and anonymous. Her decision on whether or not to trust the police could wait. For now, the first goal of the new day was to find somewhere warm that served breakfast.

8

'Already where?'

'Tottenham,' Julie replied.

Drayce looked past the stationary queue of traffic in front of them and examined the busy streets. 'Because this is where you believe Sarah is, I presume?'

'Correct.'

'You able to tell me how you were able to track her down so easily?'

Julie allowed her eyes to break away from her phone, just in time to spot Fiona turning her head to the side, her lips parted to answer his question. She made eye contact long enough to convey to Fiona she should stay quiet, then she eyed Drayce with suspicion. 'Only if you can give me a good reason as to how that information will help you keep her safe.'

'You said you're worried about a corrupt officer in the NCA...'

'Or the Met,' Julie was quick to add.

'Yes, or the Met. Well, it just seems to me that if you're able to track her down with ease, then maybe they are as well?'

'The technology we've used to find her isn't available to many people in the Agency,' Julie said, her eyes now back on the screen. 'And even fewer in the Met. The risk they'll get to her first is slim to none.'

'But not impossible?'

Julie sighed with frustration. 'No, I suppose not. But let me put it this way, if they were able to track her down using this technology, it would significantly narrow down the list of potential suspects. It's pretty high-tech stuff, access to which would require an NCA officer to have a level of security clearance that maybe only a couple of dozen people have.'

Drayce wanted to know more. 'Enlighten me.'

After a flurry of rapid finger taps, Julie said, 'She withdrew money from a cashpoint in Tottenham several hours ago, and we know from facial recognition technology that she hasn't used public transport, so we're pretty happy she's still in the city somewhere.'

'Maybe she rented a car, or stole one.'

'She can't drive. And by that, I don't mean her licence was revoked, or that she's a terrible driver. I mean she physically can't drive. She's lived in central London her whole life. Never had to learn, so never did. She'd be as much use behind the wheel of a car as I would be behind the controls of a fighter jet.'

'Perhaps she's been walking all night? She looks pretty fit in her photo. I reckon she could cover a good distance overnight.'

Julie shook her head. 'No, not possible.'

'You can't walk far in this city without walking under a camera,' Fiona said. Her eyes flicked between Drayce and Julie in the rear-view mirror. 'And with the standards of our facial recognition software, we'd know about it the moment she did.'

The vehicle lurched forwards. Drayce saw they were slowly crawling along Tottenham High Road in time with the other cars around them. An endless line of clothing stores, nail salons, barbers, cafes, and supermarkets stretched out into the distance on either side.

'This is where she withdrew the money,' Julie said.

Drayce followed her line of sight to two cashpoints in the wall of a bank. 'What time was that?' he asked.

'Just gone midnight, 12:03 to be precise.'

'How much did she withdraw?'

'Three hundred pounds.'

'That's enough walking around money to last a while.'

'Indeed.'

'And there's been no more activity on her card since?'

Julie shook her head. 'Nothing.'

'Which means it's unlikely she checked into a hotel for the night, because most demand to scan a credit card, but it doesn't discount her paying a taxi driver in cash to drive her out of London, to an area where she can travel more freely without risking walking under a camera every few steps.'

'Actually, we've discounted that as a possibility. After we picked up her credit card payment for a taxi to Tottenham, we checked with every hotel in the area that would take cash for a room, as well as every major taxi firm in this part of town, and there haven't been any fares out of the city overnight.'

'None they'll tell you about, anyway.'

Julie eyebrows lifted high again. 'If you ran a taxi firm, would you lie to a national law enforcement agency, risking your business and your freedom for the sake of a complete stranger?'

He took a moment to consider his answer. 'I guess not.'

'Me neither. And Sarah left her phone in the safe house, which means she can't summon an Uber, so I think it's safe to assume she wasn't driven out of the city, and we know she couldn't have driven herself, and we also know she didn't take a bus or a train, because they're all littered with cameras.'

'Which means she hasn't gone far, and probably spent the night sleeping rough a short radius from that cash machine.'

Julie nodded. 'That's the theory we're working with, which is why we've brought you here. She can't stay out of sight forever. When she shows her face on these streets, we'll know where she is.'

Just as Julie said this, her phone made a noise. Both she and Drayce looked down at the screen and saw a fresh window had popped up.

'Is that an update?' Fiona asked, her frantic eyes wide in the mirror, obviously frustrated that she had to focus on the road.

Julie ignored her question, too busy with her phone. Despite the poor angle at which he was reading, Drayce's heart rate spiked because of what Julie's technical support team reported.

'Is that far from here?' he asked.

'About a hundred yards up the street,' Julie replied.

He scanned the faces of pedestrians. 'How certain are they it's her?'

'One hundred percent. The technology doesn't lie, but they've viewed the footage remotely and have visually confirmed it's her.'

'How long ago?'

'Twelve seconds.'

Drayce opened his door and climbed out while the car was still moving slowly in the traffic.

'Wait!' Julie shouted, but he just ignored her and jogged up to the pavement, slipping between bodies as he joined the heavy footfall. So focused was he on covering some distance to get Sarah in sight and follow her, he didn't even notice the four men in the silver Range Rover SVR he passed in the line of traffic.

–

Finding somewhere to eat wasn't as easy as Sarah had thought; most of the restaurants she'd walked past had been fried chicken and takeaway places, and therefore shut in the mornings. The cafes that were open resembled places from which the homeless might turn down free food. She carried on along the High Road, retracing her route from the night before; she remembered passing a Costa cafe shortly after withdrawing money from the cashpoint. She had walked the entire way with her hands in her pockets and they were just starting to feel human again, the numbness that had soaked through overnight seeping away to nothing. The rest of her felt better too, no longer shivering thanks to the pleasant morning sun slowly taking the chill off her back as it peeked its head above the city landscape; the pace of her walk also generated some much-needed body warmth.

But no matter how much the winter sun shone, and no matter how fast she walked, neither would satisfy her hunger pains. Her stomach rumbled as she spotted the Costa up ahead on her right, an oasis in the desert, and she walked even faster than before, weaving between bodies as she overtook people. With her hands a little warmer, she took them out of her pockets and ran her fingers through her hair, cringing at how greasy it felt. Next on the agenda after food would be to find somewhere where she could have a hot shower.

She pushed on, ignoring her sore feet and the aches and pains from sleeping on cold concrete. She couldn't wait to get inside the cafe, but it wasn't just the warmth and the food spurring her on; she didn't feel comfortable out on the street, certainly not on foot. It made her feel vulnerable.

She found herself examining every single face she walked past with suspicion, imagining one of them reaching out and grabbing hold of her before dragging her inside a vehicle, kicking and screaming. It was crowded in this part of town, which was probably a good thing, but would it really make a difference? Would anyone step in and help her, or would the best response she could hope for by today's standards be somebody filming the kidnapping on their phone? That sort of thing went viral every time, and a viral social media platform would be far more tempting to many people than helping to stop a stranger from being abducted.

Shaking these negative, cynical thoughts from her mind, she picked up her pace even more as she darted to the side of a couple walking hand in hand, a few doors away from the cafe. She was in such a hurry that as she stepped to the side of the lady in front of her, she walked head-on into the path of a big guy in a grey suit.

'Wow, sorry,' Drayce said after Sarah's face bounced off his chest. 'You came out of nowhere.' He held her by her shoulders as she took a step back from him with a dazed and confused expression on her face.

'No, no, it's my fault,' she said as she collected herself, a smile forming from politeness. 'I'm in a hurry and I wasn't watching where I was going.'

'Yeah, you were moving quickly. Are you okay?'

She brought a hand up to her forehead. 'I'm fine.'

'All right, you take it easy. Better late than never, as they say.'

'Yes, thank you.'

They stepped around one another and carried on walking in their respective directions. Drayce glanced at the reflection in the car windows and saw her step off the pavement into the Costa cafe. He carried on walking for a few steps and then moved to the side of the pavement, his back pressed against a doorway as he took out his phone and called Julie on the number she'd rung him on earlier. She answered after the first ring.

'Where the hell have you gone?' she asked.

'A little further up the road. I'm quicker on foot than sitting in that sluggish traffic jam. And I've found Sarah.'

He heard a sharp intake of breath. 'Where is she?'

'In a Costa cafe on the main road. It'll be on your left soon. I'll keep an eye on the cafe's exit and I'll update you if she leaves.'

'Okay. Where are you precisely?'

Drayce looked behind him. 'I'm in a doorway adjacent to an off-licence, three up from the cafe. Come and get me once you've made contact with her.'

'Will do.'

He cancelled the call and put his phone back in his pocket, then tilted his head in the direction of the cafe's exit.

They'd found Sarah a lot quicker than he'd expected, but now that he thought about it, with the kind of toys the NCA had at their fingertips, it made tracking another human being across London a fairly simple task. Had Sarah been a little more switched on, she could have made them work for a few days before they got to her. Using bank cards was a hell of a giveaway, as was wandering around on foot inside the surveillance capital of Europe. Given the background information they had about her, coupled with their surveillance software and facial recognition technology, it was a wonder they hadn't found her sooner.

Drayce didn't know what kind of capabilities the people who were after her had, but it was clear he would have to teach Sarah a thing or two about staying under the radar if he planned on doing a successful job of keeping her alive.

Light rain falling increased the speed of everyone walking past. A few umbrellas popped open, carving a path through the crowds under the threat of their spiky tips. Drayce pressed himself harder against the doorway to avoid getting wet and pondered the issue of personality: always something to consider when protecting a client, especially under these unusual circumstances. He hoped Sarah wasn't averse to following orders. Their introduction would be quick and to the point, and they wouldn't have a great deal of time to get to know one another before he had to tell her exactly what to do without the luxury of standing around to debate the issue. Normally he'd have a long sit-down with a new client to establish what they expected of one another; with Sarah, they'd have to do this while on the move; very different from how he'd normally done things. Drayce hoped she'd be easy to get along with.

The sight of four men heading for the cafe interrupted his thoughts. Their body language, and the way their eyes assessed the crowds, meant Drayce clocked them immediately. He took out his phone and kept his head down, pretending to be busy with something on the screen, keeping the men in his peripheral vision. Meandering as they approached the cafe, they stopped near to the entrance and fanned out, scanning faces, as if checking for anyone paying them too much attention. Drayce stopped pretending to be on his phone and called Julie.

'What's up?' she asked.

'Do you have another team working with you and Fiona?'

'No. Why?'

'Because there's one here, loitering at the front of the cafe.'

There was a slight delay in Julie's response. 'Describe them to me.'

The four men separated into two pairs and Drayce took in their details and relayed them. One of them was much bigger than the others: a physical giant, even by Drayce's standards. Probably about 6'6'', maybe 6'7'', armoured by nature, his body thick with muscle. He had short black hair and a widow's peak, shaved down to a quarter inch. A thick slab of a forehead sloped down to a prominent brow ridge and a set of hard features: a clay bust modelled with a lump hammer by an artist short on time. A patch of rough scar tissue on the right-hand side of his head where an ear should have been completed the monstrous image.

The guy next to him was a regular gym monkey, his wide shoulders and thick neck barely contained within his clothing. He had a huge black beard that touched his chest, and although Drayce couldn't see them clearly, he had tattoos on the backs of both hands.

The other pair had the appearance of before and after photographs on a SlimFast advert: one chunky with a shaved head, the other slim with wavy blond hair. The chunky guy's complexion was a dark shade of pink, a steroid addict with a blood pressure problem. His skinny friend might have been on a register. He had black circles around eyes that belonged to a predator, his gaunt facial features drew down to thin lips, making him appear almost snake-like.

Drayce heard the tips of Julie's fingernails tapping on the screen of her phone as she noted everything he was telling her.

'What concerns you about them?' she asked.

'They're paying a lot of attention to the cafe Sarah went into, and there's something about them I don't like.'

'Explain.'

He examined them as best he could without drawing their attention to him. He parted his lips to offer Julie the explanation she wanted, but no words came out. The cop's nose he'd spent eighteen years developing told him they were up to no good, but he couldn't form a coherent reason. Julie would just have to accept his gut instinct.

'They're here to do something bad,' he said. 'I'm sure of it. And if they're not your team, then I worry whose they might be.'

'Can you get a photo of them? This might be time-critical.'

Drayce tilted his phone, snapped half a dozen photographs on the sly of the four men, and sent them to her.

'They're on their way to you,' he said. 'I'm going to move closer so I can intervene if something happens.'

'No,' Julie ordered. Drayce thought he heard car doors slamming shut on the other end of the line. 'We're not messing about in this traffic any longer, we're out on foot. Stay where you are and wait for us to get there.'

He watched the four men slip black masks over the bottom halves of their faces. The giant stayed in front of the cafe with the man he dubbed Blackbeard, a ridiculous spectacle with the mass of hair bunched up underneath his mask, while the Slim-Fast twins walked around to the back. The giant and Blackbeard turned to face the doors, giving Drayce the impression they were preparing to make their entry.

'They've covered their faces,' he said. 'They're getting ready for something.'

The giant took out his phone, dialled a number, and put it to his ear. Drayce had no doubt he was communicating with the pair who'd gone around the back, probably to ensure they were in position before they went in after Sarah. The giant put the phone away and they both moved to the doors. Drayce kept his eyes on them until they were out of sight.

'Shit,' he said.

'What is it?' Julie asked.

'Two of them are covering the back of the building and the other two have gone inside. I can't wait any longer. I'm going in after them.'

'No, wait for me and Fiona to arrive. Did you hear me, Alex? You still there? Alex?'

Julie's voice faded out as Drayce dropped his phone in his pocket. He pushed off the doorway, stepped out into the rain, and marched to the cafe.

9

Drayce covered the distance with a fast walk, his long strides giving him the pace of your average person's jogging speed. He used the rain as an advantage, a reason for rushing, helping him blend in with the other customers hurrying to get into the dry. At the cafe's entrance, he slowed and took a few deep breaths before shaking the raindrops off his shoulders, pushing open the doors, and stepping inside.

The cafe was identical to every other Costa on the planet: wooden furniture everywhere and a long queue of customers alongside a display of cakes behind glass; on the other side, baristas worked hard, their red uniforms moving back and forth amidst a cloud of steam from the espresso machines. Drayce strolled across the floor, scanning faces. He spotted Sarah at the front of the queue, paying for a big tray of food and drinks. The two men had just taken a seat at a table. He joined the end of the queue, a valid reason for standing around to watch how things played out.

After paying, Sarah picked up her tray and walked to a table in the corner of the room. The two men stood up and followed her. As she put down her tray, she slid her backside across the bench until she was right in the corner, which meant she could see the entire room, but ultimately a mistake because she was trapped between the table and two walls, unable to get to her feet in a hurry during an emergency. Drayce watched her assess the two men approaching her table; her face indicated she understood her mistake.

They slid in beside and opposite her, their body language relaxed and friendly. The masks they wore obscured their identities to any onlookers without highlighting themselves as suspicious; many people still wore Covid-19 masks while out in public. Drayce stayed in the queue, not wanting to make a move just yet, confident the two men didn't intend to execute her in a busy cafe in broad daylight. He could afford to wait a little longer for Julie and Fiona to arrive with their badges and guns to do things legally. The big guy with the missing right ear leant forwards and said something to Sarah, before nodding to his bearded mate, who opened his fleece, revealing something hidden underneath.

A gun, no doubt.

Sarah's eyelids peeled back in horror, her face the colour of fresh, untouched, powdery snow as the blood drained from her complexion. Drayce tapped out a message to Julie, warning her the men were armed, hoping it might make her reconsider a call for back-up. He knew from experience an armed response vehicle could be on scene in a couple of minutes.

The guy with only one ear gripped Sarah's arm with his big right hand. He was subtle with it; to casual bystanders, it might appear to be a caring gesture, but Drayce saw his fingers digging hard into her upper arm, their tips turning white with the pressure.

We've got you, was the clear physical message conveyed. *You're coming with us, whether you want to or not.*

The giant stood up, lifting Sarah to her feet, keeping hold of her arm as she shuffled out from behind the table. The other guy moved in close and took hold of Sarah's other arm, the tattoo of a snake's head visible on the back of his hand, the body of which slithered under the sleeve of his fleece, and would no doubt travel up his entire arm.

Drayce was familiar with abductions required to appear consensual to avoid a scene. They wanted to get her out of the cafe and into a vehicle where they'd take her somewhere to kill her quietly.

Drayce left the queue and approached the threesome as they left the table, reminding himself that the guy with the beard was armed, or at least had a weapon of some sort under his fleece. He'd deal with him first. As he crossed the cafe, Drayce shut down the civilised part of his brain and pushed aside his inhibitions. For the next few minutes, they'd just get in the way.

Between him and the men were three tables, with people sitting at them. To his right, a low wall with a wooden top acted as a barrier between the seated customers and the constant stream of people queueing for service. To his left, a staircase led to another seated area on the first floor. The route they were taking to the exit would take them right by the bottom step. Drayce timed his pace to put him a couple of steps up by the time the threesome manoeuvred their way around the furniture and walked past the bottom. They were close when his left foot touched the first step. As his right planted on the second, they were almost level with his back, and as his left touched the third, he pivoted on the ball of his foot and turned to face them.

The sole of his shoe made direct contact with the top of the bearded guy's mask, the impact on his nose resembling a baseball bat to the face. Drayce had kicked him powerfully at an angle, and instead of falling sideways into Sarah, he sailed behind her for several feet across the cafe, gliding across the room as if on roller skates, and collided with the low wall. He toppled over it into the queue of people on the other side.

The big guy with the missing ear pushed Sarah out of the way and faced Drayce, the scowl evident in spite of the mask. Capitalising on the element of surprise, Drayce jumped off the steps and cracked him under his chin with a flying knee. Bringing his clenched fists up under his chin as he weaved, Drayce loaded up on his left leg before triggering his hips, torso, and shoulders for a tiny, yet vital, pivot on the foot and hip to generate power before slamming a left hook into the guy's jaw. Every ounce of his twenty stone was behind his fist, snapping the man's head around and turning off his brain like a light switch; his body hit the table behind him and slumped to the ground.

A lady screamed. Several people jumped to their feet, some waving their phones as they tried to film what had just happened. Sarah hadn't moved an inch throughout the melee. She just stood there, ashen, as still as a statue, with her hands up to her face.

'Come with me,' Drayce said as he grabbed one of her arms to drag her to the exit, eager to get out of there. But the Before version of the SlimFast twins stood just on the other side of the doors, his fat face peering through the glass. Drayce made eye contact for a split second before turning around for the back exit, only to halt again when he saw the After-SlimFast man approaching from that direction.

This twin drew his pistol and the entire cafe erupted into chaos as people ran for the exits, blocking Before-SlimFast from getting inside.

With no sign of Julie and Fiona, the only option was up. He turned to the stairs, one hand on Sarah's arm and the other on the back of her neck as he covered her. He hoped the first floor might provide another means of escape, or would at least buy them some time for the police to arrive, undoubtedly on their way now that a gun had been drawn in public. But the first bullet rang out, the metal body clipping the steps behind his heels, and blocked out these thoughts from Drayce's mind, forcing him to focus on one thing.

Running.

10

Upstairs was almost identical to downstairs: a large open area full of tables and chairs. Meals and cups of coffee lay abandoned; people sprawled on the floor, cowering under tables and behind chairs as Drayce and Sarah hurtled across the room. At the far end, Drayce shouldered open a staff-only door that led to a hallway and another set of stairs to the top floor. He pushed Sarah ahead, then followed just as a bullet whizzed over his shoulder and embedded in the wall by his ear with a puff of plaster dust.

He pushed Sarah on, urging her to move faster. The staircase went up and then came back on itself, leading to two rooms used as office spaces. The one to their right had a big sash window overlooking a flat roof and a back yard. Not ideal, but by far the best option they had.

'In here,' Drayce said as he pushed Sarah inside.

He followed her in, gripped onto the edge of a desk and dragged it over to block the door. Sarah barely paid any attention to what he was doing, clearly in shock. She backed off into the far corner and brought her hands up to her face again, palms pressed to her temples as though blocking out everything happening. The desk in place, Drayce opened the sash window and pinpointed a route down to ground level. Footsteps, fast and angry, stomped up the stairs. He strode to Sarah, who, visibly shaking and terrified, stared down at her feet. She had to trust him if they were to get away from these people: he held her lightly by her shoulders and spoke softly.

'Listen to me, Sarah, I'm not one of them.' Her eyes rolled up to meet his; glistening tears reflected his image at him. 'I'm working with the authorities and I'm here to help you get away from those men.' She was trying to keep her eyes down, not wanting to look at him. 'I've been asked by the NCA to protect you, and to get away from these people who want to kill you, I need you to—'

At a sudden, forceful, blinding pain in his groin, he buckled forwards just as Sarah lowered her knee and ran around him. He collapsed to the floor, braced against the carpet with the palm of his right hand, his left tucked between his legs. He heard her climb out of the sash window behind him, her nails scrabbling at the wooden frame, the soles of her trainers scraping the brickwork. He groaned, nauseated, as he stood up and staggered to the window; he heard Sarah's feet land on the flat roof below, and saw her run across the rubber surface to an alleyway at the back. He leant against the window frame and took a deep breath to block out the pain – in vain – before a noise made him turn around.

The footsteps on the staircase were in the corridor; going out of the window was no longer an option; he'd be far too easy a target when the door flew open. In two large bounds, he reached the hinge side just as the first kick went in. As expected, the desk only provided a second's delay as the men forced their way in. The legs dragged across the carpet and, the gap wide enough, the SlimFast twins rushed into the room, pistols raised in front of them.

Instinct kicked in. As the door swung shut behind them, Drayce attacked them from their blind spot, hammer-fisting the gun-wielding arm of the one nearest to him. The fat man yelped when the bottom of Drayce's fist made contact with his bicep and the gun fell from his hand. Drayce kicked it away with his left foot and then pushed off his right as he threw a right cross into the man's jaw, sending him crashing into his skinny friend. With the pair lined up, Drayce drove the ball of his right foot through the gut of the man he'd just punched, unloading the kick with enough force to send them both careering backwards in the direction of the open window. Luckily for the pair, the backs of their thighs caught on the window ledge, wedging them, stopping them from falling out.

After-SlimFast aimed his pistol at Drayce, unable to steady himself enough to take an accurate shot because his fat friend was pinning him against the window ledge. Drayce charged, dropping his shoulder as he slammed into the fat guy's belly and collected his legs from under him, the domino effect tipping both men out of the window.

Drayce heard two dull thuds, one louder than the other as they hit the flat roof below. He peered down at their writhing bodies, heard them moaning in pain, and knew they were out of the chase. He turned around and retrieved the gun he'd knocked to the floor: a black SIG Sauer P365 XL. He checked for a chambered round, dropped the weapon into his jacket pocket, and then moved back to the window.

He reduced the drop to the flat roof significantly by hanging on the outside of the ledge, landing safely on his feet thanks to the cushioning provided by the would-be kidnappers. The air rushed out of their lungs like burst balloons. After-SlimFast's gun had fallen from his grip when he'd landed and lay on the rubber a couple of metres in front of Drayce; he stepped off his squidgy landing pads and picked it up, noticing it was the same model as the other weapon. State-of-the-art pistols: not something your average villain could get their hands on. Serious guns meant serious criminals.

Better be on my guard twenty-four seven from now on.

He dropped it into the pocket on the other side of his jacket to balance the weight, and took a moment to look at the two men at his feet, no longer the intimidating presence they were a moment ago. Both clutched their chests where Drayce's boots had impacted. The skinny twin with wavy blond hair curled up in pain as he held his knee; the fat one with the shaved head almost certainly had a broken ankle. Neither would be running after Sarah any time soon.

Rather than wait around to help detain those two – more important he catch up with Sarah – Drayce ran to the far edge of the roof, climbed down to the alleyway, and ran after her. While on the move, he took out his phone and called Julie.

'Where are you?' Her voice stern and to the point.

'I'm following Sarah. She ran off down an alleyway at the back of the cafe.'

'What happened?'

'The men I told you about tried to take her, so I intervened. Where are *you*?'

'We heard gunshots and we're clearing the cafe. How exactly did you intervene?'

Drayce slowed down at the end of the alleyway and paused on the street, checking left and right for any sign of Sarah. 'I knocked two of them out on the ground floor, and pushed the other two out of a first-floor window onto a flat roof.'

There was a delay before Julie responded. Drayce pictured her face.

'You did what?' she asked.

'Necessary, I'm afraid. They had guns and I didn't.'

'The extent of their injuries?'

'Not good, but not fatal. I doubt they're mobile yet.'

'Well, the ground floor's clear, so two of them have got away. Where's this flat roof you're talking about?'

'At the back of the cafe.'

'Hang on, we're just moving up to the first floor now.'

He explained to Julie how to get to the window he'd climbed out of, and while he waited for her to catch up, he jumped onto the roof of a taxi parked at the kerb for a better view down the street. Over the heads of pedestrians and the roofs of cars, he spotted Sarah running along the pavement in a blind panic, barging through people to get away as fast as possible.

'The roof's clear,' Julie said. 'They've all got away.'

Drayce was stunned to hear they'd been able to get up and walk, never mind cover enough distance to escape before Julie and Fiona got there. But he couldn't let the whereabouts of those men dominate his thoughts. Not until he'd caught up with Sarah.

'Alex?' Julie asked. 'You still there?'

'I've got to go. I'll catch up with Sarah and make sure she's safe.'

He ended the call, dropped his phone in his jacket pocket, and jumped down off the taxi's roof.

One of the many benefits of being six foot six and twenty stone was that other people weren't often substantial enough to be classed as obstructions. Everyone who saw Drayce coming moved out of his way, noticed by the people further ahead who did the same, creating an effect similar to Moses parting the Red Sea. The flash of Sarah's grey cardigan disappeared down a road on the right. He ran around the corner at speed, the pavement nowhere near as crowded, and spotted her ahead. The gap between them about twenty metres, he pushed on even harder to catch up before she went out of sight again, every stride bringing him closer to her. Sarah appeared to be slowing down as her initial adrenaline dump wore off.

Three shop lengths turned into two, and then one, and just as he was about to reach out and grab hold of her, she slowed to a stop and moved into a gap in the brickwork that led to two doors, which appeared to be entrances to the flats above the row of shops.

Drayce crowded the gap, casting a big shadow over her exhausted body as she slumped a shoulder against the wall, unable to run any further. Seeing the shadow, she turned around and tucked her chin in an instinctively defensive posture. He did his best to come across as non-threatening as possible – not easy for someone built the way he was.

'Listen,' he said between heavy gasps. 'I'm on your side.'

Sarah didn't reply. She just glared at him with more than a mild sense of distrust.

'Think about it. If I were one of them, why would I fight them off the way I did? I could have killed the two I threw out of that window.'

'Did you?' she asked.

He took a couple more breaths before he answered her, elated she was talking to him. Opening up communications was a step closer to gaining her trust. 'No. They got away, somehow.'

'Shame.'

Drayce smiled. 'You're not wrong.'

Sarah kept her chin tucked in and folded her arms in front of her chest. 'I need proof you are who you say you are.'

'I understand, and I'll get you that proof, but for now, we need to get somewhere safe, and then I'll contact the NCA officer who brought me into this and you can speak to her. Sound fair?'

She looked him up and down, rose slightly from her defensive posture, and nodded, clearly exhausted, her eyes puffy and bloodshot. As she parted her lips to speak, Drayce saw tears threatening.

'But where's safe?' she asked.

He peered over his shoulders at both ends of the street for signs they'd been followed. He touched his jacket pockets to check the two guns were still there, turned back to face Sarah, and held out his hand.

'Wherever you're with me,' he said.

11

The team of men sent to abduct Sarah made it safely back to their Range Rover before the police arrived and raced out of the area without doing anything reckless enough to draw attention to themselves. They headed east out of the city, searching for somewhere to stop where there weren't many people around. Stan drove, Marcus next to him, doing his best to patch up his broken nose using the rear-view mirror; Freddie and Leo were in the back, the pair of them writhing in pain. From what they'd described, they were both lucky to be alive.

Stan pulled down his visor and looked in the mirror, tracking his jawline up to the ugly patch of pink scar tissue where his left ear had been bitten off in a fight, back when he'd worked the doors years ago. He took his left hand off the steering wheel and touched his broken jaw with his fingertips, delicately, a child tentatively examining a grazed knee.

But this was no grazed knee.

Pain on a level he'd never experienced before bolted through his face and into his brain; he screwed his eyes shut. A second later, he opened them, pleased to see he hadn't lost control of the vehicle. He wanted to scream, to roar, to shout his frustrations to the world, but his broken teeth would only add to his misery. He'd learnt that the hard way shortly after he'd woken up and realised Sarah was no longer in his grasp, and he wasn't keen to repeat his mistake. He slammed the visor up, put his hand back on the steering wheel, and tried to concentrate.

Near Walthamstow, on the busy North Circular Road, in Stan's mind they were now far enough away from the carnage in Tottenham for them to stop and sort out their shit, so he took a right at the next junction and headed south. A couple of minutes later, he turned onto a quiet residential street, lined either side with a mixture of detached and semi-detached red-brick houses. Halfway up on the left, wooden boards surrounded a building being renovated. He spotted a gap where two boards had been left open, presumably to give the workmen access for their heavy plant equipment. He slowed down to a crawl and stared through the gap; it was unoccupied, with no signs of builders at work. After a quick glance around the street to confirm nobody was out on foot, he turned sharply, pulled onto the driveway, and backed in behind the boards, out of view of the road. He checked for cameras and, happy they couldn't be seen by any third parties, he took a deep breath through his nostrils – even passing air over his broken teeth hurt – switched off the engine, and turned to face Marcus.

'We should be all right here for a while.' He felt a couple of his back teeth wobble, and heard a new lisp to his strong cockney accent. 'At least long enough to get patched up and figure out what our next move is gonna be.'

Marcus nodded his head and carried on examining his nose in the mirror. Stan looked at him: the word broken didn't seem adequate. The bleeding had stopped, but at its worst, it had poured from him, soaked into his beard, and dried to form a thick, crusty mass hanging from his face. He'd initially had his hand clamped over it to stem the bleeding, and dark currents of claret tracked down his arm where it had run freely, his snake tattoo crying tears of blood. Stan turned around to Freddie and Leo.

'How bad is it?' he asked them.

'Hurts like fuck,' Leo replied, clutching at his ankle.

'Same here,' Freddie said. 'My knee's swelling up pretty bad.'

Stan opened his door, put one boot on the ground, and then turned to Marcus.

'We'll strap them up and get back on the road.' He climbed out of the car, took a single step away, and turned back to Marcus. 'And call our informant. I want to know what the fuck's going on.'

Marcus left his nose alone and stepped out of the vehicle.

—

Twenty minutes later, they'd strapped Leo's ankle and Freddie's knee tightly with old rags from the boot and had popped some painkillers to take the edge off their discomfort. Stan assessed the pair of them, sitting on the tailgate, resting their legs. In the corner of his eye, he saw Marcus a few feet away, making the call. Freddie had his cut-throat razor in his hand, flicking it in and out, while his dark, baggy eyes gazed through the curtains of blond hair that hung down his forehead, personifying the sociopath he was. Nobody had spoken for the past five minutes as each of them dealt with their own personal hell, waiting for the meds to kick in fully. Leo broke the silence first.

'What are we going to tell them?'

Stan glared at him. 'We're not telling them anything, not until she's dead.'

'But they said they wanted to know everything and—'

'I know what they said, but if you think I'll be the one to call them with bad news, think again. Unless you want to get on the phone and tell them yourself?' Leo didn't reply. He stared down at his feet. 'Didn't think so. We'll get a message to them through their solicitor once we've got her back. He's not due to visit them until late this afternoon, so we've got plenty of time.'

'Who was that bloke she had with her? I reckon he must be a copper.'

Freddie shook his head as he interjected. 'Didn't behave like any filth I've ever dealt with. What kind of copper assaults two men, throws another two out of a window, and then runs off without even attempting an arrest?'

Leo shrugged. 'S'pose.'

'It doesn't matter who he is,' Stan said. 'The important thing is we know she's not on her own anymore, so when we track her down again, we won't take the subtle approach by trying to blend in and take her without causing a scene. Next time we'll get our numbers together and go after her like the first time... masked up, gunned up, and teamed up.'

'That's what I'm talking about,' Freddie said, before wincing and bending down to hold his knee, as if it would magically make a difference to how it felt. 'I'm gonna put a bullet in that big bastard's head!'

'Me, too,' Leo said.

'And me,' Marcus added as he put his phone away and rejoined the group.

'We all will,' Stan said, touching his jaw with his fingertips. He turned to Marcus. 'What did our informant have to say?'

'Nothing useful. Struggling to keep tabs on how everything's progressing, apparently. It seems the people in charge of Sarah's safety are keeping everything very close to their chests.'

'How much do you think that bitch has told the coppers?' Freddie asked as he ran his fingers through his hair.

'Obviously enough for them to arrest the brothers and seize their assets,' Leo said.

'Perhaps, but the brothers are clever,' Stan said. 'They haven't left a shred of evidence anywhere to get them sent down. The testimonies from Wayne and Sarah were the only things that could convict them of anything. We've dealt with Wayne, and soon we'll have dealt with Sarah as well. As long as she doesn't make it to court, the brothers walk free.'

Leo clenched his hands into fists, the muscles in his forearms rippling. 'What about the other issue?'

Stan took a moment before he answered that question. 'She hasn't told them anything about that. We'd know if she had.'

'But if she does, the damage will be—'

'It's in hand. The brothers thought long and hard about it and things are in place.'

'You mean the early warning system?'

'Precisely.'

'How sure are you it'll work?'

'Absolutely sure. There are two stages to it, two tripwires if you like, and there's no indication that the first one is even close to being triggered. We'll know as soon as it is and have plenty of time to sort things out.'

Stan watched the other three men nod, no doubt reassured by his confidence.

'Do you think our informant will lead us to Sarah again?' Leo asked.

Stan turned to Marcus. 'Doesn't need to, hey, Marcus.'

Marcus addressed the group. 'Before we were ambushed by whoever that bloke is, I pinned a tracker to her clothes. Once we've regrouped with the others, we can go straight to her.'

The other men all smiled, even Stan, although aware it must have been terrifying, a crooked sneer the only shape his lips could make without causing him additional pain.

'Let's get back in the motor and on the phone to the other lads,' he said. 'The sooner we get us all back together, the sooner we can hunt that bitch down again. And this time, we'll be packing far more than that gorilla she's got with her can handle.'

12

Drayce and Sarah hurried out of the immediate area, always his first objective after any attack. No use sticking around to let the assailants have another stab at abduction. Distance from the threat was an ally in these circumstances, as was concealment.

They cut down side streets and alleyways to stay off the busy roads where they were most at risk of being spotted. Drayce had no idea who the men were or what kind of capabilities they had; until he did, he had to assume they were a huge workforce with every gadget and weapon known at their disposal. Otherwise, as Lao Tzu put it, 'there is no greater danger than underestimating your opponent'.

He led Sarah south, through street after street, all of which had long rows of Victorian terraced houses on both sides, with limited escape routes between the occasional junctions or alleyways separating the bricks and mortar. The few cars that passed, Drayce made sure he had his right hand on a gun, his eyes on the occupants, and Sarah within arm's reach at all times to push her into cover if he engaged with a threat.

Twenty nervous minutes later, they could no longer stick to the quieter streets, moving around London on foot. They had some distance to cover, which meant they required transport. Drayce took hold of Sarah's arm as they approached the junction to Seven Sisters Road.

'Hold on here for a minute,' he said.

He put his shoulder on the brickwork and slowly pivoted, moving his line of sight around the corner until he had a view across the road to the underground station entrance. Plenty of vehicles passed by, but none of them or their occupants caused him concern. A few people waited at the steps to the tube station, presumably just loitering until their friends or work colleagues joined them for their journey. He assessed their appearances individually. The girl with the bright blue headphones: no danger; the guy with the Avengers backpack: not a threat; the homeless man with the bin bag on his head, drinking from a bottle of hand sanitiser: maybe avoid that guy, but still, not one of the criminals who were after Sarah. He pivoted back into cover behind the wall.

'It's clear,' he said to Sarah. 'But you can never be certain, so when we walk across the street to those steps, I want you to stay close to me. Got it?' She nodded. 'And please, if I tell you to do something, do it straight away, because if there *is* a threat, then there's a good chance I'll spot it before you do, and we won't have time for me to explain why I want you to do whatever I've asked of you. Deal?'

She nodded nervously. 'Whatever you say.'

Drayce smiled at her. 'That might be the first time a client has ever said that to their bodyguard. I think we're going to get along just fine.'

Sarah smiled back at him, but it was forced, with an awkwardness to it. He hoped this was down to nerves and adrenaline, rather than a feeling of distrust. He put a hand on her upper arm and met her eyes.

'Before we go any further, I need to know if you have anything on you that transmits a signal. I know you left your phone at the safe house, but do you have anything else on you that someone could use to track your movements?'

Sarah shook her head. 'No. Nothing at all.'

'Good. On the same topic, keep your bank cards in your pocket. Cash is fine, but if a card is necessary, I'll be paying. They might be able to track your transactions, but they certainly won't be able to track mine.'

A more natural smile took shape on Sarah's face. 'I can live with that. Straight to Harrods it is, then.'

'Nice try,' he took hold of her elbow. 'Come on, let's go.'

They moved with a sense of urgency, but not at a speed that attracted attention. They only ran when they crossed the road, as any sane person does in London. On the other side of the street, they walked around the blue railings and trotted down the steps as if running late for a train, blending in with the other people around them. Drayce scanned the streets at the last moment before they dropped below ground level, happy nobody was following them.

Drayce used his contactless cards to whisk them through the barriers, not wanting to dawdle around buying tickets. A train pulled up after only a minute, and there were plenty of empty seats. Drayce told Sarah to sit in the middle of the centre carriage, to give them more than one escape route should he spot a tail. Seated and happy no one in the carriage presented a threat, he took a deep breath, and for the first time since he'd caught up with Sarah, removed his hand from the gun in his right pocket. He took out his phone and messaged Julie, letting her know he was with Sarah and she was safe. He put his phone away, aware of Sarah's eyes on him.

'So where are we heading to?' she asked.

Drayce studied the underground map above him. They were on the Victoria Line, heading into the city.

'I don't know exactly, but somewhere busy. Crowds and congestion are our friends at this point... they'll help us to stay hidden for the foreseeable, which is our best chance of survival. If they can't find us, they can't hurt us.'

Sarah turned away from him, her eyes darting from one passenger to the next as her imagination no doubt played tricks on her mind, making her see danger everywhere. Drayce assessed her in the reflection of the window opposite them, its pitch-black surface the perfect mirror as they hurtled through the tunnel. Despite what Julie had said to him about the serious and secretive nature of the case Sarah was a witness in, he desperately wanted to question her regarding the identities of the people hunting her. The more he knew about who they were and what they were capable of, the better equipped he would be to keep her safe. Forewarned is forearmed, as the saying goes. He looked around at the other passengers, happy they were out of earshot.

He turned back to Sarah and parted his lips. *Should I, or shouldn't I?*

While true the more he could find out about these people, the better he could defend himself and Sarah, knowing too much would put him at added risk, not just presently, but also in the future. He could become cursed with knowledge that meant he had to look over his shoulder for the rest of his life, and he certainly didn't want that. But he did need something to work with to keep them both alive in the here and now.

He shuffled about in his seat as he battled the dilemma, alternating between twisting his wedding ring and fingering the locket on his black leather necklace. The name of his late wife, Lily, was engraved on the front; inside was a photograph of her. If she were still here, she wouldn't tolerate this kind of indecisiveness from him.

You have a job to do, he heard her telling him. *So do it.*

He doubted himself right up to the point when the words came out of his mouth.

'I need to know a few things about these people,' he said.

Sarah turned her head to face him, the steady vibrations of the tube making her fringe bounce just above her eyelashes. She frowned, clearly unhappy about where this conversation was heading.

'I'm not sure that's such a good idea,' she said.

In hindsight, Drayce shouldn't have expected any other reply. The NCA had probably spent months building up trust to get her to talk to them; he'd met her an hour ago. She'd be taking a hell of a risk speaking to a stranger about the case.

However, he'd already saved her from these people once today, so trust was likely simmering somewhere beneath the surface. Plus, she'd agreed to leave with him voluntarily, after her initial resistance. This thought reminded him of the pain in his groin, so potent it made him feel sick. Sarah must have clocked on, because she spoke with what he took to be genuine remorse.

'I'm sorry for, well, you know, kneeing you down there.'

'It's fine. You were frightened and you didn't know who to trust. I'll be okay.'

He blanked out his discomfort and focused on what to say next to persuade her to open up, because if they were tracked down again, a simple piece of information about these people might be the difference between life and death for the two of them.

'I know you don't want to talk about these people,' he said.

'It's not that.' She moved a shaky hand up to her forehead and brushed her fringe out of her eyes.

For the first time, Drayce noticed a scar on the palm of her hand – a burn – in the early stages of healing. Not the product of an accident, he thought, too severe for that. Her flinch response would have pulled her hand away before the damage got that bad. To cause an injury of such magnitude, Drayce suspected someone had held her hand down on the heat source.

'It's just I've been sworn to secrecy by the NCA. I'm not supposed to speak about it to anyone. They've taken statements from me and the next time I talk about it should be in front of a judge and jury in Crown Court.'

'I don't need to know about the case, or even about how you came to be a witness. All I'm interested in is learning about what kind of people these men are. The more I know about the threat they pose against us, the more I'll be able to mitigate the risk and keep us safe until my contact in the NCA has jacked up a new protection team for you.'

He stopped talking and watched her closely, letting his words sink in. She reached into her pocket and pulled out a small photograph, not much bigger than a passport photo, and held it firmly between the index finger and thumb of each hand. She stared at the lady in the picture, as did Drayce.

'My mum would know what to do,' she said. 'She always knew what was for the best, no matter how shitty things got.' Drayce heard her voice crack a little under the weight of her emotions. 'I wish she was here now.' Tears trickled down her cheeks.

Drayce resisted the urge to put an arm around her, an instinctive reaction for him when faced with a crying woman, but they'd only just met, and there was a thin line between comforting a person and making that person uncomfortable.

'You look just like her,' he said. 'She's beautiful.'

The moment the words left his mouth, he realised the implication, even though he'd genuinely meant them to be two separate observations.

Sarah blushed. 'Thanks.'

She met his eyes, held the gaze for longer than Drayce expected. She'd probably noticed the difference in colour: one bright blue, the other dark brown. Heterochromia. It often caught people's attention the first time they noticed it.

Drayce kept his mouth shut as the train rumbled along, transporting them into the heart of the city. He turned away from Sarah and focused on the other passengers in the carriage, constantly marking their positions, tracking their movements, and evaluating their body language. If any one of them, at any point, presented a threat, he could deal with it in the blink of an eye. Sarah would talk when she was ready, he thought. For now, he had to keep his eyes open, his mind sharp, and his hands close to the guns in his pockets.

13

As soon as they established the team of kidnappers had escaped, Julie and Fiona had beaten a hasty retreat from the cafe back to their car and driven out of Tottenham. There was little point in hanging around for the police to arrive – an inevitability, considering someone fired a gun inside a busy cafe during peak morning rush hour. The nature of the case meant neither of them would have been able to tell the cops anything, so it was best they just left and focused on securing Sarah's safety.

Julie hoped Alex had caught up with her and convinced her she'd be safe in his company. Given how efficiently and effectively those men had found her, Julie wasn't confident Sarah would be safe for long if she continued running from Alex and ended up on her own again. As Fiona drove the two of them south to the river, Julie tapped a message into her phone, asking Alex for an update. Minutes after typing it, a message pinged through from him, telling her Sarah was with him and they were both okay. A big sigh of relief escaped Julie's lips.

'We should call Foster and tell him there was another attempt on Sarah's life,' she said, more as a way of thinking aloud rather than to Fiona, but her statement brought a response nonetheless.

'I wouldn't,' Fiona said. 'Not yet. Let's at least find out if your guy has got hold of her, and if he has, where. We should give Foster something besides a headache when we call him.'

Julie showed Fiona her phone. 'I've had a message from Alex. He's with Sarah. I think we should call Foster. It's not our job to protect him from the hard times, it's his job to take the facts from his case managers and coordinate the Agency's response.'

And besides, she wanted to bounce a few ideas off him, such as how on earth the brothers' associates had tracked Sarah down to the cafe. The Met didn't know she was there, so they couldn't be blamed, which ultimately shone the spotlight on the NCA harbouring a corrupt officer.

They ought to speak to Foster even if it upset him, whether Fiona thought it a good idea or not.

Julie's shoulders were broad enough to take on any angry boss for the good of a case, something she'd done countless times during her career in the Met. She tapped on his name in the contacts menu on her phone and put it to her ear, noticing the disapproving look on Fiona's face in the rear-view mirror.

For once, this is about something more important than your career, Missy.

'Julie, how are you getting on?' Foster asked after the second ring.

Julie tapped the speaker icon on her phone so Fiona could listen in on the conversation.

'It could be going better,' Julie said.

'What do you mean by that?' Foster asked, his voice filling the interior of the vehicle.

'We found Sarah.'

'Is she all right?'

'She's alive and uninjured.'

'Isn't that good news?'

'Yes, but it's not down to a lack of effort from the men who want her dead.'

'And what's that supposed to mean?' he asked, his voice higher pitched than normal.

'I don't know the exact details of what happened, but they found her, and it was only thanks to Alex's actions that they didn't take her.'

'Jesus Christ.' Julie heard Foster's footfall as he paced up and down his office. 'But she's safe?'

'Yes, thanks to him. John, those men knew where she was. Somehow, they knew she was in a cafe in Tottenham, despite the fact the Agency were the only ones tracking her.'

A thick silence hung over the line for longer than was comfortable.

'We can't be sure of that,' Foster said, eventually. 'They might have tracked her down another way. I'm not ruling it out, but we can't be certain they've got someone in the Agency helping them. Maybe she contacted someone from her old life and told them too much?'

'Like what? That she'd be in a Costa cafe in Tottenham just before eight o'clock?'

'Perhaps. She might have been meeting someone from her old life there. Maybe she bought another phone, called someone overnight, and agreed to meet at a specific time and place in the morning? Maybe they sold her out? Maybe they set her up off the back of a threat, and had someone from the brothers' organisation sitting next to them when they were on the phone, listening to the whole thing? We don't know enough yet, Julie. We can't rule anything out, but neither can we make dangerous assumptions.'

He made a good point, but it didn't do much to alleviate Julie's anxiety.

'I suppose so,' she said.

'Think about it from her point of view… who else did she have to turn to last night, other than a friend from her old life? She was on her own, terrified, and probably didn't have a clue what she should do. The idea of arranging a meeting with someone she thought she could trust would be too much of a temptation. The more I think about it, the more I see this as a far more likely scenario to explain why they were able to find her.'

'I hope you're right.'

'Me too. Where are you now?'

'Just coming through Hackney. We'll probably come back in and—'

'No, stay out. There's nothing more you can do here and I want you two mobile and ready to respond if your man needs you.'

'He won't. He likes to work alone.'

'Well, be that as it may, I want you in regular contact with him. Did you speak to Sarah before she left with him?'

'Not even close. Alex rescued her and got them both out of there immediately. We didn't arrive until after the carnage had ended.'

'In that case, get in touch with him and find out where they are.'

Julie didn't respond straight away. She wanted time to work up the courage to challenge Foster on what she believed would be a bad move.

'I don't think that's a good idea.'

Silence on the other end of the line.

'I just think…' Julie continued, seeking the right words to explain what she'd agreed with Alex, 'that it'll be safer for her if we let Alex keep their location a secret. If the brothers do have an informant in the Agency, then—'

'No, no, no. I'm not being kept in the dark on this. Until there's any substantial evidence to show that the person respons-ible for leading those men to our witnesses is a corrupt officer in the Agency, I want tabs kept on Sarah's movements. This case is too important for us to be in the dark regarding her whereabouts.'

'But John—'

'No buts, just do it. Ring me when you know where she is.'

And with that, he cancelled the call. Julie dropped her phone into her pocket and turned to face Fiona.

'What he said makes sense,' Fiona said, taking her eyes off the road for a moment, as though gauging Julie's expression.

'Does it?'

'Why wouldn't it? She's our responsibility. We need to know where she is.'

'But do we? Wouldn't it be safer if it were kept out of the Agency? Think about what's just happened. There's something going on here, Fiona, and the more I think about it, the more I worry about a mole within our ranks.'

Fiona tapped her fingers on the steering wheel. 'It's certainly a possibility, but it's not the most likely scenario. I think Foster's idea that Sarah might have contacted someone from her old life holds the most weight, given the circumstances. You and I both know how often that happens with the kind of clients we deal with.'

'I know, but I just don't think we can be too careful at this point. If Alex is the only one who knows where Sarah is, then the brothers' informant – if they do indeed have one – won't have any chance of finding her. If I update Foster, her location will inevitably be put onto the system in some shape or form, with a chance it'll leak. A chance I don't want to take.'

'Well, she can't stay with Alex forever. At some point, we have to take over.'

'I'm not talking about anything long-term, but the only people who were aware of Wayne and Sarah's locations were the Agency, and a handful of cops from the Met, and the only people who knew Sarah was in that cafe, work for the Agency. Which tells me if she stuck to the rules and didn't contact anyone from her old life, then there's a mole working for the brothers. And until we know for sure, I'd rather play it safe and keep her location a secret. Even from us.'

Fiona hit a deep pothole in the road with the front offside tyre, rattling the suspension, her perfectly styled bob-cut bouncing in rhythm. 'Fine by me. For what it's worth, I think you're probably making the right call. But just how do you expect to square that with Foster? He just said he wants to know where they are as soon as we do.'

'I know he did, and I haven't worked it all out yet, but for now… I might just ignore his calls.'

Fiona raised her eyebrows and consciously nodded, as though reluctantly impressed. 'Brave woman.'

Julie looked across at her with steely eyes. 'You bet I am.'

14

The Marlowe brothers' hitmen stood on wet, muddy ground in the middle of a scrapyard, in an area of the Docklands yet to be redeveloped. The seven men were between their two vehicles: a black Mercedes van and a Range Rover SVR. Stan and Marcus were a couple of steps ahead of Freddie and Leo, the four of them facing the other three: Chrissy, Tommy, and Daz. Everyone had their hands in their pockets apart from Freddie, who played with the cut-throat razor he took everywhere with him, the polished walnut handle nestled in his palm as he flicked the blade in and out. Stan had told him three times to put it away, but the dopey lunatic just wouldn't listen. Disobedience was rife when you were in charge of men who killed for a living, something with which Stan had a great deal of experience.

Mounds of old car parts and bare shells of bodywork decorated the surrounding landscape, the motoring graveyard blocking the view from nearby roads. Two giant machines were at work, crushing shells of cars into cubes. The only part of the world outside the yard that they could see was the Thames, visible through a gap in the junk, its greyish brown current framed left and right by the rusty piles of scrap metal. Stan couldn't see any boats, which didn't surprise him. They were a long way from the renovated part of the Docklands, with billions spent on apartment buildings, hotels, and restaurants, all of which surrounded harbours where the super-rich moored their yachts, and was full of CCTV cameras, private security, and ANPR, Automatic Number Plate Recognition. This area was different, chosen for that very reason: there was absolutely no one else around them.

Apart from the dog.

Chained up twenty yards away, one end attached to its collar, the other to the chassis of a stripped-out Ford Escort, legs ramrod straight, eyes trained entirely on their group. It belonged to the owner of the yard, purely as a means of security and trained to tear to pieces any local thieves who dared jump the fence at night, searching for something to steal. The breed was questionable. Stan thought it was as close to a wolf as any dog he'd ever seen.

'That chain look strong enough to you?'

Stan smirked at the hint of worry in Chrissy's voice.

'Ignore the dog,' Stan said. 'It's the owner you should worry about. Ugliest, most vicious man alive, he is.'

Chrissy visibly relaxed when the dog lay down on its belly, now bored with their group. He turned his head from side to side, examining their surroundings, distinctly unimpressed. 'You come here often, Stanley?'

'Are you flirting with me, Chrissy?'

'Don't be soppy. It's just an odd place to meet, that's all.'

'It's private, and with the noise of those machines crushing things up, there's absolutely no chance of anyone eavesdropping on our conversation. I know the owner, and although he's a miserable, hard-nosed old bastard, he is trustworthy. Won't let no one through those gates back there while we're here.'

'Fine. Let's get down to business, shall we?'

Stan nodded and then explained to Chrissy what had happened when they'd tried to kidnap Sarah. Earlier on that morning, the crew had decided that a subtler approach was called for after the chaos at the flat in Enfield. The seven of them agreed that Stan would take just Marcus, Leo, and Freddie with him, leaving Chrissy, Tommy, and Daz behind. The idea being that with just four of them, it would make it easier for them to blend in amongst the general public, and better able to bring Sarah in without any drama.

'Rat shit, that's what I'm hearing from you lot. Total, utter, rat shit.'

Stan threw Chrissy a scowl while he listened to him moan. He'd been expecting it, but it still pissed him off. An electric pain fired up into his brain when he automatically clenched his broken teeth, and he missed everything else Chrissy rabbited on about. Chrissy, though not as tall as Stan, was just as wide, with steroid muscles and a thick scar on his left cheek. Like Stan's missing ear, it was a keepsake from his days on the doors many years ago, before the SIA, Security Industry Authority, had stepped in and brought some legitimacy to their old profession. Violent men with criminal records as long as theirs found other forms of employment, such as armed robbery and drug dealing, before settling into their true calling in life: enforcement for the big players in organised crime.

'It's not "rat shit", Chrissy,' Stan said, 'whatever the fuck that means.'

His eyes moved to Tommy and Daz, the runts of the litter in Stan's opinion. Scrawny, jittery little things… only made it into the brothers' firm because of how good they were with a gun. Put the soppy pair empty-handed into an affray and watch them melt, Stan had told the brothers, but his criticisms hadn't made a difference; they'd still taken them on. Tommy was tapping his foot, Daz biting his lip. Stan wanted to tell the pair of them to settle down and relax.

'I knew trying to grab her in public like that was a bad idea.' This from Tommy, his blond, almost to the point of being transparent, bum-fluff goatee wafting around his lips.

'We should have all gone together and shot the place up,' Daz said, picking at a spot on his chin, his short, dark, curly hair wafting in the breeze.

'We didn't know she had protection,' Stan said, although why he was making excuses to them, he had no idea. 'We won't make the same mistake again.'

'Too right we won't,' Chrissy barked, before spitting on the ground. 'Who's this geezer who was with her?'

'No idea.'

'Police?'

'Doubt it, judging by the way he behaved. Doesn't matter though. Now we know he's a factor, we can be properly prepared next time.'

'Just like I said, we should have been last time, instead of you four heading off on your own to get her. Well, there'll be no more stupid games this time round, tryin' to grab her so you don't cause no scene. We can't afford to be cute with this slag. She needs to die.'

Stan was tempted to remind Chrissy of the mistakes he'd made the day before in Enfield that had resulted in the decision to take a subtler approach in their next attempt. It had been his rush to force their way into the flat that led to the ensuing chaos, the death of one of the team and, more importantly, Sarah's escape. But he didn't want the argument to escalate into a full-blown gang fight. They didn't have the time to waste.

'Shame about Liam,' Stan said, his mind conjuring up images of them carrying the dead man's body out of the flat to the van.

The expression on Chrissy's face didn't alter one bit. He didn't even blink. 'He knew the risks.'

Stan shrugged. 'S'pose.'

In the corner of his eye, he detected Freddie limping over to the chained-up dog, his cut-throat razor extended in his right hand. He oozed excitement at the prospect of doing something terrible to the animal. The smile on his face didn't portray joy. It was too evil for that. More a depiction of barely restrained cruelty. His entire expression was malevolence personified, a child squatting over an ant's nest on a hot summer's day, magnifying glass in hand.

'Freddie!' Stan called, closing his eyes at the pain shouting caused. 'Get back here.'

The man offered a slight turn of the head in response, but his feet continued in the direction of the animal, now back on its feet, eyes locked onto Freddie, a menacing curl on its lips, fangs bared in readiness in the presence of a predator.

'Bloke's a fucking psycho,' Chrissy said, shaking his head.

'Freddie! Back here now!' Stan's voice, louder this time, had a deep tone that more than conveyed his anger. Freddie stopped three feet from the dog and turned his head properly this time.

'What? I'm only gonna pet it.'

'I said get back here. And if you cause me anymore pain by making me shout again, I'll fucking kneecap you and feed you to that animal myself.'

With a kick of the dirt and a bow of the head, Freddie reluctantly folded the blade away and returned to the group.

'Fucking evil bastard,' Stan said, taking a couple of deep breaths to try to settle his blood pressure. He turned to Chrissy. 'The rest of the kit still in the van?'

Chrissy nodded at Tommy and Daz and then flicked his head sideways at the vehicle. The younger men scurried off, making several trips back and forth to deliver the giant black rucksacks. They lined them up in the middle of the group. Stan heard a succession of sharp metallic clatters as they hit the dirt.

'More than enough there to finish this job,' he said with a fractured smile that left him wincing.

'Don't you fucking know it,' Chrissy said. 'We're hitting them hard this time.'

'About that... we better discuss exactly what our limits are.'

'We have none.'

Stan shrugged. 'Fine by me, but we all have to read from the same page. And what about a plan? Are we killing them wherever we find them? Or following them and picking our moment?'

Chrissy scratched the scar on his cheek. 'I know what I want to do, and that's hunt her down straight away and kill her and whoever's protecting her. But we should be careful. This geezer she's got with her knows what he's doing. Maybe following them and waiting for an ideal ambush point would be the smarter choice. I think that's what the brothers would want… the smart, clean option.'

'Perhaps. But what if an opportunity to ambush them never shows itself? What if we find them, follow them, and watch them go from strength to strength all the way to Scotland Yard? What then?' Stan waited for an answer. When he didn't get one, he carried on. 'I'll tell you "what then". We'll have lost her forever, that's what. If they get her back into the safety of their protection, they'll tighten things up and the next time she shows her face will be in the dock. Is that an acceptable risk to take?' He turned from side to side, staring at everyone in turn. 'Is *that* something the brothers would want?' A resounding shake of the head from everyone was the unanimous response. 'In that case, I suggest we kit up and close the net around her, then kill her at the first opportunity. No waiting, no hesitations. Wherever they are, we gun them down where they stand. Agreed?' The word echoed back at him from the others. 'Good.' He locked eyes with Chrissy. 'I think we best check that this stuff's in proper working order one more time before we head off.'

Chrissy held his hand out to the bags. 'Go ahead.'

All seven of them stepped forwards, one man per pack. They leant over their rucksacks and undid zips that ran around almost the entire circumference, opening each one like a book. Strapped to the inside was the body armour they'd worn when they attacked the safe houses, along with the firearms, explosives, and other miscellaneous weaponry.

Seven bags for seven killers. No brides.

Velcro straps fixed the weapons in place, securely held but readily ripped free in an instant. Stan's pack held a VZ–58 assault rifle – the Czech version of the AK-47. Strapped to the bag separately were four magazines, all fully loaded. Marcus's held a Skorpion machine pistol, along with a Kalashnikov AK-12. As Stan glanced at the other packs, he saw a variety of assault rifles, shotguns, and pistols, each with countless rounds of ammunition, along with a number of hand grenades. He took a deep breath and smiled as he surveyed the arsenal laid out before him.

The last item to catch Stan's eye was inside Chrissy's rucksack. A small square electrical device, black in colour, several antennae protruded from the top. 'Make sure that signal jammer's ready to go,' he said. 'When we do find that bitch, we're gonna want to delay witnesses calling the police for as long as possible.'

Chrissy nodded his head. 'Any news on the tripwires?'

'You mean, have they been triggered yet?'

'Well, have they?'

'We wouldn't be hangin' round here if they had, would we?'

'S'pose not.'

'None of us need to worry about that until something gets triggered, and then it's all we need to worry about. For now, we just focus on killing the only witness left and remove the threat against the brothers' freedom, it'll probably negate any worries we might have about what the tripwires are protecting.'

Chrissy shrugged. 'Fair enough. This tracker of yours still working all right?'

Stan turned to Marcus, who glanced at his phone and replied with a short swift nod.

'Seems so,' Stan said. He flicked his head at the Range Rover. 'Shall we get to it?'

'In a minute. First, describe this geezer she's with.'

Stan turned back to face him. 'Well, he probably outweighs me by a stone or two and knows how to fight. Doesn't matter this time round, though. He'll die just like the others who thought they could keep her safe.'

'You sure about that?' A smirk broke out across Chrissy's lips at the same time his eyes dropped to Stan's jaw, then across to Marcus's nose, and finally to Freddie's knee and Leo's ankle. 'Gave you lot a good hiding by the looks of it. Good job you've got us coming along this time, hey, boys?' He glanced over at Tommy and Daz – his audience whenever he told a shit joke – whose lips twitched, ready to grin. That is, until they saw Stan's eyes.

103

'You bedwetters find this prick funny, do you?' Stan asked them.

Tommy shrugged his shoulders. 'Just a joke, innit, Stan. No offence.'

'Calm down, Stanley.' This from Chrissy, laughing as he picked up his bag of guns. 'That temper of yours rarely does you any favours.'

The hair on the back of Stan's neck stood up as he tried to hold it together. He bent down and picked up the assault rifle from his bag, along with a magazine. The others visibly stiffened.

'That temper,' he purred, as he loaded the gun and racked the charging handle to chamber a round, 'is what keeps me in a constant supply of murderous rage.' The skin around his eyes pulled tightly against his skull, exposing the whites as he stared at Chrissy, Tommy and Daz. 'And that's quite useful for a man in my profession.'

He aimed the gun at the wide-eyed and rigid Chrissy, the laughter that escaped his lips moments ago vaporised in the chill. Tommy and Daz broke away from Stan's eyes, to the gun, then back to Stan, undoubtedly weighing up the threat to Chrissy – and themselves.

Relishing their diminished confidence in their own sense of humour, Stan's tightly wound expression fell into a smile, showing both rows of loose teeth, pain shooting up through his skull.

'Save your shit jokes for someone who finds them funny,' he said. 'I'm off to finish this job for the brothers. I suggest you follow.'

Everyone visibly relaxed when he lowered the gun, picked up his bag, and strode to the Range Rover, leaving Chrissy to expel a cold shudder, felt so deep it made his bones quiver.

15

The recorded voice came over the train's intercom to announce the stop. Drayce turned to face Sarah.

'We'll get off at the next station.'

'St Pancras?'

He nodded. 'Like I said, busy is safe. The less crowded somewhere is, the more emboldened these people will feel to have a pop at us if they find us. There's little to no chance they'd try something overt in an environment such as St Pancras.'

Sarah bit her thumbnail. 'If you say so.'

'With the terrorism threat at the level it's at, the staff there is trained to watch out for anyone who might present a threat. Anything suspicious and they'll be straight on the phone to the police. They'd be insane to try to take you by force there.'

Sarah's eyes told him the motivating speech wasn't working. 'They *are* insane,' she said. 'That's what worries me.'

'Trust me, witnesses are our friends.'

'They weren't much help in the cafe.'

Drayce nodded. 'That's a fair observation, but don't forget, those men only approached you there because they knew they could do it quietly without causing a scene.'

'What's different now?'

Drayce smiled. 'They know I'm with you, and after what I did to them last time, they'll know being subtle with me isn't an option.' He nodded at the photograph in her hand. 'I'd put that somewhere safe if I were you, we'll be getting off the train soon.' She hesitated, unsure which pocket would be safest. 'Try one of the front pockets… it's too easy for it to fall out if you slip it into a back one.' He hooked his necklace with a finger and pulled it out from under his shirt. 'I use this. Guarantees I won't lose it.'

Sarah examined the engraved silver locket where the two lengths of thin black leather met. 'Who's Lily?'

'My wife.' He flicked it open to reveal the photograph of her. A tangle of dark, shoulder-length brown hair cascaded down either side of her bright green eyes, one side swept back behind her neck, while the other continued down past her smile. She had the back of a hand under her chin, a delicate touch rather than a prop. He snapped it shut and tucked it away.

Sarah's lips cautiously parted ways. 'Is she no longer—'

'Alive?'

'I was going to say "with us."'

'She passed away three years ago, shortly before I left the police.'

'You were a police officer?'

He nodded. 'Eighteen years.'

'Doing what?'

'Armed policing, mostly.'

When more wasn't forthcoming, Sarah asked, 'Care to expand?'

Drayce didn't reply straight away; he hated talking about himself. But after a rapid deliberation, instinct suggested he should share the bare bones of his previous career; it might instil some confidence in his abilities. 'I started out in Manchester where I first joined the ARVs, then I transferred to Birmingham and trained to be a CTSFO, and then to the Met where I was with SO19 for a while, and then finally with RaSP as a close protection officer.' He recognised the bewilderment on her face. He'd forgotten he wasn't talking to a cop. 'Armed Response Vehicles, Counter Terrorist Specialist Firearms Officer, and Royalty and Specialist Protection.'

'Royalty? Did you protect the Queen?'

'No. I had the Home Secretary for a year, and then the Prime Minister for two.'

'You were the Prime Minister's bodyguard?' Sarah's eyes widened, her jaw slack. 'What went wrong in your life to bring you here, protecting me?'

'I prefer what I do now.'

'Really? I mean, it's a pretty big drop down the ladder, isn't it?'

'My employers didn't really give me much choice.'

'You were fired?'

'No, I mean they left me with no choice but to leave.'

'Did it have something to do with the death of your wife?' Sarah immediately slapped a hand over her mouth, the words having tumbled out, almost uncontrollably. 'I'm sorry, I shouldn't have…'

'It's okay. Really. It—' He stopped, unsure exactly how much he should say. He didn't want to talk about Lily, but opening up a little to Sarah might encourage her to do the same further down the road, and that was something he was keen to hasten: the more he learnt about her background, the more he might learn about the people who wanted her dead – and why. He took a deep breath, as though he needed a little something extra to get the next sentence out, but when he parted his lips, the words just wouldn't form.

Perhaps another time, he thought to himself.

'It's complicated,' he said.

She nodded. 'I understand complicated. My life might be the very definition of it.'

Drayce forced a smile onto his face. 'I was in a bad place when Lily died, no kind of a mental state for a serving police officer, that's for sure. But things are good now. And I meant it, I much prefer this job. I'm my own boss. I work for who I want, when I want, and if I don't get on with a client, I can walk away.'

Sarah smiled nervously. 'Not thinking of walking away from this one, I hope.'

'No chance. I'm sure you and I will get along just fine, and besides, I made a promise to Jules a long time ago.'

'Jules?' Sarah asked. 'Do you mean Julie Adler?'

He nodded. 'She's the one who brought me on board and led me to you. I owe her for something she did for me years ago, and she's decided your safety is important enough for her to call in the favour.' He smiled. 'She must really like you. I was expecting her to keep that one in her pocket for years and years.'

'I've just realised something,' she said, studying his face.

'What's that?'

'I don't even know your name.'

He held out a hand. 'Alex Drayce. Nice to meet you.'

'Nice to meet you, too,' she replied as she shook it. 'Tell me, Alex, why have the NCA sent you and not a serving police officer?'

Drayce hesitated, wondering whether it was a good idea to let Sarah know of Jules's suspicions that there might be a corrupt officer somewhere in either the Met or the NCA. No point trying to bullshit her, she didn't seem the type to fall for lies, and he didn't want to instigate any distrust between the two of them by telling any.

'She's worried there might be a leak somewhere within the authorities,' he said.

'A leak?'

'I'll be blunt. She thinks that whoever wants you dead might be getting help from a corrupt officer in either the Met or the NCA.'

Sarah paled.

'It's not a certainty by any stretch of the imagination.' Drayce regretted being so honest with her. 'But she needs to factor it into her plans to keep you safe, because it is a possibility. That's why I'm here, to keep you safe by making sure nobody knows where you are.'

Sarah gave him a nervous grin as she slid the photograph of her mother into the front right pocket of her jeans, before running her fingers through her hair and blowing her fringe out of her eyes.

'There's something I have to tell you,' she said as she laced her fingers together on top of her thighs and gazed down. 'Something about what happened in the safe house, when they tried to take me.'

'I'm all ears.'

She made eye contact with him. 'I killed one of them.'

Drayce put a hand on top of her clasped pair, the giant slab of meat and bone covering them both. 'I'd say that was reasonable under the circumstances. They were intruders, committing a crime, and you were in fear of your life. I don't think you have anything to worry about.'

'It's not just the trouble I might be in that worries me. It's also how I feel.'

'If by that you mean you feel guilty, I'd encourage you not to. Those men were trying to kill you. Taking another person's life is never pleasant, but when you have no choice, you have no reason to feel guilty.'

'But that's just it,' Sarah said. 'I *don't* feel guilty. I don't feel anything, in fact. That's what worries me. I know I killed a man, an evil man, and I just don't care.'

Drayce smiled. 'A girl after my own heart.'

The train slowed as they approached the station, and emitted a high-pitched squeal from underneath the carriage as the brakes did their work. Seconds later, the brightly lit platform came into view.

'Come on,' he said as he stood up and walked to the nearest doors.

Off the train, he stayed close, covering her back with his body as they walked down the platform. He watched everything and everyone in front of her with a finely honed threat perception, keeping the wall line to her left and him to her right, offsetting himself from her shoulder, back a couple of feet. Experience had taught him it was the best position to not only view her and her personal space, but also to engage with a threat, or alternately, lay hands on her to remove her from her surroundings. Every so often, he put his arm out to politely redirect other travellers who were too close.

At every corner was a mirror, placed for when the crowds were busy, so people didn't march around corners and clatter into one another. Drayce used them to check for threats before they committed to their new route.

'I think we're going the wrong way,' she said.

'Ignore the signs, they're wrong. They direct people along the longest route possible to try to prevent bottlenecks. When I was a CTSFO, my team and I memorised plans for all the main stations in the city, so in the event of a terrorist attack, we could quickly navigate our way around the tunnels and deal with the threat as early as possible. I know this place better than the back of my hand.'

When they finally walked out into the main station, they were on the lower level, surrounded by shops. A banner hanging vertically from the ceiling had an upwards arrow, advertising that travellers could 'Eat, Drink and Relax' on the upper concourse.

'Head over to that staircase,' he said to her as he pointed in its direction. 'We'll find somewhere busy to get a bite to eat. The best places to hide are sometimes right out in the open.'

She glanced his way briefly. 'So I'm beginning to learn.'

As they ascended the stairs, Drayce marched ahead to get an early view of the upper concourse. Happy there weren't any groups of men up there who rang alarm bells, he let Sarah catch up.

'As long as we're careful,' he said, in a tone intended to comfort her, 'then we'll be safe here.'

16

Stan pulled up on Railway Street, just around the corner from St Pancras. He saw Chrissy's black van in his mirror, sitting in the middle of the road because there were no parking spaces left. Before leaving the Docklands, they'd swapped the plates on their vehicles for cloned sets. They carried several with them and discarded used ones regularly to make it harder for the police to track their movements. Stan felt the pain in his jaw gather strength. He turned around in his seat to face Freddie and Leo in the back.

'I'm sure you've guessed by now that I can't let you take part in this.' He got disappointed nods from both men. 'We've got to be in and out, running every step of the way if we're to finish this without getting arrested or killed by armed police.' He nodded at their strapped-up legs. 'And in your current conditions, I'm not sure you'd keep up.'

'We really doing this?' Marcus asked.

Stan turned to him. 'You got a problem with that?'

'No, not really, I guess. It's just that… St Pancras?' He checked his watch. 'At this time of day, it's gonna be heaving. It's one thing shooting up a flat, and some shithole in the middle of nowhere. But here?' His eyes found the station entrance through the window. 'Maybe—'

'Maybe what?' Stan growled, daring Marcus to challenge his decision. The energy radiating off Stan made it clear there was no arguing the point.

'Nothing.'

Stan put a hand on Marcus's shoulder. His grip was tighter than necessary. 'Remember… we know exactly where she is, which means we can go straight to her and be in and out before the police get near us. And besides, with that little signal-blocking gadget that Chrissy's got with him, the 999 calls will take ages to get through. We'll mask up from this point on, and we won't take them off for any reason until we've done the job and are out of the area, somewhere safe. Then we'll change the plates, get out of the city, and contact the solicitor to let the brothers know it's done.' He turned to face Freddie and Leo and nodded down at their legs. 'Which one of you pair will be best to drive?'

'I'll do it,' Freddie said. 'Leo can't, not with his ankle in that condition. It's my left knee that's hurt, so driving an automatic won't be a problem.'

'Good. Make sure you cover your face before you climb in the driver's seat, then get out of here and wait somewhere close by for us to contact you when we're ready for the pick-up. Got it?'

Freddie nodded.

'How's the tracker doing?' Stan asked Marcus.

'Good. The signal's nice and strong, and it's showing them on the upper concourse in the main station.'

'Magic.' Stan reached into his pocket and presented a small silver case to Marcus. 'I reckon a little energy boost is in order.' He placed it on the centre console and opened the lid, revealing a small metal tube buried within a mound of white powder on a mirrored surface. He fished out the tube, separated the powder into two fat lines, and snorted one with all the vigour of a pig at feeding time. Finished, he handed the tube to Marcus, who took it with one hand while exploring his broken nose with the other. Deciding the pain might not be worth the reward, he handed back the tube, licked his fingertip and scooped up his line, rubbing it around his gums.

'What about us?' Freddie asked.

Stan blinked a few times, rubbing the bridge of his nose, his eyes wild. 'All you're doing is driving. Me and Marcus need this for what we're about to do.'

Freddie sat back in his seat with a petulant face. Stan reached down to pick up his body armour from the footwell and slipped it on, then did the same with his balaclava, pulling it down over his head, the thick black material covering everything apart from his eyes. Marcus and Freddie both did the same.

'Are we ready?' Stan asked.

'Ready,' Marcus said.

'Ready,' Freddie echoed.

And with that, all three men climbed out of the Range Rover. Freddie hobbled to the driver's door, while Stan and Marcus hurried to the boot and then jogged over to Chrissy's waiting van, their rucksacks full of guns bouncing on their backs as they did so.

17

Inside St Pancras, Drayce and Sarah sat at a table at Carluccio's, underneath the Olympic rings and the giant clock, and only a few feet from The Rendezvous sculpture, more commonly known as The Lovers statue: a huge bronze depiction of a man and a woman embracing one another. A constant stream of travellers walked past in either direction, some heading casually out into the city, others running to catch a train. Drayce watched them all carefully for missing ears and giant beards.

He'd chosen to be out on the concourse to give him a good view of everyone who approached, picking a table close to the wall. They weren't far away from an entrance to the restaurant, and had an exit from the station close by if an escape were necessary.

From where they sat, his view spanned the entire station: the complete length and breadth of the concourse, above which was the breathtaking ceiling, the giant glass and iron structure stretching off into the distance. He spotted another bronze statue closer to the train line, this time of the poet John Betjeman, a strong advocate of Victorian architecture, gazing up in admiration. All the tables around them were occupied, providing the constant hum of chatter from the other diners engrossed in conversation.

Drayce scanned the other customers. A young couple were enjoying coffee and pancakes at the table next to them, neither of whom rang any alarm bells with him. The same went for the young mother and her little boy at the next table; she chatted on her phone as she tucked into a pink grapefruit; he sat quietly enjoying a bowl of porridge. No threat at all.

They'd ordered food and drinks because Sarah had complained about being hungry, having missed out on the food she'd bought from Costa earlier that morning. Shortly after they'd finished eating, Drayce's phone rang. Julie.

'What's up?' he asked.

'I've been trying to get hold of you.'

'We've been on the tube. Bad signal.'

'How is she?'

'Doing well, considering everything she's been through.'

'Good. I need to speak to her.'

'Give me a second.'

He held his phone out to Sarah. 'It's Julie. She wants to speak to you.'

Sarah took the phone and pressed it up to her ear. 'Hello?'

Drayce inspected their surroundings, not listening to their conversation, but he got the gist, nonetheless. From this side of the discussion he understood that Julie was reassuring Sarah that she could trust him, and Sarah was happy to agree. A sense of achievement washed over him; it wasn't easy to win over a client, thrust together in these strange and difficult circumstances. But then the conversation took a turn. Julie was clearly doing most of the talking, Sarah both nervous and guarded with her responses.

'No, definitely not,' he heard her say as her voice took on a higher pitch. 'I wouldn't lie about a thing like that.' Then a moment later, 'It's all well and good telling me not to worry, but after what you've just asked me...'

Drayce frowned. After getting Sarah to relax and be comfortable around him, he didn't want to take a step backwards as she panicked about something she had no control over. As far as he was concerned, Julie could keep her bad news to herself. He gestured to Sarah with his hand, asking for her to pass the phone back.

'Why are you stressing out my client?' he asked Julie.

'I had to ask her something. It's to do with the informant these people may or may not have in our organisation.'

'Are you allowed to tell me anything more than that?'

To his surprise Julie went ahead and told him, revealing her supervisor's theory that Sarah might have contacted someone from her old life after escaping from the attack on the safe house and set up the cafe as a meeting point; information that could have been picked up by the people who wanted her dead.

A cute theory, Drayce thought, which would take weight off the corrupt officer narrative – something Julie's supervisor would be desperate to do. Of course, if Sarah hadn't let her location slip, then the only other answer for how the hit team had known she'd be at that cafe was that someone in the know had informed them. And from what Drayce had heard of Sarah's side of the conversation, it wasn't promising for the authorities. 'From what I heard of her answer,' he said. 'I take it she didn't contact anyone?'

'No.' The word was spoken sharply, with more than a hint of exasperation. 'No, she did not.'

'And I take it from your tone that's not what you wanted to hear?'

She sighed with such frustration that her breath whistled down the speakers. 'It does complicate things slightly.'

'It's time you stepped things up to find out where the information's leaking from.'

'It's not as simple as that, Alex. Not until I've convinced my supervisor there's definitely a problem.'

'Well then, perhaps leave him out of it and figure it out on your own. Either way, that leak must be plugged. In the meantime, do some digging into the identities of the men who tried to take Sarah.'

'Agreed.'

'Did you get the photograph of them I sent to you?'

'Yes, I got it. Fiona and I are on our way back to HQ now to run it through the facial recognition software.'

Drayce was about to ask why she didn't just send it to someone else who was already at headquarters, to speed things up, but then remembered how close to her chest Julie was keeping everything. If the attackers discovered she had the images of the four men, they might pull them out and replace them with people Drayce wouldn't recognise, giving them the edge in any future kidnap attempts.

'Providing you find out who these men are, what's the likelihood of you telling me anything about them?' His question was met with silence. 'Because the more I know about the people coming after us, the better able I'll be to defend us against them.'

As the silence continued, Drayce listened hard, and not only did he not hear Julie reply, he no longer heard the background noise that hummed along so consistently. He took his phone away from his ear, checked the screen, and saw that the call had cut out.

'That's weird,' he said.

'What's weird?' Sarah asked.

'The call's died.'

'Maybe she hung up on you?' Sarah's top lip curled in a show of disapproval. 'She was in a mood when I spoke to her.'

He checked the signal strength. 'No, I don't think she did.'

He examined his phone more closely: no signal whatsoever. Not even a single bar. Not even an empty row of bars, in fact. There was just a cross in its place, indicating that it couldn't find the network provider in one of the busiest, most well-connected capital cities on the planet.

Unease burgeoned in the pit of his stomach.

Then he noticed the body language of the young mother at the next table, glaring at the screen of her phone with an angry frown after her call had also been abruptly terminated. He looked all around him and saw that everyone who'd been doing something on their phone just a moment ago was now staring at their device in confusion, as though they had all suddenly stopped working.

He turned to Sarah. 'Something's not right.' He put his phone back into his pocket as alarm bells clanged in his head. He stood up, grabbed Sarah by her arm and lifted her to her feet. 'We're leaving.'

A single step away from the table, he halted at the sight of four men in balaclavas running into the station.

18

The men appeared from the other side of The Lovers statue, jogging towards the restaurant, their images creating a ripple of fright amongst the crowds as everyone backed away from their intimidating presence. The group was homing in on Sarah and Drayce, as though they knew exactly where to head.

But how? Drayce thought. *How have they found us?*

At a hand signal from the man at the front, they all grabbed handles on the sides of one another's rucksacks and ripped them open. Drayce saw how the packs unfolded down their backs and recognised what they were: he'd used them in his previous role in counterterrorism. Those packs had been designed for one purpose and one purpose only: to carry high-calibre firearms without anybody else knowing.

But Drayce knew.

He just hoped it wasn't too late.

The two men at the back tore guns from the open rucksacks of the two in front, handed them a weapon each, and then fanned out to block any escapes. Drayce saw menacing black shapes appear in their hands but didn't have time to register what the weapons were. He was already on the move.

He pulled Sarah into a bear hug, her back pressed up against his chest, and threw them both through the door that led into Carluccio's before the men had a chance to aim their weapons at them, both landing with a grunt on the floor.

Screams from members of the public echoed across the station as the men opened fire, their bullets only narrowly missing Drayce and Sarah as they took cover behind the restaurant's walls. Drayce rolled her over and lay on top of her to shield her from the bullets that whizzed through the doorway, the rounds tearing chunks out of both the frame and the wall on the opposite side of the restaurant.

Terrified travellers sprinted in all directions. Those previously seated in the restaurant battled their way to safety, clattering through the tables and chairs. Others ran for the exits, no doubt afraid this was a terrorist attack. Loud bloodcurdling cries echoed around the station. In mere seconds, the entire space was almost deserted. Only the four gunmen remained, facing Carluccio's in a semi-circle as they fired sharp bursts of fully automatic gunfire, sending wave after wave of hot metal at their targets. A sudden pause in the rate of fire told Drayce they were reloading their weapons.

Time to move.

Staying crouched low, he got to his feet and hurried to a staff-only door, pulling Sarah with him. A three-round burst exploded from the muzzle of the gunman with the smoothest, fastest reload, the first to fit a fresh magazine and get his weapon back in play. The bullets missed their target, narrowly, the rounds singeing Drayce's jacket as they clipped his shoulder before embedding in the wall. With his heart in his mouth, he pushed Sarah through. The pair of them vanished as bullets peppered the door behind them.

–

'Shit!' Stan faced Chrissy. 'Take your man outside to cut them off,' he said, shouting to be heard clearly through his balaclava. He turned to Marcus. 'We'll go in after them.'

Chrissy and Tommy ran out of the station to cut off their targets. Marcus stayed close to Stan as they moved to the restaurant's doors, their guns up on aim. They clambered over the toppled tables and chairs, the soles of their boots crunching on broken glass and crumbled brickwork, and positioned themselves next to the staff-only door.

Stan reached inside his pack and removed a grenade.

–

The staff-only door led down a small corridor to a kitchen. Drayce scanned the interior. Empty, the cooks had run for their lives after hearing the gunfire, no doubt. Behind him, footsteps crunched on broken glass in the restaurant. His senses in razor-sharp alignment – adrenaline pumping through him – forcing an idea, any idea, from somewhere.

Across from the stainless steel work surfaces was a door and he raced to it, pulling Sarah with him. If his sense of direction was accurate, it would lead to a walkway between the station and the hotel.

An escape route.

Close to it, he thought better of it, ducking out of sight of the window at the top, just as two of the gunmen ran into view.

'Get down,' he said to Sarah, who instantly dropped below the window pane. He snapped shut the metal deadbolt fixed to the door to slow them down. His eyes scanned the kitchen again, desperate for a plan B.

A walk-in pantry in the corner of the room had a substantial steel door. He dragged Sarah over to it, pushing her head low to keep her out of view of the window, bundled her inside and shut the door with him on the outside. He took one of the pistols out of his pocket and cupped the grip with two hands, the index finger on his right feeling for the trigger.

Whirling around at the staff-only door being kicked open, he readied the pistol, prepared to shoot the first gunman who came into sight. The door swung on its hinges, and a metallic tinkling heralded something rolling across the floor.

His breath caught in his throat, the shape of the device registering in his brain. An offensive concussion grenade. The good news was no fragmentation, but the shockwave of air pressure created in the enclosed space would have a kill range of roughly twelve metres.

The kitchen measured three by four.

If it hadn't been cooked by the guy who threw it, then Drayce had five seconds before the explosion. He counted in his head as he reached the pantry door.

One.

He flung the door wide open, pushing Sarah back inside as she tried to leave, before scrambling in after her and slamming the door shut.

Two.

He pushed her down and dived on top of her, protecting her.

Three.

The grenade went off early, which meant it had been cooked, but not for too long. After all, even for the person using the weapon, it was dangerous: a ticking bomb in the palm of their hand.

The shockwave rocked the pantry walls and shook the floor like an earthquake, sending small plastic containers raining down on the two huddled figures. Once things had settled, Drayce stood up and patted himself down. He wasn't in any pain and he couldn't find any injuries, but the silence in the immediate aftermath of the explosion turned into a high-pitched wail as his eardrums screamed. He touched them gingerly with his fingertips, relieved to feel nothing. No bleeding; no fluids at all. Limited damage.

He checked on Sarah: visibly confused, frightened, and badly shaken up, but physically she was fine. The pantry's solid structure had saved their lives. He moved to the door as the buzzing in his ears faded; the blast had destroyed the latch. Slightly ajar, it had opened outwards by a couple of inches. He watched that gap with fierce eyes and listened carefully. Footsteps. Two pairs of feet, slow and careful as they searched the kitchen.

Once they established there wasn't an immediate threat, they would search wherever a human being could hide: cupboards, fridges, freezers.

The pantry.

The deadbolt unlocked as the two who had cut off their escape were let inside; pans crashed as they ransacked the big storage cupboards. Then nothing but footsteps again: quiet, cautious, stealthy, from the other side of the pantry door; soft murmurings just behind him, testimony to Sarah's terror. He put a finger to his lips, then turned, his pistol up on aim, ready for the first target. His grip tightened. His jaw clenched. He was ready.

The door opened, slowly at first, then violently, swinging wildly and clattering against the wall.

The lead man entered, his weapon first, fast and careless, his attention on the opposite corner to where Drayce and Sarah were.

Drayce closed in on the man's back, cupping his left hand around his chin and pulling him in tightly, simultaneously turning him to face the doorway and reaching past his head with the pistol, aiming it into the kitchen. Locked in his vice-like grip, Drayce pulled his hostage back the way he'd come, blocking the pantry doorway, before creeping his line of sight to the side of the man's head.

Three barrels were directed his way, all of them as steady as rocks. Total silence had descended. Drayce studied their eyes through the holes in their balaclavas, wide and unblinking as they faced his muzzle, their only option to shoot *through* their teammate. The standoff didn't last long.

'We don't care about you,' one of the men said. In the middle of the three, he stared down the sights of a compact machine gun. Drayce heard a London accent, East End. 'It's the woman we want. Hand her over and you walk away from this.'

Drayce recognised him despite the balaclava, from his build and the lack of a bulge where his right ear should have been.

The same went for the guy to his left; a giant beard wasn't easy to hide with a balaclava.

'I walk away no matter what,' Drayce replied, practically growling the words. 'First through you, then your friends, and then out of that door.'

Drayce thought he saw a movement underneath the big man's balaclava, right where his mouth would be. Perhaps a smile.

'Listen, you stupid bastard,' the man said, 'just step back and let us have her. She's not worth dying for.'

Drayce shook his head slowly and tightened his finger around the trigger. 'You've misjudged me. I'm not that guy. I'm an entirely different beast.'

The eyes of the man in front of him conveyed he could not believe what he was hearing. Drayce watched him, hoping he would make the right choice. But then he saw his upper body fold around his weapon, pulling the stock a little tighter into his shoulder, preparing to take a shot.

Fine, Drayce thought, *if that's how you want it.*

He pulled his trigger and swept the weapon from side to side as he sent a single round to the centre mass of each shooter – the best chance of hitting them. Pained groans mingled with the loud cracks of the pistol and the clattering of bodies bouncing off counters and walls as they dived for cover. They returned fire, their efforts wasted, the bullets spraying a giant U-shape up and over him and his hostage, to embed in nothing more than the kitchen walls and ceiling.

Concentrating through the chaos he glimpsed the wide-open door to the rear exit. He eased out of the pantry, his hostage still pinned to his chest, and saw the other three gunmen cowering behind the steel counters at the opposite end of the kitchen. He fired a couple of shots their way to encourage them to keep their heads down, then told Sarah to get behind him. Thankfully she had the courage and presence of mind to follow his instructions.

Keeping the struggling mass of limbs between him and the threat, Drayce dragged his human shield with him as he moved for the exit, the man trying, but failing, to fight his way out of Drayce's grip. Every second or two, Drayce fired a single, deliberate shot to keep their heads down. Palpable relief flooded through him when they made it to the exit; first Sarah, then him, then his human shield. He halted in the doorway and turned to Sarah.

'Run!'

She didn't need telling twice. She spun on her heels and sprinted down the alleyway to the front of the hotel, her soles drumming a fast beat, her breath laboured from exertion and fear.

An elbow strike to his gut made Drayce wince. His hostage slipped out of his grip. The man turned, a hand slipping into his jacket, the dull black metal of a pistol visible as he drew his arm back. Drayce pushed him away and stepped back, creating distance as he aimed at the man's face – his only option due to the body armour – and shouted a command.

'Don't—'

But that was all he managed before the threat presented itself, the man bringing his gun up on Drayce, negating the use of verbal commands. Drayce squeezed the trigger in response to the threat, a sudden thought as to the human being in front of him invading his mind: certainly someone's son, perhaps someone's husband; a father with a family to go home to; a man with loving people in his life who relied on him, and who would live through terrible grief when he was gone. Drayce thought of the times he'd been forced to kill people in the past, and how painful and hollow he'd felt afterwards.

His gun fired; the man's body hit the ground. Drayce turned and hurtled after Sarah.

19

Drayce bolted down the alleyway without glancing behind him. He caught up with Sarah and pushed her ahead of him, shielding her. Any of the gunmen not injured would soon be on their tail. Their soles slapping against the flagstone floor echoed around the brick-and-stone structure as they raced for their lives. At the archway at the end, Drayce pulled Sarah behind the cover of the brick wall and caught his breath while he checked nobody was following them.

Just a few moments earlier, he'd doubted they'd make it out alive, backed into a corner of that kitchen, their exit blocked by murderous gunmen. He dropped the magazine from the used pistol: only two rounds left, which included the one in the chamber. Not a great deal of use should he find himself in another gunfight. He stripped them off into the palm of his hand, slipped the weapon back into his jacket pocket, and then lifted out the unused pistol and thumbed the two rounds into the already stacked magazine. Happier with a fully loaded gun in his hands, he slipped it behind the cover of his jacket, took Sarah by the arm and set off walking, checking their surroundings.

They emerged next to the main entrance to the St Pancras hotel on their right, the ramp leading down to street level about fifty yards to their left. The entire area was eerily quiet, the streets devoid of the city's usual hum because everyone in the vicinity had fled the attack. But this peaceful façade wouldn't last long.

'Keep moving,' he told Sarah, pulling her along with him. 'The more distance we can put between us and them, the better.'

Her expression, rather than the frightened, vulnerable person he'd expected to see, was the fierce glare of an angry, determined woman.

'Well, we'd better get moving,' she said as she picked up her pace.

Drayce let go of her arm and examined the line of cars parked outside the hotel lobby: three black Hackney cabs and an Audi estate car, with no sign of the owners. With Sarah at his shoulder, he ran up to the nearest one and reached for the driver's door handle: locked. The same was true of the next two, but as he passed the third taxi, he noticed the driver's door of the Audi wasn't flush with the bodywork, ajar by roughly an inch. The engine – something big and fierce – rumbled under the bonnet, the boot was partially open, and a suitcase lay abandoned on the pavement. At the sound of gunfire, the owner must have dropped his luggage and run inside, in such a hurry he forgot to turn off the engine and lock it.

'Get in,' Drayce told Sarah. As she reached for the front passenger door handle, he added, 'In the back.'

'Why?'

'Because there's more room for you to stay out of sight.' He shut the boot and ran to the driver's door. 'Hurry!'

They both opened their doors and climbed in at the same time. Drayce instructed Sarah to strap in and then lie down across the seats. As he dropped his gun back into his pocket and buckled up his seatbelt, he saw the RS6 badge on the steering wheel.

Well, that explained the noise coming from the idling engine.

Figures emerging from the shadows of the archway caught his eye, balaclavas still covering their faces and assault rifles still in their hands.

'Don't move,' he whispered to Sarah.

The human eye was acutely sensitive to movement, especially when the brain was in hunting mode, as those of the men chasing them undoubtedly were. The best chance he and Sarah had of remaining unnoticed, and escaping, was to stay absolutely still. Drayce watched the gunmen closely through the front windscreen. One clamped a hand to his shoulder as though he'd been shot, and two appeared relatively uninjured, one of whom was carrying the body of the man Drayce had shot. Drayce remained statue-still, happy that, so far, he and Sarah had not been seen.

Something else happened in their favour.

Police sirens wailed in the distance, echoing off the nearby buildings as they raced to the scene. One of the gunmen spoke into a phone and seconds later, a van and a Range Rover ascended the slope to the hotel entrance and drove up to them. The side door of the van slid open, the back doors of the Range Rover swung wide, and the body was unceremoniously dumped onto the floor of the van. It was clear the man was dead. Drayce pushed aside a feeling of guilt, reminding himself he'd had no choice.

The sirens drew closer every second. Drayce had a decision to make: if they drove away, it risked them being seen by the gunmen; if they stayed, it guaranteed they'd get caught up in the police response. Drayce had no desire to explain things when they arrived. It would be safer for him and Sarah if they vanished into the city. He kept his eyes on the van and the Range Rover, and reminding Sarah to keep her head down, pulled out from the line of vehicles, spun around, and drove down the slope to street level.

–

Stan dumped his rucksack into the front passenger footwell of the Range Rover, then slipped a hand under his body armour. The centre of his chest hurt like hell; broken ribs for sure, but hopefully not a cracked sternum. Every breath was agony as his ribs expanded and contracted, forcing him to belly breathe to limit the pain. A glint of brass caught his eye: the mushroomed bullet embedded in the front of his armour. A growl born of pain and anger escaped his lips.

The force of the bullet had sent him flying to the kitchen floor, where he'd scrambled behind the cover of the giant steel counter. Only Tommy and Marcus had suffered from the shootout, a bullet currently lodged somewhere in the latter's shoulder.

'Fuck me, that hurts!' Marcus said as he climbed onto the back seats of the Range Rover while applying pressure to the wound; dark red blood oozed between his fingertips.

Stan appreciated he would be in a lot of pain, but the bleeding wasn't catastrophic. Treatment could wait until they were out of the immediate area. Marcus was lucky compared with Tommy, who had been shot dead by that bastard protecting Sarah.

Stan made sure Tommy's body was safely in the back of the van, and then shut the sliding door and banged on the side panel to tell Daz he could move off. Marcus climbed into the back of the Range Rover, tentatively, cupping his injured shoulder. Fury swept through Stan at the reality of their fuck-up.

'What happened?' Leo asked from the back seat. He leant forwards between the front headrests, utter incredulity and confusion etched into his face, ignoring Marcus, who was trying to get in his seat without banging his shoulder.

'Doesn't matter now,' Stan said. 'Let's just get out of here before those sirens arrive.'

'I thought Chrissy's gadget was supposed to stop that lot being called?' This from Freddie in the driver's seat, his curly blond hair bouncing as he nodded at the van reversing past them.

'Not stop, *delay*,' Stan replied as he climbed into the front seat. 'It's only got a reach of fifty metres and the people running from the station would have soon covered that, plus those gunshots were loud enough to hear across the city. It was only a matter of time before the police started travelling, and by the sounds of it, they're nearly here. So get a fucking move on!'

Stan shut his door as Freddie reversed.

'Arrrgh!' Marcus screamed. 'Watch my shoulder, you dopey prick!'

'I've moved over all I can!' Leo shouted back. 'You want me in the boot?'

'Shut up, the pair of you!'

Stan's glare in the rear-view mirror stopped them from bickering, and the interior of the car drifted into a tense silence.

Something whipped across the back window; something big, moving fast. Stan abandoned the reflection and turned around in his seat. A grey Audi disappeared down the ramp.

Stan reached across Freddie and hit the horn, signalling for Daz to stop the van. Freddie pulled alongside it. The passenger window of the van buzzed down and Chrissy peered out.

'What's the matter?' he asked.

Stan leant out his window. 'Tell Daz to get in here and swap places with Leo! He's gonna put those trigger skills of his to some use!'

'What d'you mean?' Chrissy yelled, demonstrably irritated that his escape was being delayed. 'I thought we were getting out of here!'

'Just fucking tell him! There's no time to discuss it!'

As the men hurriedly swapped places, Stan locked eyes on the ramp, working hard to memorise the registration of the Audi. He'd caught a glimpse of the driver, and that glimpse had lasted long enough for him to see the man's face.

—

'Stay down,' Drayce said when he saw Sarah sit up in the rear-view mirror. 'We're not in the clear yet.'

After leaving the station, they'd headed west through Mayfair and were now travelling south on Park Lane, with Hyde Park on their right and a string of luxury hotels on their left. They'd just passed The Dorchester when Sarah sat up.

'How the hell did they find us?' she asked as she dropped back down, her cheek pressed tightly up against the leather seat, verging on tears, masking her fear with anger; a classic coping mechanism.

'I'm trying to work that one out myself,' he replied.

'Did you tell anyone where we were?'

'No, of course not.'

'Not even Julie?'

'No, not even Julie.'

Which was the truth; he hadn't. But maybe she had worked it out based on the background noise during the conversation at Carluccio's; the conversation that had cut out before the chaos had begun. If someone was hacking her calls, and listening in, they might also have narrowed down their location. Or maybe they didn't need to. Perhaps they had the resources – from what Drayce had just witnessed of these people, their resources were hardly lacking – not just to hack and monitor the call, but also pinpoint the location of each device, leading them straight to St Pancras. He reached into his pocket and turned off his phone as a temporary precaution.

'Well, they found us with someone's help!' Sarah said, tears threatening.

'Perhaps.'

'What do you mean, *perhaps?* Of course they had help! How else do you think they tracked us down?' She sat up and leant forwards between the two front seats. '*You* said we'd be safe!'

'Lie down.'

'*You* said they wouldn't find us!'

'Sarah, please, lie down.'

'No! You said we'd be safe somewhere busy and congested. You said it'd be easier for us to hide in a crowd. Well, it wasn't, was it? They found us, and even with all those people around, they still tried to kill me! How? How did they find me?'

'I don't know.'

'Did you tell them?'

'What?'

'Where we were! Did you tell them where we were?'

'Of course not.'

She leant even further forwards, her hot breath wafting across Drayce's face as she berated him. 'But if we were the only ones who knew our location, and I obviously didn't tell them, then that only leaves you.'

Drayce grabbed the rear-view mirror and tilted it until he made eye contact with her.

'Did you see what I did to those men in that kitchen? Why would I have done that if I was working for them?' He checked the road ahead – the car in front of him was a good twenty metres away. He turned back to Sarah. 'I don't know how they found us, but I—' His voice stuck in his throat as something caught his eye. The front of Sarah's cardigan dangled over the handbrake as she leant forwards: a tiny metal pin pierced the material, like the back of a badge. His hand reached to touch it.

'Watch out!' Sarah cried.

Drayce spun his head back to the road and slammed on the brakes. His seatbelt dug into his chest and smoke gently rose from the tyres; the scent of burnt rubber and brake pads filtered through the air vents. He couldn't see the registration of the car in front, but did see the wide eyes of the driver, glaring in his mirror and making obscene gestures with his hands. Drayce didn't blame him; it had been far too close for comfort. Now they were stationary, he turned back to Sarah and grabbed the front of her cardigan.

'Hey!' she said. 'What the hell are you doing?'

'What's this?'

'What's what?'

'This badge.'

'I'm not wearing a badge.'

He turned it over and saw it wasn't a badge pin at all. It was a small metal cylinder – half the size of a match – clinging to a tiny disc on the other side of the material. He pinched both sides and they fell apart. He collected the two pieces – cylinder and disc – in the palm of his hand, and examined them closely.

'What the hell is that?' Sarah asked. 'I've never seen that before.'

Drayce pushed them around his palm with the index finger of his other hand, desperately wishing to find something to negate his fears when they snapped together. Magnets. An interminable second or two ticked by, then with a sigh, he wound down his window and tossed the items into the road.

'Well?' Sarah asked.

'It was a tracker. They've been following our every move.'

Sarah's lips parted, her jaw slack from disbelief. 'How did they get that thing on me?'

'They must have clipped it to you in that cafe in Tottenham.' Drayce punched the dashboard in anger. 'I should have foreseen the possibility of a bug being planted on you. I should have checked you over.' He caught her eye in the rear-view mirror. 'I'm sorry.'

Sarah slumped back in her seat, her anger somewhat assuaged. 'It's not your fault. But I'm relieved that being found had nothing to do with you. I worried about taking a chance on you after all that's happened.' She relaxed back into her seat. 'At least it's no longer on me.'

'It was probably the only one, but we should pull over soon and check for others, just to be sure.'

Sarah nodded. Drayce watched her in the mirror and smiled. She'd only see his eyes in the reflection, but they must have echoed the shape of his mouth, because she smiled back.

Trust restored. Bond repaired.

After a deep sigh of relief, he reached for the steering wheel, about to move the Audi forwards with the slow-moving traffic, when a silver Range Rover SVR in the mirror paralysed his breathing.

Two cars back, a Kia Sportage and a Mercedes A-Class provided it with some cover. Drayce gripped the steering wheel, released the breath trapped in his chest, and took his foot off the brake, rolling the Audi forwards with the traffic.

'What's the matter?' Sarah asked, clearly picking up on the tension emanating from him.

'We might have a problem.'

His eyes flicked between the mirror and the windscreen, concentrating on the Range Rover while planning an escape route. They were approaching Hyde Park Corner, with its multiple lanes and numerous junctions; plenty of options there. The line of traffic halted again and he left enough room between them and the car in front to pull out and get past if needed.

He stared hard in the mirror. Was it the same one?

Thousands of Range Rovers populated that area of London, but gut feel screamed 'hitmen'. The traffic moved again, creeping nearer to Wellington Arch. The Kia behind indicated as Drayce checked the mirror, then turned off Park Lane, heading into the heart of Mayfair. Then the same from the Merc. He watched the Range Rover carefully as it closed the gap; his eyes dropped to the registration. It was different – a good sign – providing momentary relief from the adrenaline flooding his system.

Means nothing, his instincts told him. They'll have changed them… no way would they ride around on the same ones picked up by the cameras outside St Pancras.

As the Range Rover drew closer, Drayce focused on the two guys sitting in the front.

Goosebumps broke out.

Balaclavas no longer covered their faces: they were easily identifiable. The guy in the front passenger seat was the man with the missing ear, and the driver was the blond guy Drayce had thrown out of the first-floor window of the cafe.

'Alex?' Sarah said. 'What's the matter?'

'Nothing I can't fix.' He carefully slid the loaded pistol out of his jacket pocket and wedged the muzzle between the cushions on the front passenger seat, grip facing up, keeping his eyes on the road the entire time. Sarah stiffened when she saw the gun and gazed left and right to work out what he'd seen.

'Keep facing forwards,' Drayce said. 'I don't want them to know I've seen them.'

Sarah stilled. 'Where are they?'

'Doesn't matter. Are you still wearing your seatbelt?'

'Yes.'

'Good. Press your back into your seat and hold onto the door handle.'

Her knuckles turned white as she throttled the leather. 'What are you going to do?'

Drayce slipped the drive mode into sport, turned off the traction control, and selected first gear. 'I'm going to lose them.'

20

10:39 a.m.

Sharp fragments of broken lights and bodywork scattered across the road as Drayce overtook the vehicle in front, scraping deep gouges along both sides of the Audi as he forced his way between two lanes of traffic. In the mirror, he saw the Range Rover launch itself forwards to follow in his wake. As he burst free from the queue of traffic, horns blared at him as he swung wildly onto the ring road orbiting Wellington Arch, narrowly missing a white van, a red double-decker bus, and a black Hackney cab, all forced to swerve to avoid colliding with him.

Impatient to get out of sight of the crew in the Range Rover, he used all six lanes to make progress through the chaotic maze of traffic, weaving from lane to lane and using every gap the Audi would fit through. As he emerged from a line of cars he had just overtaken, a bus moved out of its lane without indicating, forcing him to drive dangerously close to the stone wall that surrounded Hyde Park Corner. His jaw clenched when he saw the gunmen making progress. He cursed the bus driver as he hit the brakes, manoeuvred around the back of the giant vehicle, dropped down a gear and floored the throttle, the huge exhausts roaring with fury as he crossed all six lanes in a single swoop, narrowly avoiding a collision with a taxi as he took the junction onto Constitution Hill.

'Alex!' Sarah cried.

Startled by her frightened voice, he turned his head and saw what she'd seen: their pursuers were level with them on the left, able to take the junction at greater speed, unimpeded by the bus. Drayce planted his right foot to the floor and blasted down the long straight road, the trees lining both sides whizzing past in a hazy green blur. But it wasn't enough. The immense power of the Range Rover SVR, along with the higher speed as it turned onto Constitution Hill, brought it alongside them.

Drayce lowered the front passenger window and snatched up the pistol. 'Get down!' he shouted to Sarah.

The driver's window shattered as he opened fire at the Range Rover, thousands of tiny pieces caught in the wind and blown through the cabin, scattered all over the occupants. The driver had seen the gun just in time and ducked out of sight, leaving the front seat passenger in the firing line. He winced at the impact, the rounds presumably having hit his body armour.

Drayce watched the driver sit up, his blond curls clinging to his sweaty brow, above a tightly packed expression that flipped between the Audi and the road ahead. After narrowly avoiding a bullet that whizzed past his head, Drayce had expected him to back off from the chase. But there was no reduction in the speed of the Range Rover.

You're tougher than you look, Goldilocks.

As he prepared to fire again, the tinted rear window lowered, revealing the muzzle of a black assault rifle aimed his way.

A sharp dab of the brakes and the Audi dropped back several feet, slotting in behind the Range Rover, out of sight of the weapon's aim. Thrown against her door, Sarah let out a soft cry. About to ask if she was all right, movement inside the vehicle in front distracted Drayce. The men in the rear seats were changing positions, their silhouettes climbing over one another as they repositioned themselves. A second later, the boot opened: one of the gunmen lay prone on a folded-down rear seat, his body wrapped tightly around an assault rifle, his left eye closed, concentrating down the sights with his right. His trigger finger primed for the right moment to shoot during the continuous rhythm of the vehicle's movements.

Time to make that job even harder.

Drayce swerved to the right as the man opened fire, spraying short sharp bursts of fully automatic gunfire in their direction. His driving pure instinct, Drayce whipped the steering wheel from left to right avoiding one head-on collision after another to survive the relentless torrent of lead raining down on them. *Ting ting tings* clattered all around the bodywork, bullets hit the front windscreen and travelled through the cabin to exit through the rear. He backed off from the Range Rover, swerving the Audi from side to side at random intervals.

So focused on making them as hard a target as possible, Drayce barely noticed Buckingham Palace to his right, or the crowds of people around Victoria Memorial running for their lives, taking directions from the Palace's armed police officers, some frantically talking into their radios, while others shouldered their weapons. But both vehicles were travelling far too fast for any of the cops to take a worthwhile shot as they joined The Mall at over one hundred miles an hour.

Then came a pause in the chaos.

The shooting stopped.

Drayce gambled on the gunman reloading, and carpe'd the heck out of the diem. He closed the gap between them, positioned the Audi along the left-hand side of the road, and took aim with his pistol, emptying his magazine into the rear nearside tyre. The Range Rover shuddered then swerved violently from side to side, a plane passing through a nasty pocket of turbulence. Drayce's heart sank as he watched it settle into the same unstoppable momentum as before.

Damn run-flat tyres.

He dropped the empty pistol into his jacket pocket to join the other one, and glanced ahead in time to see he was closing on the three underpasses at Admiralty Arch with frightening speed. To make matters worse, a closed gate blocked the middle archway and the one on the right was full of oncoming traffic, leaving just one archway clear, which was only the width of a single vehicle.

Decision time: get past the Range Rover and through the archway first, or slam on the brakes, spin the car around, and find another escape route?

Brake lights on the Range Rover forced his hand.

He stamped on the throttle and swerved violently to the right, overtaking the Range Rover and its hesitant driver. He flew under the arch and into the widest gap in the traffic ahead – speed imperative. A Fiat 500 and a Toyota Prius both fell victim to Drayce's getaway. The Audi's wing mirrors cleanly removed, they fell underneath its wheels, spat out at the rear end as he forced the vehicle through another gap that was not wide enough. Ignoring the horrific sound of tearing metal, he pushed the Audi through gaps equally too small, the threat of the heavily armed men in the Range Rover ever-present in his rear-view mirror.

Negotiating the fast-approaching roundabout by conventional means would be impossible: the traffic was just too heavy. A hasty analysis of the spaces between cars identified a route *through* the roundabout, using the clear space around the Charles I statue.

Horns blared and obscenities bawled, Drayce ignored it all as he manoeuvred through and continued down the Strand: a wide road that soon turned into a dual carriageway, offering much easier progress. Behind him, the Range Rover followed his every move, and even closed the gap; it crossed the roundabout at greater speed with its significant ground clearance.

Drayce gritted his teeth, flying the Audi down the Strand before mounting the central reservation and turning into Savoy Street on his right, tearing downhill to the river.

Wind blew through the bullet holes in the windows and swirled around the cabin as he neared the T-junction at the bottom. With a gentle touch on the brakes, he swerved left, a cloud of smoke marking his route as all four tyres fought for purchase. Engulfed by the shadow of Waterloo Bridge, the Audi hurtled along Victoria Embankment. Red lights, other motorists, pavements and pedestrians: all negotiated as he carved a route along the river to escape the gunmen. His rear-view mirror indicated this chase would soon be over, one way or another.

About fifty metres behind the Range Rover, blue and white lights flashed maniacally, steadily closing the gap. A convoy of at least six vehicles.

The cavalry had arrived.

Between the CCTV at St Pancras, the ANPR cameras on the route they'd driven, and the carnage they'd left in their wake, it was no wonder the cops had caught up.

Drayce increased the gap between them and the Range Rover as they entered the tunnel on Upper Thames Street, his eyes adjusting to the gloom until emergency lights on the police vehicles reflected wildly off the walls, the deafening echo of their sirens flooding the tunnel.

To undertake a line of traffic up ahead, Drayce reduced speed and crossed over onto the white hatchings, forcing the gunmen to slow as well: the police convoy closed the gap even tighter. The end of the tunnel rushed up, and they exploded back into the daylight. Ahead was another set of red lights to ignore if he wanted to escape their pursuers.

The unmarked police vehicles came out of the shadows like ghosts and blocked the traffic-light-controlled junction side-on. The front grilles lit up, blue and white, and the occupants flung open the doors and leapt out with large black carbines in their hands.

Drayce swerved to the right, not even touching his brakes as he skirted past the end of the central reservation and careered down Queen Street Place, glancing off lampposts and mounting pavements to avoid the roadblock.

The Range Rover followed in Drayce's wake. Two pairs of CTSFOs on off-road motorbikes, the only cops able to follow the chaotic path, loomed in Drayce's rear-view mirror as he approached Southwark Bridge. They wore the same grey tactical suits and black body armour he'd worn when he'd done their job. They all had carbines strapped to their backs, and the pillions cradled shotguns – to disable each vehicle before engaging with the occupants.

He could not allow that to happen.

On Southwark Bridge, the dark river water passing underneath, the gunmen behind took a sharp turn to the left, abandoning the chase, no doubt because of the Met's elite counterterrorist unit. One of the bikes followed the Range Rover, while the other pursued Drayce and Sarah onto the bridge. Drayce concentrated ahead, planning his route, but there was something wrong: the Audi's throttle wasn't responding. He dropped down a gear and floored it. No difference. No power. The exhausts coughed and spluttered with the cadence of an old chain smoker's lungs. The forced reckless journey had killed it: it crawled to the middle of the bridge and stopped, dead. The approaching CTSFOs appeared in his rear-view mirror. If caught, they would be arrested pending the investigation into events at St Pancras; they'd spend a significant amount of time in police custody for questioning.

How far was the reach of the people who wanted Sarah dead? Could he trust the criminal justice system to keep her safe? These people, and the corrupt officer Julie believed worked for them, might get to Sarah while she was in a police cell.

That was not a risk Drayce was willing to take.

He told Sarah to get out, grabbed her arm and dragged her to the bridge's barrier as the CTSFOs screeched to a halt behind them. Shielding his face, he climbed up on top of the barrier and pulled Sarah up with him.

'What are you doing?' she asked, terror vibrating in her voice.

'Do you trust me?' Drayce dumped the two empty pistols into the fast-flowing water and shuffled his feet to the edge. Shouts of 'Armed police!' dominated the background as the officers climbed off the bike, their weapons rising on aim.

'What?' she uttered, frowning, the rest of her face screwed up tight in fear and confusion.

He held her by her shoulders and watched her eyes. 'Do you trust me?'

'Yes,' she said breathlessly as a cold wind whipped her hair up into the air.

'Good.'

He pushed her, her thrashing form plummeting as she screamed. He followed her just as the officers levelled their weapons, locking his body straight to enter the water with minimal impact. A brief feeling of weightlessness engulfed him as he fell to the murky river. He ignored the panic brought on by having absolutely no control. Freefalling, he heard more shouts from the officers on the bridge, blanketed when he entered the cold water.

Pure shock consumed him. He only just kept his lips pressed tightly together, preventing his lungs from filling with water. As he broke the surface, he saw Sarah frantically flapping her arms, spluttering as she struggled to keep her head above the water. Drayce reached out and grabbed her arm as the current swept them underneath the bridge and out the other side. He pulled her close, propping her head on his chest, her mouth and nose out of the water, and swam hard. A glance at the bridge showed the two officers watching, their hands punching the railing in frustration.

21

Drayce let the current take them both, his head swivelling from side to side to get his bearings. He blinked hard to rid the dirty river water from his eyes: they were floating underneath London Bridge, drifting closer to the left side of the river than the right, and up ahead was a pier on large concrete stilts. If he could make it there, he could pull them from one stilt to another to a small beach with stone steps leading up the embankment to street level. The urgency to avoid capture and arrest meant the beach was their best chance.

Drayce encouraged Sarah to kick her arms and legs – hard – and realised she couldn't swim. Keeping an arm wrapped around her chest, he did all the work, sweeping long strokes with his free arm and kicking with all his might to get them across to the pier before the current swept them past. The armed police officers who patrolled the river would form a search party: they had to get out of the water, quickly.

Far easier said than done.

For every stroke he took to the riverbank, the current swept them downstream six feet. The pier was fast approaching, and as he looked further downriver, it was obviously their only option. If they missed this opportunity to get out, there was nothing else in sight; the embankments on the next stretch were far too high, and the police would be swarming the river on boats before they reached the next pier. He kicked harder and powered his free arm through the water, turning his head from the waves breaking across his face, stinging his eyes and making him cough as water flooded his nostrils and hit the back of his throat.

Dragging Sarah's dead weight as he fought against the current, his wool suit clinging to his frame, as heavy and cumbersome as a suit of armour, threatened to drag him under. He focused on the stilt he wanted to reach, and swam hard.

They weren't going to make it.

The length was too great, the angle too severe, and the current too strong.

In the distance: sirens, on the water, heading their way.

A fresh burst of adrenaline fuelled him through the water. His eyes fixed on his goal, the shrill sirens motivated him through the burning pain in his muscles. They'd miss the stilt he'd originally aimed for, but he might catch the last one. Their closing speed was such that he'd get one fleeting chance at success. He stretched his arm as far as it would go – it was now or never – and precisely at the moment he thought he'd missed it, the cold hard slap of slimy concrete hit the palm of his hand.

It took all his strength to hold on, fighting the pull of the current, but he clawed from one stilt to the next, pulling Sarah upstream to the beach. After the fourth stilt, he put his legs down and felt the soft riverbed with the toecaps of his shoes. A little further and he was able to put his soles down and walk. They emerged from under the pier and waded through the waist-high water to the steps, the level gradually dropping until they were on the muddy beach.

His gait uneven, Drayce glanced down. He was missing a shoe, lost in the thick mud he'd just waded through. He took off the one that had survived and then checked his necklace, giving a big sigh of relief when his fingers tugged the leather cord, the locket bouncing against his chest. He drew in some deep breaths, exhausted and freezing now he was out of the water. Sarah, frozen to the spot, was hugging herself and shivering; he took her by the arm and made her walk to the steps.

'Get your hand off me!' she said as she pulled away from him.

Shocked by her tone, Drayce almost let go. Almost.

'We've got to hurry,' he said. 'It won't take the police long to surround this area and drag the net in. If we're still around when they do, we'll be in it.'

'I'd rather take my chances with them than with you. You pushed me off a bridge!'

Drayce almost said 'calm down', but then he remembered what had happened in the past when he'd said that to an angry woman.

Sarah shouted at him again. 'I can't swim. I just nearly drowned!'

'But you didn't,' Drayce replied. 'And if you want to wait here for the police to come and arrest you, then I can't stop you.' The word arrest changed the expression on Sarah's face. 'That's right, I said arrest. Because after what happened at St Pancras, that's exactly what they'll do, and only once they've interviewed you for three days straight will they move you into the victim category as opposed to the suspect one, but it'll be too late by then, because if Julie's right, and there is a corrupt officer working for these people, having you trapped in one place for three days will be a gift for them to execute your murder.'

Sarah's shivering increased, along with the misery on her face. Drayce couldn't distinguish between the tears and the river water dripping down her cheeks, but he was pretty sure she was crying. Downriver, he heard the wailing sirens getting louder. He moved his hand from Sarah's arm to her shoulder.

'If these people have someone with power helping them, I can't risk you being swallowed up into the system, because I don't know how far they reach.' He took his hand off her shoulder and held it out, gesturing for her to take it. 'With me, you're safe.' He turned his head to the sirens. 'With them, you're not.'

Sarah folded her arms across her chest as she gazed down at his hand.

'You pushed me into the river,' she said again, softer this time.

Drayce made eye contact with her. 'I'm sorry, I really am, but I'd run out of options. Keeping you safe means keeping you well out of reach of the people who want you dead.' His eyes flicked back to the approaching sirens, which he estimated were less than a minute from the beach. 'Now, if you don't mind, I think we should get moving.'

Sarah stared down at his hand, as if contemplating reaching out for it.

'You don't have long to decide,' he said. 'They'll be here any second.'

Reluctantly, she reached out and took it, but brought her other hand up, the index finger pointing sharply up into his face. 'Just give me some warning next time you have another stupid idea, okay?'

He smiled. 'Deal.'

They started for the steps, but only got a few feet when Sarah pulled him to a standstill.

'Wait!' she said, her free hand patting down her pockets. 'Mum's photograph!'

'We don't have time.'

'I can't go without it!' She let go of his hand and turned back to the river. 'I have to go back!'

'Sarah, we need to get moving.'

'It's laminated, it'll be floating out there. I can get it back!'

Red and blue lights reflected off the water.

'There isn't time!'

'It's the only one I have of her. I've got to get it back!'

Drayce grabbed her and spun her around to face him, about to throw her over his shoulder and carry her when he saw something fall in the mud. He bent down and picked up the photograph, wet and muddy, but in good condition thanks to the plastic coating. 'Can we go now?' he asked as he handed it back to her.

She nodded and took it from him, clutching it to her chest before taking his hand again.

Then they were running, through the mud, up the steps, and between a set of four black bollards set side by side at the top. Drayce ditched his ruined shoe in a bin with a heavy heart – Church's Oxfords weren't cheap – and then they ran away from the river and into an area of the city teeming with tourists. The expressions on the faces of the other pedestrians they passed were mostly blank; the majority followed the city's rule of avoiding eye contact with strangers at all costs. But some stared, concerned, others with contempt. They stood out more than two homeless people who'd wandered into the lobby of the Ritz. Drayce tilted his head down to Sarah.

'We should get off the streets. In our current state, it won't be long before someone calls the police to report two crazy people running around in soaking wet clothes, one of whom isn't wearing shoes.'

Sarah nodded back, her teeth chattering too violently for her to speak.

Drayce spotted a taxi without a fare on board. He waved it down and opened the door for Sarah, before climbing in after her. They sat, eyes forwards, dripping wet from head to toe. When the driver saw the state of them, he turned around with a scowl, his lips fracturing as he prepared to tell them to piss off. But at seeing Drayce's face, the presence of a man literally twice the size of most others, instead of ordering them out of his taxi, he asked politely where they wanted to go.

Drayce hesitated about breaking one of his rules by introducing a professional situation into a personal space, but with the pair of them now soaking wet, freezing and on the run from violent hitmen and the police, he was out of options. He swallowed his doubts and gave the driver an address not far from his flat in Southwark.

22

11:13 a.m.

Sombre during the entire journey, Sarah gazed out of the window, no doubt processing everything that had happened. After checking her for any other trackers, Drayce stayed quiet as well, monitoring the streets for any tails and checking the occupants of other vehicles in case anyone paid them too much attention. Around the corner from his block, he tore open the Velcro pocket inside his jacket, took out his keys, paid the taxi driver – slipping him an extra hundred from his stack of wet notes – 'You never saw us' – apologised for the puddles on the seats, and led the way to his flat. It wouldn't be the hardest thing in the world for the police to link two suspects who'd jumped into the river to a soaking wet man and woman who took a taxi out of the area. Drayce hoped the extra money would ensure the cabby's discretion. But at least he didn't have Drayce's address.

He unlocked his door and held it open for Sarah, who stepped over the threshold and walked down the narrow hallway. To her left and right, open doorways faced one another: a small bathroom to the left and a double bedroom to the right. Seeing her head turn from side to side as she slowly walked ahead of him, a mild panic stirred within Drayce as he questioned how tidy he'd left the place before setting off for the snooker club that morning. The door locked behind him, he glanced into both rooms, pleased to see the bed made and the towel from his morning shower hanging neatly on the rails.

'This where you live?' Sarah asked from the middle of the open-plan kitchen and living room area, turning on the spot. A grey fabric sofa faced a glass coffee table and a flat-screen television mounted on the right-hand wall. Below the TV was a square gas fire encased in metal, a layer of white pebbles visible through the glass screen. The far wall was mostly windows overlooking a large communal park area. A kitchen counter ran along the left-hand wall, below which were the washing machine, fridge and oven; above were several white-gloss cupboards. The colour scheme was typical for flats rented on short-term contracts: lots of different shades of grey and white, with little in the way of a personal touch. The only thing Drayce had on display that hadn't come with the flat was a set of picture frames on the kitchen work surface, six in total, linked with hinges so they could be folded up and packed away. Each photograph was of Lily with a beaming smile. The frames all black, their plastic corners chipped and their edges scratched: evidence of numerous knocks and bumps from travels with an international bodyguard.

'At the moment,' Drayce replied as he placed his keys in front of the picture frames. 'It's just a temporary place I'm still renting after a few jobs here in London. I don't have a home, as such. Certainly nothing permanent. No point when I travel for work as often as I do.'

He grabbed two clean towels from the bathroom, keeping hold of one and leaving the other next to the basin. Back in the living room, he offered Sarah the use of the shower. He waited until she was out of sight and then he stripped off, piling his sopping wet clothes on the tiled floor before wrapping the clean towel around his waist. Happy it wouldn't fall, he bent down, tore the Velcro that clasped his jacket pockets together, and took out his phone, his stainless steel wallet, and the stack of cash he'd taken from the snooker club, praising the person who had discovered how to waterproof modern smartphones, along with the genius who had decided to make banknotes out of plastic. The Velcro strips were an idea he'd had after losing a set of keys on a job a few years ago: an idea he'd initially thought to be ingenious, despite his tailor's grimace. After spreading the contents of his pockets, along with his belt, on the kitchen granite work surface to dry, he moved to stuff his suit into a bin liner ready for the dry cleaners, halting when he noticed the black, frayed scorch mark to the shoulder of his jacket, a reminder of how close he had come to taking a bullet at St Pancras.

Ditching his other items of clothing in the washing machine, he set it on a hot wash and sat on the edge of the sofa's back support, inhaling deeply and holding his breath as he replayed his trigger pull in the kitchen doorway at St Pancras; straight-away, he considered self-preservation. Were there cameras covering that position? Could he have been recorded with the gun in his hands and a clear shot of his face, marking him out as a suspect?

No.

He'd checked for cameras in that alleyway, and tucked the gun away when they'd got to the Audi and driven off. If any cameras had caught him after that point, and the authorities were able to identify him, he'd have to tell the truth, and argue, quite justifiably, that he was acting in defence of both himself and Sarah. But without CCTV footage of the shoot-out in the kitchen, and no witnesses, Drayce doubted he'd be getting his collar felt any time soon. Everything considered, he was pretty safe from being marked as a suspect in the gunman's death. Once this was all over and Sarah was safely back in witness protection, Drayce could debrief the authorities, confident his actions would be justifiably seen as self-defence. A tired sigh escaped his lips as he released the breath he'd been holding.

Instinctively, he turned to face a movement: Sarah had left the bathroom door slightly ajar. Before he had time to look away, he caught sight of her in the mirror, as she pulled her wet t-shirt over her head.

His eyes widened. Across her back was a horrific pattern of scars. Some resembled small round burn marks from the tips of cigarettes. Others were long, the brutal scar tissue like long serpents slithering across her back. It took Drayce a second to realise they were actually a series of vicious strokes from a whip.

Gathering himself, he forced his eyes down to the floor, padded over to the fireplace, and lit the gas, warming himself in front of the instant heat. He knelt in front of the glass and held out his hands, rubbing them together. His flesh welcomed the warmth as a starving man would a plate of food, absorbing it hungrily and distributing it around his body, his extremities tingling in the process. The goosebumps that decorated the deep ridges and undulating curves where one muscle group flowed into the next gradually dissipated.

From across the flat he heard running water hitting the shower tray from head height. Despite the pleasure of the fire, the image of Sarah's back was forefront in Drayce's mind.

What on earth had she been subjected to?

The list of possibilities for how and why she had sustained those injuries was a long one, but as Drayce sat in the glow of the fire, he was pretty sure he could narrow it down. They were torture marks, that was for sure, so the *how* was covered; the *why* was the difficult part.

Had she once been a key element of the criminal organisation that now wanted her dead? Had she betrayed them, resulting in kidnap and torture?

Drayce didn't buy that narrative; she just didn't seem the type. He would have expected her to be a lot more arrogant, and far more difficult to deal with if she'd played any significant part in organised crime. Sure, her personality until now could have been an act, but he doubted it. Acts couldn't be kept up for long; they all withered at some point, especially under stress, and the two of them had certainly been subjected to plenty of that since this morning.

So, Sarah probably wasn't a gangster.

So what then?

Drayce had helped protect a number of investigative journalists since he'd left the police and become a bodyguard; people who had dug a little too deeply into the affairs of extremely dangerous people, uncovering information worth killing for.

Could that explain it? She'd infiltrated a criminal gang, had her cover blown, and been tortured as a result… exposed the activities of a group of people so dangerous they were hell-bent on tracking her down and killing her?

Speculation, Drayce told himself. Nothing but speculation. The only way to know exactly how much danger the pair of them faced, was to get her talking.

A noise made him sit up straight. He wasn't sure how much time had passed but Sarah was in the hallway, engulfed in his giant dressing gown, her hair wrapped up in the towel. Her cheeks were pink and her eyes bright and alert, no longer on the verge of hypothermia. He stood up, slightly embarrassed at his state of undress, and hurried to the bathroom, the two of them smiling awkwardly as they crossed paths.

Ten minutes later, showered and dressed, he reappeared from the bedroom wearing dark blue Olympvs jeans – the only make he ever bought, the only make that fitted around his thighs and backside comfortably – a black sweater, and a dark blue wool overcoat. On his feet were a pair of warm socks and sturdy brown Altberg boots. Sarah was by the kitchen counter, tall and rigid, her hands clasped together.

'Try to relax,' he said. 'We're safe here.'

'I've heard you say that before.'

He raised an eyebrow. 'Touché.'

She walked over to the fireplace and knelt in front of it, exactly how Drayce had done earlier. She unfurled the towel, tilted her head back, her long black hair cascading down her back. Drayce suddenly realised he was staring, as though he could see through the dressing gown, right at those scars.

'I'm just nipping out,' he said.

Her head spun to face him. 'Out? Where?'

'To buy you a new outfit. I'm not the kind of guy who keeps a stash of women's clothes, and I don't think any of my gear will fit you.' His smile wasn't reciprocated. 'Don't worry, I won't be long. Make yourself at home while I'm gone. And not that anyone will, but don't answer the door if someone knocks.'

She turned away from him to face the fire. 'I'm not a child.'

'You know what I mean.'

She bent forwards, embracing the warmth as she hugged herself. 'Don't worry, I'm not leaving this fireplace for quite some time.'

'I don't blame you,' Drayce said as he collected his wallet and moved to the door.

'Aren't you forgetting something?' she called out.

He stopped just as his hand touched the handle, turning his head back down the entranceway. 'What's that?'

'My sizes. Or were you just going to guess?'

He squinted. 'I hadn't thought of that.'

Sarah flicked her head at the pen and notebook on the kitchen counter. 'Pass me those, would you?'

Drayce walked back, picked up the notebook and pen and passed them to her. 'You meant it when you said you weren't leaving that fire, huh?'

'Absolutely.' She scribbled down a list of everything she'd need – including toiletries and a toothbrush – along with her sizes, then handed it back. It was longer than Drayce had expected. His face must have made that obvious. 'Thought I'd spell it out for you. I'd hate to think of you wandering around the women's aisles with no idea where to start.'

'Good job I didn't lose my credit card in the river.'

Now Sarah smiled. 'See you when you get back.'

'You know,' Drayce paused at the front door again, waving his wallet in the air. 'Normally, people say thank you for this sort of thing.'

Sarah raised her eyebrows and dipped her chin in a how-dare-you look. 'Normally, people don't throw others into freezing rivers.'

He pondered that thought as he opened the door. 'I suppose I had that coming. Just don't try to hold it against me forever. These things have a shelf life.'

'Not with me, they don't.'

He turned around and cocked his head to one side as he backed out of the doorway. 'Go easy on me. You see how much trouble I've got myself in repaying the last woman I owed?'

He could tell she was trying, but failing, to let his sense of humour take effect on her. She appeared sad, dejected, and rundown. After everything she'd been through, he couldn't blame her.

'This is never going to end, is it?' she said. 'I'll always be on the run from these people.'

Drayce tried to find the right words. 'It all seems too big to comprehend now, but you will overcome it. Your life won't always be this way. You've got to break the problem down into small chunks, and deal with them one at a time. And I promise I'll be with you every step of the way.'

And with that parting comment, he backed away and closed the door, unable to take his mind off those scars, and prevent his imagination from conjuring up a list of horrific scenarios for how they were inflicted, and why.

What on earth happened to you, Sarah?

23

11:17 a.m.

Julie and Fiona parked on a nearby side street after picking up lunch. They walked into the NCA HQ site on foot, and crept through a side entrance to avoid being spotted by Foster. Julie checked her phone in case she'd had a message from Alex, but all she had to greet her was a notification from her BBC news app. That could wait. They found an empty office on the ground floor and ate while they downloaded the photographs Drayce had taken outside Costa.

'I'm not massively comfortable with this,' Fiona said as she picked at her salad box with a tiny disposable fork, her eyes gazing warily over Julie's shoulder at the screen.

'Your comfort isn't important right now,' Julie replied through a mouthful of burger, hunched over the keyboard, typing. 'You just need to help me do what's right.'

'But—'

'And as it stands,' Julie snapped, 'what's right is for us to make certain nobody can find out where Sarah and Alex are while we figure out the identities of these four men. Got it?'

Fiona leant back in her chair, quiet, her attention on her efforts to spear a slice of radish, apparently resigned to Julie's way of doing things, albeit unwillingly. Julie caught sight of Fiona's reflection in the computer screen and smothered a retort at the sulky, pouting expression on her face. She stopped typing, swallowed her mouthful of burger, placed the giant stack of bread and meat back in its carton, and turned around to face her.

'Let me tell you something, because although you're a bright woman, you clearly haven't worked it out yet. Sometimes orders are to be ignored if you want to get the job done. Now, you can accept that as fact, or you can waste time figuring it out for yourself, but I suggest you listen to someone who's been there and back and learned from her mistakes.'

Fiona shrugged. 'It's just that sneaking around and hiding things from Foster doesn't sit right with me.'

'I seem to remember you not wanting to tell him about what happened at the cafe right away.'

Fiona cocked her head to the side and frowned. 'It's one thing to delay telling him about something he knows nothing about, but to disobey a direct order from him just doesn't seem right. You might be at the tail end of your career, but mine's only just getting started. I can't afford to burn bridges with a line manager.'

Julie restrained the urge to give her a hard slap. 'I get that, but these are strange circumstances, and we have to improvise if we want to guarantee the right result. And besides, I'll be the one to get it in the neck if Foster finds out, not you.' She forced a smile, trying to bring her on board. 'Okay?'

A neat little grin bloomed over Fiona's face, the corners of her mouth tilting upwards. 'I guess.'

Julie turned back to the computer. 'Good.' She raised her newly refilled tumbler of coffee to her lips, pushed through the burn, sighed with satisfaction, and placed it back on the desk when her tongue and lips could no longer take the heat.

'You look tired,' Fiona said.

Julie rubbed her eyes with her knuckles. 'I'm always tired.'

'Still not sleeping well?'

'I can't remember the last time I did. Probably as a teenager, before I made the mistake of becoming a cop.'

She reached for her burger and took another bite.

'Is that burger kosher?' Fiona asked.

'Not all Jews eat kosher,' Julie replied, flatly. 'And I'm one of them.'

156

'Oh.'

'I don't have time for all that, much to my mother's annoyance.'

'I see.'

Julie used the hand that wasn't holding her burger to click on the magnifying glass icon, beginning the search. She heard Fiona shuffle up behind her to get a better view.

'So how does this work then?' Fiona asked.

'The software uses biometrics to map the men's facial features, and then it compares the information with images we have on record from mug shots taken in police custody.'

'Which means if they've ever been arrested, we'll know who they are?'

'Precisely. And I'm sure men in their line of work will have a long list of convictions.'

Julie's phone rang, distracting her from the computer screen. Dereck. She put down her burger, washed her mouthful down with a greedy slurp of coffee, and answered it on speakerphone so Fiona wouldn't be left out of the conversation.

'Dereck,' she said. 'What's up?'

'I bring news from the Met.'

'Good or bad?'

'Both. Which do you want first?'

'Let's get the bad out of the way.'

'All right. Well, the bad news is that the neighbours who heard and saw the attack at the flat can only give very vague descriptions of the offenders, and when I say vague, I mean men in black clothing and balaclavas with guns in their hands.'

'Not helpful, but not surprising.'

'True. There's no CCTV in the area, and no information regarding any vehicles the offenders might have used.'

Julie sighed. 'Are you close to getting to the good news yet, Dereck?'

'Yeah, the good news is that one of the offenders was seriously wounded somehow, maybe shot by one of Sarah's protection officers.'

Julie sat up a little straighter. 'Is there a body?'

'No, but there's the next best thing: blood, and lots of it. We won't know much regarding forensics until the CSIs have finished at the lab, but they've spilt a couple of pints all over the hallway floor, so they'll definitely get a full DNA profile.'

'And hopefully a hit from the database.'

'Hopefully.'

'That's great news, Dereck.'

'How are things going your end?'

Julie watched the flashing icon on the computer screen that indicated the search was ongoing. 'Good, thanks.'

'Have you seen Sarah? Is she okay?'

'Not seen, but spoken to. She's okay. She's with Alex and he's taking care of her.'

'Good to hear.'

'Yeah, and thanks to him, it appears we might be well on our way to identifying the people who are trying to kill her.'

'Really? Do tell.'

'He took a photograph of four men we believe are connected.'

As soon as the words had left her mouth, Julie realised her mistake.

'How did he get that?' Dereck asked in shock.

Julie remained silent. She saw Fiona lean in and part her lips to reply for her. A sense of panic prompted Julie to react immediately, clamping her right hand on Fiona's arm and pinching her thumb and index finger on her left to draw a line across her lips, as if closing a zipper. Startled, Fiona got the message and leant back into her chair, staying quiet.

'Well?' Dereck asked.

'It's complicated,' Julie replied, keeping her eyes and hand on Fiona. 'We'll explain all when we debrief later on.'

'But—'

'It might be nothing, the photo is really unclear,' she said, wishing he'd shut up or move on. 'We're probably wasting our time, to be honest, so don't mention it to Foster. The DNA profile at your end is the best evidence we have.'

Julie heard him huff down the line, then he said, 'Talk about an anti-climax.'

She let go of Fiona and tried to laugh it off with Dereck. 'Yeah, tell me about it. Got a bit carried away there.'

'That's not like you.' Suspicion crept into Dereck's voice. 'You don't normally reveal something until you know it's a fact.'

'Anything else your end?' she asked, to change the topic.

'Don't think so.'

'Okay. Gotta go. Speak soon.'

Julie reached forwards and tapped the screen of her phone to cancel the call, then leant back into her chair, closed her eyes, and took a deep sigh of relief that the conversation was over.

No more opportunities for me to put my foot in my mouth, she thought.

'What was that all about?' Fiona asked, her voice shrill and angry.

Julie opened her eyes to address her. 'What was what all about?'

Fiona's eyelids pulled back in an expression of exaggerated shock. 'You grabbing hold of me like that when I was about to speak.' She swiped at her arm. 'You got ketchup on my shirt.'

Julie sat up and spun her chair to face her. 'Don't panic, it'll wash out. And I'm sorry, but we can't risk the information we're discovering getting talked about, or mentioned to Foster, or even worse, fed into the system.'

Fiona jabbed a finger in her direction. 'But you started talking about it, so I thought it was okay.'

'I know I did, but I shouldn't have done. I made a—'

'He's our colleague, for Christ's sake,' Fiona waved her hands about, gesticulating in frustration. 'We're supposed to be able to trust one another.'

'Well, we can't.' Julie heard the aggression in her voice and warned herself to keep a lid on it. Fighting anger with anger rarely made things better. 'Not yet.'

Fiona turned her back, hostility personified. Julie scooted her chair up to her and put a hand on her shoulder.

'Listen, it's not that I don't trust Dereck. Of course I do. It's just I worry he'd mention it to Foster, who'd then feed it back to his supervisors in a tasking meeting, as per his job – which, let's face it, he'd definitely do because he's thorough and by the book with everything he does – which means it'd get fed into the intelligence system and read by whoever's working for the brothers.'

Fiona spun her chair to face her. 'But we don't know there is anyone working for the brothers. You heard Foster's theory, and I don't see any evidence to suggest otherwise.'

Julie shook her head. 'His theory doesn't explain how they found Wayne. Sarah knew nothing about where he was.'

'Well, maybe he did the same thing. Maybe neither of them followed the rules we gave them, making *them* responsible for all this chaos. The point I'm making is that until there's actual proof, I will not believe someone inside the Agency is working for the Marlowe brothers.'

Julie thought about everything Fiona had just said and shook her head. 'They knew how much danger they were in, and they'd come to us for help. Why would they jeopardise their safety by giving away their locations?'

'Because they're stupid criminals! That's who we deal with: criminals ratting on other criminals, who by their very nature, do not follow rules.'

Julie let it go; it was clearly a losing battle. Silence descended on the room. Fiona hunkered down in her chair, arms crossed. Julie watched her closely, hoping she understood the potential of what was happening, and why they had to be so careful. Julie certainly understood why Fiona was so unwilling to believe there might be a corrupt officer in their midst, as well as uncomfortable with keeping their colleagues in the dark. But whether the risk was high or low, likely or unlikely, as things stood, there was still the danger of an information leak to the brothers, regardless of whether Fiona was comfortable with that possibility or not. It was imperative they take precautions with every detail they uncovered. In Julie's opinion, it was the only safe, sensible thing to do.

She'll come around. In time.

The high-pitched buzzing of Julie's phone cut through the air like a raid warning, dissipating some of the tension in the room as it broke the awkward silence.

'It's Chris,' Julie said to Fiona, before answering it. 'Hi, Chris.'

'Hi, Julie. You hear me okay?'

'Yeah, fine.'

'Good. Just a heads-up that the line might not stay this clear throughout the call. The signal's poor out here in rural Suffolk.'

'No worries. If we sound a little funny, it's because you're on speakerphone. It's just Fiona and me.'

'Okay. Hi, Fi. Play me a song.'

'It was a rubbish joke the first time you told it, and it doesn't get funnier over time,' Fiona said. 'And that's not even how the abbreviation of my name's pronounced. It would be Hi Fee, but then it wouldn't even work on your moronic level, would it?'

A moment of dead air while Chris absorbed this response. 'All right, take it easy. It's only a joke.'

'Well, I'm not in the mood.'

'Yeah, I got that.'

'How's it going with the locals?' Julie asked Chris, drawing him out of the firing line of Fiona's temper. She felt responsible for having stoked it in the first place. 'Have they been helpful?'

'Yeah, very. I spoke to the SIO Suffolk Constabulary has assigned to the murder investigation, and she added me to the scene log and showed me around. Hell of a mess they made down here.'

Julie listened intently as Chris went on to describe the layout of the country house and the crime scene as he'd witnessed it, including the internal and external damage from an explosion and subsequent fire. Sadness washed over her as Chris talked about finding the bodies of Wayne and one of his protection officers – a Sergeant Michael Scott – both gunned down in the woods.

'What about the other officer?' Julie asked. 'There were two assigned to Wayne's protection detail.'

'His name was PC Daniel Moss. They found his body in an upstairs room in the main house, and what's left of him is nothing more than a blackened human figure. Pretty gross, really. His body and limbs are all curled up from the heat of the fire. Because of how remote the place is, the blaze wasn't spotted for hours until a farmer saw the glow in the distance. Add that to the response times of the fire service around these parts and it meant the inferno took hold and destroyed the entire interior and the roof. The stone walls are about the only parts of the structure still standing. The poor man cooked for hours.'

'Jesus,' Julie said.

'They're going for dental and DNA to confirm it's PC Moss, but say it's just a formality, because they're pretty sure it's him.'

'How come, if the body is so badly damaged?'

'He's still wearing his watch, which is uniquely identifiable… it's engraved with his name underneath the dials. The watch survived enough for forensics to read the engraving – once they'd cleaned it up – thanks to the protection from the sapphire crystal face. He also had his warrant card in his jacket pocket, which melted into the wallet. Remarkably, enough of it stayed intact for the police to identify it as his. Oh, and his police-issue firearm strapped to his torso, the serial number matches the one he signed out for the deployment.'

Julie conceded. 'I can see why they're so confident it's him.'

'What about forensics on and around the bodies of Sergeant Scott and Wayne?' Fiona asked.

Julie heard Chris suck air in through his teeth, in the same way an old mechanic would, when appraising the engine bay of a car owned by someone he was about to rip off.

'There's a little more hope there, but not much. I don't think they've been moved, which is good. Looking at the branches, leaves, and the bed of woodland around them, I'd say they're still where they were shot. Trouble is, the weather has been horrendous here overnight, and where they've fallen is right underneath a gap in the canopy, so both bodies are drenched.'

'Meaning any fingerprints or DNA the killers might have left behind will likely have been destroyed,' Fiona said.

'Precisely.'

'So what are we left with?' Julie asked.

'Well, they've still got to recover PC Moss's body from the fire scene to see what evidence that can give them.'

'Not much, if it's as fire damaged as you described.'

'Probably, but you never know your luck. Also, some fresh tyre tracks leading into and out of the farm don't match those fitted on the unmarked police vehicle Sergeant Scott and PC Moss were using. They might be good enough to narrow down the type of vehicles the killers came in, but not much more because the treads are fairly common. After that, it's pretty much down to the ballistics evidence recovered. The CSIs estimate that dozens of rounds were fired into these woods, and probably quite a few inside the house as well, and the police have managed to recover a few spent casings the killers left behind, which they can use to link or rule out any weapons they seize in the future.'

Julie put her head in her hands and ran her fingers through her hair. 'I was hoping for more than that, Chris.'

'It is what it is. Can't magic these things up.'

'I know. Sorry for being negative.'

'How are things at your end? You found Sarah yet?'

'Yeah, she's okay. She's with Alex, as planned.' A loud ding erupted from the computer's speakers. Julie smiled. 'Got to go, Chris. Something's come up. Great work you're doing. We'll speak soon.' She hung up before he had the chance to reply.

'Here we go,' she said, excited, as she examined the computer screen. A result notification window had opened.

She moved right up to the screen as another three popped up in rapid succession and clicked on each one to read the full details, comprising of police mug shots, full names, dates of birth, current and previous addresses, known associates, and offending history.

The wheels on Fiona's chair squeaked as she moved up close behind Julie.

'Wow,' Fiona said with more cheer in her voice than before. 'That was easy.'

'Yep.' Julie's smile had grown wider. 'Now we know who the brothers are using, we have the advantage.' She detected worry on Fiona's face in the screen's reflection. She turned her head. 'What's up?'

'You're going to want to keep this from Foster, aren't you?'

'Only for a little while.'

Fiona gazed down at her lap, her hands clasped together tightly above her salad box, her thumbs twiddling nervously. Julie turned her chair to face her properly and put her hands over hers, stilling her fidgeting.

'We have the advantage here. I can communicate with Alex, tell him who these people are, and it'll make his job of keeping Sarah safe much easier. If I tell Foster what we've discovered, it'll be fed into the intelligence system... and if I'm right, and the Marlowe brothers *do* have an informant in our ranks, they'll know their people have been identified, and hire another bunch of thugs to do their dirty work. We'll be back to square one, with no idea where the threat's coming from. We've got to retain this advantage if we're to do our job and keep Sarah alive.' She tilted her head down, trying to catch Fiona's eye. 'Make sense?'

Fiona slowly lifted her chin. 'I guess.'

Julie smiled. 'Good.' She turned back to the computer screen. 'Just one more thing left to do before we get out of here.'

'What's that?'

Julie opened her emails and started typing. 'I have a friend who works in the vetting department. I'm going to ask him to send me a list of everyone in the Agency who has the level of security clearance necessary to allow them to access our case records. That'll give us a list to work through to narrow down who the rat could be.'

Julie finished typing and clicked send. She picked up her phone to read the notification she'd spotted earlier on her BBC news app. It expanded when she tapped on it. The headline read LONDON SECURITY SERVICES ON HIGH ALERT AFTER SHOOT-OUT AT ST PANCRAS. Julie's stomach sank, the remainder of her burger dropping back into its carton.

Surely not, she told herself. *Surely this has nothing to do with us.*

But her gut told her otherwise.

She dialled Alex's number.

24

Drayce marched with long strides to a clothing store five minutes away from the flat on foot, arriving in three. He grabbed the first pair of dark blue jeans he saw in Sarah's size – the last pair with extra-long legs – a pair of plain white trainers, a long-sleeved black t-shirt, underwear and socks, and a thick grey jumper. As he walked to the tills, he passed a rack of winter coats, picked a black parka with a brown fur-lined hood, and paid as fast as he could. On his route back to the flat he stopped at a pharmacy to collect the toiletries Sarah had asked for.

She'd moved from the fireplace, perched on the edge of the sofa, leaning forwards with her arms crossed, as if cocooning herself from the world.

'Got sick of the fire, huh?' he asked.

'Your dressing gown's too warm.'

'I see. Here.' He dropped the bags on the floor next to her feet. 'See if that lot's suitable. And don't blame me for the dinosaur toothbrush. They were out of the adult ones.' He walked to the kitchen while she rummaged around in the bags. 'You want something to eat?'

She gave him a disapproving look. 'We ate at St Pancras. How are you hungry already?'

He shrugged. 'I'm thinking maybe I burned a few calories rescuing you from the Thames.'

She smiled, despite her efforts not to. '*Rescued* me? You were the one who pushed me in in the first place.'

Drayce got busy in the kitchen, rummaging through the fridge and cupboards. 'True. But, hey, can't go back in time. All's well that ends well, so why don't you get changed into your new clothes while I feed myself?'

She stood up with the bag and walked into the bathroom. Drayce made three tuna sandwiches and a bowl of salad, and had just finished plating it all up when Sarah came back in wearing her new outfit, the parka tucked under her arm.

'Feel better?' he asked as he carried the food over to the coffee table in the middle of the living room.

'I guess.'

He took a seat on the sofa, picked up a sandwich, and started eating. Sarah looked on, trying to contain her envy. 'You going to eat all that?' she asked.

Drayce swallowed his mouthful with a grin. 'Don't tell me you're hungry already? You ate at St Pancras, remember?' She joined him on the sofa and flashed him the same don't-you-dare expression as earlier, so he pushed the plate of sandwiches her way, her hand grabbing the bigger of the two that were left before he'd even let go of the plate. 'I made extra because I knew you'd be hungry. After the morning you've had, you'll be craving some energy.'

They sat in silence while they ate everything in front of them. Drayce made some coffee when they'd finished, to stave off the fatigue that would soon be setting in. Sarah took her cup over to the fireplace and sat cross-legged in front of it, holding up the photograph of her mother close to the flames. When she noticed Drayce watching her, she said, 'I ran it under the tap to get the mud off and it's still a bit damp.'

'You'd have gone back into the water for that if you'd had to.' He said it as a statement, rather than a question, airing his mind as he verbalised his thoughts.

'Yeah.'

'But you can't swim.'

'No.'

'And it's the Thames in winter – filthy and freezing – which you'd nearly just drowned in.'

She didn't reply. She focused on the flames flickering out from the pebbles, then rubbed the photograph with her thumb and, happy it was dry, put it in her pocket.

Drayce watched her, the desire to get her to open up about her past beaming to the front of his mind. The terrifying scene at St Pancras and the chase through the city had been far too close for comfort. If they were to avoid something similar in the future, he needed to know everything he could about the woman sitting in front of him. It might lead to him learning about the people who wanted her dead. He didn't want to be overbearing with questions, but he had to try something.

'Tell me about her,' he said.

She lifted herself up on her hands and spun around on her backside until she was facing him. 'What do you want to know?'

'You were obviously close. What kind of person was she?'

Her eyes dropped down to the floor. 'She was the perfect mum. Kind, loving, and a wonderful example of who I should grow up to be.' She paused, the hint of a smile showing on her lips, but not enough to affect the rest of her face. She brushed her hair out of her eyes with her fingers and cleared her throat, her emotions visibly mounting. 'She was always there for me whenever I was in trouble and never judged me too harshly when I'd done something wrong. She worked in a casino in the city, which is where she met my father. Had quite a rough upbringing in Peckham and struggled in school, but you'd never have guessed it. She was so smart. She always knew how to solve problems, and never panicked about anything. She'd always say, "worse things happen at sea, my darling. Tell me what's wrong and we'll work it out together." And we always did. The two of us.'

Her eyes flicked up at Drayce, then back down again. He contemplated staying quiet, leaving the silence there for her to fill, but now that she was talking, he wanted to encourage the flow.

'You mentioned your father—'

Her sharp eyes skewered him, cutting off his words. 'He's a different story,' she said. 'We didn't bond in the same way Mum and I did. I didn't really have much to do with him while I was growing up, to be honest. After Mum died, I was shipped off to boarding school. During school holidays, he left the house for work before I woke up, and wouldn't be back until after I'd gone to bed. It was as though he wanted to keep his distance from me. He'd had a good upbringing, far better than Mum's... went to a public school somewhere in Surrey, but I don't think he enjoyed himself there. He certainly never talked fondly of it... too rebellious for the teachers by his own account, but I think he was popular with the other kids. He had one of those personalities that could really win people over. "A natural salesman," Mum would say. I was the complete opposite. I did well in lessons and exams, but I didn't really fit in. I took after my mum – too down to earth for most of the other posh kids. Didn't have many friends. Maybe that's why he was never close to me. Maybe I just wasn't the person he wanted me to be.'

Her voice faded out. She reached back into her pocket and took out the photograph of her mother, staring at it.

Comforting herself, Drayce thought.

'What about you?' she asked.

'What about me?'

She shrugged and brushed her fringe out of her eyes. 'Seems weird me telling you all about myself. I've talked enough, it's your turn now.'

Drayce didn't reply straight away. He still didn't know what she'd got herself embroiled in to warrant a group of professional killers coming after her: if he wanted to walk away from this job when it was over, it was important he be guarded with how much he told her. On the other hand, he wanted her to continue opening up to him, and that would only happen if he played the game of give and take. He heard Lily's voice in his head, giving him the advice he so badly needed.

It's the only way she'll trust you, but there's a balance to be had here, Alex, so get it right.

'Not much to say, really. I joined the police in Manchester when I was eighteen, then transferred to Birmingham when I was twenty-five, and finally to London when I was thirty.'

'Is all that moving around normal in the police?'

'Not really. I found it hard to settle down in any one place. Always had this desire to keep moving. Until I met Lily, of course. Then the idea of settling down felt like the most natural thing in the world.'

The thumb on his left hand twisted his wedding ring around his finger as his right hand found its way up to the locket, feeling its smooth oval shape through his sweater. He swallowed the pain.

'What happened to her?' Sarah asked.

A wave of sadness washed over him, flooding his mind with painful memories. As before, when they'd been on the tube, he didn't want to talk about it. But unlike then, his mouth worked independently of his mind, spilling the information out as fast as his lips could move.

'Lily was a police officer. We met shortly after I transferred to London. She was a detective in Islington CID. We bumped into each other at a few jobs when I was a CTSFO and really hit it off. Usual story, I guess. We went on some dates, moved in together, and then about a year later got married.'

His mouth dry, he stopped talking, working his tongue around his gums until things felt normal again. 'We bought a house together in Hertfordshire, not long after I'd transferred to the protection teams. A rubbish commute, but our slice of heaven, far enough away from the city that work wasn't on our minds when it didn't need to be. We were really happy.'

His thumb moved back to his wedding ring, turning it gently around his finger as his mind drifted back. 'Lily was walking from the police station to the tube to catch her train home when someone attacked her.'

That last word froze in his mouth. He tried to hold it together.

'She fought back, but he had a knife.' He paused again when he realised how fast he was talking. He heard his breathing, nostrils flaring, huffing like a bull. He did what he knew would work and focused on controlling each breath in through the nose, out through the mouth, conscious of Sarah's eyes on him.

'She survived the initial attack, but her wounds were horrific. I needed time off work to be with her, but they wouldn't give it to me.' His right hand bunched into a fist. A couple of breaths later and it relaxed. 'Said they'd have someone to take my place as the PM's bodyguard in a few days. So I ignored them, and stayed by Lily's hospital bed right up until she took her last breath.'

'I'm sorry,' Sarah said, with what appeared to be genuine sympathy.

Drayce fought back his emotions and forced a smile her way. 'Bet you wish you'd never asked.'

'No, not at all. Did they catch who did it?'

Drayce shook his head. 'The CCTV was crap. It was too dark, his face was covered, nothing distinctive about his clothing, average build and height. No murder weapon, no fingerprints. I thought they'd get him when they found someone else's blood on Lily's hands, giving them a DNA profile of the suspect. But it wasn't on the database, and whoever killed her has never been arrested, before or since. It remains unsolved to this day.'

'What did they say about you not coming in for work?'

'They were going to discipline me, but I saved them the trouble and resigned.'

Sarah stuck her neck out as she frowned at him. 'That's terrible. You should never have been put in that position. Your wife had just died.'

He shrugged. 'London's a big city, with tens of thousands of cops. I was just a number to them, as was Lily. After Lily died,

I just didn't want to be around the bureaucracy, or the politics, or the violence anymore. I'd had enough of that world.'

'So you became a private bodyguard?'

Drayce heard her tone loud and clear. 'It suited my skill set, and to be honest, there's normally very little violence. It's closer to a PA's role most of the time… checking locations, planning routes, and working out the logistics of a client's day-to-day activities. Pretty boring stuff.'

Sarah glanced back down at the photograph of her mum, brushed her face with the pad of her thumb, and then looked back at Drayce. 'Did you grow up in Manchester? I don't hear a regional accent in your voice.'

'No, I didn't grow up in Manchester. I didn't grow up anywhere in particular. My parents died when I was two, and with no other family, I moved from one children's home to the next, all around the north of England and the Midlands, until I turned sixteen, old enough to get a job and a place of my own. Probably why I couldn't settle in any one force area for very long. I was so used to being moved from pillar to post as a kid.'

'That sounds tough.' Sarah was wide-eyed. Whatever she'd been expecting to hear, that evidently hadn't been it.

Drayce took a sip of coffee, conscious of the fact he was letting his mouth run away with itself. The balance he'd been hoping to strike, he'd missed completely. He knew he was telling her too much about himself, but he wasn't sure how to stop now that he'd started. He could count on one hand the number of times he'd told someone about Lily and his upbringing, but at that precise moment, he couldn't understand why. It felt good to talk.

'It was all I knew at the time,' he said with a shrug.

'How was school? It must have been hard to concentrate under those circumstances.'

He nodded. 'It was, but I was different from most of the other kids around me. I actually wanted to be there because it provided some order to the chaos. I did all right in my exams, but I was in no position to go to college or university. After I left school, I found work in a boxing club for two years in exchange for a roof over my head.'

'A boxing club?' Sarah asked, palpably astonished.

'It was just around the corner from the kids' home in Nottingham, and I'd seen the fighters coming and going, all of them hard, giant men. I snuck in a few times to watch them train, and then, feeling brave, I tried to blend in, mimicking what I'd seen them doing on the bags.

'I must have stood out like a sore thumb… a tall, skinny kid amongst a dozen grown men. I thought the owner was going to smack me around the head and throw me out when he first saw me, but when I told him I was from the kids' home, he offered me a job. Turns out he'd grown up in the same home, so I guess he felt sorry for me. I worked and trained there every single day of the week; before then I'd been virtually homeless and sick of the bullying and fighting that went on in the home.

'The owner caught me sleeping in a storage room one night at the gym and offered me a place to stay. An empty flat above the gym was in too poor a condition to rent out, so he gave me the keys and said I could live there in exchange for helping him smarten the place up.'

He smiled at the memory, a warm feeling spreading out from his chest. 'He had such a big heart. His name was Jack O'Leary, but everyone knew him as Old Man Jack. He taught me the value of hard work, and how much meaning can be derived from shouldering responsibility. After six months of mopping up the blood and sweat in the gym and painting and decorating the flat, I think Old Man Jack felt I'd earned his trust. He had a bunch of professional boxers signed up with him, and he let me help with the training. Over the next eighteen months, I sparred with every pro who came through the gym.'

His hand came up to his face, pinching the bridge of his nose. 'Never been broken, which any boxer will tell you, is a trophy all on its own.'

'You must have been pretty hard to reach.'

He smiled. 'Still am.'

He noticed Sarah paying a lot of attention to his ears.

'Is the boxing how your ears got so...?'

'Cauliflowered? No, a youth programme in Wigan wanted to teach kids like me a sport, as a way of instilling some discipline, I think. I went to a wrestling club called The Snake Pit. They taught an old English style called catch-as-catch-can. Brazilian Jiu Jitsu made it worse... practised that in the police. Brutal stuff, but it kept me out of trouble.' He rubbed the calcified lumps with his fingers. 'My own fault... I didn't like wearing headgear.'

Sarah shuffled closer to him. 'What made you join the police? I'm no expert, but I wouldn't have thought many kids with your type of upbringing would aspire to a career in law enforcement.'

Drayce nodded. 'You're right. A bit of an outlier, I was happier in the gym or the library, rather than out on the streets. I wanted to do something productive as an adult.'

He paused, thinking back. 'Leaving Old Man Jack's gym one night, I came across three lads from the same kids' home as me. Their names were Stephen Daines, David Hunt, and Shawn Yardley. Vicious bastards with a habit of picking on the vulnerable, weaker kids. They were on the street corner, watching a cash machine outside a newsagent across the street, and I knew exactly what they were up to. They were the types I tried to steer away from, bigger, stronger, older kids who were always looking for someone to rob and beat up.'

'Bigger and stronger than you?' Sarah asked as her eyes moved up and down his giant frame.

'I haven't always been built this way. It's taken a lot of hard work in the gym, with a lot of heavy weights.' He nodded at the empty plates on the coffee table. 'And a lot of food as well. Back then, I was a shy, skinny teenager, so I avoided bullies like the plague. When I spotted Stephen, David, and Shawn that day, I kept my head down and crossed the street, hoping they wouldn't see me. Turns out they didn't, or perhaps had bigger fish to fry that night. I turned down an alleyway, out of their sight. I remember checking over my shoulder to see if they'd followed me. I saw them sprint past, pulling their scarves up over their mouths and noses.'

He wondered why he was telling this story to someone he'd only met that morning; a story he hadn't told anyone but Lily before.

'I remember breathing a sigh of relief that they weren't chasing after me. But then I heard the screams and stopped dead in that alleyway, unable to move another step. I wanted to run away, grateful it wasn't me they'd decided to target that day, but my legs just wouldn't work. Something stronger than the fear kept me rooted to the spot.

'Before I knew it, I was running. I remember speaking to myself – no, *screaming* at myself – in my head, asking what the hell I was doing, but my legs just ignored my brain and took me back across the road to the cashpoint. Those screams… they'd awoken something in me, some instinct overpowering everything else, demanding I help.'

Drayce realised his hands were clenched into fists, dissipating his energy as he recalled what had happened next.

'They'd surrounded a young mother, blocking her in against the cashpoint as she tried to shield her child in a pushchair. Stephen had a knife in his hand, waving it at her as he smiled. The other two were being their vile selves, throwing insults and spitting on her jacket, taunting her, before robbing her.

'She had her purse wide open in one hand and a couple of notes in the other, terrified, in real fear for both her life and her child's. I slowed to a steady jog as I got close, surprised they hadn't heard me.'

'What did you do?' Sarah asked.

Drayce relaxed his hands. 'As soon I was within reach of Stephen, the fear vanished, replaced with more anger than I'd ever felt before, outraged that they thought they could treat someone that way. I wanted to give them a taste of their own medicine.

'I saw the knife in his right hand, so I hit him with a left hook. He went straight down, so I came back with a right hook that hit David on his chin, who collapsed and cracked his head on the pavement. Shawn wasn't quick enough to react even if he'd wanted to. He just stood there, all the arrogance and menace evaporated, and stared at me, as afraid as his victim. He mumbled something that might have been an apology – something about it being their idea, not his – and then I hit him as well. As he dropped to the ground, I turned to the lady, but she must have seen her opportunity and run off, so I legged it.'

Sarah leant forwards and cupped her face in her hands. 'What happened next time they saw you?'

'Nothing. Any time I'd see them around, they avoided me with their heads bowed. A few days later, an officer came to the gym... the whole thing had been caught on camera. I thought I was in trouble, but he arrested Stephen, David, and Shawn. Later, he came back to thank me and said they could use someone like me in the police.

'I guess that planted a seed. Greater Manchester Police was the only force recruiting when I turned eighteen, so that's where I started my career.'

'Well, looking at what you've grown into,' she nodded her head up and down his body, 'I'm glad you chose a life of enforcing the law, rather than breaking it.'

Drayce smiled briefly before his phone ringing distracted him. He took it out of his pocket.

'It's Julie,' he said.

'I wonder if she's got good news for us. We could use some.'

'Only one way to find out.'

He tapped the screen to answer it and raised the phone to his gristly ear.

25

12:08 p.m.

In the empty office at NCA headquarters, Julie leant on the desk with her arms crossed, staring at the screen of her phone lying flat on the desktop and still on loudspeaker. Fiona was right behind her, craning her neck over Julie's shoulder to make certain she didn't miss any of the conversation.

'It's Julie. You two okay?'

There was a pause before Alex replied.

'Yeah, considering.'

'Considering what?'

'Considering they found us.'

'St Pancras?'

'It's in the news already?'

'Machine guns were fired inside St Pancras, Alex. Of course it's in the news.' She closed her eyes and gave a big sigh. 'Tell me what happened.'

As Alex ran through the attack and how they'd escaped, Julie kept her eyes closed, processing everything.

'I should have searched her,' he said afterwards. 'If I had, I'd've found the tracker sooner. It's my fault.'

'Where's this tracker now?'

'Flattened somewhere on the Park Lane tarmac. I doubt it's still transmitting a signal, but if it is, we're nowhere near it.'

'Good. And you're sure Sarah's all right?'

'Yeah, she's okay. How are you getting on with those photographs?'

Julie checked the computer screen. 'The results have just come through. Want to know who those men are?'

She heard him shift position as though preparing to listen hard.

'Yes, I do,' he said.

'Let's start with the biggest of the four, the man with short dark hair and a missing ear.'

Again, Julie saw Fiona's expression in the reflection from the computer screen. She exuded worry, rocking back and forth, as though she wanted to put a hand on Julie's shoulder and stop her from passing confidential intelligence on to Alex.

Julie ignored her and talked faster. 'His name's Stan West, forty-two years old. Previous convictions include armed robbery, extortion, GBH, and conspiracy to supply class A drugs. Born and raised in east London. Intel suggests he wanted to move up in the world of organised crime, but struggled to muscle in on the big fish in the city. He ended up working as the head doorman at a chain of venues owned by some very serious criminals, who over time decided his talent for violence was wasted on drunks, and took him on as an enforcer for their illegal operations. That was twelve years ago, when he dropped off our radar and hasn't been seen or heard from since.'

'He's one of the guys I dropped in the cafe.'

'Well, I'd say he's been moving up in the world of organised crime these past twelve years. Killing and kidnapping witnesses is a few steps above what's on his pre-cons.'

'What about his three friends?'

Julie glanced behind at Fiona: she was looking at something on her phone, not paying any attention to the conversation.

Strange, Julie thought, considering Fiona had been peering over her shoulder not so long ago, desperate to be involved. *Perhaps she's still sulking from our disagreement, or Chris's terrible joke.*

Too busy to dwell on her colleague's current mood, Julie turned back around, reached for the mouse, and scrolled down the screen. 'Marcus Bone, Leonard "Leo" Durham, and Freddie Dawes. Marcus is the guy with the beard, Leo the thickset one, and Freddie the blond. They're all a similar age to West and have a similar list of convictions, hard men who do the dirty work for the ones with real power.'

'What are the chances of you sending me their mug shots? I think they'll be clearer than the photographs I took.'

'I'll take photographs of them on my phone and send them to you. But please keep them to yourself, and if anyone asks, they didn't come from me. I could get into real trouble if anyone finds out.' Julie lowered her voice as she said that last part, her eyes watching Fiona's reflection closely in the computer screen.

'No worries,' Alex said. 'I appreciate everything you can do to help me spot these people coming. Thank you.'

'No problem. Keep your eyes peeled, Alex.'

'I will. You planning on doing anything with those names?'

'Not for as long as possible. I still don't know whether the brothers have their tentacles inside the Agency. If they have, it might leak back to them that we know who they are, which means they'll be pulled out and another team sent after you.'

'Which is exactly what I don't want. As long as it's these four coming after us, I know who to look out for.'

'Understood.'

'What are you going to do about St Pancras?'

Julie took a moment to think about her answer. 'Nothing.'

There was no response from Alex.

'From initial reports, it appears no innocent people were killed,' Julie continued. 'If I reveal anything about our involvement at this stage, it'll only risk jeopardising Sarah's safety.' Her phone buzzed, the plastic case rattling against the desktop. Foster's name was on the screen. 'I better go, Alex. The boss is calling me.'

'Tell him to get busy plugging the intelligence leak. The sooner you guys identify and arrest the corrupt officer, the sooner I can bring Sarah in.'

Julie rubbed her forehead with the fingers of both hands. 'I wish it were that easy.'

'No one ever said being a cop would be easy. Speak soon.'

She cancelled the call with Alex, turned off the speakerphone, and answered the incoming call from Foster.

'Hi, John.'

'What the hell have you been up to?'

The aggression in his voice set her in place like a statue.

'What do you mean?'

'Have you discovered the identities of the men who tried to kidnap Sarah?'

Julie almost dropped her phone. She spun around in her seat and locked eyes with Fiona, grinding her teeth as she stared at her.

'Well?' Foster asked, angrily and impatiently. 'Have you?'

'Hang on a second, John.'

His distant voice ranted on in the background as she took her phone away from her ear and snatched Fiona's out of her hands. Fiona's chair rolled back as she flinched away from Julie, sending her salad box clattering to the floor, its remains scattering across the carpet. Julie saw the shock recede from Fiona's face, making way for anger. She sat up in her chair, a protest about to escape her lips, but Julie assumed the tense energy coming off her forestalled Fiona's mouth from breaking the seal.

Julie tapped on Fiona's email app, opened her sent items, and saw that while Julie had been talking to Alex, Fiona had emailed Foster, telling him all about the photograph and the names they'd found. She locked eyes with Fiona, who sank into her seat, no doubt wishing the ground would swallow her up. Julie tossed Fiona's phone at her feet and put her own back to her ear.

'Back with you.'

'I want to know why I've been kept out of the loop on this, Julie. It's inexcusable!'

'Give me a break, John. I've only just discovered their identities.'

'But you've had their images since this morning, haven't you?'

Julie hesitated. 'Yes.'

'I can't believe you've held this back from me. You should have told me straight away.'

'I was going to tell you, but—'

'But what?'

'The safer strategy was to hold on to the information until we know whether or not the Marlowe brothers have someone in the Agency.'

A heavy sigh of frustration vibrated in her ear. 'Not this again, Julie. I told you, until we have—'

'I know what you told me, but I also know my instincts have never failed me in my entire career, and right now, my instincts tell me someone is feeding everything we know back to the people who are after Sarah.'

'You disobeyed my orders!'

'I did what was right!' Julie didn't mean to come across so determined and hostile, but she couldn't help it. This matter was too important. 'I did what I know is the best thing for my witness. What I know will keep her safe.'

Silence fell on the line. Julie waited for the comeback, for the reprisal, for the *you're fired, so get back here and clean out your desk*. But it never came. The only thing he said was, 'You have to trust me.'

Julie's voice softened. 'I do trust you. But I have reason – we all *should* have reason – to believe there is potentially someone in our organisation helping the brothers.'

'There isn't enough evidence, and I have orders to follow, and so do you.'

'John, please, I'm begging you, keep what Fiona told you to yourself. We can't afford for it to get into the wrong hands.'

'There's a procedure to follow, and that procedure is very clear on such matters. We can't hold information back that might assist in a police murder investigation. Those men are suspects, Julie.'

'Please, John. Just give me an hour. I'm on to something, I know I am. I can narrow down the list of who the brothers' informant might be and—'

'No!' Julie imagined his mouth making the same shape as that of an angry dog about to take a bite out of someone. 'We do this by the book. At the moment, you have no evidence there's corruption involved in this case. The only evidence you've obtained is the identities of four murder suspects, and as per procedure, I will be linking their details to our case, and forwarding everything you've found to both Suffolk Constabulary and the Metropolitan Police to assist with their investigations.'

'John, please listen. If you do that now, you're putting Sarah's life in danger.'

'I've listened to you enough. Now you listen to me – your job is to do one thing and one thing only: keep in contact with Sarah and Drayce, nothing more. If you come across anything else that might assist the police, you call me straight away. Any more independent actions from you that might jeopardise our case, or the police investigation, and I'll have you suspended. Understood?'

Julie cancelled the call.

Fiona gaped at her as though she was insane. 'Did you just hang up on him?'

'I wouldn't have needed to but for you!'

Fiona held her hands up. 'Hang on a minute. You're the one trying to hold information back from him.'

Julie stood up, took a couple of steps forwards, cucumber slices and lettuce leaves crunching under her feet, and leant over her. 'Don't pretend what you've done is down to your unbreakable honesty and integrity. You're too clever not to understand that sometimes information must be held back. You were thinking about your precious career. Nothing more.'

Fiona visibly held her resolve, her self-righteous entitlement no doubt cementing her actions as justified. 'You can't hold back information on the identities of four murder suspects for any reason.'

Julie's index finger hovered in front of Fiona's face. 'You need to take a good honest look at our world if you want to make a difference in it. I did what I did to give Alex the best chance possible of keeping Sarah alive. And now, thanks to your desires to stay in Foster's good books, if I'm right about the brothers having an informant somewhere along the intelligence chain, they'll be sending a whole new group of killers after them.'

Julie took her finger out of Fiona's face but stayed where she was, hovering over her. Fiona had nothing else to say.

Behind her, Julie heard an email ping through to the computer. She turned around and opened it. It was from her friend in vetting, and judging by her first glance of the contents, he'd come up with the goods. She tapped on the print icon, logged off, then picked up her tumbler of coffee, the liquid sloshing from side to side as she angrily turned back to face Fiona.

'You've made it clear I can't trust you,' Julie said, 'so from now on, you'll have nothing to do with me or my handling of this case.' She walked around Fiona and headed for the door. 'I can't work with someone I can't trust.'

'But—'

'I don't want to hear it, Fiona.'

And with that, she snatched the sheet of paper the printer had spat out, pushed open the door, and walked out of the room, leaving Fiona in her chair, speechless and alone.

–

Through the thin office walls, Dominic heard the phone slam onto the receiver as the conversation between his boss and Julie ended abruptly. Although he hadn't heard everything Foster had said, the man's voice was loud enough for him to get the gist of his side of the conversation. He presumed Julie was making progress.

He took his phone out of his pocket and opened WhatsApp, tapping on the conversation thread started just four weeks ago, but which felt as if it had been controlling his life for years. If he didn't keep the information flowing their way, he was pretty sure they'd go ahead with their threats, something he was desperate to prevent.

He scrolled to the beginning of the thread to view the very first message he'd received from the anonymous number all those weeks ago; the message that started this horrendous chain of events, changing his life forever.

> Have fun last night, did ya?

Mild anxiety had crept in as he'd read the short sentence, his mind casting back to the night before. To what he'd been doing, and with whom.

> Who is this?

> It looked like you were having fun, that's for sure! Do your bosses in the National Crime Agency know you enjoy visiting brothels?

That mild anxiety had instantly made way for a full-blown face-flushing-heart-pounding-sweat-inducing panic attack. He remembered stabbing at the phone's keyboard, wanting to shut this person up, to erase them from his memory, to make it all go away, the adult version of when a child clamps their hands over their ears, shuts their eyes, and shouts *la la la la la la la*.

> Leave me alone! I'm blocking your number.

> You don't get rid of us that easily. And if you're having a bout of amnesia, this should stir your memory…

The video clip was only short, but long enough to tell the full sordid story of what he'd done. His face was in the centre of the screen, framed by the bright red bedspread and two naked bodies, their shiny, sweaty limbs coiling over one another like a pit of snakes. The clarity was unblemished; his identity unmistakable.

> Think your wife might fancy seeing this?

> Please don't! I have some money – inheritance – I can pay you!

> You will pay, believe me. But not in the way you think. We'll be in touch.

And so it had begun.

Foster's office door burst open. Dominic, a well-practised liar and cheat, didn't panic. Calmly, he lowered his phone under the desk, out of sight, as the smile broke out across his face.

'Everything all right, sir?'

'No, it isn't.' The straight-talking Irishman rarely minced his words. 'I've sent you an email. It needs proofreading and then forwarding on to the Met SIO, whose details are at the bottom of the page.'

'Yes, sir.'

'And on the double, Dominic, you hear?'

'Of course. I'll do it immediately.'

He opened the email straightaway, watching Foster march away out of the corner of his eye. After reading just the first paragraph, he couldn't believe his luck. They'd be pleased with him for this, surely they would. And that was all that mattered: show them how hard he was working for them, keep them happy, and ensure the video stayed out of his wife's inbox.

The email read in its entirety, he made sure Foster was out of sight, then lifted his phone from underneath the desk, opened his camera app, and carefully aimed the lens at the screen.

26

As Freddie brought their new Mercedes to a stop, Stan flung open his door and launched his head and shoulders out to avoid vomiting over the dashboard. The contents of his stomach hit the tyre tracks in the mud and splashed over the front wheel. Such was his desperation to throw up outside of the vehicle, momentum carried the rest of his body out, tumbling him to the ground on all fours – his hands saving him from face planting – his back rounding as he heaved.

A few well-placed shots from Daz through the back window of the Range Rover with one of the assault rifles had forced the cops to back off, providing enough of a gap to allow their escape. They'd switched the registration plates three times on their journey out of London, before swapping the dented Range Rover, with its smashed windows and bullet holes, for a black Mercedes GLC – one of a dozen stolen vehicles held by the firm in a warehouse in Croydon. Confident they hadn't been followed, they crossed the M25, heading south-east, and passed through a couple of villages before turning down a narrow dirt track for about half a mile, where they found a clearing in the middle of some woods, somewhere they wouldn't be disturbed.

Stan had taken another round in his body armour during the car chase, exacerbating his chest injuries, hence the mounting nausea throughout the journey, culminating in the sudden urge to puke. He heard the others talking through the open car door.

'How the fuck did they get away?' Freddie asked. 'She had a tracker on her. They should have been sitting ducks.'

'That bastard she's got with her killed Tommy,' Marcus said. 'The brothers are gonna be pissed at us. We shot up St Pancras and didn't even get the job done.'

Stan heard the squeak of leather as Freddie leant across the passenger seat. 'How bad is it, boss?'

Overwhelming rage gripped him as he rose from the vomit. 'This should all be over by now. She should be dead, just like Wayne. I should be lying in the sun somewhere hot and far away, counting my money.'

Instead, Stan was broken, spewing up his guts from the pain and blunt trauma. All because of the man protecting Sarah. A red mist descended when he pictured his face. He slammed his door shut and pounded his fists into the bodywork, the combination of punches eventually denting the panel. His knuckles left behind dabs of blood. The others looked on through the glass as he released a torrent of fury from his system.

'Judging by his reaction, I'd say it hurts pretty badly,' he heard Daz say, the words muffled through the closed door.

Exhausted, Stan opened the door again, stepped back, and drew in a series of rapid breaths until he was calmer. 'How the fuck did we lose her again?' Shaking, blood and vomit dripped from his knuckles. 'She was right there. We fucking had her.'

Silence from the others met his tirade. He unclenched one of his hands and brought it up to his chest, wincing as he felt the spot where the second bullet had landed during the car chase.

Freddie read his expression, and after catching his eye, flicked his head at the back seats. 'At least your face isn't as bad as Marcus's.'

Marcus brought up a bloodied hand from his shoulder to his beard and gently patted his features, avoiding his swollen nose as he moved warily, wincing as he found open wounds. He lowered his hand, fresh blood glazing his fingertips.

Freddie's right, Stan thought, *he was one hell of a mess.*

'Bastard!' Marcus growled. 'I've got shards of glass in my face!'

Stan opened his door to take a closer look. 'They're only tiny. One of the bullets must have brought some of the glass with it as it passed through the window. I reckon your beard limited the damage it might have caused otherwise.'

'I'm gonna kill him,' Marcus hissed through clenched teeth, his face turning red, his eyes bulging, his giant bloodied hand in line with his jaw as it clenched into a fist, shaking with fury. 'I'm gonna kill that bastard.'

Stan inspected the other two. 'You pair collect any injuries?'

'No,' Daz said. 'I wasn't hit.'

'Me, neither,' Freddie said from the driver's seat.

Stan glanced back at Marcus. 'You gonna be all right to carry on?'

He clamped a hand back over the bullet wound to his shoulder. 'Of course I am. Never felt better.'

'Don't be sarcastic with me.'

A fake smile appeared from within the giant mass of blood-clotted hair. 'It's stopped bleeding, so it can't be that bad.'

Stan took out his phone, then put it away again as a grey Audi Q7 drove into the clearing. Chrissy pulled up alongside them.

'I was just about to call you,' Stan said as Chrissy climbed out of the driver's seat. 'How'd you get on?'

Chrissy shrugged. 'Nothing I ain't done before.'

'Van destroyed?'

'Good and proper.'

'And Tommy?'

'On ice with Liam. I'll deal with them properly later. Too much for us to be getting on with for me to spend time burying them now. That sort of thing needs careful planning, and we've got us a witness to hunt down – again.'

Leo hobbled round from the other side of the Audi.

'How's that ankle?' Stan asked.

'Still fucked. But I can walk.'

'Good, 'cos we've got work to do if we want to salvage this job and avoid the brothers' wrath.'

'On the plus side, it means more money for us,' Leo said.

Stan's expression hardened. 'How do you work that one out?'

'Well, it's simple maths, innit? First we lost Liam, now Tommy. The price for the job hasn't changed, and now there are less of us to share it. Half a mill between six, instead of the original eight.'

Stan glanced at Chrissy, trying to judge his reaction. Liam and Tommy had been his boys, after all. 'Bit cold of you, Leo.'

Chrissy stared right back at Stan. 'Ice cold. Which is why I raised the point to him on our journey over here. No point being sentimental. Tommy and Liam would be thinking the same thing if they were still here, and it was one of us who'd got a knife in the neck and a bullet in the nut.'

'Well, we'll be lucky to get a penny each from the brothers at this rate.' Stan swept his arms out wide and held them at shoulder height, his palms facing Leo and Chrissy as though framing their surroundings. 'Take a look around.' He pointed at Leo. 'Your ankle's knackered.' Then at Freddie. 'His knee's ruined.' Then at Marcus. 'And he's got a bullet in his shoulder.' He bent his arms at the elbows and pointed two thumbs at himself. 'And I've got a fractured jaw, ribs, and now a cracked sternum.'

Stan screwed his eyes shut as a bolt of pain fired up from his teeth to his brain. When he opened them, he caught sight of something, over by the treeline on the other side of the clearing. The bushes were shaking, something moving through them, too big to be an animal. He listened hard as he watched the quivering branches, expecting to hear the *beep* of a police radio any second now.

The others followed Stan's line of sight.

'What have you seen?' Chrissy whispered.

Stan didn't reply straightaway; he didn't want his voice to camouflage the movements of a team of coppers about to surround them. He heard twigs breaking under a person's weight, and leaves rustling as whoever it was pushed their way through the foliage. Then came voices, close by. More than one.

'Someone's coming,' he said.

They all reached for their guns at the same time.

A child burst out of the bushes into the clearing: a small boy, maybe nine or ten years old at the most, running with a smile as though being chased in a playground. He stopped dead about fifty yards away and planted his feet in the thorny undergrowth when he saw the six of them, his gleeful expression giving way to fear. A second later, his mate joined him, the pair catching their breath as they stared at the big cars and the six scary men. They were wearing school uniforms, their top buttons undone and their ties pulled to one side, their knees muddy from playing in the woods on their route home. Stan's pistol had gone back in his waistline the moment he'd seen they were only kids, just as the others had. Apart from Freddie.

'Put your gun away, you idiot!' Stan told him. 'They're just kids.'

'They've seen our faces.'

Stan regarded him as though he was insane. 'So what? They've got nothing to link us to. Unless they see what you've got in your hand and decide to tell their parents that some nonce-looking geezer pointed a gun at them in the woods. So put it away!'

Reluctantly, Freddie tucked his pistol out of sight.

'Hello, kids,' Stan shouted with his best attempt at a smile, trying to appear friendly despite the pain in his jaw. He knew it was a lost cause; he must have looked terrifying. 'Having fun?'

Neither replied. They faced one another, coming to the subliminal agreement that it was best to give these men a wide berth. One turned and ran, but his mate froze when he saw

Freddie bolt towards him. Stan started after Freddie, but in his current state couldn't match his speed and agility, despite the smaller man's injured knee. The schoolboy's feet were rooted to the ground, eyes wide and unblinking, his arms visibly shaking as Freddie got to him and grabbed him roughly by his shirt.

'Who's your friend?' Freddie said, towering over the small boy. 'I want his name, you hear?'

'Freddie!' Stan shouted as he fought to catch up, wincing at the dagger of pain in his jaw. 'Let him go!'

'I want your friend's name, I want your name, and I wanna know where you both live, got it?' He produced his cut-throat razor and flicked out the blade in front of the boy's wide, unblinking eyes. 'Otherwise, I'll cut your nose off, you dirty little—'

Stan's fist cut Freddie's sentence short. Freddie's teeth collided together with a *crack* and he hit the ground, dazed and confused, barely holding onto his consciousness. Stan took a deep breath, panting from the exertion of the sprint. He looked at the boy and gave him his best attempt at a friendly smile. 'It's all right, mate. My friend here was only mucking about. You head off home.' The boy took a single step back, struggling to break free from his frozen state. 'Go on, mate. Head off home. And no need to tell anyone about this, yeah?'

The boy snapped out of the trance, turned, and ran.

Stan turned to Freddie, his smile vanishing. 'What the fuck was that all about?'

Freddie sat up, spat blood on the ground, and gave a lazy shrug of his shoulders. 'We needed the option.'

'What *option*?' Stan's face flushed, his blood pressure escalating. 'Hurting children? That's an option for you, is it?'

Another bored shrug. 'They saw our faces, clocked the wounds. Maybe they'll go home and tell their parents what they stumbled across in the woods. Maybe their parents watch the news, saw what happened in the city, and put two and two together. Maybe they phone it in. Maybe it causes us problems.'

He gazed over to where the kids had stood, as though picturing himself executing the pair of them, then looked back at Stan. 'If it needed doing, then yeah, why not?'

Stan drew his gun, marched forwards, and pressed the muzzle to Freddie's forehead, parting his blond fringe. He towered over him just as the maniac had done the boy, feeling good about giving him a taste of his own medicine.

'We do not hurt children, you fucking monster! Not under any circumstances. Got it?'

Freddie ran the tip of his tongue across his thin, bloodied, lizard lips, collecting beads of perspiration, while he contemplated his answer. His eyes rolled up to meet Stan's. 'Sure.'

Stan pressed the gun into his skull a little harder, tilting his head back. 'You get your act together from this point on, or you're done. Understand?'

Freddie nodded his head, just the once, his blond locks caressing the top slide of the pistol. Stan held the gun there for a moment longer, driving the point home, then tucked it back into his waistline. A small circular indent remained in Freddie's forehead. Stan walked back to the others.

'Got your hands full with that one, ain't you, Stanley?' Chrissy said.

Stan sighed as he rubbed his forehead. 'Not half.' Once Freddie had rejoined them, Stan addressed the whole team. 'We've got to come up with a plan, and that plan needs to involve some help. Because let's face it… none of us are in any fit state to finish this job ourselves.'

A moment's silence fell on the group as they grasped their dilemma.

'I can't believe they got away,' Leo said.

'It doesn't make sense,' Chrissy said. 'They didn't know we were coming, and she had a tracker on her. It should have been easy.'

'They got lucky,' Stan said, 'that's all.'

'That fella she's got with her must be the luckiest man on the planet.' Marcus stroked his beard, tentatively pushing his fingers through the matted hair to the pieces of glass decorating his skin, mimicking a teenager picking at his acne. 'That's twice he's seen us off now.'

'His luck won't last forever. We'll corner them again. Mark my words.'

'It would give me great pleasure to cut the pair of 'em,' Freddie said, his hands toying with his cut-throat razor, his fingers stroking its edges.

Stan assessed him out of the corner of his eye. 'I'm sure it would.'

'I'm gonna put a bullet right between their eyes,' Daz added.

Stan took out his phone. 'You'll get your chance, but for now, we've got to call the brothers' solicitor.'

The others all regarded each other, tension thickening the air around them.

'And say what?' Freddie asked, flicking the blade in and out.

'We tell him we can still coordinate the efforts to track her down, but after what we've come up against, we need fresh bodies when it comes to the violence. The brothers can provide that.'

'They can.' The blade moved in and out of its handle as Freddie flicked his wrist up and down with the carefree energy of a child with a yo-yo. 'But they won't want to.'

'They're gonna be really pissed,' Chrissy said. 'They were adamant they wanted it to stay within the firm, and we told them we could handle it.'

Stan took a deep breath, wondering if contacting the brothers was the right move. They were not the type of men who took bad news well.

'Any of you lot got a better idea?' he asked, assessing the blank faces. 'Thought not.'

As they stood in silence, Stan's phone vibrated twice in his hand. He read the message to himself, blood rushing to his face as he processed the contents, sweating, prickly heat breaking out across his face and neck. He read it again from the beginning before throwing his phone into the car in frustration. It bounced off the seat and landed in the footwell.

'What's the matter?' Freddie asked, the look on Stan's face putting a stop to his fiddling with the razor.

'They know who we are.'

'Who's *they*?' Chrissy asked.

'The police,' Stan kicked the door panel of the Mercedes in frustration, creating yet another dent. 'They're onto us.'

The others went white.

'How the fuck has that happened?' Freddie asked.

Stan put his hands on his hips, his eyes gazing off in a thousand-yard stare. 'The NCA has photographs of us. They know we're the ones who tried to kidnap Sarah from the cafe in Tottenham, and they suspect we're responsible for the murders at the two safe houses.'

None of them moved an inch, all six men rocked by the news.

'We're cop killers,' Leo said. 'We're as good as dead.'

'Has this come from our informant?' Marcus asked Stan.

Stan managed a single nod in return.

'So it's one hundred percent legit then?' Leo asked.

Stan didn't respond, lost in his thousand-yard stare.

'If it's come from our informant, then it must be,' Chrissy said. 'He wouldn't risk pissing us off by lying about this. Dopey prick's scared to death of his wife finding out what he's been up to.'

'What about the other thing?' Leo asked Stan. 'Dominic mention anything that suggests the brothers' first tripwire's been triggered?'

'That's untouched. The filth only knows about us, nothing else.'

'Well, that's a blessing at the very least.' The others frowned at Leo. 'What? It is. The police might suspect us, but we can still finish this job, get paid, and disappear. We know how to hide from the police, we've been doing it our whole lives. But hiding from the brothers?' He swallowed, his Adam's apple bobbing nervously in his throat. 'Let's just say I wouldn't want to have to tell them everything they've worked for was at risk. They might want to take it out on us, and I'd rather be on the run from the police than from them.'

Stan processed Leo's words, thinking it through carefully. 'You're right. We can still get through this with the money and our freedom, but we've got to be careful. We tidy ourselves up, regroup with some other lads, and finish this job. Then we can get our money and leave the country before the police catch up with us.'

'So we're calling the brothers' solicitor?' Leo asked, a tremor in his voice.

'Don't worry, sweet cheeks, *we're* not doing anything. *I'll* get it done.' He nodded to the vehicles. 'Let's get in the motors and clear off before any more kids come this way. I'll make the call on the move.'

Stan retrieved his phone from the footwell, and after taking a moment to rally his courage, dialled the solicitor's number.

27

12:35 p.m.

'You ever heard any of those names before?' Drayce asked Sarah.

He read out the four men's names and showed her their mugshots. She remained cross-legged on the floor with her back to the fire while she examined them. At no point did Drayce detect recognition.

'No, never heard of them.' She blew her fringe out of her eyes and pulled her hair through her fingers, testing it, as though assessing how well it was drying. 'Sorry, not being very helpful, am I?'

'It's okay. At least we know who they are, which is something.'

He watched her closely as she tucked her knees up to her chest and hugged her legs. Her intense focus told him she was thinking things through carefully. The enormity of everything she was going through was, no doubt, taking its toll. After a while, she met his eyes.

'I saw what you did,' she said.

Her tone made it clear this was a slight change of topic. Drayce was pretty sure she meant the part he left out when he explained to Julie what had happened at St Pancras. He'd wait until the debrief to tell the authorities he'd been forced to kill one of the attackers, once Sarah was safely back in witness protection. Sarah must have glanced over her shoulder as she ran down the alleyway, or perhaps turned at the sound of the gunshot and saw the man fall.

'What did I do?' he asked, just in case his interpretations were wrong.

'You killed one of those men, the one you were holding onto.'

He nodded. 'Yes, I did.'

'Because of me.'

'No, because of him. He was going to shoot me, so I stopped him.'

'But you wouldn't have been put in that position if it wasn't for the mess I'm in.'

Drayce adjusted his seating position and looked her in the eye. 'Don't you dare blame yourself for any of this. You were brave enough to be a witness and I chose to help you. I chose to be here. None of this is your fault.'

Sarah's expression softened.

Drayce's phone buzzing broke their conversation. He read the message from Julie. Sarah unfolded herself and sat up on her knees, her figure blurry in the background. Her movements were tense and rigid, perhaps through worry. She must have seen the look on his face as he'd read Julie's message.

'Is everything okay?' she asked.

Drayce put down his phone. 'Well, that didn't last long.'

'What didn't?'

'Our little ace up the sleeve... that we know the identities of the people coming after us. Julie wasn't able to contain it. There's a good chance they're aware we know who they are.'

Sarah shot to her feet. 'How?'

'A colleague of Julie's fed it to their boss, who fed it to his bosses, and to the Met's murder detectives, all via an intelligence system that, if Julie is right, can be accessed by the corrupt officer who is working for the people who want you dead.'

Sarah brought her hands up to her forehead, her fingers parting her fringe, the worry contorting her face. 'That's it then.' She took her hands out of her hair and slapped them down on her hips, tears glistening in her eyes. 'It's over.'

'What do you mean?'

'The witness protection programme. It'll never be safe for me to go back into it.'

'Why do you say that?'

A single tear broke free and ran down her cheek, but she held it together enough to speak. 'Think about it, Alex. If they have someone in the NCA who Julie's superiors aren't able to identify, they'll always be a step ahead, right up to the point when they eventually track me down again. And the odds say there's no chance of us being as lucky next time. We don't know who to look out for anymore. We're back to square one, being hunted by an invisible enemy.'

Drayce stood up and walked over to her, placing his hands gently onto her shuddering shoulders as she desperately tried to hold it together.

'Not necessarily,' he said.

It was obvious she wanted to reply, but would burst into tears if she tried. Drayce held her shoulders a little tighter. He'd waited long enough for the right moment to question her background. A panic attack might be far from perfect timing, but if he waited any longer, he ran the risk that the right moment wouldn't come until it was too late.

Now or never, he told himself. 'I *will* keep you safe, I promise, but I need you to help me.'

The tears flowed freely now. 'Anything,' she said, her voice barely a whisper behind the emotions.

'I want to know everything, despite the fact you've been sworn to secrecy. Every little detail, the background, your connections to these people, the trial, what you know, and what they want to stop you from saying in court. Absolutely everything.' He watched her study her feet, patently unsure about whether she should tell him. 'The more I know,' he pressed, 'the more I have to work with.'

She pulled away from his grasp, walked over to the sofa, and sat down with her legs crossed. She placed her hands gently on her lap, her fingertips laced together, and composed herself. Drayce sat down next to her.

'Have you heard of the Marlowe brothers?' she asked.

If Drayce had been doing something other than listening to her, he would probably have frozen to the spot. If he'd been carrying something, he might have dropped it. As it was, his appearance on the outside didn't change much, but the way he felt on the inside certainly did. He cleared his throat.

'Yes. Yes, I have.'

Francis and Nathan Marlowe were international criminals based in London. Drayce didn't know much about them personally – during his eighteen years as a police officer, he'd only ever been involved in a handful of arrests of associates who had committed violent crimes on their behalf – but the word amongst the serious organised crime teams had always been that they were the most powerful crime family in the UK. During his time in the Met, Drayce had heard of dozens of beatings, kidnappings, and murders linked to the brothers. Extremely violent men, with little regard for human life other than their own, they had more than enough money and power to send teams of armed men after someone they wanted dead. The pursuit of Sarah wouldn't end just because one team had been identified, Drayce now understood. They would send as many men after Sarah as it took to get the job done.

'They're the ones who want you dead?' he asked.

She nodded.

'But why?' he asked. 'What on earth could you have done to warrant them taking so many risks to have you killed?'

Sarah kept her eyes on her hands as she spoke, her knuckles white. 'Two weeks ago, they were charged with criminal offences for the first time in their lives and remanded in custody to await trial. Two people provided the evidence that led to their arrests and charges… a man named Wayne Hardwick…' Her voice stumbled away to nothing, her lips moving but no words forthcoming. She bit down hard and inhaled through her nose before continuing. 'And me.'

Drayce waited. Telling him all of this was manifestly distressing for her, and he knew to take his time with the questions, or risk her clamming up and seeking comfort in silence. He gently asked, 'How do you two know so much about their organisation?'

'Wayne worked for them. Not as an enforcer... he was far too soft for dishing out any violence. He was just a dogsbody. Francis and Nathan pass physical messages on to others in the organisation. They're terrified of technology, they don't trust it. Wayne handled the messaging, delivering notes to various associates every day, and Francis and Nathan treated him like garbage. If he was early, they berated him, if he was late, they beat him. If at any point they caught wind of an attitude from him, guess what they did?'

'I'd heard they were violent men,' Drayce said, allowing Sarah's rhetorical question to go unanswered.

'You can say that again. I remember hearing about one occasion when Wayne answered them back. He swore at them after they'd taken turns slapping him around the head in front of a room full of associates, just because they thought it was funny. The story goes they had the entire room, maybe thirty or forty people, in total hysterics, although I'm sure most of them were only laughing to keep the brothers happy. Apparently, the room hushed as the words left Wayne's mouth, Francis and Nathan's faces transforming from manic hysterics to calm anger in the blink of an eye. Next thing you know, Nathan's pulled out a gun and put it to Wayne's head. He made him strip naked, then made everyone else watch as he forced Wayne to crawl around the room on his hands and knees while everyone took turns beating him with their belts, buckle side down.'

Sarah paused, the story of the brothers' brutality taking its toll. 'They're monsters, and the pair of them deserve to be locked up for the rest of their lives.' She paused for a moment, swallowing her emotions. 'As you can imagine, Wayne's treatment made him the perfect candidate for turning into an informant.'

Drayce pondered that thought. 'You'd think the brothers would have foreseen that risk and perhaps have treated him better as a result.'

'I think their arrogance blinded them. They could never have imagined anyone having the courage to rat on the fearsome *Marlowe brothers*. And that was ultimately their downfall. The police approached Wayne because they got wind of how badly he was treated, and they also knew how much of an asset he could be to them. He quite literally had at his fingertips all the moves the brothers were making. It was an intelligence goldmine for them.'

Drayce nodded. 'You can say that again. No wonder they had enough to charge the pair of them.'

'Indeed.'

Drayce watched her closely, waiting for her to continue. She was still staring down at her hands, avoiding eye contact with him. Her side of the story was obviously more complicated than Wayne's.

He coaxed her a little. 'So that's Wayne's connection to the Marlowe brothers… a poorly treated dogsbody who decided to tell all to the police.' He leant a little nearer to her. 'What's yours?'

She looked up at him, her amber eyes fiery, flames around her pupils. 'I'm their sister.'

28

Julie turned off her phone's screen and clipped her seatbelt. She'd just sent Alex a message to alert him that, despite her efforts, the hitmen's identities were now with the Met's murder team, as well as linked to their case on the NCA's intelligence system. She took a sip of her tepid coffee, grimacing, and reading the printed email from her friend in vetting, when she heard a tap on the passenger window. Fiona clutched her handbag in front of her, remorse etched across her face. Julie hit the central locking button to secure the doors, then lowered the window a centimetre or two, just enough for her to hear what she had to say.

'What do you want?' Julie asked.

'I want to apologise.'

'Not interested.'

Fiona took a step closer to the window and bent down to the gap. 'Please, Julie. I didn't mean to go behind your back. I wasn't thinking straight. Please, can we talk?'

Julie glanced down at the printout. She wouldn't be able to progress things until Fiona got whatever was bothering her out of her system and left her alone.

'Go on then,' she said. 'Say what you've got to say.'

Fiona's eyes dropped to the ground and she cleared her throat. 'I'm not a rule-breaker,' she said somewhat defiantly. 'And I make no apologies for that. I am who I am. You are who you are, and there's nothing either of us can do about that.

We've just got to learn to work together. I know you say that sometimes it's necessary to break the rules, and maybe it is, but it's just not something I've ever done, and neither is it something I'm likely to do in the future.'

Julie considered her own face in the window reflection: brow furrowed, eyebrows raised, and her mouth turned down. Not friendly.

'This might be the worst apology I've ever heard,' she said as her finger moved to the engine's start button.

Light rain started to fall, motivating Fiona to slip her handbag underneath her coat and clutch it to her chest. Julie leant a little closer to the window, if for no other reason than to take pleasure from watching Fiona get cold and wet.

'I'm getting to the apology,' Fiona said, 'but I want to say something first. I know we're very different, and I know you're not my biggest fan, but I'm always honest and I'm sure that must count for something.'

Julie's expression softened, her finger hovering gently over the ignition button. 'Sure.'

'We're both at very different stages of our lives. I've only been doing this job for a couple of years… you've been living it for the past three decades. I'm sure you've made plenty of mistakes during your career, and I know I'll make a few during mine.' She paused, taking a deep breath. 'And messaging Foster was definitely one of them.'

Julie took her finger away from the ignition button. 'A big mistake.'

Fiona nodded her head and the tiny raindrops that had accumulated on her hair broke free and scattered down the front of her coat. 'Yes, a big one. I don't apologise for wanting to be honest with our boss, but I do apologise for going behind your back. I shouldn't have done that, and I hope you can forgive me.'

Julie crossed her arms in front of her chest and sighed. Despite her desire to remain angry, she was starting to sympathise with Fiona, standing there in the rain, bleeding her heart out.

'I've built a good name for myself in the NCA,' Fiona said. 'And keeping Foster out of the loop risked damaging my reputation with the people who make the kind of decisions that affect careers. I have a long future ahead of me... I can't afford to burn bridges with a boss this early on. But I understand why you wanted us to keep what we'd discovered to ourselves, and I promise, if you let me work with you again, I'll learn how to keep things between just us two.'

Julie reached for the window button, lowering it down all the way. 'I need to be able to trust the person I work with.'

Fiona smiled. 'You can trust me, I promise.'

Julie pressed the button to unlock the doors. 'Get in before you get drenched.'

Fiona did just that. She shut the door behind her, took her handbag from underneath her coat, and placed it in the footwell between her feet. She pulled her seatbelt across and clipped it in place, then turned to the sheet of paper Julie held out.

'Take this,' Julie said as she started the engine and pulled out of the parking space.

'What is it?' Fiona asked, taking the printout from her and examining it closely.

'Those are the names of everyone in our organisation with the authority to access information regarding Wayne and Sarah's protection details. Whoever led those men to the safe houses, and to Sarah in Tottenham, is on that list, but there are twenty-eight names in total, so we've got to narrow it down.'

'Okay. What's the plan?'

Julie drove under the rising barrier at the exit and turned onto the city streets. 'The plan is for us to pay a visit to an old colleague of mine I think might be able to help.'

'What kind of a visit?'

'I want to ask him some questions. His name's Brian Spelby and he works for the prison intelligence section in the Met.'

'What are you hoping to find out from him?'

Julie deliberated for a moment and realised she wasn't one hundred percent sure of the answer.

'I just think he might be able to help in some way. I want to know how the Marlowe brothers behave inside. I want to know who visits them, who they call, who they write to, that sort of thing. I'm not expecting to find out that someone on that list has been in direct contact with them, but… I don't know, maybe Brian can tell me something that might narrow down the list, or maybe point me in the direction of someone who can.' She shrugged her shoulders. 'It's worth a try, that's all. Just a quick chat to get a feel for how much the brothers are giving away from their behaviour inside. There might be a clue there.' Julie paused, doubting herself for a moment. 'That is, if Brian is happy to speak to me.'

Julie noticed Fiona's eyes narrow, and immediately worried she'd said too much.

'Why wouldn't he be?' Fiona asked.

Julie bit her bottom lip; she'd certainly said too much. 'We didn't exactly part ways on the best of terms when I left the Met.'

'Was he a supervisor you fell out with or something?'

'Bit more personal than that.'

Fiona grinned, her expression as exuberant as a teenager. 'Don't tell me he's an old flame?'

Julie sighed. 'Something like that.'

'And I suppose this is another inquiry Foster doesn't need to know about?'

'Correct.'

Fiona's smile vanished. 'Can I ask if this visit is above board? I mean, you're not going to try to get anything out of him he's not supposed to tell you, are you?'

Now it was Julie's turn to grin. 'That depends on whether or not you can handle an honest answer.'

Fiona finished reading through the list of names, folded the sheet of paper in half, and placed it in the centre console. She gazed ahead at the road, her hands clasped together on her lap. 'I'm probably best off not knowing.'

Julie's grin turned into a teeth-baring smile. 'That might be the first thing yet that we have agreed on.'

29

'I didn't know they had a sister,' Drayce said, his jaw slack at the shocking revelation.

Sarah sat cross-legged on the sofa, Drayce perched on its edge as he listened to her tell her story.

'Yes, they have a sister. Sarah Elizabeth Marlowe.' She gave him a nervous little wave. 'Nice to meet you.'

'Well, I didn't see that coming.'

'I've had very little to do with my brothers since we were teenagers. After our mother passed away, we went to different boarding schools, Francis and Nathan to an all-boys, me to an all-girls. Our father was too busy running his little empire to have us around, getting in his way.'

The muscles around Sarah's eyes drooped slightly, her face collapsing into despair. 'He didn't really know what he was doing in the father department. Before her death, Mum had done the raising, and after she died, well, our father either wasn't interested, or was so terrified of the prospect of raising three children on his own that he handed over the responsibility to the British public-school system. Which, I must say, worked well for me, because I loved school. Home was a nightmare after Mum died.'

Drayce was sure he already knew the answer, but he asked the question anyway. 'Why was that?'

'My brothers were just as cruel when they were children as they are as adults, which meant whenever I was around them,

I didn't have an easy time of it.' She lifted her jumper to show Drayce a three-inch scar on her midriff, the fossil of a slash wound. 'Francis did that with a potato peeler while Nathan held my arms behind my back. I was twelve years old, and they were fifteen and seventeen. We were at home during the school holidays, and I'd been washing the dishes. They decided I hadn't cleaned them properly and were going to teach me a lesson.' She pulled her jumper back down. 'There are other scars as well.'

Drayce was unable to find any words.

'Because of their violence, it got to the stage where I hardly saw them. When the holidays came around, I used any excuse I could to stay at school… summer camps, expeditions, school trips, student exchanges. Whatever I could do to stay away from home, I did.'

'So your dad was…'

'The late great Terrance Marlowe? Yes, unfortunately. He built the foundations that Francis and Nathan's criminal empire now sits on. I, on the other hand, turned my back on them all after I left school and went to university. Which, I must add, I paid for with a student loan just like everyone else. No way was I taking my father's money, not with how he'd made it. I changed my surname to Bennett – Mum's maiden name – and was quite happy living my own life away from my family's awful crimes, with nobody knowing I was connected to them. I just wanted to be normal. Just a normal person, living a normal life.' Disgust permeated her face. 'The opposite of my brothers – the type of people who are more than happy to kill anyone who gets in their way.'

'What did you study?' Drayce asked.

Sarah's expression brightened somewhat. 'Veterinary science.'

'Impressive. You must have really enjoyed school. Got to get good grades to study that course.'

She nodded. 'I've always loved animals. I graduated with a first from the Royal Veterinary College here in London, stayed on to work at their research centre for a few years, and then went on to practice at Battersea Dogs and Cats Home.' The earlier sadness in her eyes came back, more intense than before. 'Until all of this happened.'

Drayce sat back, conscious that perching on the sofa's edge might not give off much of a relaxed vibe. He wanted Sarah to feel comfortable so she'd carry on opening up to him. 'So what did happen?' he asked, unable to keep the question from his lips. 'What was it that brought your brothers back into your life?'

'Our father had lung cancer. It was a late diagnosis.'

'I'm sorry to hear that.'

'It's okay. We were hardly close, but he was still my father, you know?'

Drayce didn't; his father had died when he'd been too young to remember him. But although he couldn't relate enough to empathise with her, his compassion meant he had a huge amount of sympathy for her. 'It must have been hard for you.'

She nodded. 'It was. He had his people track me down after his diagnosis. Turns out even a hard-nosed old gangster such as him can soften up on his deathbed. He wanted to see me, because, you know, he knew he was going to die, and didn't want to go without saying goodbye to his only daughter.'

'What did your brothers think of that? Were they happy to see you again?'

She shook her head. 'They wouldn't have been, I can tell you that with confidence. But they didn't know anything about it. I visited my father in secret. I didn't want to have anything to do with my brothers. My father had reached out, and I wanted to say goodbye, because after all, he did his best after Mum passed away.' Drayce noted the change in Sarah's expression. 'But I had nothing to say to the evil men who literally tortured me during our childhood. As far as I was concerned, I didn't want to see them again for as long as I lived.'

Drayce watched her carefully. 'But you did, though, didn't you?' Her eyes met his, the answer obvious. 'How did that come about?'

Sarah took a deep breath. 'My father left me some money in his will, quite a lot of money, as it turned out. He told me all about it from his hospital bed. He said that Rupert, the family solicitor, would handle everything once he'd passed. I was shocked and must have come across as a little reluctant because he was extremely persistent, telling me I must take what was rightfully mine, which amounted to a third of his assets, with my brothers also taking a third each. He told me his one and only skill as a father was as a provider, and he wanted everything divided fairly between the three of us.'

Drayce thought of everything he'd heard about how much Terrance Marlowe had been worth. 'That must have been a substantial inheritance.'

Sarah's eyes fell back to her clenched hands. 'It would have been, but I didn't want to keep it, not a penny of it. The third left to me was the legal assets my father had accrued over the years, but every penny of those assets originated from his crimes. All the profits he'd made from inflicting misery on other people had been squirrelled away into investment portfolios and properties, and laundered through cash-dependant private companies. I didn't want to touch it because it was all dirty in my eyes. I didn't tell my father how I felt because I didn't want to break his heart, but I just couldn't have lived with myself if I'd kept it, not when I knew where it had come from. I made a good, honest living, and I didn't want any of his blood money on my conscience, no matter how good his intentions in leaving it to me.'

The despair in Sarah's voice touched Drayce as she spoke about everything that had turned her peaceful life as a vet around and forced her to go on the run. He stood up and walked to the kitchen counter to give her a minute to settle down.

'You want another coffee?' he asked.

She turned to face him. 'Please.'

He got to it, cleaning out the cafetière and refilling it with fresh grounds as the kettle boiled. Ready, he brought it over and set it down on the coffee table, the two of them sitting in silence while it brewed.

He pressed the plunger and poured them both a mug, handing Sarah hers. She took a sip and her reaction made it plain it was too hot for her to drink. She gently blew on its surface.

'What did you do with the money?'

'Gave it away,' she said, a cheeky smile creeping over the rim of her mug as she hugged it in both hands.

'Just like that?'

'Yep. I didn't want it, and I knew lots of charities that could put it to good use. Mostly animal charities, considering my line of work. So that's what I did… sold my share of everything and gave every penny of it to charity.'

Drayce's eyes widened. 'And your brothers found out about that?'

The smile left Sarah's face. 'Yes, and they weren't happy, as you can imagine. You see, I didn't just inherit a large sum of money to be transferred to my account. Everything was tied up in shares and investments. When my brothers found out what was in our father's will, they wanted to buy me out to keep everything under their control, with the pair of them owning all the family's assets fifty/fifty because of the danger of a third party seeing the paper trail and unearthing the details of their criminal empire. They sent some heavies to speak to me, but I shut the door in all their faces. I didn't even want to discuss it. The shares and investments were mine to do with as I pleased, so I sold the shares on the stock exchange, and the properties went to the highest bidders. Then I gave the money away, and that was that.' She took another deep breath. 'Or so I thought.'

Drayce gave her a second or two while they sipped their coffees. 'How did your brothers react?'

'They paid me a visit in person, at my home address. I hadn't seen them in nearly fifteen years, and there they were, on my doorstep in suits and ties, all grown up. Nathan – that fat, ugly thug – barged past me and walked inside. Francis followed calmly in his wake, as always, the pair of them acting as if they owned the place. I didn't want them in my home, but they said they didn't want to discuss family matters on the doorstep.'

Sarah exhaled out of her nose, an angry dragon huffing. 'The arrogance of them. I hadn't seen them in fifteen years, but suddenly they're at risk of losing some money and, hey presto, I'm family again.'

Drayce waited.

'I can picture them now, in my kitchen, side by side in sharp suits with scowls on their faces. You'd think they were the Kray Twins. They said because I'd sold my third, it had brought outsiders into the fray, and because the family assets were so closely intertwined with criminal enterprises, it had brought serious unwanted attention to them. They'd received letters from HMRC, and swore they were under constant police surveillance, which they attributed to me allowing strangers into the family's business affairs. They threatened me and swore revenge. When I told them to piss off, and waved a hand at them as I shouted that they didn't scare me, Nathan grabbed hold of me by my hair and dragged me over to the stove.'

Her right hand instinctively went to the burn mark on her left palm, touching it delicately with her fingertips. 'Francis watched with a smirk on his face, just as he'd done when we were children. They had to leave in a hurry because my screams got the attention of the neighbours, but they made it clear they'd get revenge for what I'd done. I knew then that I had to do something.' She closed her fingers around the burn mark. 'Before they sent people to kill me.'

He put his mug down on the coffee table. 'So you contacted the police?'

'Yes. It started with me filing a complaint for the assault, and after sitting down with a pair of detectives and explaining what

I'd done to upset my brothers so much, it led to them inviting two senior officers into the room to speak with me, and ended with them making me an offer.'

Drayce couldn't help himself. 'And that offer was?'

'To identify all my brothers' assets and to talk the detectives through all the ways in which they'd been laundering their illegal earnings over the years, in exchange for a place on the witness protection programme. As you can imagine, before I sold my third of the family's assets, I'd been privy to all the documentation my father had on file. I knew everything, and I said if they could give me a new identity, somewhere safe and far, far away from London, where I could practice as a vet, then I'd give them everything they required to bring my brothers to their knees.'

Drayce reached for his coffee. 'I bet your evidence has the ability to put them in prison for the rest of their lives.'

Sarah didn't reply, drinking her coffee instead, avoiding eye contact with him.

He had the distinct impression she was holding something back. 'What is it?' he asked.

Sarah lowered her mug. 'The threat of prison isn't the only thing I have to wield against them.'

Drayce put his cup down and frowned. 'What do you mean?'

She leant forwards. 'I left something out when I told the police what I knew of my brothers' crimes.' She licked her lips and hesitated, as if unsure how much she should tell him. 'Something that would cause far more damage to them both than any prison sentence ever could.'

30

NCA ID cards meant that both Julie and Fiona avoided the lengthy security checks essential for all other visitors to New Scotland Yard. Pleasantries exchanged with the guards, the bollards lowered into the ground and the gates opened for Julie to drive into the secure car park. She found a space and called the man she'd come to see.

He didn't exactly sound thrilled that she'd turned up at his workplace unannounced, but he said he could spare her a few minutes, somewhat reluctantly, if Julie read his tone correctly. She thanked him, told him she'd wait by her car, and hung up. She tried to convince Fiona to wait in the car, but Fiona was having none of it, and sat next to her on the bonnet.

Brian Spelby appeared from a side entrance to the main building, gazed around for a moment and then spotted Julie, smiling at him from her perch on the car's bonnet. He hadn't changed in the three years since Julie had left the Met and joined the NCA, which, now that she thought about it, was the last time they'd seen each other. He was still trying too hard in the looks department, and in Julie's humble opinion, would be better suited to a more understated appearance. His navy suit with little room left in the cut must have cost him an entire month's wages; his hairstyle was far too fashionable and trendy for a forty-eight-year-old: shaved at the sides with a longer cut on top held back with wax. Downwind of him, Julie smelt his aftershave from seven car lengths away. He walked over, produced a forced smile, stopped about eight feet away, and stood with his arms folded.

'Hello, Julie,' he said, his flat tone intimating regret for meeting her.

'Hello, Brian.'

'It's been a while.'

'Yeah, three years or something, right?'

He nodded. 'Something like that.'

'I meant to call before now but it's just been so—'

'Spare me the excuses,' he interrupted.

Julie stood up from the bonnet, already bored with being overly polite. 'Don't make this weird, Brian. I've just come to you for help with something on a purely professional basis. Let's keep the personal stuff to one side and leave the past in the past, where it belongs, shall we?'

'Fine.' His expression altered a little when he said this, as though he might be a little embarrassed at his grumpy and somewhat juvenile re-introduction after all these years. He looked at Fiona, as though noticing her for the first time. 'Who's this?'

'My colleague,' Julie said, venom in her eyes and enough sting in the words to let him know she wouldn't tolerate any more of his rudeness.

Fiona stood up from the bonnet, shoulder to shoulder with Julie, and stuck her hand out. 'My name's Fiona. Pleased to meet you.'

He shook her hand but didn't return the pleasantries. Julie remembered why she'd never called the sulky man-child back. She decided to get straight to business.

'I've come about the Marlowe brothers, Nathan and Francis.'

'What about them?'

'They're in HMP Leeds, awaiting trial for a string of offences, and you work on the Prison Intelligence Unit.' She hardened her expression, making it clear she wouldn't be fobbed off easily. 'I thought you might be able to answer some questions for me.'

'What's wrong with an email?'

'This is time-critical. I wanted to get some answers straight away.'

'You ever heard of a little invention called the telephone?'

Julie resisted the urge to punch him in the throat. 'Something told me you might not answer my call, Brian. And judging by your attitude right now, I'd say I was right.'

He shrugged. 'Fine. Fire away. But make it quick, I don't have long.'

'Have you got surveillance on them?'

Brian laughed. 'Blimey, you haven't changed. There's no skirting around the issue with you, is there?'

'Have you?'

'I don't see how that's any of the NCA's business.'

'This is a serious matter, and the last time I checked, the NCA and the Met were on the same team. Work with me on this.'

His expression softened a little, as did his body language. He unfolded his arms and stuffed them into his trouser pockets. 'Yeah, sure, there's a team watching them.'

She took the printed list of names from her pocket and handed it to him. He unfolded it and started reading.

'What's this?' he asked.

'I want to know if any of those names have come up on the surveillance transcripts.'

Brian pushed the sheet of paper back at her, half-chuckling to himself. 'You're pushing your luck, Jules.'

She left it there, stretched out in his hand, hoping she could change his mind. 'I don't need anything official. But if you just run those names by whichever team is keeping an eye on them, and let me know off the record—'

'No chance.' He shook his head with determination. 'I'm sorry, but I'm not privy to those details, and it would be amateurish for me to even attempt to find out. Even if I were to be stupid enough to approach the department I know is watching them, they'd quite rightly tell me to bugger off until the relevant details from the transcripts had been placed on the intel system and approved for dissemination.' He forced the list back into her hand. 'I don't know what kind of influence you think I have, but surveillance operations are kept a secret for a reason.'

Julie folded the sheet of paper and put it back in her jacket pocket. 'What about the brothers' behaviour, do you feel brave enough to tell me a bit about that?'

'It's not about being brave, Jules. It's about procedure. You're supposed to put a request in for this sort of thing, not just come on down to Scotland Yard to find out for yourself.'

'I'm pragmatic in that way,' she said with an aggressive, none-too-friendly smile. 'And I already told you I don't have time to waste by funnelling everything through the official channels. Don't forget what department I work in, Brian. I'm trying to stop that pair from having an innocent person killed.'

Her eyes locked onto his. He tilted his head up to the grey London skies and let out a big sigh. 'Fine. What do you want to know about, specifically?'

'Specifically, I want to know who visits them, who calls them, and who writes to them. In a general sense, I want you to paint me a picture of how they behave in prison. I want to know if they've struck up any close bonds with any other prisoners, or guards for that matter.'

'You don't want much then.'

Julie bit her teeth together, clenching her jaw hard to stop herself from saying something she'd regret. Back in control, she said, 'They're communicating with someone on the outside, and I want to know who.'

He looked over both shoulders, presumably to make sure there was no one within earshot. 'Without saying too much, I can tell you that if they *are* communicating with someone, they're smart about it.'

Julie frowned. 'How so?'

'They never make phone calls, they don't receive any letters, or send any out. They barely speak to any of the other inmates and the only person who visits them is their solicitor, and the conversation takes place in a private consultation room that for legal reasons cannot be bugged.'

He held Julie's eye contact, his expression genuinely apologetic. 'I'm sorry, Jules, but if they *are* coordinating something from inside prison, then they're doing it in a way we haven't been able to trace yet.' He nodded at her pocket. 'If you want to know if anyone on that list is communicating with the brothers, then investigate the list and trace something back from their end, because I'm telling you now, you won't pick up anything from the brothers' side.'

Julie's energy seeped out of her. 'I don't have the evidence to investigate anyone on that list, Brian.'

He smiled, but not in the arrogant, mocking way she'd come to expect of him. This time it appeared to be honest sympathy. 'Well then, you just said it, Jules, you don't have the evidence. We've all been there. Not much can be done in the absence of evidence. Maybe you can think of another way to narrow down that list.'

'Yeah,' she replied, sounding as dejected as she felt. 'Maybe.'

'Anything else I can help you with?'

She shook her head. 'No. Thanks for everything, Brian. And sorry for dropping by unannounced. I promise I'll give you the heads-up in the future.'

'No worries. And I'm sorry for the hostile reception. It was just a bit of a shock, to be honest. You know, after all this time.'

Julie nodded. 'Sure. I get it.'

'It was good to see you.'

'You too.'

He turned and walked away, his potent aftershave – something with a strong citrus note – dissipating as he went. Julie watched him go and then swivelled to face Fiona, who was fighting back a smile itching to break out across her face.

'*Aaawk*ward,' she said, stretching the word out for emphasis.

'You could have waited in the car.'

'And miss the reunion?'

Julie shook her head and laughed. 'Come on, let's get out of here.' She walked around the car to the driver's door.

'Where next?' Fiona asked.

Julie thought about her answer as they both climbed in, but it wasn't until she'd clipped her seatbelt in, started the engine, and driven through the gates, that she realised she didn't have one.

31

'What would frighten your brothers more than prison?' Drayce asked Sarah.

She reached forwards and put her empty mug down on the coffee table. 'Losing all their money,' she said, leaning back into her seat.

'Based on what you've told me about the case the police and the NCA have against them, I'd say they've already had all their assets seized. Both the Proceeds of Crime Act and the Unexplained Wealth Orders will have seen to that.'

'True, they've had a lot of assets seized. Deeds to various properties, stocks and shares, bank accounts in the UK and abroad, they've all been taken over by the authorities.' Sarah brushed her hair out of her eyes. 'But they can't seize what they don't know about.'

Drayce wanted to dive right into the questioning, but fought his natural urges and held off. Sarah's body language indicated questions were unnecessary; this was something she'd been itching to get off her chest for a while.

'My grandfather died from Alzheimer's disease, and after witnessing what he'd gone through in the later stages of life, my father was terrified the same fate might await him in old age. Hence, he kept diaries. I guess he felt writing down his thoughts might help stave off the disease if he were destined for it. These diaries had been gathered up along with all the paperwork relating to the family finances, and when I went to meet with my father's solicitor, there they were, stacked up next to his desk. He left me alone during the meeting because his secretary needed him for something more important than supervising me, and while he was out of the room, I flicked through one of them.'

On the edge of his seat, Drayce was desperate to interject, but reluctant to derail her thought process.

'The solicitor took much longer than expected,' Sarah continued, 'and when he eventually walked back into the room, it was as though he'd seen a fire. He hurried over to where I was sitting, snatched the diary out of my hands and slammed it shut. He was quite flustered, and mumbled some sort of an apology about being sorry but those books had nothing to do with my father, which of course I knew was a lie, because I'd read quite a few pages of the one I'd opened.'

'What was in it?' Drayce asked, unable to resist the urge.

Sarah took a deep breath. 'He hadn't just written about personal stuff, such as his fear of dementia. He wrote about everything to do with business matters as well. The one I picked up from the top of the pile was the oldest, the very first one he started shortly after my grandfather's death, back in 1989. He wrote about his plans for securing the family's finances for the future, and in 1989, cash was king, especially in criminal matters. He explained everything in detail so that in the event of him losing his mind, he would have it all written down, never to be forgotten.'

Sarah paused for a moment, setting up the punchline. 'My father had a huge cash reserve hidden away that the authorities knew nothing about. The only written record of it was in that first diary, and the only people alive who have read that diary are me, my brothers, and two others.'

'And those two others are?'

'Well, their solicitor, I'm sure, because he kept hold of the diaries for my brothers. The other will be a man known as the Accountant.'

Drayce's eyes narrowed. 'Who's the Accountant?'

'I don't know his real name but he's responsible for guarding the money. It's buried in the grounds of a farm in rural Essex, sealed within a container. It's all detailed in that first diary.'

'And where's that diary now?'

Sarah's eyebrows lifted, as though the answer was obvious. 'My brothers will have destroyed it. I think they were planning on keeping them all, initially, hence why they were with the solicitor. Perhaps they intended to read through them to see if our father had any other hidden cash reserves he hadn't told them about. But after I'd seen them, there was no way they'd stay in existence. As soon as my brothers knew I was a threat to them, they'd have burned the lot. Can you imagine if the police laid hands on a physical record of where several million pounds of my family's ill-gotten gains are stashed, along with details in that record of how the money is protected?'

'And how is it protected?'

'My father had certain things set up to warn him if the police were onto him. He called them tripwires. He ran an informant in law enforcement during his entire career, just as it seems my brothers do now within the NCA. The first tripwire was the informant. The second was the Accountant. If the informant triggered the first tripwire by letting my father know the police knew about the farm, he'd contact the Accountant and set things into motion. Alternatively, if the police kept their knowledge of the farm a secret prior to the raid, cutting my father's informant out of the loop, then the Accountant would set things into motion when the police turned up.'

The sun disappeared behind a vast curtain of clouds, sinking the flat into gloomy darkness. Drayce switched on the lights, then returned to his seat and waited to catch Sarah's eye.

'Tell me more about the Accountant,' he said.

Her eyes came back into focus as she met Drayce's. 'My father's diary described the farmhouse where the Accountant lived as being set within twenty-five acres of land. To any passer-by, it was a typical farm, surrounded by grazing fields, nothing suspicious whatsoever. Even if the police had discovered it, the Accountant would have seen them coming from a mile away and have plenty of time to enact the final part of my father's plan.'

'And that was?'

Sarah smiled. 'The Accountant's a qualified pilot – although he'll be too old to fly now – and the cash isn't just in a container. It's in a container, loaded onto a plane, and hidden underground.'

Sarah laughed; Drayce's astonishment was genuine.

'I'm telling the truth,' she said. 'It was all written down in his diary.'

'I believe you,' Drayce was quick to say. 'It's just so—'

'Unbelievable?'

'Yeah.'

She nodded. 'I felt the same way when I read it. It seemed so implausible and yet I knew it was true. The cash and the plane were buried together, twenty feet below the surface. They dug a tunnel leading from the house to the plane, and another tunnel, wide enough for the plane, up to the surface of a field, at a gradual angle to serve as a runway for the Accountant to fly the plane out and take off as it hit fresh air.'

She shook her head at the ingenuity of it all. 'Even if the police found out about the farm and tried to raid it, they wouldn't stand a chance of getting their hands on any of the cash before it was airborne.'

'Do you know where this farm is?' Drayce asked.

Sarah nodded. 'The address was in the diary.'

'And the only people who know about it apart from you, and now me, are your brothers, their solicitor, and this Accountant character?'

She nodded again. 'That's right.'

Drayce regarded her with a sceptical eye. 'Why didn't you tell the police about this when you gave them your statement?'

Sarah locked her fingers and rubbed her thumbs together as if to dispel some nervous energy, her mind delving deeper into her thoughts. 'I don't know, is the honest answer. I wanted to teach my brothers a lesson, and I wanted them to pay for the way they'd treated me. But the farm was… well, it was my father's, not theirs. I know they've inherited it along with all the other criminal matters my father had established, but it had been my father's idea. If you'd read his diary, and seen for yourself the way he talked about that farm, then it might help you to understand what I'm trying to convey. He was just so proud he'd figured out a way to make sure that money stayed safe… for us, not him. He made it clear in his writing he never planned to spend a penny of it. It was all for his three children.'

A dark expression fell on her face. 'Not that my brothers were ever going to share any of it with me.'

The vengeful energy vanished and Drayce reflected this might be because her thoughts had switched back to her father again, a parent with whom it had taken her nearly thirty years to bond. 'I suppose I felt I owed it to him to keep the farm a secret. Handing it over to the police just seemed like a step too far. It was my brothers I wanted to punish, not my father.'

She appeared to gauge whether Drayce understood. She pulled the sleeve of her sweater over her hand and brought it up to each eye, dabbing at them as the emotions got the better of her. 'He confided in me, shortly before he died, that he couldn't have been prouder of me for the way I'd chosen to live my life.'

A shy smile stole onto her face: the kind of smile seen on any son or daughter when they reflect on a proud parent. 'He didn't want any of us to go down the same path as him. He told me he did what he did so we wouldn't have to, and that he'd tried to steer my brothers away from that life.'

She shook her head, deep in thought. '"But they are who they are, Dad," is what I told him. "They are who they are as much as I am who I am, and as much as you might want to change them, you can't." Maybe it was the wrong decision to keep that farm to myself, but at the time, I just felt I owed it to my father to keep that place a secret.'

Drayce didn't throw any more questions her way. He understood her reasoning.

'Besides,' Sarah said, 'telling the police about it probably wouldn't have done much good. I'm sure my brothers will have moved it all on and hidden it elsewhere by now.'

Drayce wasn't convinced of that. 'I doubt it. Think about it... your father wrote his first diary over three decades ago. Since then, your brothers have earned a huge amount of money from their crimes, and much of that will have come from cash-dependant enterprises. They'll have laundered a significant amount and filtered it into offshore accounts, but a lot of it will have stayed as cash. They would have faced the same problem your father faced all those years ago... that cash had to be stored somewhere.'

Sarah's eyes widened. 'You think it's still there?'

Drayce nodded. 'Why else would their solicitor have been so keen to snatch your father's diary out of your hands? I think he did that because the cash your brothers have added to the family business over the years has been accumulating on that farm. There would have been no need for them to move it until you found out it existed, and that was only a few weeks ago, most of which they've spent in prison. Contemplate the logistics of moving a set-up of that magnitude: finding a new location, digging fresh tunnels, moving the cash. They haven't had time.'

Sarah's eyes lit up. She stood up in a hurry, her hands bunched into fists and full of energy, as though she'd had an epiphany.

Drayce eyed her cautiously. 'Why do I feel I should have kept my thoughts to myself?'

She hovered on the spot, a ferocious energy descending over her eyes. 'What do you think we should do, in your professional opinion, to keep me safe from this point on?'

Drayce had the answer prepared and ready to go. 'I know a person, here in the city. In half an hour, I can have enough guns and ammunition in this flat to fight a small war. I can set up cameras at every entrance point to the building, reinforce the door to the flat, and sit here, ready and waiting for anyone who comes looking for a fight.' He watched Sarah process everything he said. 'Even if they find out where we are, they won't make it over the threshold. We wait it out, let Julie find the informant, and then put you back into witness protection when it's safe.'

Sarah gave it some thought once he'd finished. Then she shook her head. 'We're not staying here. I can't hide forever. Eventually, they'll find me. Running and hiding isn't in their rulebook. If I'm to survive this, I've got to be as aggressive as my brothers.' She smiled. 'I need to take the fight to them.'

Taken aback, Drayce said, 'I'm not sure that's a good idea.'

'Well, if I have to,' she turned and picked up her coat, shrugging it on as she walked to the entranceway, 'I'll do it on my own.'

Drayce shot up and ran after her, placing his hand against the front door as she got to it. 'Just wait a minute.'

'Get out of my way,' she said as she pulled on the handle. 'I need to do something.'

'What do you need to do?'

'Something! Just something!' Her efforts to pull on the handle more frantic. Drayce leant a little harder against the door. 'I'm sick of hiding from them. I'm going to the Accountant's farm, and I'm going to burn every note I find!'

'You can't go anywhere on your own.'

She glared at him with fierce eyes. 'I can do what I want!'

Drayce kept his voice calm, hoping she'd lower hers to his level. 'I made a promise to an old friend that I'd keep you safe.'

'But you don't control me! If I want to leave here, I can!'

'True, but I have a responsibility to keep you alive, so I can't let you go on your own.'

Her efforts to get out of the flat relaxed a little. 'So you're coming with me?'

Drayce sighed. 'I'd rather you stayed here, hunkered down behind me in body armour, while I point a machine gun at the front door.'

'I told you… I'm not hiding anymore. They've bullied me my whole life. I'm taking a stand.'

Drayce took a deep breath. 'Okay. But you can't take the fight to these people on your own. It'd be suicide.'

Her eyes lit up. 'So you *are* coming with me.'

The impending doom Drayce always sensed when trouble was on the horizon enveloped him. 'Is there anything I can say to talk you out of leaving this flat?'

She leant in close to him, her face just inches from his, and her voice much calmer now. 'Absolutely not.'

'Fine, but if we're to be proactive against these people, it's imperative we be smart.' An idea swimming around in the back of his mind as he'd listened to Sarah talk surfaced. 'And I think I might know of a way to go about it.'

He walked back into the living room, turned off the fire and the lights, and then reconvened with her at the door. 'Remember when I dragged you out of the Thames and you made me promise to tell you the next time I had a stupid idea?'

'Yes,' she said, cautiously. 'I remember.'

Drayce opened the door, and as they walked out together, told her all about his stupid idea.

32

All Rupert Jones could think about was the smell.

It was everywhere around him, the stench wafting down the endless white-walled corridors and under the numerous steel doors, all the way to his poor nostrils. He didn't know the cause, but guessed it had something to do with the many degenerates who made up the substantial population of prisoners housed in HMP Leeds. It was the same the last time he'd been summoned to the wretched complex, making the tedious journey north from London. His visits were always just long enough for him to get used to the smell – if such a thing were possible – before he was back out in the fresh air again.

He removed his bright yellow pocket square from his black Hugo Boss suit jacket and held it up to his nose, having sprayed it that morning with his favourite cologne – Tom Ford Tobacco Vanille – in preparation for the prison's odour.

He'd already suffered the indignity of being searched by a man whom one could only presume had an objection to bathing – the stench emanating from that particular guard had been so awful that Rupert had nearly resorted to pinching his nose – and now he just wanted to sit down with his clients. He had a home visit booked with an escort that evening – one of his regulars – so he was keen to get this latest visit over with so he could get back to London in plenty of time. He observed the giant lump of meat to his side, not bothering to hide the disdain he felt for a man who was so stupid he had resorted to working in such a place.

'This is ridiculous,' Rupert had to remove the pocket square from his face to enable him to spit out the words with all the contempt he could muster. 'The governor will be hearing from me about this. Delaying meetings between a solicitor and his clients is utterly unacceptable.'

The guard's head turned in his direction, the skin on his fat neck rolling over the collar of his white shirt as he did so. Dark splotches on the sleeve nearest to Rupert had the mark of bloodstains that hadn't successfully washed out. Probably not his own blood, Rupert thought. The expression on the guard's face was one of indifference, as though he didn't understand a word of what had just been said. After glaring down at Rupert, the guard faced the front again, his neck fat rolling back into its default position.

Rupert all but stamped his feet in frustration; he wasn't a man accustomed to being ignored. What he *was* accustomed to was impeccable timekeeping, which certainly wasn't one of this guard's strengths. Rupert questioned whether he'd even be able to tell the time. He was wearing a cheap digital watch, something a child might sport before they learnt what the big hand and little hand were for. Rupert examined it for a moment. It had a thin black plastic strap straining around his fat wrist, every bit as tasteless as you would expect from such a dullard. Rupert admired his own timepiece: a Patek Philippe Chronograph with a dark brown leather strap, a gift he'd bought for himself following his second divorce, which had really just been a way of hiding some capital from that blood-sucking whore. He tilted his wrist up in front of his face, making a big song and dance of checking the time in front of the guard, and was just about to remind him again of his close acquaintance – the governor – when a loud buzzer rang from somewhere near the ceiling. The metallic *clunk* of the lock's bolt sliding out of the big metal door in front of them was apparently the signal for the guard to move, because he gripped the handle and pulled it open, revealing a long corridor expanding away from them, on either side of which were doors leading to various consultation rooms.

'Room number seven,' the guard said in a deep and lazy voice.

'Oh, it speaks!' Rupert replied, moving swiftly down the corridor and out of reach of the brute. He walked briskly, the hard leather soles on his handmade shoes tapping out a rhythm as he counted down the numbers on the doors. Number seven had another two guards standing in front of it.

'Make way! Make way!' Rupert barked, waving his fragrant pocket square at them as though that might encourage them to part faster. 'I will not be delayed any further!'

The bored guards shuffled apart just enough for Rupert to squeeze between their shoulders sideways, admonishing the pair of them as he hurried inside. 'The governor will be hearing from me about this. Mark my words.' He shut the door behind him and turned to face his two clients.

Francis and Nathan Marlowe sat next to each other at a white table positioned in the centre of the room. Francis had one bony leg folded over the other, his sinewy arms crossed. As always, his jet-black hair was combed in a side parting, slick with gel. Behind his gold-framed glasses were eyes that barely moved, his pupils as black and as soulless as a great white shark's. Quiet and calculating, Francis had a presence that could make the average man feel a chill in a sauna.

Nathan, on the other hand, was a less subtle individual and twice the size of his sibling, thanks to an unhealthy obsession with fried foods and sugary drinks, coupled with a steroid addiction and a daily visit to the weights room. His thick, meaty hands lay flat on the table, his giant sausage fingers spread wide. His once-black hair was turning grey at the sides and falling out at an increasing rate. His widow's peak had succumbed to almost total baldness, the skin around his neck and cheeks scarred from several nasty breakouts of acne, both of which were repugnant side effects of the steroids. A fierce man, Nathan was prone to spontaneous outbursts of violence. Rupert knew from experience it was best to tread carefully in his company.

The two men regarded Rupert with expressions of mild irritation, the best he had ever known them to have. Even as children, when Rupert had been their father's legal representative, the two brothers eyed everyone outside of the family with the same hostility. Nathan shifted his reptilian eyes to the empty chair on Rupert's side of the table, while Francis kept his eyes on Rupert.

'Stop flapping around and take a seat,' Francis said, his calm and measured voice almost a whisper in the quiet room.

Rupert tucked his pocket square away and straightened his tie and suit jacket, both dishevelled after squeezing through the two guards. He set his briefcase down on the floor, sat on the empty chair, and straightened his back.

'Well?' Francis asked. 'What have you got for us?'

Rupert swallowed, his mouth suddenly dry. 'Earlier today, I received a call from Stanley.'

Nathan leant forwards, his big meaty forearms pressing even harder onto the table; the legs uttered a creak under the strain. Rupert smelt prison food and cigarettes on his breath.

'And?' Nathan asked.

'And I'm afraid there's some bad news.' His eyes darted between the brothers. Undiluted hostility replaced the mild irritation.

'What bad news?' Francis asked.

Rupert ran his tongue around his mouth, in vain, to stimulate some saliva flow. His lips were sticking to his teeth. 'It would appear your sister has sought the help of a man from outside the regular authorities.'

'Don't call her that,' Nathan said.

'Indeed,' Francis added. 'She's no sister of ours.'

Rupert practically bowed his head. 'I'm sorry. Slip of the tongue. Won't happen again.'

'What of this man?'

'Yeah,' Nathan said. 'What difference does one bloke make?'

'Well, I'm afraid the difference is that we no longer have a link between ourselves and her movements. The informant you put me in touch with is a little out of the loop now.' He rubbed the nape of his neck, noticing how clammy his palms were. 'With this outsider protecting Sarah, it has become difficult for Stanley and the others to track her down, and when they did, this man – how can I put it…?' Time ticked by while Rupert chose his words. 'Proved quite the challenge.'

Nathan pushed his meaty forearms off the table, leant back into his chair, and sighed. In the same way a wolf's breath passing over its fangs would make a sheep bristle, the ominous whistle of air through Nathan's teeth awakened the hair on Rupert's neck.

'What are you saying?' Nathan asked. 'Have those dickheads got themselves nicked?'

'No, no. They've not been arrested, but they have suffered some injuries, and are… unable to complete the job on their own.' Rupert paused to allow the brothers to interject, but they didn't say a word, which was somehow worse than if they'd started shouting. The duo stared at him with open mouths as though the update had sent them into a state of shock.

'They're asking for help,' Rupert continued.

Nathan was the first to break out of the spell. 'Help?' he asked with all the derision he could muster. 'Fucking *help*?' His voice rose. 'That's not how this works, Rupert. *They* work for *us… we're* paying *them* to get the job done.' He turned to his brother. 'What kind of people go to their bosses to ask for help completing the job the bosses are paying them to finish?' He turned back to Rupert and leant forwards onto the table again, this time with just one forearm, his other raised as he pointed a rigid index finger. 'You wouldn't pay an exterminator to kill a rat, and then expect the exterminator to come and ask you to lay the traps for them, would you?'

Rupert didn't know what to say to that; the man had a point.

Nathan turned back to his brother. 'They must think we're a pair of mugs.'

With a quiver to his voice, Rupert met Francis's gaze and said, 'They understandably want your approval before they bring in reinforcements. Stanley assures me they can complete the contract, they just want a few extra bodies to help with the... erm... heavy physical aspects. And with this being such a delicate operation, they seek your approval regarding who they might use.'

Francis turned to his brother but didn't speak. Rupert wondered if they might be communicating via telepathy.

'I told you it was a mistake using them for something as important as this,' Nathan said.

'They've done good work for us in the past,' Francis replied.

'Sure, some leg-breaking or a show of muscle when we've needed it. But nothing on this scale. We should have used a contractor, someone ex-military. A professional.'

Francis shook his head. 'We wanted this to stay within the firm, remember? The further we go outside our circle of trust, the easier it'll be for the police to get wind of what we're trying to do. And Stanley's done right by coming to us with his problems, rather than burying his head in the sand, or worse, lying about it. And besides, we have other resources we can send their way.'

'Who?'

'The Russians.'

Nathan's nose crinkled. 'The Russians? You want to involve those devious bastards in the job our freedom relies on? Are you mad?'

Unlike his more emotional brother, Francis's face hadn't changed. It rarely did.

'No, dear brother, I am not mad. I have thought long and hard about plan B in the event Stanley and the others couldn't get the job done, and the Russians are our best option. If we're to involve individuals outside of our organisation, we need them to be capable, with no direct connection to us. The Russians fit that mould perfectly. Plus, they owe us.'

'Yeah, and do you remember *why* they owe us?'

Francis closed his eyes for a moment, perhaps so Nathan couldn't see him roll them, Rupert thought.

'Yes, I remember. They weren't our number one choice for a reason, but what happened last year wasn't entirely their fault. And besides, mistakes are made. Nobody is perfect, especially not men who kill for a living.'

'What mistake did they make?' Rupert asked, forgetting his place in a moment of sheer intrigue and curiosity. Francis shot him a look that made him feel he might be turning to stone.

'None of your fucking business. I pay you for your legal skills, nothing else, so unless I volunteer something, you keep that giant beak of yours out of it. Got it?'

Rupert dutifully nodded several times, his hand absent-mindedly rising to the tip of his nose. Francis's use of the word 'giant' had hit a nerve.

'They lost a quarter of a tonne of our cocaine to the authorities,' Nathan blurted out, eyeballing his brother as he did so.

Francis stared at Nathan in the same way a bitter teacher might the class idiot, whom he'd got sick and tired of a long time ago. 'You really are a fat, loud-mouthed simpleton, aren't you, brother?'

Nathan ignored Francis and spoke to Rupert. 'The only thing that stopped a war breaking out was their promise to repay the money lost, which they have, plus the promise of a favour when the time came.'

'Which we'll call in now,' Francis said, in a manner that made it clear the decision was final. 'With the money and resources those Russians have in London, they'll track down Sarah in no time, ending this period of misery we find ourselves in. They're more than capable.'

'That's what you said about Stan and Chrissy, and look what a mess they've made.'

Francis sighed as he turned to face Rupert. 'Do you know how it feels to work with a man who cannot focus on the objective?'

'I *can* focus,' Nathan interrupted.

'Who gets distracted by every little bump in the road,' Francis continued, 'and can't keep his mind on the desired destination?'

'That's not fair, Francis,' Nathan said, his tone resembling that of a whining child. He turned to Rupert for support. 'Tell him, Rupert. You know me. Tell him I *can* focus.'

Rupert glanced between the two men, cognisant that no matter what he said, he would offend one of them. 'Erm… well… I suppose…'

'We focus on the objective,' Francis said to his brother, rescuing Rupert from his dilemma. 'We focus on what must happen for the trial to collapse. We're halfway there, brother. Just one more to go and the CPS will have nothing to present in court but two statements that Rupert and his team can pull apart, and two dead witnesses we can easily discredit.' He turned back to Rupert. 'Contact the Russians. Give them the relevant information, along with Stanley's number, and tell them that once she's dead, the favour's spent and we're back on equal terms.'

'Yes, Francis. I'll call them from the car on my way back to London.'

Francis nodded his head vaguely in response to Rupert's reply, but his eyes were staring at nothing, unfocused and wild, as though contemplating something deeply important. 'Have you heard from the Accountant?'

'No,' Rupert replied.

Francis nodded. 'Neither have we, which I suppose is a good sign.'

'Indeed. It means Sarah must have kept her mouth closed about that part of it all.'

'I suppose that's something to be grateful for amongst all this chaos. Maybe that dreadful woman does have some family values after all.'

'And, of course, there's still the chance she didn't read anything significant in your father's journal. After all, I'd only left her alone in the room for a few minutes.'

'I told you before,' Francis said sternly. 'We have to assume the worst, which means she knows what was in that journal.'

'Yeah,' Nathan said, jabbing a giant sausage finger at Rupert once again. 'You don't row out of your fuck-up that easily, mate.'

'No, of course not,' Rupert spluttered. 'I was merely—'

'How's the relocation project for the Accountant coming along?' Francis interrupted. 'Have you found anywhere suitable for him yet?'

Rupert placed his hands on the tabletop, wringing them together. 'Nothing's finalised yet, but I'm visiting another two sites tomorrow. If they are as suitable as they appear, then I am confident we can secure a quick sale and exchange.'

'Time is of the essence. Just because she hasn't told them yet, it doesn't mean she won't.'

'Of course,' Rupert stuttered. 'I'll see it's progressed as expeditiously as possible.'

'Nice watch,' Nathan said out of the blue.

Rupert turned to see him ogling his Patek Philippe, which, with his hands out in front of him on the tabletop, peeked out from behind his left cuff. Hastily, he pulled it down to cover the timepiece.

'Well, thank you. It's nothing special, just a little gift to myself from—'

'Show me,' Nathan growled.

Rupert caught Francis's eye, hoping the only man capable of reining in Nathan Marlowe might say something. No such luck.

'Come on, you old poof.'

'I'm not a—'

'Show me your fancy watch.'

With a heavy heart, Rupert pulled his cuff back.

'I can't see it properly,' Nathan barked. 'Take it off and hand it here.'

Rupert reluctantly undid the supple leather strap and cautiously handed it over to Nathan's fat, hairy, eager hands.

'Fancy,' Nathan said as he pawed it. 'Very fancy.'

Rupert abhorred the greasy fingerprints he was leaving all over the crystal face. His heart sank every time the cretin tugged on the straps, giving the oaf the appearance of a child who expected sweeties to drop out if he yanked on it hard enough.

'Please be careful, Nathan.'

'I'm just looking.'

'I know, it's just that—'

'Don't be such an old queer!'

'I told you before I'm not a—'

'Well, you dress like one. Doesn't he, Francis? Doesn't he dress like an old queer?'

Nathan watched his brother expectantly as Francis examined Rupert's expression, the corners of his mouth kinking as though enjoying his anguish, soaking it all up in the way a daemon would, feeding on the misery of others. Rupert's eyes never left his precious watch.

'Enough,' Francis said to Nathan, the kinks falling away, his bored demeanour ending the game.

Nathan stuck his bottom lip out and shrugged in response as he draped the watch over his wrist.

Rupert looked on in horror. 'Erm, Nathan?'

'Strap's a bit small.'

Rupert longed to retort, *it would be, wouldn't it, you blithering imbecile? It wasn't made for your fat wrist.*

'Anything else to report?' Francis asked, demanding Rupert tear his attention away from the obscenely expensive watch just stolen from him.

'Erm… no. That was all.'

'Make another appointment to visit us when you've heard from the Russians that the job's done.'

Rupert nodded and returned his gaze to the watch. 'I will.'

'Good,' Francis said as he got to his feet. 'Then we're done here.'

Nathan stood up with him.

Rupert rose to his feet as well, a hand pawing the air around Nathan's wrist. 'Could I just...?'

'I said we're done here,' Francis stated, matter-of-factly.

The two brothers walked around the table and left the room, leaving Rupert alone, his painfully light wrist breaking his heart. The giant guard appeared in the open doorway, the same one who had accompanied him to this room, and who would now escort him out of the prison. He'd obviously seen what Nathan had been wearing as he'd left, because he had a big, mocking smile on his face, his eyes darting between Rupert's sad eyes and his naked wrist.

'This way,' the guard said as he tilted his giant forearm and checked his cheap digital watch. 'I think it's time you were leaving.'

33

'I think that might work,' Sarah said.

They'd rented a car using a fake ID Drayce kept handy for such eventualities, choosing a white Kia Sportage because it was reliable and discreet, and headed northeast on the M11, with Drayce behind the wheel.

Shortly after leaving the city, he'd stopped off at a variety of shops and bought a slew of items required for his idea to work. Two bags of equipment were in the boot, with a new pay-as-you-go phone charging up in the car's USB port. Sarah had turned away from him, gazing straight out of the windscreen, no doubt mulling it all over in her mind as he paid attention to the road.

Travelling through the Essex countryside, they had nothing to view other than miles and miles of fields and hedgerows on either side of the road. He blindly reached inside the open bag of biltong in the centre console – something else he'd bought before leaving London – and tossed a few pieces into his mouth.

Sarah turned back to face him. 'Explain it all to me again,' she said, 'just to make sure I understand you correctly.'

Drayce waited until he'd finished his mouthful. 'Well, as I've made clear, I'd rather we turn around and head back to the flat for plan A.'

'I told you, I'm not—'

'I know, I know, you're not hiding anymore. I get it. In which case, if you insist on being proactive, and there's nothing

I can do to stop you, then I might as well help you, and the way I see it, the best thing we can do is to help Julie identify who the informant is so they can be arrested. Then, with them out of the picture, you can go safely back into the witness protection programme, give your evidence in court, and live the rest of your life in peace. With me so far?'

She nodded, so Drayce continued.

'I believe the best chance we have of making that happen is if we force your brothers' hands. I started to think about the ways in which they might be communicating with their informant. I have no doubt they'll do it in a secretive way, hidden from the prying eyes and ears of the authorities. Most likely, the messages are passed on through a trusted third party, maybe in coded communications, or maybe just in a way that will prevent the authorities from getting access to them. In that case, it'll need to be planned, because they won't be able to communicate whenever they decide they've something to say, or whenever they want an update, not if they want to keep it secret.

'Criminals as high profile as them, waiting on remand on serious charges, will have a lot of eyes on them. Legitimate phone calls are monitored, and their cells regularly searched for mobiles. Consequently, they'll either have occasional pre-arranged meetings with their middleman to pass messages to their informant, or if there's no middleman, and they're somehow smuggling letters and notes in and out of prison, it'll take even longer, and communication with their informant will be even more intermittent. That intermittence is a weakness, and I aim to capitalise on that weakness.'

Sarah looked at him quizzically. 'And you think the best way of doing that is to raid the farm?'

'Well, not an actual raid, just a staged one. If the Accountant believes the farm's being raided by the police, he'll follow the plan, escape with the cash, and get a message to your brothers. And what's the first thing your brothers will do?'

Sarah didn't reply. She waited.

'They'll contact their informant wanting to know what they're playing at, and why the police got so close without any warning. Either they'll have paid or threatened this person to give them the heads-up, so they won't be happy that the Accountant had to enact their emergency plan of flying the money out of the farm. And they'll want to contact the informant straight away, not through any sort of pre-arranged meeting with a middleman on the outside, but more than likely from a mobile phone that's been smuggled into prison, because they'll want answers immediately. Not in a week's time, after messages have slowly gone back and forth. We can take advantage of the mistake we force them into making by having Julie's people waiting to intercept that line of communication, tracing it to the informant's phone.'

'But if they don't know which phone my brothers are using to communicate from prison, how is Julie supposed to trace it to the informant?'

'The surveillance team will use an IMSI catcher, also known as a Stingray, which will intercept all text messages, calls, and any other data sent from the brothers' cell. They can send everything they catch to Julie, who can sift through the communications, using her three decades of experience as a detective to identify the informant. Shouldn't be too hard, though. Your brothers won't expect the authorities to go to these lengths, especially if they don't realise they're on to a leak, so it's likely they'll speak freely in the messages.'

He took his eyes off the road for a moment to read Sarah's face; he had the impression she might be on his wavelength.

'I was right the first time I heard it,' she said. 'I think it might work.'

Drayce focused on the road. He took his phone out of his pocket and handed it to Sarah. He didn't want to call Julie – she'd fire question after question at him – so he asked Sarah to send a message informing Julie that the brothers would be contacting their informant tonight, likely on a mobile phone, so she needed everything in place to trace those communications.

'What are we going to do once we get there?' Sarah asked as she hit send and gave Drayce his phone back.

'We?'

'Yes. We. You weren't thinking of leaving me out of it, were you?'

'Yes, I was. I'll drop you off at a hotel, pay for a room in cash, and you can sleep off the stress of today's events while I do what must be done. It's too dangerous for you to come along.'

Sarah shook her head. 'No chance. I'm coming with you. Going on the attack was my idea.' She leant across in her seat, her fiery amber eyes just inches from Drayce's face. He was about to try to talk her out of it, but then she spoke again, loudly and forcefully, pinning his lips shut. 'You could use an extra pair of hands to make this work, and I'm not in the mood for debating it, so I'm coming with you.' She sat back. 'End of.'

Judging by the expression on her face, he wouldn't convince her otherwise. And besides, with everything she'd read in that journal, she was probably right about him needing her.

'Fine,' he said. 'And for the record, I didn't think there was any chance you'd let me leave you out of it, but I had to at least try. You know, if I were to actually do my job properly.'

She glanced across at him, her expression that of holding back a smile. 'Understood.'

Drayce's phone rang. Julie. He asked Sarah to switch the settings to silent when the call ended. There was no point talking to Julie yet. The message Sarah had typed out explained everything Julie needed to know to trace the brothers' communications. If he spoke to her over the phone, she'd likely try to talk him out of his plan.

He knew it was far from the smartest idea in the world to take Sarah along with him, but what else could he do? It was either this, or let her go off on her own and put herself in God-knows-what kind of danger. At least with his idea, they stood the chance of identifying the brothers' informant, hopefully with little risk on Sarah's part. But as he hurtled along the motorway, he had regrets for not having just handcuffed her to a radiator in his flat while he went out to collect those machine guns.

Plan A would have been so much simpler.

—

By the time they got to the lay-by Drayce had spotted on the map, it was fully dark. A few miles from the farm, it was quiet and hidden from view by woodland on both the field side and the roadside. The lay-by fed off and onto a small B-road that ran west and east through a long stretch of the remotest part of the county. Sarah leant across the centre console as the pair examined a satellite image on Drayce's phone. She used the tip of a pen she'd found in the car to point out exactly where the farm was located. The satellite image showed the entire area separated into various farming plots for miles around, the borders denoted by lines of hedgerows in a darker green than the fields, all fitting together like a jigsaw. The Accountant's plot was in the shape of a slightly melted square, with the farmhouse in the centre.

A long driveway ran to the house from a main road to the south, but other than that, the perimeter was contained by other fields. Drayce examined the surrounding landscape and found what he was looking for: a dirt track on the far side of a line of trees to the north. He took the pen and talked her through his plan.

'Once I've set up the equipment close to the entrance, I want you to wait there, hidden in the undergrowth, while I take a wide arc around the plot through the fields, until I get to about here.' He used the pen to point to the dirt road north of the farm. 'They're bound to have cameras covering the gates at the entrance – big, obvious things, I'm guessing – and I'm betting they'll have sensors and hidden cameras set up around the perimeter. Once we're in position and ready, we'll use those cameras and sensors to our advantage. Sound good?'

Sarah nodded. 'Sounds good.'

Drayce noticed her legs and hands shake a little, no doubt the effects of the adrenaline surge through her system. 'Are you sure this is what you want?' he asked as he put a hand on her forearm. 'It's not too late to turn back.'

She shook her head vehemently. 'There's no turning back. I have to stand up to them. And you're right… identifying their informant is the best way to get rid of the threat they pose once and for all.' Voicing this appeared to raise her spirits. She stopped shaking and sat up straight. 'Let's do it.'

Drayce unplugged the pay-as-you-go phone and handed it to her, then they both climbed out of the car. He collected the two black nylon bags full of equipment from the boot, locked the vehicle, and placed the keys inside the exhaust pipe, just out of sight. With the amount of ground to cover on foot, the last thing he wanted was to risk dropping them in one of the fields, leaving them both stranded. Happy they had everything they'd need, he led the way for Sarah.

With the farm's entrance in sight, he told her to hunker down in the roadside ditch while he continued. The closer he got, the more delicate his steps, and the more aware he was of his shape, shine and silhouette, careful not to walk in view of the CCTV cameras mounted on either side of the gate. About fifteen metres away was as close as he dared to go. He removed some of the equipment from his bag and set it up in the undergrowth. Working mostly by touch – hard going in the faintest glimmer of moonlight – he got it all in place within a few minutes. He snapped a glow stick and dropped it in the grass verge to mark where the equipment was, then picked up the bags again and retraced his steps to Sarah.

'Take this,' he said, handing her one of the bags. 'Inside are the clothes and other things you'll need.' She took it from him without any hesitation, determination evident in her eyes despite the darkness. 'Keep hold of the phone, and when you feel it vibrate, move up to the equipment and switch it on. I've left it in the undergrowth for you, in line with a glow stick I placed on the grass verge. When you're done, run back to the lay-by. I'll meet you at the car when I've finished my part of the plan and we'll get out of here. Got it?'

She nodded and moved further into the ditch, squatting low as she clutched her new phone in her hands. Drayce threw the second bag over his shoulder and retraced their route before darting through the hedgerow and walking a wide arc around the perimeter of the farm's plot. At several locations along the route, he took torches from his bag and taped them to branches in the hedgerow at shoulder height. Each one he fixed to face the Accountant's farm, switching them on once he was happy they were secure.

Despite how boggy it was underfoot, and hard going because the hedgerows that separated the fields were difficult to push through, Drayce made good time, arriving at the dirt road to the north only twenty minutes after leaving Sarah. He slowed down when he had the perimeter of the Accountant's land in sight; using a line of trees as cover, he moved closer. The dirt track and treeline were higher than the Accountant's land, providing an elevated view of the plot.

The building was exactly what he'd expected: a large brick-built main house with a pitched roof and large windows and a courtyard about half the size of a football pitch at the back, leading to a row of stables and a large barn. A few lights were on in the house, and three powerful security lights illuminated the courtyard, but there were no signs of life. Mostly by touch, he made his way back to the dirt road, dumped his bag on the ground, and opened it.

He had ten blocks of lights – battery-powered disco lights, to be precise – fitted with a mixture of red and blue tints. He walked down the track, placing one in the centre of the muddy road every six paces, which he judged was roughly a big car's length between each one. The last block of lights in place, he turned around to face back up the road, squatted down, and took out his phone to call Sarah, ignoring two missed calls from Julie.

As the phone rang, he worked back, switching on each block, the night brought to life in bright strobes as the flashing lights lit up the treeline, in semblance of a hive of police activity along the dirt road. He cancelled the call as he ran back to the treeline and worked his way through the woodland until he had a clear view of the Accountant's home again. His only movement the rise and fall of his chest, he watched carefully for any signs of activity.

More blue and red lights strobed in the distance, visible for miles around in the darkness of the countryside. Sarah had successfully switched on the lighting equipment on her side of the farm, before slipping into the fake police jacket and cap he'd bought, and running up to the cameras at the gate to spray them with black paint, as planned. Far off to his left, the beams of the torches he'd set up swayed from side to side as the wind shook the branches. If he didn't know better, he might think those torches were gripped in the hands of a determined team of police officers, their arms swinging back and forth as they crossed the fields to the Accountant's boundary.

Would it be enough? Drayce wondered.

The entire concept was amateurish at best, but when he put himself in the Accountant's shoes, he thought it had a good chance of working. If he were guarding millions of pounds of cash for two of the most powerful criminals in the country – the only finances they had left that hadn't yet been seized by the authorities, making it all the more valuable – then he would probably be a little twitchy when it came to keeping it safe and out of the hands of the police. And if one night, while said criminals were locked up awaiting trial, he saw police lights at the front and back of his property, torchlights dancing around the fields, and a police officer blocking out the camera at the gates, would he calmly wait to clarify what was happening?

Or panic and raise the alarm, believing it was a raid?

Drayce knew what he'd be inclined to do in that man's shoes.

The hairs on the back of his neck warned him of something in the vicinity that didn't belong. It wasn't anything too threatening, not a footstep breaking twigs as a killer stalked him, but more mechanical, the grinding of gears: metal on metal with a dash of oil to smooth things along. He couldn't immediately identify its origin, but thought it came from somewhere amongst the Accountant's fields. He held his breath and tried to block out the wind howling in his ear by moving behind the shelter of a tree trunk.

He heard it again, louder this time.

His mind conjured images of what would make such a sound in the middle of empty fields in a remote stretch of countryside. Was it the brothers' employees in off-road vehicles, heading his way to investigate the lights and torches? It was certainly mechanical, but more of a persistent hum, rather than the ever-changing pitch of a vehicle's engine. He kept his eyes on the fields as a light appeared between his position and the Accountant's farmhouse.

Headlights? he asked himself.

No, his mind threw back at him. This was something else entirely.

He took a few steps forwards for a better view. The light grew stronger, a giant, steady beam slowly rising from the ground.

Was this it? Had his plan worked?

He stopped just a few metres past the treeline, gazing across the Accountant's land in wonder, as he saw something on a scale he could never have imagined in his wildest dreams.

34

Stan walked through the automatic doors that led outside to the helipads, the others following behind. Leo and Freddie limped along, doing their best to mask the pain from their injuries; they'd received some off-the-books treatment from a consultant on the firm's payroll, but he was a doctor, not a magician, so they were still hurting. Marcus's arm was held in a sling, his face now clean of blood, nose reset and bandaged like a mummy. Chrissy and Daz were the only ones walking with the confident gait of the uninjured.

Outside, they were surrounded by the bright lights of the heliport, located on the south bank of the Thames, just opposite Chelsea Harbour. A T-shaped platform extended into the river with a giant letter H painted on its surface, crashing waves beating the pillars beneath. In the dark sky, a bright cluster of lights gradually approached the platform. The six men stood still and watched carefully.

After Stan's phone call to him, Rupert reported the problem would be discussed during the scheduled visit to the prison that day, and that he should wait for a message with the brothers' orders. That message arrived within a few hours, telling them to be at the heliport at six o'clock to meet the help that had been arranged.

As the black helicopter flew out of the darkness, its outline taking shape amongst the bright lights that decorated it, Stan felt his breath whipped away from him as the downdraft swirled all around him. He shielded his mouth with his hand to help him draw breath, his eyes never once leaving the aircraft, wondering about the men aboard. Rupert had assured him the Russians had a great incentive for helping to bring all of this to a neat conclusion.

The helicopter touched down, the men on board not bothering to wait for the rotors to stop. The side door slid open and out poured six men, ducking low as they jogged over to Stan, each one with a peaked cap on his head and a rucksack on his back. They had the bearing of the young and fit, somewhere in their twenties perhaps, dressed in the kind of rugged outdoor clothing reminiscent of a bunch of soldiers on leave. Stan studied them as they approached, wondering who the hell Rupert had sent him.

'You work for mutual friend, yes?' the man at the front of the group shouted to make himself heard over the noise of the aircraft. He had messy dark hair spilling out from underneath his cap, above a jawline that could have been carved from granite.

'Yeah,' Stan replied, watching him carefully.

'You want help with mission, yes?'

'Yes, very much so.'

Their formidable presence, coupled with a closer look at the guy at the front, made it clear that Stan's first impression of the group had been fairly accurate; they were ex-military for sure. Their youthful physiques, however, had less to do with age, and more to do with the punishing exercise routine they undoubtedly followed. Crow's feet creased the corners of the man's watchful eyes; he was far older and more experienced than Stan had initially given him credit for. He'd heard of Russian gangs employing former soldiers, such as Spetsnaz operators, but he'd never actually seen it with his own eyes. Rupert had done well.

'We leave now,' the Russian said. 'No time to waste.'

Stan nodded. 'Yeah, all right, mate, but we need to get you some weapons first. I've got a lock-up across—'

'No.' The man readjusted his rucksack. 'We have our own.'

Stan glanced around the group and for the first time noticed the straps digging hard into their shoulders. There was some real weight to those rucksacks.

'All right,' Stan said as he turned to leave. 'Let's go.'

As he led the way back across the heliport, his phone beeped. A message from the Accountant. What he read made him stop dead.

'The farm's being raided,' he said.

The others gathered around him.

'Are you taking the piss?' Chrissy asked.

Stan glared at him. 'Do you think I'd joke about something like that?'

'She must have told the police about what she saw in those journals,' Leo said.

'Or Dominic's let us down,' Marcus suggested.

'Nah,' Stan said. 'He'd know about it as soon as Sarah opened her mouth, and with what's at stake for him, he'd tell us straight away.' He re-read the message, shaking his head. 'Something's not right.'

'What do you mean?' Freddie asked.

'I want to go and see for myself whether or not there's a raid.'

'Are you mad?' Marcus said. 'Can I remind you we're currently wanted men? I don't think driving past a location that's swarming with police officers is a very good idea, do you?'

'But that's just it, Marcus, I don't think it is. Something else is going on, and I want to know what.'

'What are you suggesting?' Chrissy asked. 'That we just drive past the gates and look out of the window? Not very subtle, is it, Stanley?'

Overhearing the conversation, the leader of the Russians placed a hand on Stan's shoulder.

'I know a better way,' he said.

35

Drayce backed up to the treeline and hunkered down on one knee, making sure he was out of sight amongst the foliage as he watched the earth come alive.

At first, he couldn't believe his eyes. The ground opened up in the middle of a field, a thin beam of light spilling out, the first visual sign as the crack appeared as though it was a portal to hell. A giant trapdoor, the glare from within more prominent as it rose higher, radiating across the fields and lighting up everything in front of him.

As his eyes adjusted to the brightness, he identified support beams at the front corners, a hydraulic set-up pushing it open and revealing a rectangular hole he estimated to be the size of a football pitch. A metallic support structure at the mouth of the opening lined the walls of a tunnel with triangulated beams, to give integrity to the underground network and stop it from collapsing in on itself.

His plan had worked: the Accountant had initiated the evacuation.

Another noise erupted from within the tunnel, echoing off into the distant night: the whine of a powerful jet preparing to take off. Drayce watched with amazement as a large cargo plane flew out of the opening, its wheels lifting as it climbed steadily into the night sky.

Soon the plane was nothing more than blinking lights amongst the stars, and the trapdoor gradually lowered to ground level, sucking the light away and returning the fields to the quiet, dark scene they had presented just minutes ago.

Drayce stayed still, down on one knee, waiting for his eyes to adjust to the darkness sufficiently for him to move without tripping over a root or bumping into a tree. He pushed himself up off the ground, went back to the dirt road, and switched off each block of lights, before retracing his route back to the main road.

He ran, wanting to get across the fields and back to the car to meet Sarah as fast as possible. Once they were both out of danger, he'd call Julie to find out if she'd picked up any communications from the brothers in prison.

Only then would he know whether his plan had truly worked.

—

Seven men in the Russians' helicopter was a tight squeeze.

There was enough room for one extra passenger and Stan had taken it, leaving the others behind in London; they were following to the farm in the Mercedes and the Audi. Stan mapped the helicopter's progress during the first part of the journey, quite easy given the huge network of streetlights around London and its satellite towns. All he had to do was look down at the ground to judge quite accurately where they were. He told the pilot to follow the motorway that headed northeast, its lights snaking off into the distance as far as the eye could see.

However, now that they were closing in on rural Essex, things were a little trickier, a little darker. There weren't anywhere near as many sources of light for him to keep track of their progress now that the motorway had ended. The pilot's navigator handed him a map and asked him to mark precisely where the farm was, so he could cross-reference it to the aircraft's navigation system. They were approaching their destination. Stan moved his headset microphone closer to his lips and spoke to the navigator.

'Hover above the area I showed you and you should see a large house with outbuildings in the centre of the plot.' The navigator gave the thumbs up. 'Good. Do you have night vision?' Another thumbs up, before producing a monitor for the helicopter's camera with his other hand. Stan took it and examined the farm's plot in the green tinge. He zoomed in on the farmhouse, impressed with the clarity of the picture. The lens on the camera was state of the art, the house almost as clear as in daylight.

These Russians sure aren't short of a bob or two, he thought to himself.

From their position, only the front of the main house was visible, so he asked the pilot to circle the buildings slowly, allowing him enough time to examine each aspect.

As the aircraft banked round, he felt increasingly confused by what he could see, or rather, what he couldn't see. There was nobody in sight, not a soul, and no sign of any vehicles. The only thing that stood out was the glare through the windows from the lights in the house. If what the Accountant had told him was true, he should be staring down at an army of coppers swarming the entire premises by now. He frowned at the monitor. His suspicions were right: something was definitely wrong.

'There's a hedgerow marking the perimeter of the plot,' he said to the navigator as he leant forwards and pointed at the screen. 'You see this right here? Follow it so we can search the fields and the surrounding land.'

'What are we looking for?' the navigator asked.

Stan lifted the monitor to within inches of his nose, the glow from the screen illuminating his face, his eyes wide as he searched for signs of life.

'Anything that doesn't belong here,' he replied.

36

Drayce made difficult progress through the fields. He'd nearly stumbled twice on his journey back, the uneven ground difficult to negotiate in the dim moonlight. He pushed on as fast as conditions allowed, navigating mostly from memory, wanting to limit the number of times he checked the map on his phone because the bright screen diminished his vision in the darkness. On a few occasions when he crossed ditches, he got lucky and spotted the outline of boot-prints in the thick mud, their damp surface reflecting the moonlight; he recognised the outline as his own, confident he was retracing his route successfully. He also found the holes he'd created in the hedgerows when he'd pushed through them earlier on, and from memory, he had only two more fields to cross before he reached the road with the lay-by.

Just as he picked up his pace, his desire to get back to Sarah forcing his legs to work even harder, he heard something in the sky and looked up to see the flashing lights of an aircraft heading for the Accountant's farmhouse. He stopped running and distinctly heard the tell-tale *thud-thud-thud* of a helicopter's rotors. He watched it for a moment and saw it slow and hover above the farm, his anxiety mounting. He took out his phone to ask Julie if it was the NCA or the police, and to call Sarah to make sure she was back at the car, ready to leave, but he put it away when the screen illuminated. No signal.

It can't be the police, because they don't know the farm exists.

So who was it?

The lights moved. Drayce watched it circle the farmhouse before following the perimeter and the surrounding land, which would bring it his way in no time at all.

Not good.

With his heart pounding, he turned back to the road and legged it. He didn't know who was in that helicopter, but whoever it was, they had a connection to the farm, the Accountant, and the Marlowe brothers, and he wanted nothing to do with them.

At the other side of the next field, he ran head-on through the hedgerow, ignoring the thorns and branches tearing his clothing and cutting his hands and face, feeling none of it, adrenaline coursing through him. As he sprinted across the last field, he checked the lights moving fast in the sky behind him as they swept around the perimeter, banking off to the side in a sudden movement, before they settled on a direct trajectory.

Towards him.

Summoning reserves he didn't know he had, he tore towards a hedgerow maybe fifty metres away, the helicopter chasing him. The hedge was ten seconds away from him on a good day, in trainers, on a hard, flat surface. In boots, on tired legs, through a muddy field... Determined not to look back, he concentrated ahead instead, those rotors getting closer and closer.

The world around him changed from night to day as a powerful searchlight lit him up from above. The aircraft roared overhead, so low to the ground, the downdraft nearly blew him off his feet. Its menacing shape came to life as it banked around to face him, before gently landing in the field.

With his route cut off, he darted to the right and ran to the nearest hedgerow, aiming to reach the ditch at the field's edge before the crew disembarked. The skids sank in the mud, the searchlight operator no longer able to rotate it; the beam of light fixed straight ahead, Drayce disappeared into the darkness. He slid into the ditch just as he heard what he thought might be the side doors sliding open, and immediately lay with his chest flat to the earth to keep himself hidden from view.

A shiver rocked his entire body as he partially immersed himself in the several inches of filthy drainage water in the ditch. Several torchlights lit up the lip of grassy earth and hedgerow above him as the helicopter crew tried to get him back in view. He crawled on his stomach, wading with his arms and legs through the mud and water, until there were no longer any torchlights above him. Keeping low, he inched to his feet and crept his head above the lip of the ditch to view who had alighted the helicopter.

He didn't like what he saw.

Seven figures headed to the spot where he'd dived into cover, moving rapidly. He watched the dark, menacing figures carefully as they got closer to the ditch. More details came into focus: all fit, strong men, moving at a speed, experienced in chasing people over rough terrain; the distinctive bulk of plain black heavy-duty body armour visible on their torsos, with no police markings or insignia; their torches, held out in front of them, ramrod straight, indicated they were mounted to something large and solid, held steady in their hands.

Long-barrelled assault rifles, he presumed.

Feeling the same rush he'd always felt when he knew a fight was on the cards, he backed off along the ditch, hoping to reach the road before they saw him. His hopes dashed when the men slowed down to a walk just a few metres away from the edge, before spreading out in a long line to cover the entire length of the ditch with their guns.

He ducked down before torchlight reflected in his eyes. He stayed low and stopped moving, aware he'd been making a lot of noise squelching through the thick mud to make ground. A barked command – perhaps Russian, he thought – and they moved again, the torchlight on their guns getting brighter as they drew closer.

Drayce ran through his options, and he wasn't keen on any of them. These people obviously worked for the Marlowe brothers, and effectively had him surrounded. He couldn't move any further along the ditch because they'd hear, and if he tried to get out to make a run for it, they had the space and time to gun him down easily. Escape at this point was unachievable and he wasn't persuaded popping his head up with his hands in the air in surrender would work in these circumstances.

Which, unfortunately, meant there was only one other way to go.

At the sound of boots trampling through mud just above the lip of the ditch, Drayce tensed his legs. He looked up, pressed his chest against the muddy embankment, and slowly raised his hands. While he waited, he heard more chatter, definitely Russian, but quieter this time because they undoubtedly knew they were gaining on him. Rustling clothes indicated they were close enough. He kept his eyes on the lip of the ditch as he listened, and squatted down until his thighs were parallel to the ground.

When the first torch appeared above him, he launched his upper body out of the ditch, took hold of the weapon with one hand, latched onto the man's groin with the other, and pulled him into the ditch. It happened so fast, by the time it registered that a giant creature covered in mud had dragged one of their men underground, Drayce was well underway with the next part of his hastily formed plan.

Having fallen backwards into the shallow, muddy water, pulling the gunman on top of him, face to face, he wrapped his legs around the man's waist and clinched his neck, using his body as a shield as they were lit up by the other torches. He felt a pistol holstered to the man's hip and reached for it, feeling for the retention clip and then the grip, before drawing it and aiming at the nearest torch.

Bright flashes lit up the ditch as he shot at anything that moved. The man on top of him let out an angry roar, the whites of his eyes prominent in the darkness, glaring at him from just a few inches away, above white teeth clenched hard as he strained to free himself. But Drayce's focus was beyond those eyes and teeth: he took a shot every time someone peered into the ditch, impatient to get out from underneath his hostage, steal his assault rifle, and make a break for it.

A sudden, sharp pain in his left arm made him drop the pistol. His opponent had created enough room to draw a knife from somewhere and slash Drayce's upper arm. A split second later, the man's other fist flew out of the darkness and cracked Drayce on his jaw, rocking his head so far back, it was almost submerged in the mud and water. In a panic, he let go of the man's neck and gripped onto his knife-wielding arm to limit the damage, the blade glinting in the moonlight as it danced in the air above him. He sat up and wrapped the man's arm in a double wrist lock, bending the limb back in a way nature did not intend; about to twist the man's elbow and shoulder joints out of their sockets, he heard a loud splash to his right, then one to his left, as two figures landed in the ditch. Before he could react, something hard and unforgiving hit him across his temple. Bright stars filled his vision and a light-headedness overcame him. Warm liquid ran down his face with the urgency of water from a broken tap. He let go of the man's arm and covered his head in time to absorb the next blow, and the one after that. Then hands were around his neck, and boots on his face, pushing his head underwater.

Drayce held his breath as the other man wrestled his way out from between his legs, and then a whole barrage of punches, kicks, and stomps rained down on every part of his body. He hinged his hips and kicked to the side, fighting his way above the water line to take a breath, not suffocate, and stay in the fight. He curled into a ball, protecting his head and vital organs, expecting the edge of a cold blade against his throat, or the flash of a muzzle reflected in the surface of the water.

The beating stopped.

A strong hand gripped his hair and pulled up his head and shoulders, his arms seized by more hands and pinned to his sides.

With one eye swelling, he peered gingerly out of the other at the shadowy figures of the men crowding him in the ditch. Another, who squatted down near the lip, stared from above, switched on a torch, lighting up the grisly scene and the man's face. A face he recognised.

'Well, well,' the man said through a twisted grin that dominated his expression. 'Didn't expect to find you all the way out here.' He turned his head from right to left, theatrically, as though he was looking for something. His missing ear confirmed the man's identity. 'You hiding that lady friend of yours somewhere near here? I bet you are. Maybe if you tell me where she is, my mates here will go easy on you. How does that sound?'

Drayce spat a mouthful of blood into the ditch; his fierce glare told Stan West exactly how that sounded.

Another hard blow struck him to the back of his head. He stayed conscious just long enough to feel all seven of them struggling to drag his body out of the ditch, before his eyes rolled back into his head and he slipped gratefully into a pain-free unconsciousness.

37

Julie cancelled the call and dropped her phone onto the kitchen counter in anger. Four times she'd tried to call Alex, and he'd ignored every single one of those attempts. After attempt number three, she'd contacted her office and requested them to trace his phone. Still waiting for an answer, she walked through to the living room and picked up her pizza box from the scratched and chipped wooden coffee table in front of her, stained with water rings from spilt mugs of tea and coffee drunk by the countless witnesses who had stayed there. She sat down in an armchair opposite Fiona, perched on the edge of the big three-seater sofa with another uninspiring salad box. Julie picked up a slice of pizza – pepperoni with extra cheese – folded it in half lengthwise, and bit off a huge chunk at the tip of the triangle, willing Alex to see the missed calls and ring her back.

They'd gone to one of the many safe houses in the city at the NCA's disposal; somewhere private to kill time, eat dinner and wait to hear from Alex, as well as Brian. Julie had called Brian after she'd read Alex's message, asking him to alert the surveillance team that the Marlowe brothers would be contacting someone from prison tonight. The house wasn't in use, so no chance of being interrupted while they waited.

More importantly, it was private, secure, and not NCA headquarters, where they had every chance of running into Foster, someone Julie was keen to avoid. Although if things went to plan, that might change once she'd heard back from

Brian and Alex. If Alex was right, they might be close to identifying the brothers' informant and solid evidence to show Foster to make him take the notion of a corrupt officer more seriously.

'How long are we going to wait here?' Fiona asked, shivering as her eyes scanned the cold, sparsely furnished front room of the terraced house in Bethnal Green, picking at a mound of wilted lettuce.

'As long as we need to,' Julie replied through a mouthful of pizza. 'I don't want to risk bumping into Foster until I've heard from Alex.' She finished the slice, put the pizza box back on the coffee table, and wiped her hands and face with a napkin. 'The message he sent gave me the impression he was onto something.'

'But the message didn't tell you what that something was?'

Julie shook her head.

'And he hasn't answered your calls since?'

Julie's anxiety ramped up. 'That's right.'

'What about that phone call you made to Brian? Was that connected to what Alex told you?'

'Yeah, he wanted me to pass a message on to the surveillance team watching the Marlowe brothers.'

Fiona sighed. 'Sarah's obviously been talking to him about the case.'

Julie nodded. 'Inevitable, I suppose. He thinks whatever he's going to do will cause the brothers to contact their informant from prison. God knows why.' She checked her watch as a larger knot formed in her stomach. 'It's already seven o'clock. I was expecting to hear back from him by now.'

'Maybe it's worth calling him again? We need to know what he's up to, or at the very least, speak to Sarah to make sure everything's okay.'

'Yeah,' Julie said, knowing that trying so soon after the last attempt would be a waste of time. 'Maybe.'

Fiona raised her eyebrows. 'There's no harm in trying.'

Julie nodded, and motivated by Fiona's encouragement, stood up from her chair to go to the kitchen. Her phone rang and she ran to snatch it off the counter. Her heart sank when she saw it wasn't Alex.

'Chris, what's up?'

'Julie, hi, I just wanted to give you an update regarding the investigation here in Suffolk.'

'Yeah, okay.' To say Julie was a little disappointed was an understatement. 'What have you got?'

'You all right? You don't sound too happy.'

She walked back into the living room, shook her head solemnly, and mouthed 'not him' at Fiona, who gave her a reassuring smile back.

'I'm fine, really. I'm just waiting for an important call back from Alex, that's all.' She tapped the screen of her phone to switch it to speaker and laid it down on the coffee table next to the pizza box before reclaiming her seat. 'What's the update?'

'Well, there's been an interesting turn of events down here. You remember me telling you about PC Moss's burned-to-a-crisp body?'

'Yes, I remember. What of it?'

'Well, I've just had a briefing from the SIO, who just minutes before had received the results of the autopsy. And guess what.'

Julie pulled a face at Fiona. 'Spit it out, Chris. I'm not in the mood for playing guessing games.'

'Okay, here goes: it's not him.'

Julie leapt to her feet, picked up her phone, lifting it right up to her mouth. She caught a glimpse of Fiona in the corner of her eye, who appeared every bit as shocked as she was. 'What did you just say?'

'You heard me,' Chris said, gleeful in his revelation. 'The body recovered from that house, with the engraved watch, the police warrant card, and the police-issue firearm, is not that of PC Daniel Moss.'

'Well, then who the hell is it?'

'Unidentified at the moment, unless they get something back from dental or DNA.' Chris paused for a second, then said, 'You know what this means, right?'

'Yes. It means someone planted PC Moss's ID card, watch, and firearm on a dead body, and left it to burn in the inferno, presumably as a way of trying to make the police believe he'd died in the fire.'

'Correct. Which means the next question is—'

'Where the hell is Daniel Moss?' Julie asked, finishing the sentence for him.

The smell might have been the worst of the prison's qualities in Rupert's opinion, but for Francis, it was the noise. During the day, the entire establishment echoed with the activities of the population: shouts, arguments, banter, and insults, culminating in spontaneous bursts of sickening cruelty, alongside the uninterrupted jangling of keys and slamming of heavy metal doors. Even during the hours of darkness, there was no peace. Despite having a cell to himself, Francis was regularly woken by the crying of a new inmate, followed by the loud mocking and jeering from the more institutionalised individuals on the wing.

Tonight would be no different, he thought as he lay back on his bed and stared at the blank grey ceiling above him. He closed his eyes and contemplated his current situation – a familiar routine of an evening – fantasising gleefully about the moment in which he would be told of Sarah's death, thus relieving the Crown Prosecution Service of their remaining witness. These revenge fantasies were the only pleasures he'd enjoyed in the hell of his confinement.

A knock at the door made him sit up; visitors were the last thing he wanted or expected at this time of the evening. The entire wing knew this, which meant an interruption to his evening routine must be important. He turned to the doorway and saw his brother, Nathan. He swung his feet to the ground and stood to face him.

'I've got someone here you're gonna want to speak to,' Nathan said.

'Who?'

Nathan stepped aside and turned to face the man standing behind him. Jonny Curtis waddled into the gap and stood in front of the glare of the two brothers. A weak, pathetic vision, Francis thought, short, fat, and about as ugly as a man with only one head could be. Francis, as usual, was not pleased to see him.

'What do you want?' he asked.

'You've got a message,' Jonny replied. 'On the phone you gave me to look after.'

A nervous tingling fluttered within Francis's chest; it was doubtful a message sent to that phone would be good news. It was purely for emergencies, with all other communications handled via Rupert in a private, secure setting, just the way Francis wanted it. He hated using phones; the interconnectedness of modern technology made it far too easy for the authorities to eavesdrop on conversations. At times he'd feared his resistance to technology had held his criminal empire back, but when the NCA had busted a number of his contemporaries following their infiltration of EncroChat in 2020, he'd been glad of his wariness.

For that reason, a great deal of effort had gone into keeping that phone a secret. Hiding it in either his or his brother's cell was far too risky, despite having a handful of guards in their pockets. Regular searches were the norm for prisoners of their notoriety. They'd had to come up with an idea for how to safely store something so important. Replacing phones seized by guards wasn't an issue, there were hundreds of them circulating around the prison. The issue was getting the new number to the Accountant.

To resolve this, Francis made an arrangement with chubby little Jonny – a minor league criminal who was always eager to bum-lick his way into the favour of the big players – who guaranteed the phone would always be charged, switched on, and in a place the guards would never be keen to look.

'You sure?' Francis asked.

Jonny was hesitancy personified. Everyone in Francis's life was wary of delivering bad news to him. He understood why.

'Yeah, pretty sure,' Jonny eventually said. 'The vibration setting's whacked all the way up.'

Francis unfolded his arms and dropped them down to his sides, his hands clenched into fists, his knuckles as white as his complexion.

'I need to read that message,' he said.

Jonny didn't move straight away, presumably because he was unsure whether to go back to his own cell to retrieve it, or there, in front of Francis.

Nathan clarified. 'Get a fucking move on then,' he said, shoving Jonny to the toilet bowl.

Eager to please the two most powerful criminals, not just on the wing but in the entire prison, Jonny dutifully shuffled over to the toilet in the corner of the room, untying the drawstring on his tracksuit bottoms.

Nathan walked out of the cell to keep an eye on the wing for approaching guards. Francis walked up to Jonny, stood with his arms folded, and watched him, taking in the nervous, frightened expression on his face, as though unsure whether he would be able to produce the goods. With Jonny's joggers and filthy skid-marked underwear around his ankles, he stood with the toilet bowl behind him and squatted down. Francis kept up the pressure and stared at him the entire time.

Exasperated after more than a minute of waiting to hear the *plop*, Francis barked at him to get on with it. Red-faced and sweating, Jonny reached around behind him and delved his hand into the bowl, reaching inside himself to encourage things along. After another minute, he groaned and pulled his arm back, the smile of a victor spread widely across his face. In his hand was a small rectangular package, wrapped tightly in cling film. He held it out to Francis.

The look he got wiped the smile off his face.

'Have you lost your mind?' Francis asked him.

'Sorry,' he replied, reeling his arm back in. 'I'll wash it.'

The package cleaned, Jonny unwrapped it to reveal an old Nokia phone hidden underneath. He left it on the edge of the sink, switched on, with the screen facing up. Jonny stepped back and childishly played with the drawstrings on his tracksuit bottoms as he waited expectantly, eagerly anticipating a pat on the head.

Francis scrutinised him with all the affection a gardener has for an unexpected cat turd. 'Fuck off then,' he said, and watched as the little man scurried out of his cell, shoulders slumped and head bowed.

Francis read the message, touching the phone as little as possible. A hot flush suffused his face, a panic sweat breaking out across his forehead. He put the phone down, took a moment to gather himself, then called his brother back in and told him what was in the message.

'Impossible,' Nathan said.

Francis's discipline prevented him from wasting time with denial like his brother. 'It's not impossible though, is it, brother? It is, in fact, the opposite of impossible. It's everything we've feared since we learned that bitch had read Dad's journal.'

'But what about the informant?' Nathan countered. 'It shouldn't have got this far! As soon as the police found out about the farm, we should have been told!'

Francis removed his glasses and rubbed his face with the hand that hadn't touched the phone. 'I agree, but it appears we've been let down.'

Nathan punched the solid cell wall, his giant meaty fist slapping against the painted concrete, indistinguishable from a raw joint of beef that fell off a kitchen counter and landed on a tiled floor.

'It's not good enough, Francis. All that work, all those deals. Everything we have left is on that farm!'

Francis examined his red-faced brother carefully. 'Calm yourself. These emotional flare-ups of yours are of no use while we're trapped in here. We just have to hope that all the money was flown out of there in time. Remember, the entire location is set up precisely with this eventuality in mind. It's what our father planned for.'

'So that's it? We just sit here in hope?'

Francis turned to the phone. 'Not exactly.'

He put his glasses back on, opened a blank new message, typed out what he wanted to send, and then keyed in the number stored in his head and nowhere else.

38

The pain hit Drayce with a sledgehammer before he'd even opened his eyes.

It started in his head as a piercing ache that felt as though an ice-pick had been rammed down his ear, then as a throbbing sensation across his entire face – his nose and cheeks had a heartbeat of their own – before showing up all over his arms and legs, which would no doubt be covered in horrific bruises. The tight sensation across the skin on his face and neck, he took to be crusty dried blood from the split to his scalp.

As he gradually regained more consciousness, he had the distinct feeling he was in a hard, unforgiving chair, with a series of vertical struts in the back support, the edges of which dug into the blunt trauma injuries along his spinal column. He tried to move his arms, but the tight, sticky resistance of thick insulation tape bound his wrists together.

A warm sensation trickled down his left arm as the knife wound opened a little wider after trying to move. Only his right eye obeyed the order to open; the other felt as big as a cricket ball. His equilibrium was so out of tune, he hadn't realised his head was slumped, chin on chest. Lifting it fired up a horrific sensation from the base of his neck into his brain: an electric shock firing pulses into the back of his eyes. He'd been in some fierce fights in his time, but never before had he received a beating on this scale.

But you're still alive, he told himself. *So make use of it.*

Taking it slowly, he brought his head up, a forceful and potent feeling of nausea surging. Then, with his good eye, he surveyed his surroundings.

'Wakey, wakey.'

The speaker stood ten feet away, and even with his compromised vision, Drayce recognised the shadowy profile of Stan West: the hitman with the missing ear. Six other men, three on Drayce's right and three on his left, fanned out in a V-shape, stared at him with their arms folded in front of their chests, the whites of their eyes prominent from within their balaclavas. Not exactly the friendliest of welcomes.

Apart from the group of men, and the chair Drayce sat on, the room was empty. The walls, constructed of wooden slats, old and poorly maintained, had mould and rot infecting the surface. The wind whistled through the gaps, corroborating they were in one of the farmhouse's outbuildings, an old barn which, from his memory of the view from the edge of the woodland, was accessed from the courtyard at the rear of the property.

He shivered in the cold air, his body convulsing as he did so; stripped of his jacket and sweater – presumably as they'd searched him for weapons – the muscles on his bare torso broke out in goosebumps. As his body shook, his boots scraped on the rough concrete floor. He watched his warm breath rise into the air: three large fluorescent light tubes hung end to end along the centre of the pitched roof, each one sheltered from above by a sheet of curved metal that reflected the light onto the group of men casting their shadows in Drayce's direction.

Stan walked to Drayce and bent down, his face centimetres away.

'I've been looking for you all day long,' Stan said, with what Drayce could only presume was an attempt at a smile. 'I want to know where Sarah is, and you're gonna tell me. Whether it's in a few minutes, or a few hours from now, eventually you'll tell me what I want to know. And I'll be honest with you… seeing the state you're in, I don't think you'll last long.'

He grabbed Drayce's head with his right hand and dug his thumb into the badly swollen eye. Drayce screamed at the top of his lungs, writhing, straining his head away. He stamped his feet on the ground and rocked back, throwing himself to the floor out of the sadist's reach.

The drastic action worked, mercifully, but numerous hands soon pulled him back up. Stan towered above him, laughing. Someone stood behind him, holding the chair in place to prevent him from pulling the same trick a second time. Panic overwhelmed him as Stan grabbed hold of his head again, flexing his thumb in preparation for inflicting more torture. A vicious growl burst out from deep within Drayce's chest when the tip of the man's nail touched his eyelid.

But then the door swung wide open, and Stan let go of his head as he addressed the newcomers. 'You boys have made good time.'

'Easy to ignore speed cameras when you can swap number plates regularly,' one of them replied. Drayce's good eye followed the voice and saw Stan's sidekick from the cafe, Marcus Bone.

'Eager to get here and join in the fun, weren't we fellas?' another said.

Drayce turned his head slightly, the blond hair and shadowy eyes coming into focus. Freddie Dawes.

'Yeah, well, you're here just in time for the good bit,' Stan said.

'The best bit,' another said, a man nearly as big as Stan with a thick scar on his left cheek.

'The bit we've all been waiting for.' This from someone else Drayce didn't recognise. He was younger and slighter than the others, with short, dark, curly hair.

'You found him,' Leo Durham said, clocking Drayce as he brought up the rear with a limp to his gait. 'Good work.'

'Spotted him from the helicopter,' Stan said, scowling at Drayce, utter contempt on his face. 'Skulking around in the fields not far from here, like a snake. I knew something strange was going on.'

Drayce heard the door swing open again on its squeaky hinges, calmer this time. An elderly man with a crooked back, in obvious pain, hobbled into Drayce's view. Dressed in beige trousers, with a white shirt under a grey cardigan, he wasn't a day younger than eighty, perhaps ninety on closer inspection. He hobbled as he walked, a wooden stick in his left hand for support. Wispy strands of white hair decorated his scalp, and his deformed fingers, clamped onto his walking stick, gave testimony to arthritis in more places than just his back. The Accountant, Drayce realised. Too old and disabled to fly the plane himself, someone else with the necessary qualifications and experience had been employed to live at the farm. Maybe more than one. Perhaps a small group of them, spending time at the farm in shifts so there was always someone ready to fly the cash to safety.

'You were tricked, old man,' Stan said, still glaring at Drayce. 'This prick here did a good job of making you think the farm was surrounded by the police.' He turned, walked to the shadows at the back of the room, and picked up Drayce's bag.

'He used this lot,' Stan said, dumping the contents on the floor for everyone to see. The lighting equipment fell to the ground, clattering loudly on the concrete. 'Had it all set up at the back of the farm.' He picked up one of the blocks of lights, examined it for a moment, and then tossed it back on the floor. 'You sneaky, sneaky bastard.'

The Accountant slowly staggered to Stan, who bent down for the old man to whisper something in his ear.

'Don't worry about that, old boy. They'll understand it wasn't your fault,' Stan said. He turned to face Drayce. 'It's this one they'll want to punish. Stick around if you want. You can watch us kick the shit out of him.' He left the Accountant's side and walked up to Drayce, bending down so they were nose to nose. 'I can see you're hurting, but I really don't give a shit.'

He pointed at his own disfigured jaw. 'This thing has been screaming at me all day long because of you, so I'd say I've got a score to settle, wouldn't you?' He flicked his head at the rest of the gang. 'As have those boys. And the only chance you've got of making the pain stop, is if you tell me where Sarah is.'

Drayce's fierce eyes and hard, unforgiving expression broadcasted what he thought, but to make his feelings truly known he spat a mouthful of blood down at his feet in a show of defiance.

'Fine,' Stan said. 'If that's how you want it, that's how you'll get it.' He turned to face the Russians. 'You lot get back in that chopper and search further out. She'll be somewhere nearby. He wouldn't have left her far away.'

The six men who'd beaten Drayce in the ditch nodded their heads and jogged out of the barn. He heard the aircraft's engine start up from somewhere outside.

'Gather round, boys,' Stan said to the remaining five. 'It's time for us to even things up with this slag, don't you think?' He tossed his phone to the Accountant. 'Record this next part for me, would you? I've got a feeling this'll be so much fun that I'll want to watch it over and over again.'

The six of them approached Drayce with their fists clenched. As he prepared for another beating, he hoped Sarah had taken the initiative and fled the area, on foot if need be, when he'd failed to return to the lay-by. He couldn't stomach the thought of what might happen to her if she hadn't.

As the shadows of the men reached him, he spotted the Accountant in the background, filming the grisly scene unfolding in front of him, certain he saw a faint smile edge across the old man's wrinkled and bitter face.

39

Sarah was back at the lay-by, digging her nails into her palm as panic set in.

He's not coming back, she kept telling herself. You're on your own, in a car you don't know how to drive. What the hell are you going to do?

She'd retrieved the keys from the exhaust pipe and settled in the passenger seat, hoping he would appear through the darkness. After everything he'd done for her, she owed it to him to wait. But for how long? He should have been back by now. He should have been back over half an hour ago, if she was brutally honest. Her eyes regularly darted from her watch to the treeline, telling herself she'd give him just another minute before she had to think of something.

But she was still there, watching for movement, praying he would appear, the situation increasingly desperate. She'd even considered getting in the driver's seat and trying to operate the damn thing herself, but after staring at the pedals and steering wheel for five long minutes, she'd make that a last resort.

Of course, there might have been a perfectly innocent reason for his late return, Sarah told herself. He was navigating in the dark, after all, across unfamiliar terrain. It was perfectly reasonable to assume he'd simply taken a wrong turn, delaying him enough to leave her waiting. But after recent events, her mind rarely latched onto the positive explanation.

Terrible, violent scenes took shape in her mind as she imagined what it might have taken to stop Alex from returning on time. Guilt seized hold as she took ownership of the fact it was she who'd forced him to come up with this crazy plan.

This is your fault, you idiot. This was all your idea. We should have just stayed in the flat as Alex said. Oh Alex, what on earth has happened to you?

Lights in the sky caught her attention, flashing, and moving at speed, low flying, darting one way and then the other as though searching for something. At first, she thought it might be the plane returning, but it more closely resembled a helicopter, considering the rapid movements. She watched it cross the fields on the other side of the road, following a wide arc that would eventually bring it around to the lay-by.

Was it the same one she'd seen circling the farm earlier?

If so, it was highly likely connected to the people who worked for her brothers, which meant as those lights in the sky drew closer, her thoughts as to who might be in control of them were making driving away in the car a more and more desirable option.

She climbed out and walked around to the driver's side, thinking she should at least get a feel for it. The steering wheel felt awkward in her hands as she gripped it and pulled it around, first one way, then the other. It was hard work and took all her effort to turn it even a little.

Is this how driving feels for everyone? she wondered. Can't be. It must be something Alex chose. He'd be one of the few people strong enough to turn this thing for more than a few minutes.

The pedals felt in the way, but she guessed that was the point. Wouldn't be much good if they were out of reach. She could only see two, thinking to herself she was sure there should be three.

This is ridiculous. You can't control this thing safely. Get back in the passenger seat and wait for Alex.

She opened her door to the hum of the helicopter circling in the sky, somewhere across the fields near the Accountant's farm. The interior light of the car came on, a beacon in the dark wilderness. She slammed the door shut again. What if that was them? What if they knew they'd been tricked and were out searching for the people responsible? Maybe she'd messed up and they'd recognised her from the cameras at the gates?

Alex isn't coming back any time soon, she told herself sternly. *And you're no good sitting on your backside in this lay-by. Go get some help.*

Julie would know what to do, but her number was in Alex's phone, which he had on him. Perhaps the time had come for Sarah to call the police? Alex had been dead against that idea because of how far he suspected her brothers' informant could reach, but what other choice did she have now? If he was in trouble, then he needed more help than she could offer on her own. She had to ring 999 and take her chances, for Alex's sake. But first, she had to get away from whoever was in that helicopter.

She pushed the button she'd seen Alex press earlier to make the vehicle come to life, and once it had, she followed the same steps he had: seatbelt on, lights on, and the handle to the D position. Everything felt clunky and awkward, and at one point, she sprayed the windscreen with water unintentionally, but eventually she was ready to move off. She touched the pedal on the right just a tiny bit, causing a noise somewhere at the front, and a split second later, it rolled forwards. She grabbed the steering wheel in a panic and frantically turned it one way, then the other to straighten it up and stop it rolling onto the grass. It felt much lighter now, which she couldn't understand, but was grateful nonetheless.

Taking it steady, she pressed on the pedal a little more and steered it out onto the road, trying her best to keep it between the lines.

This isn't so hard, she thought, as she pressed the pedal a little more to go faster.

She switched off the headlights so she wouldn't attract the attention of the helicopter, but abandoned that idea when the nearside wheels slid along the grass verge for a short distance, before gripping tarmac again a heart-stopping moment later. In panic, she flicked them back on, spraying the windscreen with water again as her flapping hands hit several switches and stalks. Shaking off her nerves, she focused on the illuminated road in front of her and put her foot down a little further, driving as fast as she dared.

After a few minutes she felt comfortable enough to look in her mirror at the sky behind her. She searched for the flashing lights, but saw nothing other than the occasional star. Her fear subsided somewhat. She moved her attention back to the road ahead and was forced to slam her foot on the other pedal, which she hoped was the brake. She missed it the first time but caught it the second, throwing her body into her seatbelt as she came to an abrupt stop. She heard a loud squeal as the tyres dragged along the tarmac. A plume of smoke crept up the side windows. Gripping the steering wheel as hard as she physically could to stop the rest of her body from trembling, she concentrated on the object that had caused her to react so suddenly.

Twenty metres ahead, the helicopter lowered into the middle of the road, side-on to the Kia. With the giant rotors still spinning furiously, the side door slid open and six men jumped out, all of whom were dressed head to toe in black, their menacing shapes spreading out to block the entire road.

Once the shock of the emergency stop had worn off, Sarah noticed they were all wearing balaclavas. But although they'd landed in front of her, blocked her path, and had their faces covered in evil masks with holes around the eyes, none of those factors were the most terrifying things about the men.

The guns pointed at her were.

Sarah stamped her right foot on the pedal without even thinking about the consequences, so desperate and immediate was her urge to get away from those men. The engine revved loudly, the wheels spun, and then the car lurched forwards violently and uncontrollably, pushing her back into her seat.

She aimed for a gap to the left of the road, in front of the helicopter's nose, avoiding the rear rotor that was undoubtedly capable of blending the car into a smoothie.

The men opened fire immediately. Sarah screamed as a flurry of bullets smashed through the windscreen, whizzed past her head, and continued out through the rear window. As more flashes erupted from the men's weapons, she dived onto the passenger seat to get out of their sight, the seatbelt stretched tight, abandoning the steering wheel as she gave up any semblance of control of the vehicle. She lay across the seats, screaming with her eyes shut tight, unsure which of the two experiences was the more terrifying: hurtling along in an out-of-control vehicle, with no sense of direction, or being shot at.

That was no kind of a decision for anyone to have to make, she thought, huddled in fear.

Shouting in a foreign language conveyed she'd just passed the men, giving her enough courage to risk peeking out of the window – just in time to see she was rapidly bearing down on a ditch at the side of the road. Her hands jerked at the steering wheel in a futile attempt at evasive action; too little, too late. She shut her eyes as the chaos unfolded. The front wheels entered the ditch at speed, into the mud and water. The grille continued with the momentum, crashing into the bank on the other side. An explosion erupted and a punch thudded into her face, her world spinning as the car flipped over and landed on its roof in a field.

The sensations that dominated Sarah's consciousness were blood rushing to her head, and the force of the seatbelt digging into her shoulder; she was hanging upside down. She opened her eyes to a blanket of white, her hands automatically freeing her face from the deflated airbag. Branches from the hedgerow on the other side of the ditch now punctured the broken windscreen, the sharp, broken edges almost touching her face. The stalled engine ticked and clicked, steam hissed from somewhere, and fluids poured out of what she hoped wasn't the fuel tank.

She took some deep breaths and tried to move her arms and legs. Relieved she wasn't in any serious pain, with one hand pressed into the roof, she used the other to frantically fumble for the seatbelt clip, desperate to escape before the gunmen got to her.

The door opened and the beam from a powerful torch blinded her; strong hands gripped tightly onto her clothes. About to fight back, she braced when the glint of a knife appeared in front of her eyes. A scream roared from her lungs as it dropped to her throat. She shut her eyes instinctively, expecting the sharp punch of the blade at any moment, but instead felt nothing but a split second of weightlessness, followed by an almighty thud to her head.

Her seatbelt no longer restraining her, hands dragged her from the wreckage; paralysed by shock and fear, she offered no resistance. Lifted and on her feet, the same hands searched and carried her away, a hand clamped onto each arm, her legs dragging in the mud.

Within seconds, her feet scraped along tarmac. She raised her chin enough to see the side door of the helicopter held open for her, before she was manhandled to whatever hell her brothers had waiting for her.

40

After combing through the finer details with Chris, Julie ended the call, slumped back into her chair and stared open-mouthed into space, shocked by what had been uncovered in Suffolk.

'What does this mean?' Fiona asked as she placed her empty salad box on the coffee table and scooted to the edge of the sofa.

'It means we may have just identified the brothers' informant.' Julie blinked a few times and turned to her colleague. 'It would appear, upon first impressions, that Constable Daniel Moss might have leaked the locations of the safe houses, faked his death in the fire, and vanished.' She dropped her phone in her lap and brought her hands up to her face, massaging her tired eyes with her fingertips.

'But why would he do that? What possible motivation would he have for helping the Marlowe brothers find our witnesses?'

'Who knows?' Julie lowered her hands and settled them on the armrests. 'Maybe they're paying him… maybe they're threatening him… maybe the three of them are old friends who have been helping each other for years. We won't know *why* until we find him, which we will, wherever the dirty little rat's hiding!'

Fiona puffed up her cheeks and let out a big huff. 'Well, that won't be easy. Where on earth will we start looking? Moss has had an entire day's head start on us.'

'Well then, we best get some troops out searching for him, hadn't we?'

Julie picked up her phone and was about to call Foster when it rang in her hand. Brian. She answered with a flutter of excitement as she hoped that maybe whatever Drayce had done had worked.

'Brian, please tell me you've got some good news for me.'

'I have, but this hasn't come from me. Got it?'

'Of course,' she said. 'I'm a very discreet lady. What do you know?'

'Okay, well, you were right, the brothers are contacting people from prison, using a mobile phone they had hidden somewhere. The team watching them intercepted the communications with a Stingray. They recovered a single message sent to the brothers from a phone that pinged back to a mast in Essex, and there's a string of messages that have gone back and forth between the brothers and another number that clearly belongs to someone on the outside who's working for them. I can email you the entire message thread if you'd prefer?'

'Yes, please.' Julie stood up from her chair with a flood of new energy. 'As well as emailing me the thread, can you read out the numbers now, while I'm on the phone to you? I think we might know who one of those numbers belongs to, so the sooner we can track it, the sooner we can get the bastard locked up.'

'Of course. Just give me a second.'

Julie heard Brian clicking on a mouse at the other end of the line. In the meantime, she tipped her handbag upside down and spilt the contents on the carpet at her feet, the fastest way to find her pen. When Brian came back on the line a moment later and read out the numbers, Julie was ready, scribbling the digits on the edge of her grease-stained pizza box.

Her eyelids narrowed at one of the numbers she'd written. It was familiar. Something was wrong. She read it again, three or four times, to make sure her mind wasn't playing tricks on her.

She knew that number, and as she read it for the fifth time, she realised her earlier presumption about whose phone it was, was wrong.

She turned to Fiona as she reached for her gun.

41

Something hit Drayce square in the face – the sole of a boot, perhaps? – a split second after he'd taken a punch to the solar plexus. He absorbed the full force of the kick, because not only was he leaning forwards when it hit him, but he didn't even see it coming, and the ones you don't see coming always hurt the most.

The force of it rattled his brain against his skull. A sharp pain erupted in his head, a bright flash of light exploding behind his closed eyes. His chair tipped back onto the rear legs as weightlessness engulfed him, floating in the air for an instant, before he was hit from behind, not by a person, but by the ground. A loud crack rang out as he hit the concrete floor.

'Fuck's sake, Chrissy!' he heard Stan say. 'I told you to hold the chair from behind to stop that from happening!'

'It's all right for you,' Chrissy replied. 'I'm feeling every one of these punches and kicks while I hold onto him back here. Swap places with me.'

'No way. You'll get your chance. I've got plenty more in me yet.'

Hands pulled Drayce up. Another crack came from behind him, quieter this time, a branch creaking in the wind. The chair's back support was compromised, flexing in a way it hadn't done before. He opened his good eye to see Stan in front of him, grinning with both hands clenched into fists, his knuckles raw and bloody. A droplet of clinging blood let go and fell to the floor where a small pool had formed. But Stan either didn't notice or didn't care. Drayce wondered if he might be enjoying himself too much to take in that sort of detail.

'You ready for round two?' Stan asked.

Drayce rolled his head from side to side and heard a crunch in his neck. The goosebumps had gone, his muscular torso now coated in a sheen of sweat. He spotted the black grip of a pistol peeking out from Stan's beltline. He glared up into his face with his good eye and then spat out another mouthful of blood, which landed on Stan's boots.

'That supposed to piss me off, is it?' Stan asked with a smile. 'By the time I'm done with you, my insoles will be squelching with your blood.'

Drayce tensed when Stan took a step back to power up for another kick, relieved to see him stop dead in his tracks when his phone rang. He took it from the Accountant and answered it.

'You what? You've found her? Where was she?'

The pain from the beating was nothing compared to the sick feeling in the depths of Drayce's stomach. Stan's voice faded as he walked away, but Drayce had heard enough.

'Bring her back here,' he heard Stan say, who turned around to face him. 'I'm gonna kill her in front of him.'

A surge of adrenaline more powerful than anything Drayce had ever felt before pumped around his body, his skin tingling, his bones trembling, his muscles flexing against the restraints. This was no longer a case of dragging the torturous turn of events out for as long as possible to give Sarah time to get away – this was now a ticking clock counting down to his and Sarah's deaths. He needed to do something, but first, he had to free himself from that chair.

'That was my Russian friends,' Stan said as he ended the call, handed the phone back to the Accountant to resume the recording, and walked back to Drayce. 'They've found Sarah and they're bringing her here. Looks like we don't *need* to torture you anymore.' He glowered at Drayce with pure hatred, the maniacal smile still dominating his expression. 'But I still *want* to, you get me?'

The punch came out of nowhere, whipping from Stan's hip and catching Drayce on his cheekbone. More stars flashed in front of his eyes. He thought he was about to lose consciousness. Stan put his phone away and bounced on the balls of his feet, a boxer getting ready to pound on a heavy bag.

Freddie appeared in front of Stan, the glint of a chrome blade on a cut-throat razor sparkling under the lights.

'Out of my way!' Stan barked.

'Fuck off!' Freddie replied. 'It's my turn.' He grabbed Drayce by the ear and lined the blade up, preparing to lop it off. 'I'll give him your look, Stan. Make him an ugly bastard like you.'

Stan grabbed Freddie's shoulder and yanked him back. Luckily, Drayce's ear remained intact.

'You can have your fun when I'm finished,' Stan snarled.

'Get your hands off me!'

Freddie spun around and slashed at Stan with the razor, who let go and darted out of its reach just in time. Stan backed away, huffing with anger, barely restraining himself as he stared Freddie down, his malice transferring from Drayce to Freddie in a heartbeat. Freddie held the blade out in front of him, a sinister smile on his face that practically goaded Stan to make a move. The pair reminded Drayce of hyenas fighting over food, lost in the frenzy of a feed. With his kidnappers distracted, Drayce pressed the edge of the tape that bound his hands against the splintered wood and began a gentle sawing motion of his wrists.

'Have you gone mad?' Stan asked.

Freddie nodded. 'A long time ago.'

Chrissy walked from behind the chair into Drayce's view. A thought materialised in Drayce's mind: there was nobody standing behind him.

'Calm down, fellas,' Chrissy said. 'Don't lose sight of the job. It's nearly done, remember. Soon that slag and this big bastard will be brown bread. And that means we're definitely getting our money from the brothers.'

'Yeah,' Freddie said, drawing the word out menacingly, his eyes never leaving Stan. 'Split between six, instead of eight. Ain't that right, Chrissy?'

'That's right, Freddie. And it's got me wondering something.' Chrissy paused, a sudden chill affecting the air in the barn. 'Maybe we can do better than six.'

Stan stiffened. 'The fuck's that supposed to mean?'

Chrissy glanced at the shadows behind Stan. 'Not yet, Daz. Keep your cool, son.'

Daz walked into the light, two hands cupping a pistol, aimed directly at Stan's head. Daz caught Chrissy's eye. They smiled at one another.

Stan turned to Daz, no doubt assessing the threat posed as he came to terms with precisely what was unravelling. After some time, he glared at Chrissy. 'So, it's like that is it, Chrissy?'

Chrissy shrugged. 'Yeah, it's like that, Stanley. Been a pleasure, mate.'

A nod from Chrissy was all it took. Daz's pistol barked in his hand, the round spinning Stan's head as he collapsed to the ground.

Chrissy assessed the others. 'Anyone got a problem with what's just happened here?'

'No complaints from me.' Freddie gazed down at Stan's lifeless body, his smile widening as he licked his lips. 'I never did like the prick.'

Marcus and Leo stayed silent, their eyes flirting with Daz's gun.

Chrissy squared up to them. 'I need an answer, gentlemen.'

They glanced at one another, then back at Chrissy.

'No problem here,' Marcus said.

Chrissy regarded Leo carefully. 'And how about you?'

Leo's lips parted to give an answer. He hesitated.

'Too slow,' Chrissy said as he turned to Daz and nodded.

Leo raised his hands. 'Wait—'

His plea was cut short by the bullet that entered his forehead, dropping him to the cold concrete floor like a stone.

'Right then,' Chrissy said as he approached Drayce with the energy of a man itching for a fight. 'Let's have some fun with this one while we wait for those Russians to bring Sarah here.'

Blinding lights exploded in Drayce's vision as another punch landed, this time a hook to the side of his head, turning his upper body and pulling the tape away from the splintered wood. A loud ringing in his ear canal gradually dissipated to reveal cackles of laughter. The remaining four had gathered close in, each wanting their pound of flesh. Drayce feared if this beating went on for much longer, he'd pass out, waking to find Sarah kneeling in front of him with a gun to her head. He drew a series of deep breaths in through his mouth and forced himself to stay conscious as he realigned the tape and sawed again, never taking his eye off Chrissy, who was bouncing on the balls of his feet and feinting a few times to try to provoke a reaction, before lunging in with a hard shot.

'Let me have a go,' Daz said as he tucked his gun away.

'Later!' Chrissy barked.

'I wanna cut him.' Freddie inched forwards, flicking his blade in and out of the handle. 'I wanna cut his fucking face off!'

'I said *later*!'

Drayce saw the next punch coming – a body shot – and tensed in time for his core muscles to absorb the impact. Chrissy stayed in close, bending down as he clinched Drayce's neck with his left hand and butted their foreheads together.

'You having fun yet?' he said, the words riding a wave of foul breath as saliva sprayed over Drayce's face. ''Cos I know I am!'

Drayce felt the world around him start to slip away. He groaned loudly and pressed his head hard into Chrissy's as a way of keeping himself awake.

'That's more like it!' Chrissy shouted in his face. 'Come on. Fight back if you think you got it in yer!'

Drayce wasn't sure if the sensation was real or if he imagined it, but the tape was loosening. He pulled his hands apart, creating as much tension as possible. Either it was stretching, or it was tearing, because he was sure his hands were separating, millimetre by millimetre. He bit down hard, glaring into Chrissy's eyes as he tensed every muscle in his upper body and pulled on the tape with everything he had. Chrissy's grip tightened around his neck, his other fist drawing back. Drayce saw something on it – knuckle-duster, perhaps – glinting in the bright barn lights from above, just as Chrissy's lips parted.

'I'm gonna beat you with this until you black out, and when you wake up, the first thing you'll see is that bitch right here at my feet, with a gun shoved in her fucking grassing mouth!'

The sudden release of the tension in Drayce's arms made them swing around to the front, clapping Chrissy's ribs, the cheers and laughter dying so quickly it was as if they'd been switched off. The smile left Chrissy's face, immediately replaced by fear as he stared at Drayce's free hands, his expression that of a zookeeper who had just witnessed the fence collapse around the lion enclosure.

Gunfire snapped everyone out of their shock.

Chrissy's head lolled forwards, an exit wound the size of a coke can now in his face. He collapsed at Drayce's feet to reveal Stan, alive with a gun in his hands, stood tall behind the group of men facing Drayce, blood pouring down his chest, the bullet from D az seemingly having passed through his cheek and jaw, missing anything vital. Stan turned the gun on Daz. Everyone stilled with fright.

Everyone except Drayce.

Seizing his opportunity, he leapt out of the chair and launched himself at Stan, who was so focused on Daz that he didn't even see the attack. Drayce batted Stan's gun-arm out the way, the weapon firing into the barn's ceiling, and clinched his neck with his left hand as his right slipped underneath Stan's chin, his huge fingers clamping around the man's broken jaw and crushing it with every ounce of grip strength he had. Blood sprayed from between Stan's lips as he squealed in pain, instinctively letting go of the gun, which hit the floor with a *thud*. He tried to pull Drayce's hands away, but Drayce wasn't going to let that happen. He lifted Stan onto his tiptoes as he ground the pieces of broken jawbone together with his fingertips.

Movement to the side caught Drayce's attention. Daz was backing away, as though frightened of the escalating melee, but Freddie was coming forwards, the blade lifted to shoulder height, his thin lips pulled tightly over his front teeth, face contorted in anger as he slashed at Drayce's face. Drayce caught his wrist with both hands. He shouldered Stan out of the way, turned to the side of Freddie's arm, and slammed his body into the back of his elbow, snapping the joint and collecting the razor that fell from his grasp. A shriek burst free between Freddie's lizard lips. He reached for a gun with his free hand, his venomous eyes locked on Drayce. With a split second remaining before Drayce was shot, he whipped the blade across Freddie's neck. The gun tumbled from Freddie's waistline and hit the floor as he clamped the hand of his working arm to his severed windpipe. He staggered backwards, gurgling and hissing as air passed through the slit in his throat.

Back in the fight, Stan swung a punch at Drayce's head with a powerful hook. Drayce weaved under the man's fist, and as he came up, sliced the blade across Stan's face, cutting him deeply from earlobe to nose. The man's flesh opened up, briefly revealing the severed muscle fibres and layers of subcutaneous fat, instantly camouflaged by a torrent of blood. Stan stilled in shock, a hand to his face, confused, as he felt teeth where his cheek should have been.

More movement made Drayce turn to Marcus, whose hand disappeared into his clothing and reappeared gripping a black pistol. Emboldened by Marcus, Daz reached for his gun. Drayce threw the razor at him, the blade's edge slicing through his scalp as it spun past his head like a propeller, giving Drayce time to swipe Stan's discarded gun off the floor.

In need of cover, Drayce forced Stan into a spin to take his back and slip on a rear naked choke hold with his left arm. Instinctively he backed up until the barn wall hit his shoulder blades, putting the threats in front of him. Using Stan's body as a shield from the guns pointing his way, Drayce brought Stan's pistol up on aim at the other men in the room to complete the standoff. He clamped his left hand around his right bicep and applied more pressure, hearing the shards of broken jawbone grinding together as he squeezed. Blood poured down his left elbow from the wounds to Stan's face.

'Put that fucking gun down!' Marcus shouted, his own weapon pointing at Drayce as he stepped over Freddie, motionless on the floor in a pool of blood, his shadowy eyes lifeless, his limp hand having fallen away from his neck.

'Yeah. L-l-let him go,' Daz stammered, one hand holding a pistol, the other clutching the wound to his head.

Drayce tightened his finger on the trigger and examined the arena, limited by the condition of his left eye. Figures moving left and right meant they were fanning out to get a shot at him. Directly in front, the Accountant slowly walked out of the shadows with a small revolver in his hand, wearing that same hateful expression as he hobbled forwards with his cane.

Drayce tucked himself even tighter behind Stan's body, pressing his face against the back of his head as he tried to stay out of sight of the three guns aimed his way. Daz appeared on the right with his gun raised to eye level, squinting down the sights, a split second before Marcus did the same on the left. Flanking him, their panicky energy changed into a plan. The barn turned deathly silent but for their footsteps as they tried to line up a kill shot on him. He knew it wouldn't be long before they'd see an opportunity and take it. It was now or never. Time to act. His pistol moved to the nearest figure almost of its own accord.

Everyone opened fire.

42

'Don't even think about it,' Fiona said as she jabbed the barrel of her gun at Julie.

Julie eased her hand away from her pistol.

Fiona's voice was different, Julie thought, her delicate and graceful tone replaced by an angry shrill. She *looked* different too. Her pretty face contorted into a fierce scowl, her lips thin and tight with rage, flecks of spittle rested on her chin, such was the viciousness with which she had barked the command.

'Now throw your phone to me,' Fiona demanded.

'Okay,' Julie replied as she edged down and slid her phone across the floor to Fiona's feet, hoping Brian was listening. 'Just, please don't do anything with that gun you might regret.'

Fiona smiled mockingly. 'Oh, I'm a long way past that stage, I'm afraid.' She bent down, picked up the phone, cancelled the call, and dropped it into her coat pocket, keeping her gun trained on Julie. 'Now get down on your knees and put your hands on your head.'

Julie did as she was told, all too aware she had no other option. As she knelt, her eyes flicked between the pistol and the madness in her colleague's eyes. She saw Fiona slip her other hand into another coat pocket and reappear clutching her own phone. She made a call and put it to her ear.

'Change of plan, I've had to speed things up. No choice. How far away are you?' A pause. 'Good, come straight here as fast as you can. After this, you're done.'

She hung up and put her phone away.

Julie's breathing rate picked up, along with her heart rate, beating an audible rhythm against her ribs. Blood rushed to her face as her anger spiked.

'How long?' she asked.

Fiona took a couple of steps nearer and gazed down at her with scorn. 'How long what?'

'How long have you been a part of all this?'

Fiona took a moment to consider her answer. 'Well, Francis and I met about a year ago, if that's what you mean?'

The muscles in Julie's face relaxed in shock. 'Francis Marlowe?'

Fiona giggled, her face lighting up as the pretty girl came back just for a moment. 'Oh, you do catch on fast, don't you? Yes, Francis Marlowe. We've developed quite the working relationship.'

Julie found it hard to articulate herself, the shock making it difficult to speak. 'How?'

Fiona shrugged. 'It was quite simple, really. He made me an offer, and I accepted.'

'And that offer was?'

'Just a little information exchange, to start with. You scratch my back, I scratch yours. How do you think I really caught those people traffickers?' She grinned, gloating in the face of Julie's incomprehension. 'He gave me the intelligence I needed to move on in my career, and I fed back to him everything the NCA had, helping him stay one step ahead of his competitors. When I got wind that the NCA and the police were going after him and his brother, we came up with a plan together.'

Julie clenched her fists, her knuckles cracking. 'You've led quite the double life.'

Fiona licked her lips. 'I suppose I have.'

'So it was you who led them to the safe houses?'

'Yes. The witnesses needed to die if Francis and Nathan were to beat the case against them, and I knew all the weaknesses they could exploit.'

'I'm guessing PC Daniel Moss was one of those weaknesses?'

Fiona nodded. 'He was, indeed. Quite a heavy gambling problem, it turned out. The man was massively in debt, several credit cards maxed out, numerous loans he couldn't pay back. He was in serious financial trouble. A little olive branch from Francis, offering to pay it all off, was all it took to bring him on board with our plan.'

Julie shook her head, bewilderment and anger on her face. 'So he gave you the addresses and you passed them on to Francis?'

'Pretty much, but he also helped things to go nice and smoothly on the ground at the house in Suffolk. It was a shame I couldn't think of a way to have the same influence within the other team. Sarah might not have escaped if I had.'

Julie's teeth clamped together. 'You won't get away with this, you psychopath!'

Fiona eyed Julie as a snake might a mouse. 'We'll see.'

A knock at the door snapped both women out of the confrontation. Fiona walked backwards, keeping the gun trained on Julie, and unlocked the deadbolt.

'Come in.'

The door opened and a man walked in, quickly shutting it behind him. He was of average height and build, and wore black boots, blue jeans, and a padded winter coat. The woolly hat on his head and the scarf wrapped around his mouth made it hard for Julie to see his face. He stayed by the door, his eyes moving between Fiona and Julie.

'What the hell happened?' he mumbled through the wool. 'How did you get found out?'

'Doesn't matter,' Fiona replied. 'What's done is done, Daniel.'

'Don't use my name, you idiot!' Obviously terrified, his eyes darted to Julie.

'She already knows,' Fiona snatched the scarf from around his mouth. 'And this isn't fooling anyone. She's not stupid.'

He pulled the material back over his mouth in a panic.

'Don't waste your time, PC Moss,' Julie said. 'I know all about your part in this deception. Out of interest, which poor sod's body did you leave in the fire?'

'That was them,' he said in a fluster. 'Not me. I could never have—'

'Don't play innocent now,' Fiona said. 'It's far too late for that.' She smiled at Julie. 'It was just some homeless guy they grabbed off the street who was roughly Daniel's height and build.' She spoke with a casualness that framed the information as an insignificant detail, rather than an innocent person's life. 'Made sense really... there was nobody in his life to notice he'd vanished and report him as missing.'

Daniel bowed his head in shame.

Julie felt sick at the level of inhumanity these people had displayed. 'What now?' she asked.

'What now,' Fiona said, 'is that I shoot you in the head, and Daniel here disposes of your body.'

'Are you capable of that, Fiona? It's one thing to help mastermind all of this, but pulling the trigger yourself is entirely another thing. And I meant it when I said you won't get away with this. Even with me dead, the police still have your number, along with the precise communications you had with Francis in prison. When I go missing, they'll investigate, and it won't take long for them to discover what you've done.'

Fiona appeared to consider Julie's observations. 'Perhaps, but what's done is done. At the very least, I can eliminate you.' She moved the gun back in line with Julie's face, squinting one eye as she carefully took aim. 'With you gone, it should buy me enough time to disappear.'

Julie saw the tendons on the back of her hand ripple underneath her skin as she tightened her grip, her trigger finger moving back, ever so slightly. Any second now, Julie thought. She had to think of something.

Fiona was aiming with her left eye, her right closed, Daniel in her blind spot. Julie looked at Daniel with fake horror and screwed her face up into an expression of shock and fear.

'What the hell are you doing?'

The acting was apparently enough to fool Fiona, because she opened her right eye and spun to face him... enough of a distraction for Julie to reach for her belt and draw her own pistol, just as Fiona turned back to face her. They stared at one another down the sights of their weapons.

43

The pistol kicked repeatedly in Drayce's hand, his point of aim directly on Daz's centre mass. The volley of bullets forced Daz to double over, clutching his abdomen, exposing the crown of his head. Drayce took advantage with the next barrage. Daz's skull cracked in the way an earthquake splits the ground along a fault line, a wet slap audible amongst the chaos as it ruptured its contents on the floor.

Returning fire from the other two men cut through the air to the side of Drayce's head, angry wasps in full metal jackets buzzing past. Then more, closer this time, a swarm rallying upon him. He felt rounds hitting Stan, jolting him every time they landed. Thick stakes of wood clattered over them as the wayward bullets shredded the barn wall. He hugged Stan even tighter, shrinking behind the man's body for cover, expecting a white-hot bolt of pain to sear his flesh at any moment.

He tracked his muzzle to the Accountant and fired a single shot into his chest, putting him down instantly. Drayce kept his pistol in motion, sweeping it to Marcus, who didn't appear to care about hitting Stan in his attempts to kill Drayce. Stan got heavier as the life rushed out of him, turning him into a dead weight. Drayce held him up with one arm as he took aim at Marcus, whose feet were planted, torso square on, out in the open with no cover, his vital organs suspended in mid-air, motionless, a sacrificial offering.

Amateur.

Drayce fired a double tap at Marcus's centre mass, raised his sight picture, and shot him in the head.

The barn fell silent.

Gun smoke hung between them, a thick fog dancing in the air. Breathing heavily, Drayce relaxed his left arm, letting Stan slowly slide down him until he was nothing but a crumpled mess at his feet. Stan's chest was rising and falling, but only just. Blood gushed from several bullet wounds. Wouldn't be long now. Drayce kicked him over so he could look him dead in the eye.

Stan's ruined lips sagged apart, his fractured words spoken through a gurgle of blood. 'Who's… Sarah to you? Who could she possibly be… to make everything you've done… worth it?'

Drayce chose his words carefully. 'She's an innocent, caught up in a world she wants no part of. A world divided in two, split between the civilised and the lawless. Men like me guard that divide with our lives.'

Stan seemed to regard him intently. 'I really did… misjudge you… didn't I?'

'Yes, you did.'

'Are the others… dead?'

'Almost certainly.'

'Well… at least that's… something. Treacherous bastards.'

'No honour amongst thieves, Stanley.'

'Very… true.' Stan coughed violently, a mouthful of blood spewing down his chin. 'I should have walked away… when I first laid eyes on you… in that cafe.'

'Yes, you should have.'

'I knew you'd be… more trouble… than it was worth.'

'Bit late now.'

'Isn't it just.' Stan's breaths became shallow and rapid, his heart fighting for the oxygen his vastly reduced blood supply couldn't provide. 'Best… get on with it. You've still… got those Russians… to deal with.' Stan smiled for the last time. 'Good luck.'

His facial muscles sagged as he passed away, his head lolling to one side, eyes lifeless. Drayce moved his attention to the other three. He circled to the right and approached them in a straight line to keep his eyes on them, stepping over the discharged shell casings that glinted in the pools of blood. Daz and Marcus were certainly dead, their injuries catastrophic, their bodies still with a completeness only the dead can manage. But the Accountant was still breathing. Lying on his back, claret spreading wide across his chest, the hammer on his revolver clicking on nothing but spent casings as the cylinder spun in his hand. Drayce considered the frail old fool for a moment. The revolver was becoming too heavy for him as his life seeped away. He glared at Drayce, a snarl appearing on his lips as the gun clattered on the ground, his resentful expression sealed as he exhaled for the last time.

As Drayce turned away from the men's bodies, a sound, faint for now, introduced itself from off in the distance, getter louder. Drayce recognised the source, lifting his chin to its mechanical drumbeat that reverberated through the ceiling, cutting through the night air as it returned from its mission. He dropped his pistol's magazine into the palm of his waiting hand, checked the load, then slammed it back in place and moved to the barn door.

44

The helicopter touched down in the field next to the farmhouse. Sarah's neck hurt, which she put down to whiplash and landing on her head when her seatbelt had been cut. She struggled to breathe through her swollen nose, certain the airbag had broken it. Both of her knees and shins were grazed and bleeding from being dragged across the rough tarmac to the helicopter. She winced as she surveyed the men surrounding her, their cold, dark eyes staring back from the holes in their balaclavas.

The two rows of seats inside the aircraft faced one another, with barely any legroom between them. Sarah had to stop herself from crying out in pain every time she banged shins with the man sitting opposite her. As she did her best to ignore the pain in her legs, she focused on the pain she felt it in her wrists – the hard, thin plastic restraints dug so hard into her, she thought they were sawing through bone. She wiggled them around, to manoeuvre them so they didn't hurt so much, but also as a means of testing them. Straightaway, the man opposite delivered a hard slap to the side of her head. He was leaning forwards, his eyes full of threat and intimidation, but behind the balaclava Sarah was sure he was smiling: the cruel bastard enjoyed dishing out punishment to his hostage. She got the message and kept her wrists still.

The door opened and they poured out, dragging her with them. Most of the group walked ahead to the courtyard that separated the main house and the barn, but two of them gripped tightly onto an arm each, their guns banging into her as they swung back and forth from their chests with every angry step they took. Bright lights lit up the courtyard as the men in front triggered the motion sensors. They turned and took a diagonal line straight across the open space, heading for the doors at the front of the barn.

What on earth do they have planned for me in there?

She desperately wanted to fight them off, but what use would it be to even try? Instead of fighting, she pretended to fall, collapsing to the ground from exhaustion, a dead weight in their grasp, a vain attempt at slowing down whatever hell awaited her inside that barn. But it didn't last long. A hard punch to the ribs, followed by a tight grip of her hair, and she was back on her feet, forced to march on.

The bright lights of the courtyard blinded her. The barn doors were now just twenty feet ahead. The man at the front of the group was almost there.

Should I fight?

She wanted to, God knows she wanted to. Every fibre of her being screamed at her to get on with it, to kick, punch, bite, and run. But what chance did she have of escaping? Although maybe, she thought, it wasn't about escaping. Maybe it was simply a choice between dying quickly, kicking and screaming in that courtyard, or slowly in a dark corner of that barn, after hours of being tortured for everything she'd disclosed to the NCA. She tensed her leg muscles and stood up tall so she walked with the two men at her sides, rather than being dragged.

She took a deep breath. *If I could get an arm free from the grip of one, maybe I could turn to the other and get my hands on his gun…*

Yes, she thought. *I'm going to do it. I don't have a choice. I'll count down from three in my head, and when I get to one, I'll fight like I've never fought before.*

Three.

She tensed her legs again, keeping her arms loose so as not to instigate a tighter grip from the men holding her.

Two.

She took a deep breath and held it, visualising in her mind how she wanted the altercation to play out.

One.

Surprise overcame her as her right arm came free with relative ease, slipping with barely any resistance from between the fingers of the man to her right. He turned to her, confusion in his eyes, which swiftly changed to hatred as his hands came up, palms facing her, his fingers clawed talons as he prepared to grab her again. Instinctively she wanted to lash out at him, stamp on his leg, or knee him in the groin, then turn and fight to free her other arm.

But she hesitated, distracted by something in the corner of her eye: some sort of scuffle at the barn doors. A blaze of light flashed from within the barn's dark interior. The angry expression on the face of the man next to her fell away as though a switch had been flipped, his eyes rolling back into his head and his hands collapsing to his hips, as the talons withered away to nothing but ten limp digits. His entire body lost balance and tilted to one side, before falling to the ground in one rigid piece as an ironing board would when knocked over. A wet, meaty thud as he hit the stony ground, followed by his lungs expelling his last breath, signalled the end of the man's life.

Mystified, she turned to face the man holding her left arm, initially halted by his resistance. Another flash of light came from within the barn and his strength vanished. His hand released her and she finished pivoting to see him lying motionless on the ground.

Heavy gunfire erupted in the courtyard.

–

Drayce had waited patiently inside the barn, lights off, poised in the shadows. As the first Russian entered, his movements were slow, threat perception lazy, tactics non-existent. As far as he was concerned, the inside of the barn was a controlled environment. He wasn't to know Stan's game plan had been turned on its head.

At the sight of the bodies, the Russian hesitated, unable to comprehend the gruesome scene that lay before him, causing a fraction of a second's delay in his response.

It was all Drayce needed.

He shot an arm out of the shadows, snatched the man by his weapon's sling, and yanked him out of sight. With the man blinded by the darkness and the surprise of the attack, Drayce wrapped his neck in a guillotine choke, silencing any attempt at warning his friends. He fought against the strangle hold, but it was no use. Seconds later, his thrashing subsided.

Hurried footsteps galloping across the courtyard revealed the other men's guards were up. Drayce drew his pistol and slowly opened his view through the barn doors, his figure practically invisible from within the dark interior. In the bright lights of the courtyard, he saw Sarah being unceremoniously dragged towards the barn. The two men holding her were the biggest threat to her, so Drayce took careful aim and fired, dropping them both before the others could shoot back.

Bullets peppered the barn doors, showering him in splinters. He ducked into cover, unclipped the dead Russian's assault rifle, and stripped the magazine. He pressed the top round. It didn't budge, the spring fully compressed, meaning it was loaded to the max. Drayce refitted the magazine, shouldered the weapon and backed up, vanishing deeper into the dark room. At the first pause in their rate of fire, he aimed at the doorway and moved across, opening his view of the courtyard.

Three men approached the barn doors in a V formation, illuminated by the powerful lights, their route across the court-yard offering no cover from view, or from fire. Drayce moved his point of aim past the first man he came to, who was still reloading, and onto the next, whose rifle was already back in play, the muzzle pointing directly into the barn. Drayce shot him in the head to account for the fact he was wearing body armour. Before the man's body hit the ground, Drayce returned to the first, who had rammed his fresh magazine home and was taking aim, having spotted Drayce's muzzle flash. Drayce gave him the good news, the round creating a third eye dead centre of his face.

As his body fell, Drayce moved across the barn door's wide expanse, searching for the final threat. The man was sprinting, rifle in high port, improving his angle of attack as he aimed for the cover of a stone building. Drayce let rip, his rounds visibly hitting their target. The man buckled, lost his balance, and collapsed to the ground in a heap. Drayce stepped cautiously out of the barn.

Sarah stayed in the middle of the courtyard, lit up brightly by the harsh security lights, shivering, her feet rooted to the spot as she stared at the dead bodies of the men who had tried to drag her to her death. A large figure appeared from the shadows of the barn's interior and walked towards her, the light gradually working its way up his body, revealing first his boots, then his jeans, then the gun in his hands, before travelling up his bloodied torso and illuminating his face.

45

'I think you'll agree this changes things,' Julie said.

Furious she'd allowed Julie to distract her with such a simple trick, Fiona's face turned red and her eyebrows locked in an angry frown. The gun in her hand quivered slightly and she shifted her weight from one foot to the other, the calmness she'd displayed just moments ago nowhere to be seen now that she had a gun pointed back at her.

Daniel had backed away into the nearest corner, as far out of the firing line as possible; no threat without his own weapon. Julie, on the other hand, hadn't moved a millimetre. The rear and foresights on her Glock as steady as they would have been in a vice and lined up right between Fiona's eyes.

'This changes nothing,' Fiona replied.

Julie shook her head. 'Don't be ignorant of the facts. The barrel of your pistol is dancing around the room like a drunk uncle at a wedding. You can't keep it straight. And you never have been much of a marksman, have you, Fiona? You've scraped through every single one of your qualification shoots that permit you to carry that thing. In your current emotional state, I'd say your chances of hitting me are about fifty-fifty, and if you do hit me, the chance of it being so accurate it inflicts a wound that kills me instantly, is so low as to make it negligible. I, on the other hand, am a natural with my Glock. I can hit a target between the eyes at ten metres, single-handed. There's three metres separating us, and I have both hands cupping my weapon. Which means if you do pull that trigger, I will absolutely still be breathing long enough to respond in kind.'

Fiona scowled fiercely, panting and blinking rapidly, sweat stinging her eyes, the hand holding her gun increasingly unstable. Julie worried she might fire it unintentionally.

'Talk to me, Fiona. This doesn't have to end in bloodshed.'

'You're right. It doesn't.' She glanced at Daniel. 'Go and take that gun off her.'

'Try if you want, Daniel, but it'll end badly for you.'

'She can't shoot you,' Fiona said. 'If she moves her point of aim off me, I'll kill her.'

Daniel took a step forwards.

'Stand still!' Julie barked, her pistol held steady on Fiona.

Daniel froze.

'Get on with it!' Fiona commanded.

'Don't you dare move an inch,' Julie ordered him, her eyes locked onto Fiona.

'You're not in control here,' Fiona said. 'I am. And once this snivelling coward has taken your gun off you, I'll kill you and leave.'

Julie shook her head. 'You're not going anywhere. You're going to answer for your crimes, as are those two evil brothers you've been helping.'

'You're w-wrong,' Fiona stammered. 'The police won't stand a chance of convicting them without the witnesses giving evidence in court.'

'But there's a witness left, isn't there, Fiona? Being guarded by a man more capable than anyone the Marlowe brothers could send after them. And you've been rumbled. So actually, there'll be plenty of evidence given in court. Enough to send you to prison, and to add even more charges to the Marlowe brothers' sheet, ensuring they stay locked up for the rest of their miserable lives.'

As the words left her mouth, Julie saw something change in Fiona. Her eyelids peeled back, exposing the burst blood vessels snaking out from her pupils. She was beaten, igniting the pure rage flooding through her. She took a step forwards, her gun no longer shaking, and curled her upper lip back, an animal about to attack.

Fiona fired, a double crack of gunfire exploding in the room. Julie felt the bullets cut through the air above her head but kept her eyes on the woman opposite. She fired back, just once, the round hitting Fiona in her chest. The gun fell out of Fiona's hand to the floor, her face no longer filled with rage. Somehow it had reverted to the pretty girl Julie had known before the revelation of her corruption.

Through the thick gunshot residue in the air, Julie watched Fiona collapse to her knees, struggling to breathe, both hands pressed firmly to her chest wound.

Movement by the door reminded Julie of the other person in the room. She pivoted her aim to Daniel, who had one hand on the door handle, his eyes on Fiona's gun, just a couple of feet away from him, as though he was considering diving for the weapon.

Julie clicked her tongue against the roof of her mouth to make sure she had his attention, then said, 'It's your choice. Six-foot high in a prison bunk, or six-foot underground in a grave. I don't care which.'

He put his hands on his head and dropped down to his knees, waiting for her next command.

46

Drayce had always hated prisons, and on first impression, HMP Leeds was no exception. He'd visited a few, early in his police career, to interview inmates for crimes they were suspected of committing before they'd been sent down, but a few was enough to have given him the everlasting impression of their depressing way of life.

The clang of doors locked behind him as he went through the various stages of the prison security system, with the accompanying bangs and rattles that echoed, had always ignited his claustrophobia. It had been the same that morning, although he'd done his best to hide it from Julie, who walked alongside him, as comfortable as he'd ever seen her. As a career detective in the Met and now the NCA, prison visits had long been bread-and-butter inquiries for her. Although, on this occasion, her motives for being there were a little out of the ordinary.

In an empty visiting room, they sat at a large white plastic table, on white plastic chairs, facing a door roughly ten feet away, expecting it to open at any moment. Everything in the room was bolted to the floor, for good reason. No use packing criminals in a room with heavy items of furniture to pick up and use as weapons.

'You sure you haven't anything you want to say to them?' Julie asked him.

Drayce nodded. 'I'm sure. I'm only here because I want to look them in the eye. It'll make their long years in this place that much more unbearable if they have the face of the man who helped beat them burned into their memory.'

While true, Drayce also didn't want to speak to them because he was wary of overstepping his mark. He already felt lucky to be in this position, tagging along for the ride, and thought it best to remain quiet and professional. Julie had stretched the truth a little to get him in there, passing him off as a consultant for the NCA who was required to witness the proceedings.

He smiled back at her as she grinned at his last comment, aware of the lingering headache that had plagued him for the past few weeks as he'd recovered from his injuries. It was just behind his eyes, coming and going with no rhyme or reason; the discomfort was one of the keepsakes from the beatings inside that barn. He touched the bridge of his nose; even with his hands tied behind his back, it had remained intact. Scars were still visible elsewhere – and probably always would be – from the knife wound to his arm and the split to his scalp, but all the other injuries he'd sustained – fractured ribs and severe bruising, to name a couple – had healed. Even his left eye, which the doctor had been concerned about, had made a full recovery, with no lasting effects to his vision. He was extremely grateful his recovery had been so short, under no illusion as to how much worse it could have been.

His thoughts moved away from his injuries when he saw Julie's head turn sharply away from him. With his mind back in the room, he followed her gaze to the door across the room swinging wide open.

A large team of prison guards accompanied the Marlowe brothers. Drayce counted eight in total, four for each prisoner. Substantial overkill, in his opinion. Drayce inspected the brothers as they walked over. If he'd been left in a room alone with them, he wouldn't have been even mildly tense. The fear their reputation invoked in people was the wave they'd been riding for years, and Drayce didn't care about reputation. In his experience, it was always exaggerated. He'd spent an eighteen-year career in the police breaking bullies with fearsome reputations. These two clowns would be no different if push came to punch.

They took a seat opposite him and Julie, the guards forming a circle around the entire table, facing inwards, all eyes on the brothers. Nobody spoke. Drayce took in their body language. Nathan Marlowe had the reputation of being a hothead, far more emotional than his brother, obvious to Drayce sitting across from him. Nathan was leaning forwards with his elbows pressing hard into the table, squeezing his right fist with his left hand, a fighter testing the tightness of his wraps. His eyes left no doubt he wanted to beat Drayce and Julie to death. Francis, on the other hand, might have been waiting for a dental appointment, his legs crossed and arms folded, bored, with a blank expression on his face. Drayce heard Julie clear her throat.

She started with the formal stuff, which amounted to reading aloud the extra charges to the brothers, the most serious of which was conspiracy to commit murder in relation to the deaths of Sergeant Michael Scott and Wayne Hardwick, and PCs Francesca Morgan and Craig Baker, along with conspiracy to commit murder in relation to the attempted kidnapping and execution of Sarah Bennett – formerly Sarah Marlowe. Sarah had gone to court and given her original evidence like a pro, receiving special mention from the judge for her remarkable bravery in the face of everything she'd been through. Both brothers had been convicted for their original crimes, and each sentenced to over forty years in prison. They'd be in their seventies by the time they were eligible for parole.

These new charges, if convicted of them, would guarantee their only route out of prison would be in a body bag.

Drayce watched their reactions. Nathan squirmed in his seat, cracking his knuckles and licking his lips at every word that left Julie's mouth as his temper got the better of him. Francis, on the other hand, barely moved. His only reaction, when Julie had finished, was to carefully adjust his glasses, pushing them slightly further up the bridge of his nose. Julie made a note that neither of them replied, then she put her paperwork away and stared at the two of them.

'So that's the official stuff dealt with,' she said. 'Now for the personal.'

Drayce noticed her glance across at him before returning her gaze to the brothers. 'If I could, I'd leave this man here to even things up between us. You see, I'm more than a little angry you went after my witnesses, and he's not very happy you sent men after him with orders to kill him. That kind of thing pisses him off.'

Drayce scrutinised the brothers, his brow furrowed, nostrils flaring, his mere breathing enough to make most people fear they were prey.

'But fortunately for you, I'm a civilised human being,' Julie continued. 'And as a result, I've been a little more creative with my ideas for revenge.' She glanced at the guards and they all took a step forwards, tightening the circle. 'You might have noticed a few faces have changed around here. Not just the guards, but the governor as well. You see, when we intercepted the phone you had in here, we discovered a whole host of communications that helped us identify all the corrupt officials who have been helping you boys. Hence, the faces that surround this table are different, and the governor has been replaced. Nice lady, this new one. I had a meeting with her just last week, and she's agreed to implement a measure I suggested to help prevent you two from conspiring to commit any more crimes on the outside.' Drayce approved the size of the smile on her face. 'You're going to be separated.'

These words brought about the first reaction from Francis. He unfolded his arms, uncrossed his legs, and leant forwards in his chair. 'You can't do that.'

'I can, and I am. You're moving to different prisons, and you won't be allowed to communicate. From the moment you leave this room, you will not see one another again for the rest of your lives.'

Nathan jumped up from his seat and lashed out at Julie. The guards weren't quick enough, but Drayce was. He caught the man's fat fist in his hand with a slap, just inches from Julie's face. Nathan was a big man, but he wasn't in Drayce's league, able to wrap his hand almost entirely around Nathan's fist. He shifted his grip so Nathan's knuckles were stacked along his palm, from top to bottom, and then crushed them together. He contemplated keeping the pressure on until he detected cartilage being damaged, similar to what's heard when a chicken wing is torn in half, but he didn't want the paperwork. He let go once the guards had their hands on Nathan and pulled him away from the table, one man on each arm and another on his neck, dragging him back to the door.

Francis got to his feet, making a move for his brother, but was tackled to the ground and dragged unceremoniously to a different door, the pair of them screaming for one another. Nathan was the first to go out of sight, the door swinging shut behind him as he was hauled away by the guards. Francis was almost crying when he reached his door.

'Wait!' Julie shouted at the guards. They paused, holding the man still. 'I haven't quite finished with *him* yet.'

Francis pulled his teary eyes away from the door Nathan had vanished through and met Julie's gaze.

'As this is the last time we'll see each other,' Julie said, 'I want to take this opportunity to tell you that you disgust me, you and all those like you, who treat other people's lives as if they're yours to do with as you please. Well, no more. Your days of victimising others are over.'

A creepy smile infected Francis's lips. 'We'll see about that.'

Julie turned to the guards and nodded her head, then stood to collect her paperwork.

Drayce stayed seated, watching Francis's feeble attempts to break free as the guards pulled him through the doorway. He caught a glimpse of his pained expression, his dark pupils visible amongst the tangle of limbs that engulfed his writhing body, portals to the man's soul. Drayce detected a rare breed of malevolence. He held the eye contact, bold and fierce, as he always did when he stared down evil.

Then he smiled and waved goodbye, just before the door closed between them.

47

Leaving the prison was far quicker than entering. They walked across the car park, through a low-hanging fog yet to be burnt away by the rising sun. Drayce inhaled deeply through his nose as he sat in the front passenger seat of Julie's car, the interior smelling wonderful thanks to the hot coffee waiting patiently in her travel mug. He watched her lift it up to her lips as she drove one-handed.

'Seriously?' Drayce asked.

Julie glanced at him out of the corner of her eye, narrowed her lids, and pouted her lips. 'Fine. Look in the glove box.'

He opened it, pushed aside the car manual and a bag of sweets, and found a stainless steel mug. He held it steady while Julie poured half her coffee into it.

'Happy now?' she asked.

His smile said it all.

The roads were a little busier now in the morning's rush hour, but not enough to stifle their journey south back to London. Julie made good progress through Leeds to the M1. They sat in silence for the first twenty minutes – Julie concentrating on the road, Drayce on the view – but then Drayce could no longer hold back the question on his mind.

'We even now?'

Julie took her eyes off the road for a second, licked a drop of coffee from her bottom lip, and smiled at him. 'Sure.'

'Maybe even tipped the balance the other way, perhaps?'

She laughed. 'After everything you've been through, I'd say you've repaid me several times over.'

He placed his empty mug in the cup holder and looked across at her. 'You know, I'm only ever a phone call away. No IOU necessary.'

Julie smiled and took her eyes off the road briefly, meeting his gaze. 'Yeah, I know. Thanks, Alex.'

She reached out with her left hand and clasped it over his right, squeezing it for a moment. Once both her hands were back on the steering wheel, Drayce admired the Yorkshire countryside, his mind mulling over recent events.

'You think the Marlowe brothers will ever get released?' he asked.

'With how lenient the criminal justice system is these days, who knows? But they certainly shouldn't. The case is rock solid.' The corner of her mouth kinked a little as though something on her mind had amused her. 'We pushed their buttons back at the prison, didn't we? Even the infamously calm Francis lost control. Did you see the look he gave you as they dragged him away?'

Drayce smiled. 'Yeah, I saw. It felt good. If men like them didn't despise me, I wouldn't be the man I want to be.'

'If there's one thing monsters hate more than anything, it's when good people fight back against them.'

Drayce nodded. 'Speaking of monsters, what's happening with the others?'

Julie's eyes narrowed slightly. 'Which others? There were quite a few.'

'Let's start with the solicitor, Rupert Jones.'

'Arrested, interviewed, and charged. We uncovered enough evidence from the brothers' prison phone, and the interviews with the corrupt guards we arrested, to add his name to the conspiracy to commit murder case.'

'Good to hear.'

'Next?' Julie's voice sounded chirpy to Drayce, as if enjoying her victor's spoils.

'How about the pilot who flew the money out of the farm?'

'Tracked down and arrested.'

'How did you achieve that?'

'It was all down to Sarah. After you rescued her and called me, she told me over the phone the full extent of what she'd read in her father's journal, namely the location of the private airfield in Norfolk where the plane was to land following the evacuation plan being triggered. By the time the pilot had finished unloading, we had him surrounded.'

'And the brothers' money?'

'Has all been seized and is waiting to be put back into communities across the country, to be used for projects far more beneficial and positive for our society than those run by the brothers.'

'Good to hear. What about their informants?'

'Charged and remanded, awaiting trial.'

'Fiona have any lingering issues from the gunshot wound?'

'She's healed up well, so I hear. I'm glad the ambulance got there so quickly. She deserves her time in court, and the many years in prison that await her. And it turns out Fiona and Daniel weren't the only two the brothers got at. After everything came to light, there was an internal investigation and a search carried out at our offices. They seized a phone from Foster's assistant, Dominic, and uncovered communications with the hitmen who'd been trying to track you and Sarah down. They had incriminating photos of him and were blackmailing him with threats of sending them to his wife if he didn't feed them information.'

'What happened to him?'

'Charged and remanded, of course. He's pled guilty and will get a lengthy custodial sentence for sure.'

Drayce nodded. 'And Sarah?'

'Is living her new life, with her new identity. Without saying too much, she has a good job in her chosen profession, working with animals out in the countryside. She's even taking driving lessons. She's happy, Alex. Really happy.'

Drayce's smile grew wide. 'That's good.'

They sat in silence for a while, eating up the road ahead. It was Julie who eventually broke it.

'About the case against you.'

Drayce kept his eyes left, staring out of his window. 'What about it?'

'Word on the grapevine is that CPS have recommended no charge, so expect a call to tell you your bail has been cancelled.'

Drayce turned to Julie. 'Seriously?'

'The video the police recovered from Stan West's phone of you being tortured, along with the evidence at the scene, and Sarah's testimony, is evidently more than enough to prove you acted in self-defence. Not worth CPS's time taking you to court. No jury on earth would find you guilty.'

Drayce took a deep breath and sighed. 'Well, that's one hell of a relief.'

Julie focused on the road ahead; Drayce gazed back out at the beautiful Yorkshire countryside. The sky was as white as snow, and a light rain had just started to fall, obscuring his view as little raindrops scurried down his window. As they drove past Sheffield, Drayce took out his phone and opened his emails, triple checking the details for his next job.

It was in LA. The contract with the client had got underway a few weeks ago, and the team leader – a guy named Nelson – was struggling with his small team of two. An extra pair of hands was required. The client must have been a wealthy individual, or at least an employee of a large corporation that cared about his safety, because the money offered was good: all expenses paid, plus five thousand dollars a week. Drayce had got in early with his CV, and because of his vast experience, Nelson had bitten his hand off. Drayce had cancelled the tenancy for the flat in Southwark and packed his bag, which he'd brought with him on the drive to the prison; Julie would drop him off at Heathrow on the journey back to London. He put his phone away, closed his eyes, imagined the sun, and smiled. When he opened them again, he squinted through the raindrops chasing each other down his window. A couple of weeks in LA would do just fine.

Before long they were hurtling through the Midlands. Drayce was exhausted, the ache behind his eyes making an unwelcome return. The stress and turmoil of recent events hadn't quite left his system yet. He tilted his seat back slightly and closed his eyes, to relax the headache away.

He must have fallen asleep, because when he next opened them, they were on the M25. He was pleased the ache behind his eyes had gone, the nap had done the trick. When he tilted his seat back up, a sign for the airport whizzed past in a blur. Not far away now.

'Sorry, Jules. I must have nodded off.'

'No problem. You sleep like an angel. It would only have been a problem if you'd snored, and then I might have punched you on the arm.'

He grinned. 'Understandable.' He blinked a few times, and as his sleepy eyes came into focus, he detected concern on her face. 'What's up?'

She took her time before replying. 'I was thinking about something while you slept... something I should probably have told you about before now.'

Drayce's radar bleeped. He sat up straight and watched her carefully. 'What's that?'

She took a deep breath. 'Lily's case has been reviewed. Word in the Met is there's new information that needs following up. They're putting a team from Major Crime back on it.'

Light-headed, Drayce made a conscious effort to pull air in and out of his lungs. Lily's locket weighed heavily around his neck, normally an unnoticed piece of jewellery, now a hefty presence. He parted his lips and considered his words carefully. They were distant in his ears, as though someone else was speaking.

'What new information?'

Julie was cautious with her words. 'I don't know exactly, but I think it has something to do with the identification of a suspect.'

The world shifted around him; he was no longer on solid earth. 'A suspect?'

'The SIO will be able to tell you the details, I just thought you should know. They'll probably be in touch, but I'm sure if you contacted them—'

'I don't think that's a good idea,' he said in a hurry. 'It's best if they just get on with it without me. I don't want to know any information about this suspect.'

'Why not?'

He looked out of his window. 'Because I don't know what I might do with it.'

His mind cast back to that day. The knock on the door in the middle of the night. Two officers on his doorstep, boots polished and uniform pristine, the dread in their eyes enough to caution him as to what was coming.

But no warning could lessen the impact. When the words left their lips, each was as stunning as physical body blows, cracking his soul into a thousand broken pieces, changing his life forever.

He wasn't even conscious of Julie, who probably wondered whether she'd done the right thing by telling him. When he eventually snapped out of it, she was navigating the colossal network of roads around Heathrow, the traffic horrendous.

'Just let me out here, Jules.'

'Are you sure, I don't mind taking you—'

He put up a hand. 'Honestly, you've driven long enough. No point you sitting through all this. I'll walk the rest of the way.'

Julie pulled over and waited on the pavement while Drayce collected his big rucksack from the boot and slung it over his shoulder.

'Thank you for the lift,' he said. 'I really appreciate it.'

'Anytime.'

'And thanks for telling me about Lily's case.'

'Like I said, I just thought you should know. The Met's team will be in touch when they're ready to update you on why they've reopened it.'

Drayce nodded.

'Don't be a stranger,' Julie said.

'I won't. I'll be back in London in no time. Keep my number close by, and if you ever need anything…'

She reached out, gently squeezed his arm, and smiled. 'You'll be the first man I call.'

He was about to turn away when she suddenly wrapped her arms around his neck and kissed him on the cheek. He hugged her back until she let go, and then he walked away, waving over his shoulder as he strolled alongside the line of traffic to the airport, thinking about those giant open roads, and the delicious food, and the hot Californian sun, all of which he hoped would overshadow the dangers no doubt waiting for him in LA.

When this latest job is over, he'll go back to London and contact the SIO in charge of Lily's cold case. He'll get an update, nothing more. He might take on board this new information about a suspect, but won't do anything with it. He won't get involved. He won't conduct his own inquiries, in his own manner, getting results in a way a warranted police officer is unable to. He'll stay out of the way of the detectives. He'll leave the investigation alone. He'll let it all run its course by the book.

Perhaps.

Acknowledgements

Writing a book is a solitary task at times, but getting it into the hands of readers certainly isn't. With that in mind, there are a few people I'd like to mention. My thanks to Jayne Southern for the help she gave me in getting this book in tip-top shape before I began approaching literary agents. A big thank you to my wonderful agent, Kate Barker, for believing in my writing and for taking a chance on me. Thank you to my brilliant editor, Kit Nevile, and the entire team at Canelo, who saw something worthy in my novel, giving them the confidence to open the door to the industry for me. And thank you to you, the reader, for buying this book. I know how busy life can be, so I hope you found my story entertaining enough to be worthy of your precious time.

On a more personal note, I owe a huge amount of thanks to my father, Clive, without whose love and sacrifice I would not be where I am today. I hope I've made you proud, Dad.

And finally, a note to my mum. When we last spoke, I promised I'd dedicate my first published novel to you, and you know I always keep my promises. During all those years I was writing as a hobby, dreaming of what I might achieve, you were always cheering me on. You told me to never give up, and I never did. You were my first reader, my first fan, and although you never had the chance to read this book, I know if you were still here, you'd have loved every page of it. If there's a bookshop in heaven (of course there is) go grab yourself a copy. I'll sign it for you when we meet again. Love you, Mum.